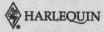
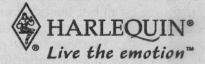

AMANDA STEVENS

is the bestselling author of over thirty novels of romantic suspense. In addition to being a Romance Writers of America RITA® Award finalist, she is also the recipient of awards in Career Achievement in Romantic/Mystery and Career Achievement in Romantic/Suspense from *Romantic Times* magazine. She currently resides in Texas. To find out more about past, present and future projects, please visit her Web site at www.amandastevens.com.

DEBRA WEBB

was born in Scottsboro, Alabama, to parents who taught her that anything is possible if you want it badly enough. She began writing at age nine. Eventually she met and married the man of her dreams, and tried some other occupations, including selling vacuum cleaners and working in a factory, a day-care center, a hospital and a department store. When her husband joined the military, they moved to Berlin, Germany, and Debra became a secretary in the commanding general's office. By 1985 they were back in the States, and finally moved to Tennessee, to a small town where everyone knows everyone else. With the support of her husband and two beautiful daughters, Debra took up writing again, looking to mysteries and movies for inspiration. In 1998 her dream of writing for Harlequin came true. You can write to Debra with your comments at P.O. Box 64, Huntland, Tennessee 37345.

Whispers
IN THE NIGHT

AMANDA STEVENS
DEBRA WEBB

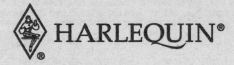

HARLEQUIN®

TORONTO • NEW YORK • LONDON
AMSTERDAM • PARIS • SYDNEY • HAMBURG
STOCKHOLM • ATHENS • TOKYO • MILAN • MADRID
PRAGUE • WARSAW • BUDAPEST • AUCKLAND

ISBN 0-373-83596-5

WHISPERS IN THE NIGHT

Copyright © 2003 by Harlequin Books S.A.

The publisher acknowledges the copyright holders of the individual works as follows:

LOVER, STRANGER
Copyright © 1999 by Marilyn Medlock Amann
PROTECTIVE INSTINCTS
Copyright © 2003 by Debra Webb

This edition published by arrangement with Harlequin Books S.A.

® and TM are trademarks of the publisher. Trademarks indicated with ® are registered in the United States Patent and Trademark Office, the Canadian Trade Marks Office and in other countries.

Visit us at www.eHarlequin.com

Printed in U.S.A.

CONTENTS

FOREWORD
by Carla Neggers

When I climbed a tree with pad and pen at age eleven and wrote my first stories, I didn't know I was writing romantic suspense. I was writing a story filled with action, adventure, danger, suspense, mystery and romance. I had a story percolating in my head, and I wanted to get it onto paper.

It's what I still do.

I've ratcheted up the suspense—and the romance—and I like to think I'm a better writer than I was at eleven. Certainly I'm more mature! But my focus remains what it was then, on the story itself. I'd never heard the term "romantic suspense" until I decided to submit my work to an agent and realized I had to describe what it was I'd written. Ah. It couldn't be "a book." That wasn't specific enough. I dug around and figured out that "romantic suspense" best described the story I'd written.

I was just out of college and knew nothing about publishing. I had no idea—none—that romantic suspense was "dead" at that time. I remember an editor saying that it would be back "when pigs can fly." But the romantic suspense she was talking about was the romantic suspense of the 1960s and 1970s, not, happily, the genre itself. I kept writing. That first book eventually did sell, and meanwhile I discovered the world of category romance. I left behind the guns and dead bodies but kept the action, the adventure, the sense of fun that I loved to write. But the guns and dead bodies crept back in, and I found editors willing to take a chance on what I was writing. So did other writers.

Readers responded—and I was one of them! From its earliest days, I turned to Harlequin Intrigue to find strong new voices and the very best in romantic suspense. I discovered writers like Amanda Stevens, Tess Gerritsen, Jasmine Cresswell, Stella Cameron and Anne Stuart, longtime favorites of mine. Now I'm thrilled to read newcomer Debra Webb, who has her own unique take on romance, suspense, mystery, danger, excitement.

When a story starts percolating for me, I'm not thinking in terms of whether it's romantic suspense or a romantic thriller or "women's suspense"—I'm thinking in terms of the story itself. The characters start to come to life…I hear snippets of dialogue… see a particular scene…until it's as if the entire book's on the tip of my tongue and I *have* to write. I let the story emerge on paper, and I go from there. Inevitably there's romance, there's suspense, there's action, there's adventure, there's danger….

Where do I get my ideas?

It's the question I'm asked most often, but I'm not sure I know the answer! I've always had a dramatic imagination. When I was seven, I moved with my parents and six brothers into an eighteenth-century carriage house that had no hot water, no bathroom, no central heat. Talk about an adventure! We had bats. We had snakes. We had mice. As kids, we'd explore our ninety acres of fields and woods. We'd grab vines and swing like Tarzan. We built tree houses. We pulled leeches off our ankles. We got banged up, we got frostbite, we got lost. I wasn't going to be happy reading or writing staid stories—I needed action, adventure, a sense of humor!

My parents also had a touch of mystery to their lives. My father was a Dutch immigrant who fought on Allied ships during World War II while his family endured under Nazi occupation. He was one of two survivors of a torpedoed ship. My mother was almost twenty years younger than he was—her Florida-panhandle family is filled with mystery and intrigue, including the unsolved murder of one family member who was shot while getting a drink of water from the cistern on the porch. My parents moved to New England just before I was born… more fodder, more inspiration.

And my mind tends to wander when I'm bored. When I was a kid, we had lots of hard, tedious work to do to fix up the place and put in a garden. I remember picking wild blueberries on a hot August morning, bored out of my mind. So I started thinking—what if I pull back this blueberry bush and find a dead guy? No. Maybe he's just wounded. Next thing I knew, I had a story in the works.

I can't trace the genesis of most of my books back to that kind of "ah-ha" moment. For the most part, I suddenly realize a story's simmering in my head and I've got to start writing. What if a woman gets shot at in the woods, then finds a dead body in Boston that's connected to the shooting? That became *Cold Ridge*. What if the murder of a cop's police-chief father turns her life upside down, until she finally returns to her hometown and finds his killer? That was the seed that turned into *The Harbor*. What if a murder suspect walks into a woman's kitchen—and she doesn't tell her Texas Ranger husband? *The Cabin*. These are three of my most recent books, but they started the same way my first books did as a kid—with a story that was in my head, that I was determined to get onto paper.

The previous owner of our old carriage house left us a turn-of-the-century player piano and shelves of musty old books in the back room. I found a copy of *The Moonspinners* and proceeded to track down every book Mary Stewart had written. I loved her settings, her characters, her sense of mystery and adventure—I still do. I didn't know she wrote "romantic suspense." To me, her books are all good stories, well written. That's what I look for as a reader, and it's what I strive for as a writer…but I'm particularly drawn to stories that intertwine romance and suspense. One isn't tacked on to the other, incidental, able to be removed without hurting the story. As far as I'm concerned, as a writer and a reader, it's the best of both worlds, and it's what you'll find in a Harlequin Intrigue novel.

Carla Neggers

LOVER, STRANGER
Amanda Stevens

Chapter One

His lungs were bursting as he thrashed his way through the jungle, trying to elude his predators. Over the lacy treetops, the moon rose full and majestic, illuminating the path of broken limbs and trampled grass he left in his wake. It was only a matter of time before they picked up his trail.

The sky was clear and inky black, like a giant, obsidian bowl that had been turned upside down and painted with thousands of tiny, white stars. Pausing to catch his breath, he searched for the brightest star among them, Polaris, the north star that would guide him toward the village. There he would hopefully find a phone, or at least transportation to take him out of this godforsaken place. If he could somehow make it to the border…

Off to the west, he heard the rumble of an engine, distant at first, but drawing steadily near. A beam of light from a high-powered searchlight arced over the terrain just missing him, and then moments later, he heard shouts. Laughter. His trail had been discovered. The killers were closing in, and they were enjoying the hunt.

Heart pounding, he plunged through the lush foliage. Low-hanging branches slapped at his face and arms while man-sized roots tangled with his feet. Amber eyes, ruby eyes, emerald eyes glowed from the trees and from the darkness all around him. Every step was a new danger, a new terror. God, how he hated the jungle!

Finally stumbling into a clearing, he found himself on the edge of a jagged precipice. Mist rose from the raging river that sliced its way through the limestone cliffs a hundred feet below him. Ahead, the ravine sprawled into a yawning gap of nothingness. Behind him, the shouts of his pursuers rose in excitement as they spotted him in the moonlight.

There was nothing to do but head back into the jungle for cover. But before he could run, gunfire echoed through the stone canyon. The noise was so muted by the mist, the scene so surreal, that for a moment, he hovered at the edge of the precipice, unsure what to do. Then he felt the sharp blast of pain in his side, looked down and saw the blood and realized he'd been hit. Realized he wasn't going to make it to the village, much less to the border.

As if in slow motion, he fell backward into nothing but vapor and air...

"Dr. Hunter? Can you hear me?"

He opened his eyes and saw a woman's face leaning over him. Dressed all in white, she looked radiant. Other-worldly. An angel, he thought. So he hadn't made it after all.

"Dr. Hunter?"

He blinked as the angel spoke again. Was she talking to him? She was gazing down into his eyes, smiling, but that name she kept calling—who was Dr. Hunter?

"He's coming around, Dr. Kendall," she said over her shoulder.

A man appeared beside her. He wore the same look of concern on his face as she did, but he wasn't smiling and his eyes were dark with something that might have been suspicion.

"Well, well," he said. "Glad to see you've decided to rejoin the land of the living, Ethan. You certainly gave us all a scare tonight."

Ethan? Who was Ethan?

He closed his eyes for a moment, trying to clear his head. Obviously he was in a hospital somewhere. These people seemed to know him, but he'd never seen them before in his life. Nor had he ever heard of anyone named Ethan Hunter. It had to be a case of mistaken identity, but—

A tiny bubble of panic floated to the surface of his consciousness. If he wasn't Ethan Hunter, who the hell was he?

He searched his mind and found no answers.

"How are you feeling, buddy?" Dr. Kendall peered down into his face.

Buddy? Did that mean the two of them were friends?

But Kendall didn't look particularly friendly. In spite of his easy bedside manner, there was something about his eyes, a glimmer of hostility that was faintly unnerving.

The man they called Ethan stared up at him, frowning. "I feel sort of…out of it." The sound of his own voice shocked him. It was raspy and coarse, and the effort to speak hurt his throat. He put a hand to his neck and winced at the pain. The skin was bruised and tender.

Dr. Kendall must have glimpsed the fear in Ethan's eyes for he said, "Take it easy. Your vocal cords and larynx have been stressed. Don't try to talk any more than is necessary."

Ethan tried to swallow past the pain and the panic. "What happened?"

"We're hoping you can tell us."

He thought for a moment. "I had this strange dream about running through a jungle... Someone was trying to kill me."

Kendall's shrug was dismissive. "I'm not surprised. You've sustained a concussion. You look like hell, but you're damned lucky to be alive."

You look like hell...

The realization hit him suddenly that he had no idea what he looked like. He put his hands to his face. The skin was bruised there as well, and a thick bandage wrapped around his skull.

Scanning his surroundings, he searched for a mirror but didn't see one. Which was probably just as well. If the pain in his face was any indication, he wasn't at all sure he was ready to see his reflection.

"What were you doing at the clinic tonight, anyway?" Kendall asked suddenly, his tone edgy.

"I'm...not sure." Ethan squeezed his eyes closed, trying to remember what had happened to him, but nothing came to him. He tried to fight back the suffocating panic that threatened to engulf him. *Who the hell am I?*

Stay calm, a little voice warned him. *You have to figure this thing out. Your life could depend on it.*

He drew a long breath. Okay. He just needed a few minutes to get his bearings. There was no cause for alarm. He had a concussion. Short-term memory loss was common enough with head injuries, wasn't it? Maybe they could even give him something—

But wait a minute. If he was a doctor—Dr. Ethan Hunter—he would know that, wouldn't he? He would know how to treat a concussion and temporary amnesia. He would know how to cure himself.

But he didn't. He didn't know anything at the moment, and his panic came rushing back.

Dr. Kendall touched his arm, and Ethan flinched. Why didn't he like this man? And more importantly, why didn't he trust him enough to confess his amnesia to him?

As if reading his thoughts, Dr. Kendall's eyes narrowed. "The police are outside, Ethan. We've stalled them as long as we can, but there's a detective who's been champing at the bit ever since you were brought in. Are you up to talking with him?"

About what? Ethan wanted to know. But he remained silent. For some reason he didn't understand, it seemed imperative that he not give himself away. That he remain calm and as much in control as he could be under the circumstances.

But just what the hell *were* the circumstances? Why couldn't he remember who he was?

The door of his hospital room opened, and a man wearing an ugly green suit walked in. He was in his early fifties, stoop-shouldered, with salt-and-pepper hair slicked straight back and plastered with hair cream. His face was deeply creviced, his eyes shadowed with years of hard service and even harder drinking.

He walked over to Ethan's bed, pulled up a stool and sat down. Removing a yellow number-two pencil and a black notebook from his inside jacket pocket, he licked the lead of the pencil, then scribbled a hasty note. Without looking up he said, "So you're Dr. Hunter."

Ethan said nothing.

"I'm Sergeant Pope, HPD."

HPD. Ethan searched his mind. Honolulu Police Department? Harrisburg? Hartford? Houston? Where was he?

Wait. There was an unmistakable twang in the detective's easy drawl. Okay, so they were probably in Houston, but why? Did he live here?

He glanced up, and as his gaze met Pope's for the first time, Ethan sensed a keen intuition and intellect that belied the faint air of ennui that settled like an old blanket over the aging detective.

Watch yourself, Ethan thought, though why he should fear the police he had no idea. Was it because in his dream, the Mexican authorities had been chasing him through the jungle? Was that why an almost innate sense of wariness had surfaced the moment the detective had walked into the room?

"I've heard a lot about you," Pope was saying. "My wife showed me an article about you in the paper a couple of months ago. Had a real nice shot of you in your downtown office, but I can't say you look much like that now."

Ethan thought about the thick bandage wrapping

his skull, the raw bruises on his face and neck. "No, I guess not."

Pope thumped the pencil eraser against his notebook. The sound was barely audible, but for some reason it grated on Ethan's nerves. "The article told all about that free clinic you built in the Mexican jungle, and how you spend several weeks a year down there, operating on underprivileged kids. They gave you quite a write-up. The wife was real impressed." The thumping stopped suddenly. "Hey, I'll have to tell her I met you tonight."

"Sure, why not?" Ethan said, because he didn't know what else to say. His throat still hurt. He reached for the glass of water on the stand beside his bed. The nurse—Nurse Angel, he now thought of her—was instantly at his side, helping him to drink. Her hand wrapped around his on the glass. Her touch was soft, caressing. Intimate.

When Ethan lay back against the pillows, he saw that Pope was watching him. The detective had seen the encounter. Ethan was sure of it.

Pope said, "She was thinking about calling you. My wife, that is." He put a finger to his nose and pressed it to one side. "She has a deviated septum like you wouldn't believe. She's been wanting a nose job for years."

So…he was a plastic surgeon? Somehow Ethan would never have guessed that.

Almost inadvertently his gaze dropped to his hands, resting on top of the sheet. There was dried blood caked beneath his nails and a wedding band on the third finger of his left hand.

His heart raced when he saw the ring. If he was

married, where was his wife? Had she been contacted? Shouldn't she be at his bedside at a time like this?

As if on cue, Nurse Angel moved back into his line of vision and gave him a knowing wink.

Pope, momentarily distracted by the nurse's dazzling smile, said, "Listen, will y'all excuse us? I'd like to speak to Dr. Hunter alone."

Dr. Kendall nodded tightly, then turned to Ethan. "Dr. Mancetti said she'd be back tonight to check on you. In the meantime, if you need anything, I'll be around for a while."

"Great," Ethan said, though he didn't have the faintest idea who Dr. Mancetti was, nor did he have any intention of calling on Dr. Kendall's services.

Nurse Angel bent over Ethan's bed, fluffing his pillow and patting his arm. "I'm pulling a double shift tonight," she confided in a throaty whisper. "If you need anything, Dr. Hunter, *anything at all,* you just call me."

"Thanks," he murmured, his gaze lingering on the sway of her hips beneath her snug uniform as she turned and walked out of the room.

Sergeant Pope seemed mesmerized by the movement, too. For a moment, neither man spoke, then the detective mentally shook himself. "The staff here seem pretty concerned about your welfare, doctor. You must be a popular guy." There was a mocking glint in his eyes as his gaze dropped to the wedding ring on Ethan's finger.

Ethan resisted the urge to hide his hands, caked blood and all, beneath the sheet.

For a moment, Pope busied himself with his notes.

Then, his voice edged with a weariness Ethan didn't trust, he said, "We may as well get this over with. I'd like to file my report and get home before midnight, and you look like you could do with some rest." He paused. "Can you tell me what happened tonight?"

Ethan shrugged. "I'm afraid the details are still a little sketchy." He made a vague gesture toward his head. "The concussion..."

Pope nodded. "I spoke with your doctor a little while ago. She said it might be a few hours, or even a few days before you could fill in all the blanks. But let's just go over what you do know."

Which is nothing, Ethan thought. *Nada.*

The only thing he could remember was the dream. Running through the jungle. Being pursued by men who wanted to kill him. And falling...falling...

Then, like a bolt of lightning, another memory shot through him. He was in a room that contained an examination table, metal cabinets and a sink. He felt groggy, out of it, but he could smell antiseptic. Knew, dimly, that he was in a place he didn't want to be.

Someone was in the room with him. Someone with a gun...

"I remember being in a doctor's office," he said, almost to himself. "In an examination room, I think."

"You were found at your clinic here in town," Pope supplied.

Ethan put a hand to his head, touching the bandage. "Someone was with me. A man. I think we fought. I heard a woman scream...then gunfire...then..." He trailed off as his head exploded in pain. He clutched his temples with his hands. "I was hit with something hard...something metal..."

"We think it was a flashlight," Pope said. "We found one with blood on it at the crime scene, but we won't know if it's your DNA until we get it back from the lab."

Ethan closed his eyes, trying to remember the rest, but his recollection was hazy at best. In some ways, the jungle dream was much clearer to him. But was it more than a dream? Was the jungle scene somehow connected to what had happened to him earlier in that office?

Why couldn't he remember? Why didn't he know who he was?

He groaned, whether from actual pain or memory, he wasn't sure.

"Did you recognize the man in your office?" Pope asked.

It had been dark inside the examination room, but the blind at the window was open and moonlight flooded in. The man was wearing a ski mask, but Ethan could tell that he was staring down at him in the pale light, grinning as he aimed the gun at Ethan's face. "Got to make this look good, pretty boy," the gunman said, as he turned to the drug cabinet behind him and rifled through the medication, choosing and discarding with an expertise that was chilling.

By contrast, Ethan's movements were slow and lethargic. Almost dreamlike. It was as if he were caught in an invisible web he couldn't break free of.

Then, unexpectedly, the door to the examination room opened and a woman screamed. As the gunman whirled toward the sound, Ethan, acting on pure instinct and adrenaline, lunged toward him. The gun went off as Ethan crashed into the man, dragging him downward. From the doorway, where the woman had screamed, the only sound was a thud, a soft moan, then silence.

The gun came free as the man hit the floor. Both he and Ethan scrambled toward it, but the weapon slid out of reach beneath a steel cabinet. As the two of them fought, Ethan became aware of a siren in the distance. Someone had heard the gunshot and called the police. The man must have heard the siren, too, for his struggles became even more desperate. More deadly. He got his hands around Ethan's throat and squeezed, squeezed, until stars exploded inside Ethan's head.

From somewhere deep inside Ethan, a primal urge, some killing instinct rose to the surface, and he reached upward, his thumbs finding the man's eyes. The man screamed and released him, but before Ethan could use his advantage, the gunman found a new weapon. He grabbed something metal from the floor and struck Ethan's head a vicious blow.

Dazed, Ethan fell back. Before he could regain his strength, his equilibrium, the man was on him. He hit Ethan's head...his face...again and again until blackness mercifully swallowed the pain.

Ethan glanced at Detective Pope. "That's all I remember." But at least now he knew how he'd gotten the bruises and the concussion, how his vocal cords had gotten stressed. What he didn't know was why. "I don't know what happened to the gunman after I lost consciousness, or why he didn't kill me."

Pope's gaze flickered over Ethan. "My guess is, he

panicked. He heard the sirens and ran. Not likely we'll find any prints on the flashlight or anywhere else. I suspect he went to that clinic prepared. He knew exactly what he was looking for.''

"Which was?''

"Drugs, more than likely.''

Ethan touched a bruise on his cheek, remembering the blows, wondering if his face resembled a slab of raw meat, because that was the way it felt.

Got to make this look good, pretty boy.

He hadn't related that part of the memory to Sergeant Pope. Nor did Ethan say what he was now certain of—that the gunman hadn't gone to the clinic looking for drugs. He'd gone there to kill Ethan.

Then why not tell the police? that voice inside him demanded.

Because his instincts told him not to. Because Ethan was very much afraid when the truth came out, when he finally remembered everything, there might be a chance a cop would be the last person he could turn to for help.

He realized Pope was watching him again, and Ethan tried to shutter his expression, tried to hide his fear and dread.

"Can the rest of this wait until morning?'' he asked suddenly, wanting to be rid of the detective. Ethan knew instinctively that he had to watch his step as he had never had to watch it before. Someone wanted to kill him. It was like a drumbeat inside his head. Someone wanted to kill him, and he had no idea who. He didn't even know who he could trust. For all he knew, Sergeant Pope was the enemy.

Was it Ethan's imagination, or had the detective's expression suddenly turned suspicious?

"I'll try to make it quick. Just a few more questions," Pope said, paging backward in his notes. "Let's see…oh, yeah, here we are." He paused, reading, then glanced up. "Dr. Kendall told me you'd been in Mexico for the last couple of months or so. He said you were due back three weeks ago, but you'd had some emergency surgery down there. An appendectomy, I think he said. You weren't supposed to travel for several more days, but then you decided to come back tonight. Why the sudden change of plans?"

The jungle dream came rushing back to Ethan. He could smell the dank scent of rotting vegetation, could see the Hummer's lights bouncing over the uneven terrain, could actually feel the throb in his side from the bullet.

Or was the pain from the appendectomy incision? Was the dream nothing more than a drug-induced vision while he'd been under the knife?

He said vaguely, "I had something I needed to take care of."

One of Pope's brows rose in surprise. "Must have been pretty important if you were willing to risk your health."

Ethan hesitated, not knowing how to respond. *You're a doctor, so think like one. Why would you come back from the jungle before you were supposed to?*

Aside from the fact that the Mexican authorities were trying to kill you.…

But Ethan didn't think he wanted Pope to know

that. So he said instead, "There's a patient I have to see."

"Is that why you went by the office tonight before going home?"

"How did you know I didn't go home first?"

"Your luggage was still at the clinic. So was your wallet and briefcase. We'll get everything back to you as soon as we're finished with it."

"Thanks," Ethan mumbled, his mind racing. A wallet would contain a driver's license, credit card, money. A home address.

Sergeant Pope said, "From your story, I gather the gunman was already inside the clinic when you arrived."

"I'm pretty sure he was," Ethan said, though he wasn't at all sure of anything. His first memory was of staring up into the gunman's masked face. Ethan had no recollection of getting off a plane, arriving at the office, or of anything else.

Except fleeing through the jungle...

He remembered that all too clearly.

"Did you call your assistant and ask her to meet you at the clinic?" Pope asked.

"My assistant?"

"The woman who walked in on you and the gunman. Amy Cole."

Dammit, be careful. "Oh, yes. Amy." Ethan wondered if he'd answered a little too quickly because Pope's gaze narrowed on him. "How is she, sergeant? She wasn't seriously hurt, was she? She saved my life tonight."

Something flickered in the detective's eyes. "Dr. Kendall didn't tell you?"

"Tell me what?"

"Amy Cole's dead. Shot right through the heart. Poor kid never knew what hit her." Pope shook his head. "Damn shame, a beautiful woman like that."

Ethan felt the air leave his lungs in a painful rush. He had no recollection of the woman, didn't even remember what she'd looked like, but he could still hear her scream. Could still see, in his mind's eye, the gunman whirl toward the door and fire.

And now Ethan was more certain than ever that the gunman had come to the clinic to kill him. Amy Cole, whoever she was, had taken a bullet that was meant for him.

Whoever *he* was...

Chapter Two

"This is suicide, Dr. Hunter. I won't allow you to do it." A middle-aged, stoutly built commando in a nurse's uniform planted her hands on her hips and blocked Ethan from the door to his room. The lines in her weathered face were deeply etched and as unyielding as the starch in her pristine uniform.

Ethan had hoped to slip out of his room unnoticed and make his exit before anyone missed him, but this woman—he glanced at her nameplate—Roberta Bloodworth had caught him in the act. What a name for a nurse!

"Don't worry," he lied as he finished buttoning his blood-stained shirt. "I'm feeling much better. All I need is a good night's sleep in my own bed."

Actually, he felt like hell. His head throbbed, his face hurt, his whole body ached as if he'd been hit by a bulldozer. But the pain was the least of his worries. At the moment, he didn't even know where his own bed was, or who he should be sharing it with.

All he knew was that he had to get out of here. He had to find some answers. Somehow he had to figure out who was trying to kill him, and why.

"Just look at you," the nurse scolded. "I hardly even recognize you, and the way you sound, like some horror movie ghoul." She wagged her finger in his face. "And I shouldn't have to remind you how dangerous a head injury can be. You shouldn't be alone tonight."

"I won't be alone." He slipped on his suit jacket. "My wife will take care of me."

"Your...wife?"

Too late, Ethan realized his mistake. He'd made assumptions about the ring on his finger that obviously he shouldn't have made. Were he and his wife separated? Divorced?

Damn. Was he widowed?

He gave her a wink. "Well, let's just say, I won't be alone, okay?"

"Same old Dr. Hunter," she grumbled, but there was a spice of mischief in her close-set eyes as she continued to challenge him.

Ethan sensed that beneath her gruff exterior, she held a genuine affection for him. It made him feel a little better. Maybe everyone wasn't his enemy after all.

But...could he trust her enough to tell her about the amnesia? Would she be able to help him?

Or would she insist on calling the police? Or worse, Dr. Kendall?

Ethan still couldn't shake the notion that Kendall held a deep malice toward him. What had happened between them in the past?

For a moment, he considered asking the nurse about Kendall, but something warned him not to. Something told him not to press his luck with Roberta

Bloodworth because she, of all people, might see right through him.

He tried to smile disarmingly. "Anyway, you know what they say about doctors. We make the worst patients. You should consider yourself lucky to be rid of me."

She threw up her hands in exasperation. "All right, it's your funeral. Why should I care?" But as she turned toward the door, he heard her murmur, "Take care, Ethan."

After she left, Ethan checked the pockets of his jacket. A stick of gum, a parking stub, a Post-it note with a phone number he didn't recognize. As if they were precious gemstones, he carefully returned the items to his pocket. Opening the door, he quickly surveyed the corridor, then stepped out, searching for the nearest exit. He spotted the elevators and headed toward them as the bell pinged on one of the cars and the door slid open.

A woman emerged, looking windblown and slightly breathless. Their shoulders touched as they brushed by each other, and for a moment, their gazes locked.

Ethan's immediate impression was that, for the most part, the woman's features were neither beautiful nor plain, but fell somewhere in the category of interesting. Her eyes, however, were extraordinary, so light a blue they almost appeared translucent.

She wore a tailored navy pantsuit, and her dark red hair was cut short and tucked behind her ears, in a style that was deceptively simple. She looked professional, no-nonsense, a woman with a definite purpose.

All this Ethan saw in a heartbeat, a man noticing and acknowledging an attractive woman. With a mumbled, "Excuse me," he entered the elevator, giving her hardly more than a second thought. But just before the doors slid closed between them, he saw her turn and stare after him, in a manner that filled him with unease.

Did he know her?

He started to press the open button to confront her, but what would he say? How could he be sure she was a friend and not an enemy? Maybe she'd come to the hospital to finish the job someone else had botched earlier.

Not a pleasant thought, but one he couldn't ignore. Truth was, he couldn't afford to trust anyone.

As he left the elevator and headed through the hospital lobby toward the street entrance, he tried to take stock of what he had learned about himself. His name was Ethan Hunter. He was a plastic surgeon. He was married...or at least, had been married. He had just returned from Mexico, where he'd undergone an emergency appendectomy, and he'd been badly beaten tonight by a man who had wanted to kill him.

The wound in his side tingled as he pushed open the glass door and stepped outside. A blast of hot air greeted him, and he realized it must be summer in Houston. Even though it was late, after ten, the cloying heat was almost suffocating.

He could see the city's impressive skyline in the distance and wavered for a moment, unsure what to do, where to go. Maybe it hadn't been such a great idea to leave the hospital. He should have at least figured out where he was going first. Maybe he should have somehow gotten his wife's number and called her to come and get him.

Somehow that didn't seem to be an option he wanted to explore. Neither was waiting around in a hospital room for his would-be killer to come and find him.

Ethan couldn't explain it, but he hadn't had a choice in leaving the hospital. He'd been compelled to flee. He knew he had to run. Knew he couldn't afford to stay in one spot too long.

Headlights arced across his face, and he threw up a hand to shield his eyes. For a moment, he thought he was back in the jungle. He could see the searchlights scouring the mountainside. Hear the rush of water below him. Feel the sharp punch of the bullet as it entered his side. Then he was falling…falling…

Someone grabbed his arm, and Ethan whirled, reaching blindly for his enemy, pulling the body tightly against him as he pressed his arm into a soft, pliant throat.

GRACE DONOVAN SAW her entire life flash before her eyes. The arm that pressed against her windpipe was like an iron vise. The more she struggled, the harder he squeezed. Forcing herself to go limp, she waited for the infinitesimal relaxation of her assailant's muscles, then she chopped upward, using both hands as she'd been taught.

His hold loosened without breaking, but at least she could breathe. She gulped air into her lungs, then stumbled away when he finally released her.

"Are you crazy?" she managed to gasp.

He was looking at her as if she were a ghost. He

stared at his hands, then back at her. Then stared at his hands again. ''I could have killed you.'' His skin looked deathly white in the sodium-vapor streetlight.

''No sh—kidding.'' Grace massaged her throat, glaring at him. Headlights swept across his face, causing the bruises to stand out starkly against his pallor. ''Why did you attack me like that?''

He was still staring at his hands. ''I don't know.''

Grace kept her own hand at her throat, suddenly feeling very vulnerable and not liking it. ''Look, you don't have to worry,'' she said dryly. ''I don't think there's any permanent damage.''

He glanced up, his brown eyes shadowed with an emotion Grace couldn't define. ''You're okay then?''

She frowned. ''I'll be fine, but I wasn't talking about myself. I meant you…your hands. You're a surgeon, right?''

He didn't answer, just stood staring at her in the gloom. Grace shivered even though it was June and the heat rising from the concrete was thick enough to cut with a scalpel. She could feel her hair curl at the back of her neck, but wasn't sure whether it was because of the humidity or the man standing before her…the way he was looking at her.

She cleared her throat. ''You are Dr. Hunter, aren't you? Dr. Ethan Hunter?''

''Do I know you?''

He took a step toward her, and Grace fought the urge to retreat. It wasn't like her to be so easily spooked, but the bruises and bandage gave him an almost maniacal look as he stared down at her. There was something about his eyes…a darkness that was chilling. She wondered, fleetingly, what she was getting herself into.

"We've never met. But I saw you briefly upstairs."

"At the elevator," he said, as if it had just occurred to him.

She nodded. "I came here to see you. The nurse told me you'd checked yourself out. Do you think that's a good idea? If you don't mind my saying so, you don't look so good."

"I'm fine." As Grace watched, he lifted his fingertips to probe his battered face. The action reminded her of a blind man, trying to "see" with his hands.

"Why were you looking for me?" he asked suddenly.

She released a long breath, not realizing until that moment she'd been holding it. "I want to talk to you about what happened tonight. I've spoken with the police. They told me about the shooting. I've just come from the morgue."

She had his full attention now. His brown gaze scoured her face. "The morgue?"

Grace wrapped her arms around her middle, shivering suddenly as if she were still in the cold-holding room where Amy's body had been taken. This was the important part. It was crucial that she convince him. "I want to talk to you about Amy Cole."

Something flashed in his eyes. Regret? Guilt? Or was it merely a trick of the light? "You knew Amy?"

"She was my sister."

He looked stunned. "I'm sorry. I don't know what else to say." He spread his hands in supplication, glancing away, then back at Grace. "She saved my life tonight."

Despite the hoarseness, his voice was deeply compelling. Dusky and sensual, it called forth emotions from inside Grace she had no wish to unveil. Not now. Not when so much was at stake. Not when her sister's death was on the brink of being avenged. Nothing else could be allowed to matter. Certainly not a man with a battered face and a voice as seductive and deadly as a storm-swept sea.

She tried to conjure up an image of her sister, but the memories had faded.

Ethan touched her arm, and Grace jumped as if she'd been burned. "Are you all right?" he asked.

She swallowed over the sudden fear in her throat. "I'm fine. But unfortunately, my sister isn't. That's what I want to talk to you about. I want to know why Amy's dead, Dr. Hunter. I want to know what you had to do with it."

The shadows in his eyes deepened. "What do you mean?"

"I think you know exactly what I mean." Grace forced herself to remember the past. To use her emotions. She unfolded her arms, letting one hand grip her purse strap. The other hand balled into a fist at her side. "I know all about you and Amy. Your *affair*." She all but spat the word at him and saw him wince as if she had physically struck him.

When he didn't try to defend himself, Grace said coldly, "She told me all about it. She also told me that you'd gotten her involved in something dangerous. Something she said might end up getting you both killed, and it looks like she was right."

This time, he didn't flinch at her words. He stared at her with eyes as cold and dark as a moonless winter night. "I don't know what you're talking about."

"Oh, I think you do." She lifted her chin. "Amy's dead, Dr. Hunter, and I think you know more about her murder than you're saying. I came here to get some answers, and I'm not leaving without them."

"Then you may be waiting a long damn time." He turned to walk away from her, then stopped suddenly, looking around at the street and passing cars.

Grace walked over to him and caught his arm. The muscles beneath her hand flexed defensively, like tempered steel. Her hand dropped to her side. "You can't just walk away from this. You owe me the truth. You owe it to Amy. She was in love with you, dammit!"

His fingertips brushed against the bandage. He suddenly looked very lost. "I didn't know."

Grace glared at him, telling herself not to react to his emotions, to the look of desperation lurking in the depths of his eyes. He was a dangerous man, and she couldn't afford to forget it.

"What do you mean, you didn't know? Amy never told you how she felt? You must have guessed. She was never very good at hiding her feelings."

He glanced down at Grace, as if on the verge of confession. Then he shrugged and turned away. "I'm sorry about your sister. Deeply sorry. But I can't help you. There's nothing I can tell you. I don't have the answers you're looking for."

"Then you leave me no choice." Grace opened her purse and took out a stack of envelopes tied with a blue ribbon. "Amy wrote to me regularly in the past few months. These are her letters. They're all about you, Dr. Hunter. About the promises you made to her. The favors you asked of her. I'm sure the police would be interested in seeing them.''

He turned at that, his expression stark in the streetlight. Whatever flash of vulnerability Grace might have glimpsed earlier had vanished. His gaze narrowed on her. ''Is that threat supposed to frighten me? Why should I assume the police would have any interest in your sister's letters? What did she accuse me of?''

Grace hesitated, meeting his gaze. Then she glanced away. ''All right, I admit, she never mentioned anything specific. But she said enough to arouse my suspicions, and I think her letters might make the police more than a little curious as well.''

''Then why haven't you already handed them over?''

''Because I wanted to talk to you first.''

''Why?''

''I have my reasons.''

He studied her for a moment. ''Is it because you're afraid your sister may not be an innocent bystander in…'' he made a vague gesture with his hand. ''…all this? Is it because if you go to the police, they may start to probe a little too deeply?''

His perception surprised Grace. ''That's part of it,'' she admitted reluctantly. ''But it's more than that. I don't exactly trust the police.''

That seemed to interest him. He lifted a dark brow. ''Why not?''

''Because Amy is just a statistic to them. Another case. One of a dozen homicides that take place in this city every week." She paused, biting her lip. "But she was my sister, Dr. Hunter, and I'll do anything to bring her killer to justice. Right now, you're the only one who can help me do that."

His brow rose again, but when he remained silent, Grace pressed her point. "I don't want to go to the police, but if that's the only way I can gain your co-operation—"

He moved swiftly, grasping her forearms and hauling her toward him. Grace started to struggle away, but something in his eyes, a terrible look of desperation, made her momentarily yielding.

"Don't you understand?" He gazed down at her, his eyes darker than Grace could ever have imagined. "I *can't* help you. I don't know anything."

"Then why are you so afraid of the police?" she asked, unable to tear her gaze from his. Her breath caught in her throat. She wondered, suddenly, if she had pushed him too far.

For a moment, he seemed to undergo some intense inner struggle. A myriad of emotions flickered across his features, then he let his hands drop from her arms and backed away from her. "I don't know anything about your sister. About those letters. About our...relationship. I don't remember her. I don't even remember my own name or what I look like. I don't remember anything. Is that clear enough for you?"

Grace stared at him in shock, watching the shadows flicker across his features. Where he stood, one side of his face was in light, the other in darkness. It was a strange illusion, almost as if she were talking to two distinctly different men. Unnerved, she said, "Are you telling me you have amnesia?"

He didn't answer, just stood there staring down at her. He was dressed in a suit, dark gray and beautifully tailored. The jacket was open, and Grace could see the dark droplets of blood on the front of his white shirt.

That, more than anything, reminded her of why she was here. Her heart jolted uncomfortably. "My God," she said. "You don't remember *anything?*"

"Not much," he muttered. His expression became shuttered again, as if he were already regretting his confession.

But had it really been a confession? Was he telling her the truth, or trying to cover his tracks?

Damn, Grace thought. *Amnesia could change everything.*

She tried to assess this new situation while wondering if she should proceed as planned. She stared at him for a long moment, watching for the telltale flicker of desperation she'd glimpsed earlier, searching for a flash of fear, anything, that might give him away.

But she saw nothing. It was as if a mask had descended over his features. In some ways, this masquerade of control frightened her more than anything else, because it showed her how easily he could deceive her if he chose to.

"What did the doctor say about your condition?" she finally asked.

He shrugged. "I understand it may take days, or even weeks, to fill in the blanks."

"From what you just said, it sounds like we're talking about more than a few blanks."

He shrugged again.

Grace glanced around, realizing how vulnerable they were standing out in the open. In spite of the intense heat, she shivered. "Look, maybe it isn't such a great idea for you to be on the street like this."

"I'm fine," he said, almost angrily. "Don't worry about me."

"You're not fine," she countered. "You were almost killed tonight. Hasn't it occurred to you that whoever did this to you…to Amy…could come back?"

"That's not your problem." But she knew he had thought of it. She could see it in his eyes. She wondered if that's why he'd left the hospital.

"Well, I'm sorry, but I've made it my problem," she said, backing her shoulders. Staring him down. "I want to find my sister's killer, and at the moment, you're my only clue. I'm not letting you out of my sight."

He scanned the night sky, as if looking for guidance. Searching for the way home. His expression looked bleak in the moonlight. "What was it you said earlier? Amy told you I'd gotten her involved in something dangerous? Something that might end up getting us both killed? Wasn't that it?" His gaze met Grace's and she shuddered. "If I were you, I wouldn't want to be standing between me and the next bullet."

SHE FOLDED HER arms over her breasts, in a manner that was unmistakably determined. He saw that same stubbornness in the set of her jaw and chin. In the way her gaze met his without wavering. "I told you. I'm not going anywhere until I get some answers."

"And I told you, I don't have those answers."

"Yes, you do. You just don't remember them. That is, if you really do have amnesia."

"You don't believe me?"

Her blue eyes flickered, but she said nothing.

Ethan told himself her opinion of him didn't matter, but for some reason, anger shot through him. She didn't even know him. She was basing her judgment solely on what she'd heard from her sister. And if he and Amy Cole had been having an affair…if the relationship had gone bad…

The wedding ring on his finger was suddenly a dead weight. He resisted the urge to remove it. For all he knew, he might still be deeply in love with his wife…ex-wife?…estranged wife?

Then why would he have had an affair with Amy Cole?

Ethan shook his head, trying to clear the fog, but the haze only deepened. So many things he didn't know. Couldn't remember. What had happened to him in Mexico? What had he been involved in that had gotten Amy killed tonight?

He stared down at her sister. His initial impression of her remained. She was a woman with a definite purpose, but there was something in her eyes that belied her tough exterior. The pain of her sister's murder?

Guilt stabbed through him. Amy Cole may have died because of him. He wouldn't be responsible for another woman's death. "Look," he said. "I don't care whether you believe me or not. I'm getting the hell out of here. And if you're smart, you won't follow me."

She took a warning step toward him. "You're not getting away from me that easily."

"Don't be stupid," he said in exasperation. "I don't want you to end up like your sister."

Something flashed in her eyes. A momentary look of uncertainty. "I won't. I'm not Amy. I can take care of myself."

He shook his head in regret. "You don't know what you're getting yourself into. *I* don't even know."

"I know that I won't rest until I find my sister's killer," she said softly. Her eyes glowed with an emotion so deep, so fierce that Ethan felt unsettled just watching her. "Can you really afford to send me away? Where will you go? Do you even know where you live? At least let me get you off the street. Let me take you someplace where you'll be safe."

He stared at her for a long moment, trying to resist the temptation she placed before him. "I don't want to get you involved in this."

"Don't be stupid," she said, flinging his words back at him. "What choice do you have?"

"Actually, there is choice," he said slowly. "I could still decide to go to the police for help."

She gave him a sidelong glance. "I don't think so."

Meaning he *couldn't* go to the police. Meaning whatever he had been involved in was not something he would want the cops to know about.

Like it or not, she had him exactly where she wanted him.

"All right," he said. "I guess we're stuck with each other. For the time being, at least."

Her expression was anything but triumphant. "Looks that way. Come on. My car's over here."

As Ethan followed her to the parking lot, he had a feeling that he was walking blindly into something every bit as dangerous, every bit as deadly as the jungle.

Chapter Three

They headed west on Memorial Drive. Ethan knew this because he studied the road signs, hoping to recall a memory. Though they were in the middle of the city, the street became progressively more wooded. The streetlights along the dark green colonnade illuminated high walls and gated drives. Ethan glimpsed large houses beyond the walls, with curving driveways and lush vegetation skillfully showcased by landscaping lights that gave everything a soft, green glow.

Ethan searched for something familiar, a landmark that would strike a chord, but the street remained as unfamiliar to him as his own name. As his own face.

He touched the bruises and grimaced. It was time to evaluate the damage. "Do you have a mirror in here?"

She threw him a surprised glance. "On the visor, but—"

"What?"

"Be prepared," was all she said.

He pulled down the visor and slid back the cover on the lighted mirror. It was so narrow, he could only see a portion of his face at a time. He adjusted the visor, staring first at the thick bandage on his forehead, then at his eyes—both of which were blackened and one almost completely swollen shut—then at the ugly, raw bruises on his cheeks, and finally his lips, cut and also swollen. Kendall had been right. He looked like hell.

He looked like a stranger.

Adjusting the mirror again, Ethan returned to his eyes. Dark brown, what he could see of them. Black lashes. Thick eyebrows. He ripped the bandage from his head and heard her gasp.

"You probably shouldn't have done that," she muttered.

Black hair, matted with blood, tumbled over his forehead, covering the long crescent of stitches over his left brow.

Got to make this look good, pretty boy.

Ethan didn't say anything for a long moment. Couldn't say anything.

She braked for a light, and he could feel her watching him. But he couldn't tear his gaze away from his reflection.

"It's all superficial," she said softly. "The cuts and bruises are only skin deep. They'll heal. In a few days, you'll look like a new man."

He studied his eyes, searching for the windows to his soul. A new man? What had the old one been like? A doctor who operated on poor children in Mexico? A husband who cheated on his wife? A man who had gotten a woman killed tonight?

He could still feel her watching him, and he turned suddenly, capturing her gaze. She looked momentarily startled, as if she'd just seen him for the very first time. Or as if she'd glimpsed something in his battered features she hadn't expected.

Was there a redeeming quality hidden among that mass of bruised flesh?

He wanted to think so. He fervently wanted to believe it.

"You're a very good-looking man," she said suddenly.

He almost laughed. "In a Frankenstein sort of way."

"No, I'm serious." She glanced in the rearview mirror. Then glanced again. The light changed, and the car accelerated. "Trust me, you're very handsome."

"I thought you said we'd never met."

He saw a brief frown flicker across her features. "We haven't, but I've seen pictures of you. Amy showed me."

Amy. He tried to conjure an image of the dead woman, a memory of his feelings for her, but he felt nothing. Saw nothing.

He studied the woman beside him. Her profile was shadowed in the subdued light from the dash, and she kept glancing in the rearview mirror, as if she expected them to be followed. He wished he knew what she was thinking, and why he couldn't bring himself to fully trust her.

There was something about her...

Something about the pain in her eyes...

He had no doubt that she'd experienced grief. That her sister's death had affected her deeply, but the pain seemed muted somehow, not sharp and fresh as one would expect. Amy had only been dead a few hours.

This woman seemed too in control. Too determined.

Her gaze left the road for a moment to meet his. He felt an odd stirring somewhere inside him. Suspicion? Desire? Funny how those two emotions weren't mutually exclusive of each other. Far from it.

"Do you look like her?" he asked.

She turned back to the road. "You mean Amy? Not really. She was fair like me, but blond. And she didn't have freckles. She was thinner than me. Taller. Very beautiful."

Was that a trace of envy in her voice? Ethan said, "I don't even know your name, or where you're taking me. I don't even know why I should trust you."

"Which question should I answer first?"

He paused. "The last one, I guess, because depending on your answer, the other two might not matter anyway."

Her blue gaze touched his again. Again he felt the jolt. "Have you ever heard the expression Honor Among Thieves? That sort of fits us, I guess. You can't go to the police without possibly incriminating yourself, and for reasons of my own, I don't want to involve the authorities, either. The only way you can protect yourself is to find Amy's killer before he finds you. And as it happens, that's the same thing I want. It makes sense that we help each other."

"Even if we don't exactly trust one another?"

She shrugged. Ethan thought her answer couldn't have been more eloquent.

After a moment, he said, "And if we do find Amy's killer. What happens then?"

She didn't hesitate. "I bring him to justice. After that, I don't give a damn what happens to you."

"That's cold."

"It's honest."

She braked for another light, but this time, she didn't look at him. She stared straight ahead, her hands gripping the steering wheel.

"So," she said, "do you still want to know the answers to the first two questions?"

He almost smiled. "Surprisingly enough, yes."

She did glance at him then. Her eyes seemed like starlight. Soft and clear. Very mysterious. "My name is Grace Donovan. And I'm taking you home."

He lifted a brow, felt the faint pulling at his stitches. "Your home?"

"No, yours."

The light changed and the car started forward.

"How do you know where I live?"

"Amy showed me once."

He paused. "Has it occurred to you that we may not be able to get in? I don't have keys."

"Did you check your pockets?"

"Of course. The police have my wallet and briefcase, along with whatever luggage I brought back from Mexico."

"Let's hope they don't find anything incriminating," she said. "At least not until we see it first."

She was blunt to the point of brutal. Ethan had to admire her guts. "What makes you think my house will be safe?"

"Wait till you see the place. It's like a fortress."

Ethan tried to picture his home. Tried to imagine himself living in a house that could be described as a fortress, but the only thing he could conjure was the smell of the jungle, the roar of the river, the adrenaline rush of danger. Somehow those things seemed more familiar to him than the estatelike homes they were passing on Memorial.

After a moment, he said, "Your last name is Donovan, not Cole. Are you married?"

"Actually, no. Amy was, briefly. Right out of high school. It lasted about a year. The guy was pretty much a lowlife. She always did have lousy taste in men." Their gazes clashed—hers defiant, his oddly defensive.

He said, "Can I ask you something? You say you want to find your sister's killer, but—"

"But what?" she asked sharply.

"You don't seem exactly…torn up about her death."

He saw her knuckles whiten on the steering wheel. "Because I'm not crying? Not falling apart? Because I want to see her killer brought to justice? There are different ways of expressing grief, Dr. Hunter. Believe me, I know."

"I'm sure that's true. But you seem so—" Again he floundered for the right words, and she turned to stare at him in challenge. "In control," he finally said.

"I don't consider that a bad thing. Do you?"

"Amy's only been dead a few hours."

"No one's more aware of that than I am." She shot a glance in the rearview mirror.

"What about your parents? Have you called them?"

"Everyone's been notified who needs to be," she said. "You don't need to concern yourself with my family. Or with my emotions, for that matter."

"But I feel responsible for Amy's death, even if I didn't pull the trigger. I need to know about her," he said urgently. "I need to know what kind of person she was. Why she became involved with me—other than the fact that she had lousy taste in men."

"I'm sorry. That was a cheap shot," she allowed almost grudgingly. "Look, I may as well tell you. Amy and I weren't very close. In fact, until a few weeks ago, we hadn't spoken in years."

Surprised, he studied her profile in the dash lights. "Why?"

She shrugged. "We had a falling out. It was stupid, but we just never made up. Resentment and jealousy have a tendency to run a little too deeply, you know?"

He heard the pain and regret in her voice and said instinctively, "Was it over a man?"

She grimaced. "How very perceptive of you. That man she married right out of high school? He was my fiancé."

Ethan didn't know what to say to that. In the silence, she laughed, a brittle little sound that didn't quite ring true. "Guess I have lousy taste in men, too." She paused again, drawing a breath. "Maybe now you understand why my emotions may not be what you think they should be. But I am grieving for my sister, in my own way. And I'll have to live with all these regrets. That's why it's so important for me to find Amy's killer. To focus on getting her justice. Because if I don't…if I let this guilt eat away at me…'' Her eyes closed briefly. Her hands trembled on the steering wheel. ''This is the last thing I can do for her, Dr. Hunter. Do you understand?''

''I think so.'' Ethan was more affected by her words than he wanted to admit. He turned to stare out the window.

Beside him, Grace murmured, ''She was only twenty-four. Just a baby. Did you know that?''

The scenery blurred past Ethan. ''Do you know how old I am?''

''Thirty-seven, according to Amy.''

''Am I still married?''

When Grace didn't answer right away, he turned to stare at her. She shrugged. ''As far as I know, a divorce was never anything but a promise.''

''Then my wife—''

She shrugged again. ''May be at home waiting for you. We'll soon find out.''

She turned into a long, circular drive, coming to stop in front of a house that could only be described the way she had earlier—as a fortress. Nestled in a forest of ancient oak trees and towering pines, the house was white and bleak, a modern, four-story structure with walled courtyards, security cameras and a windowless bottom floor.

The wall of glass blocks on the second floor reflected soft light from within, as if someone were indeed home waiting for him. Ethan stared up at the stark lines of the house and wondered what he might find inside. His past? A wronged wife?

Neither prospect buoyed him.

"How do you propose we get in?" he asked doubtfully. "I already told you, I don't have keys, and even if I did, I wouldn't be able to turn off the alarm system."

"Why don't we just go ring the bell?" Before he could protest, Grace got out of the car and strode toward the courtyard gate.

Dread hanging like a dark cloak over his shoulders, Ethan opened the door and followed her.

When he stood next to her, Grace pressed the button on the intercom, and after a few moments, a voice sputtered over the speaker. "Yes?"

Grace opened her hands, palms up, as if to say, "You're on," and Ethan cleared his throat. "It's me. Ethan. I forgot my key."

A surprised silence ensued, then a woman with a Spanish accent said, "Dr. Hunter? I'm so glad you're finally home. *Un momento, por favor.*"

Almost immediately the lock on the gate was disengaged from inside the house, and the gate swung open. They walked through the lush courtyard toward the front door. Somewhere on the grounds, Ethan heard a sprinkler, and a dog barked in the distance. He glanced up at the winking light on the security camera mounted inside the gate, and thought again of the jungle. Of eyes watching him in the darkness.

The door was drawn back, and a tiny woman wearing a gray-and-white uniform appeared in the light. She took one look at Ethan and gasped, her hand flying to her mouth.

"Dr. Hunter, are you all right?"

"I will be," he assured her.

"Dios Mio." Quickly she crossed herself, then

took his arm, murmuring in Spanish while she gently ushered him inside. "What happened?"

"It's a long story."

As she fussed over him, Ethan tried to study his surroundings without giving himself away, but it was hard to contain his reaction. The inside of the house was even more overwhelming than the outside. The jungle theme of the courtyard had been carried through to the foyer, and—he discovered moments later when they climbed a circular staircase—to the second-floor living room.

Giant palms and tree ferns stretched toward a vast ceiling of skylights, while dozens of potted orchids with magnificent purple, yellow and white blooms added to the exotic atmosphere. From his perch across the room, a huge blue-and-yellow parrot tracked them with beady, knowing eyes.

It was like being back in that jungle. Ethan suddenly felt claustrophobic. He allowed the maid to lead him to a deep leather chair, and wearily he sank into it.

She drew up an ottoman for his feet, still muttering and clucking like a mother hen. "What happened, Dr. Hunter?" she asked again when she finally had him settled to her satisfaction. "Was there an *accidente?*"

"He was mugged," Grace said.

The maid whirled, as if she'd only now discovered Grace's presence. She turned back to Ethan, her dark eyes wide and frightened. "Should I call the *policía?*"

Her English was almost flawless when she chose it to be. Ethan had the impression her lapses into Spanish were more by design, a reminder, to herself perhaps, of the heritage she'd long ago left behind.

"I've already spoken with the police," he told her.

She wrung her hands. "I knew something was wrong. I expected you home hours ago. When you called from the airport in *Méjico,* you said your flight was on time. Then you didn't come..." She broke off, her gaze easing back to Grace.

Ethan said, "This is Grace Donovan. She gave me a ride home from the hospital."

Grace walked over beside Ethan, and the maid's gaze followed her, narrowing.

"How do you do?" Grace held out her hand. The maid took it tentatively. Grace said, "I'm sorry. I don't believe I caught your name."

"Rosa."

Nicely done, Ethan thought, although why he felt the need to hide his amnesia from his housekeeper he had no idea. He hadn't told Dr. Kendall or Sergeant Pope of his memory loss, either. He hadn't confided in anyone but Grace, and again, he didn't know why, except that she was Amy's sister, and he'd felt he owed her something. Some sort of explanation.

She was only twenty-four years old. A baby.

He fingered the bruises on his throat, in some perverse way welcoming the pain.

Rosa said anxiously, "Can I get you something? *¿Agua? Té?*"

"No, thank you." For the first time, Ethan noticed a shopping bag and purse on the white leather sofa beside the chair where he sat. He glanced at Rosa. "Were you on your way out?"

She looked faintly uncomfortable. "*Sí.* I was going

to stay with my daughter tonight. She has a new *bebé*, remember? Her husband is out of town, and tomorrow is my day off. We talked about this on the phone earlier, but with everything that's happened—'' She broke off, staring down at him, shaking her head. *"Tu linda cara…tu pobre linda cara…"*

Ethan automatically put a hand to his face. ''Don't worry. It looks a lot worse than it is. You go on. Go be with your daughter. I'm fine.''

She looked doubtful, but Grace said, ''Yes, don't worry about Dr. Hunter, Rosa. I'll look after him.''

Rosa's gaze darkened disapprovingly. ''What about Señora Hunter?''

''What about her?'' Ethan asked, tensing.

Rosa hesitated. ''She called earlier. She said Dr. Kendall told her you were coming back tonight. If she comes here and finds you—'' Her gaze shot to Grace. ''Last time…the acid…your car…''

Ethan exchanged a glance with Grace. To Rosa, he said, ''Look, don't worry. I can handle Señora Hunter. You go be with your daughter and *nieto*. I insist.''

She glanced at Grace, shaking her head and muttering, ''Trouble,'' as she turned and collected her purse and shopping bag from the sofa. *"Mucho* trouble.''

GRACE WANDERED AROUND the magnificent living room while Ethan followed Rosa downstairs. She could hear them murmuring in low tones, but couldn't tell what they were saying. After a few moments, their voices faded, and Grace assumed they'd walked to the back of the house, where a rear entrance probably led to the garage.

After a few minutes, Ethan came back into the room from a different entrance, and Grace turned to him expectantly. "Everything okay?"

He nodded. "I told Rosa the concussion was playing tricks with my short-term memory. I asked her to help me with the alarm code."

"Did she?"

"Everything's set. We're armed and dangerous."

"I like the sound of that," Grace murmured. She felt the weight of her gun in her purse and almost smiled. Thank goodness it hadn't been necessary to use force to convince him to cooperate with her. Not yet at least.

"Did you get that part about your wife? 'The acid…your car.' I wonder what happened."

Ethan's mouth thinned. "I'm not sure I want to know. Sounds like we have a real loving relationship."

Grace sensed that Rosa's words bothered him more than he let on. She said reluctantly, "Do you think she found out about your affair with Amy? Maybe it was a sort of *Fatal Attraction* in reverse."

He turned away. "I really don't want to speculate on the state of my marriage."

"But we have to," Grace said. "That's the only way we'll find answers."

He turned to stare at her. "Do you really think my wife had something to do with Amy's murder?"

Grace shrugged. "It wouldn't be the first time jealousy got out of hand."

His gaze, if possible, darkened. "Is that what Amy intimated in her letters? Was she afraid of my wife?"

"She mentioned her a few times. She called her Pilar. I think there'd been some trouble. But I think the danger Amy referred to came from a different source. Something to do with your clinic in Mexico. If you're up to it, I thought we might go over her letters together. Something might jog your memory."

He ran a weary hand through his hair and walked away.

"Of course, we don't have to do it right now," Grace murmured.

He didn't seem to hear her. He wandered around the room, touching a table here, a chair there, as if he could somehow absorb the essence of the room, of who he had been, into his consciousness.

After a few moments, the almost preternatural silence got to Grace. She walked over to stand beside him. "This is quite a place."

He traced the curved stem of some exotic potted flower, then clipped a red bloom with his thumb nail, as if the delicate blossoms were no more rare or precious than a dandelion. The scarlet petals fell like drops of blood to the surface of the glass table. "It feels more like a prison than a home," he finally said.

"A prison?" Grace glanced around the spacious room. The dense foliage gave the illusion of nature at her most primal, and the enormous skylights afforded a magnificent view of the night sky. She made a sweeping gesture with her arm. "It seems more like a jungle to me. Wild. Primitive. Look, you can even see the moon."

Ethan glanced up, and Grace could have sworn she

saw him shudder. He turned away, heading toward a door at one end of the long room. He opened it and switched on a light.

Grace came up behind him. "What's in there?"

"Looks like an office or a study."

"That should be a good place to start searching for clues, right?"

She sensed him tense. He seemed reluctant to enter the room.

Grace said, "Want me to go first?"

"No," he said over his shoulder. "I'll just have a quick look for now."

Grace frowned. Obviously he didn't want her following him into the study, but why? What was he afraid she might find?

She turned and walked back to the middle of the room. A movement to her right startled her, and she whirled, automatically grabbing for the gun in her purse. But then she saw the huge parrot preening himself, and realized she'd forgotten all about him. He'd been quiet and still since they arrived, but now all of a sudden, he'd grown restless.

Grace tentatively approached his perch. His movements weren't restricted in any way. She supposed he could fly around the room if he chose to, but all he did was take a couple of nervous, sideways steps on the perch.

A cage with an open door sat on a pedestal near the perch, and Grace guessed that was where he took his meals and got his water. Maybe he was even trained to go potty there as well, she thought, because the room was immaculate.

She stood a couple of feet back from the perch and

watched him for a moment. His beady little gaze held hers. "Hey," she said softly, trying not to alarm him. "What's your name?"

He cocked his head and continued to stare at her.

"What's the matter?" Grace asked. "Cat got your tongue?"

All of a sudden, he let out a piercing squawk and flapped his wings so vigorously that Grace screeched, too, and covered her head. When he made no move to attack, she let out a breath of relief and relaxed.

"Sorry," she told him. "It was just a figure of speech." She could have sworn the bird looked sullen and put out. Grace decided she'd better make peace. Moving toward him, she made a kissing sound with her lips and crooned, "Polly want a cracker?"

"Look at the size of those headlights!" the parrot screeched.

Grace jumped at the unexpectedness of his speech. At the crudeness of his words. She gaped at him in shock. "What did you say?"

The bird repeated the line.

"That's what I thought you said."

The parrot fluffed his wings. "I don't think they're real," he said importantly.

"How would you know, you little buzzard!"

Grace's tone seemed to excite him. He raced sideways along the perch, squawking in a loud voice, "They're not real! They're not real! I should know, goddammit!"

"Why you—" Grace made a menacing move toward the parrot, but he put up such a fuss, she instantly retreated.

Behind her, Ethan said, "What's going on? I thought I heard voices."

Grace quickly took several more steps away from the bird. "Your little friend here and I were just having a rap session."

"That thing can talk?" Ethan walked toward the parrot.

"I wouldn't get too close," Grace warned. "He's a little...unpredictable."

But the enormous bird was on his best behavior for Ethan. They stared at each other for a long moment, then Ethan said, "What's your name, fella?"

"What's your name, fella?" the bird said in perfect imitation.

Ethan laughed, a sound that sent a shiver sliding up Grace's spine. "All right, I'll go first. My name's Ethan. At least...I think it is."

The parrot blinked. "My name's Ethan," he mimicked.

Ethan glanced at Grace. "This is getting us nowhere fast. You try."

Grace shook her head. "I don't think so. I don't care for birds." Not this particular bird, anyway.

Ethan turned back to the parrot. "Her name's Grace."

"Look at the size of those headlights!"

Startled, Ethan jumped, then his gaze flew to Grace. A spark of amusement—or was that curiosity?—flared in his brown eyes, and Grace's face flamed as his gaze dropped almost imperceptibly to her chest.

He turned back to the parrot. "What else can you say?"

"I don't think they're real." The bird looked straight at Grace. Then he strutted and preened on his perch.

"Proud of yourself, aren't you?" she muttered. She pointed at Ethan. "How about picking on him for a change?"

As if he understood her every word, the bird cocked his head and stared at Ethan. "Hey, pretty boy."

Grace threw up her hands. "That does it—" She broke off when she saw the look on Ethan's face. He had grown very still, his expression grim as he turned away from the parrot.

"What is it? Did you remember something?"

Behind them, the parrot gave a long, shrill wolf whistle. "Hey, pretty boy. Hey, pretty boy," he sang.

Ethan flinched. "No, it's not that." His gaze didn't quite meet hers. "I'm just tired. I think I'd like to get some rest now."

Grace got his meaning loud and clear. He wanted her to leave. He wasn't about to invite her to spend the night here.

But she was reluctant to let him out of her sight. He'd sustained a concussion, among other injuries, and probably shouldn't be alone. And, contrary to what he'd said, she was almost certain the parrot had triggered a memory for him. Why wouldn't he admit it? Why wouldn't he tell her?

"I'm a little worried about you," she said. "I don't think it's a good idea for you to be alone tonight."

He shrugged. "You said yourself, this place is like a fortress. Now that I know how to arm the alarm system, I should be safe enough."

Grace bit her lip. "Maybe. But I'm not just talking about that. You've got some pretty serious injuries. A head trauma. That's nothing to take lightly."

He looked at her then, his expression ironic. "You don't have to worry about me. I'm a doctor, remember?"

His words did nothing to reassure her. But there was very little Grace could do, short of forcing him at gunpoint to let her stay. She fingered her purse strap, considering.

"If you're sure…"

"We can talk more tomorrow." His tone was final.

"Well…I guess I'll see you in the morning then," Grace said reluctantly.

They started down the stairs together, and he put his hand on her elbow to guide her. Grace was surprised that she didn't pull away, and even more surprised that she didn't *want* to pull away. The touch of his hand sent a shiver of awareness down her backbone. It should have frightened her, but instead, it reminded her that she was still alive. Still a woman. And it had been a very long time—too damned long—since any man had done that for her.

They paused in the foyer while Ethan turned off the alarm system. Then he opened the door, and pressing another series of buttons, disengaged the lock on the courtyard gate. He followed her outside, and they stood in the driveway to say their goodbyes.

It was nearing midnight. The air had finally cooled, and a lazy breeze drifted through the ancient trees, sounding like rain. The moon was still up, almost full. The freshly watered lawn glistened like diamonds in the milky light, and on a trellis outside the courtyard, a moon flower opened to her lunar mistress.

The night was beautiful, clear and starry, but Grace knew the darkness could be deceptive. She peered into Ethan's eyes, wondering what secrets were hidden deep within those fathomless depths.

Moonlight softened his bruised and battered face, and for a split second, Grace had a glimpse of what he really looked like. She caught her breath, remembering what she'd told him earlier. He was a good-looking man, but she thought his allure had little to do with his physical appearance, and everything to do with the man beneath. The mysteries he had unwittingly buried.

She had the sudden and unexpected urge to kiss him, to see if it would stir his emotions enough to uncover those secrets.

As if sensing her scrutiny, he turned and captured her gaze. Grace wondered fleetingly if he could tell what she was thinking. If he knew what she wanted at that moment.

She was almost certain that he did.

"I'd better be going," she murmured, realizing too late just how dangerous her situation had suddenly become.

But when she would have walked away, he caught her arm, turning her back to face him. Their gazes met again, his deep and mystical; hers, she feared, open and far too revealing.

"Thank you for bringing me home tonight," he said. His voice, deep and raspy, had an unnerving affect on Grace.

"You don't have to thank me," she said. "I had my own reasons for doing so."

"Still—" He broke off, his gaze moving away from her. "I'm sorry about Amy. I hope you believe that."

At the mention of Amy, an image of Grace's sister came rushing back to her, reminding her of exactly why she was here. What she had to do.

"If you really mean that," she said softly, almost regretfully, "then I shouldn't have to convince you to help me find her killer."

"I don't think we'll have to find him," Ethan said, his gaze suddenly alert as he searched the darkness around them. "I think he'll find us. I wouldn't be surprised if he's out there right now, watching us."

Grace's gaze shot over her shoulder at his words. She shivered as her hand tightened on her purse, the urge to remove her weapon almost overpowering. "Do you really think so?"

He shrugged in response.

Grace released a long breath. "Look, you've really spooked me. Are you sure you'll be all right here alone?"

"He won't make another move tonight. It's too soon."

She frowned. "How do you know that?"

Ethan gazed down at her, bewilderment flashing across his features. "I don't know," he said hoarsely. "I don't know how I know that."

ETHAN WATCHED AS Grace eased her car around the circular drive, then pulled onto the main street. Within moments, the taillights disappeared from his sight, and only then did he walk back into the house, locking the courtyard gate and resetting the alarm behind him. He climbed the staircase again, and for several seconds, stood at the edge of the junglelike room, reluctant to enter.

A deep uneasiness came over him, but he tried to tell himself it was only natural. He had amnesia. He'd almost been killed tonight, and the sister of the woman he'd been having an affair with had all but implicated him in her murder. Why wouldn't he feel uneasy?

But it was more than that. Something other than that. He wondered if his discomfort had more to do with Grace herself than with her accusations, or even the bizarre situation in which he found himself.

She wasn't telling him everything. He knew instinctively that there was more to Grace Donovan than she'd let on, but Ethan had no idea why he felt this way. He'd seen the grief in her eyes, the pain in her expression when she talked about her sister. He was sure her emotions were genuine, and yet his earlier doubts about her came rushing back. Her reaction was not that of a woman who had just learned of her sister's murder. The guilt, the anger, the obsession to find a loved one's killer were emotions that would come much later.

So what was going on here? Why did Ethan have the feeling that he was a pawn in some very dangerous game?

Was Grace a player, or was she, too, a pawn?

She had explained her relationship with Amy. They hadn't been close. A man had come between them, and they hadn't spoken in years until recently. Until

Amy had contacted Grace and told her of the affair with Ethan.

He foraged his mind for a memory of Amy Cole, some remnant of his feelings for her. But there was nothing, and for some reason he couldn't explain, he was almost certain that she'd never meant anything to him.

So was that the kind of person he was? The kind of man who would use a woman for whatever he wanted or needed from her and then discard her without a second thought? Had he done that with his wife?

The cloying scent of the orchids made his head hurt. Ethan hurried out of the room, seeking the shelter of the study he'd found earlier. He didn't want to think about his wife or Amy Cole, and since he didn't remember either of them, it was easy enough to put them out of his mind.

Grace Donovan, however, was a different matter.

At the thought of her, Ethan's uneasiness returned full force, and suddenly he realized where his discomfort was coming from, at least in part. He was attracted to her. He had been from the first.

She wasn't beautiful by any stretch of the imagination, but she was attractive in her own way, and definitely intriguing. And those eyes...

Those eyes could melt a man's soul. He was sure of it.

Her figure wasn't tall and thin, but lush and womanly, and when he'd grabbed her earlier in the hospital parking lot, he'd felt the hardness of her muscles, the toned grace of her body.

If push came to shove, he knew she could hold her own, and that made her all the more alluring. She didn't need taking care of. She didn't need protecting, and that should have rubbed Ethan's male ego the wrong way, but instead it piqued his interest. Made him wonder things he had no business wondering. He was still a married man, even if he couldn't remember his own wife.

He'd left the light on in the office earlier, and now as he entered the room, he tried to put Grace out of his mind and concentrate on his surroundings. There had to be something in here that would trigger a memory for him. Something that would give him a clue as to what he'd been involved in. What had gotten Amy Cole killed.

Slowly, he walked around the room, studying the framed diplomas and certificates that he'd only taken the time to glance at earlier. He'd been educated at Harvard and Johns Hopkins. He was a board-certified plastic surgeon. He'd received dozens of awards and citations, and had corresponded with dignitaries all over the world.

Among the framed letters on the wall was one from the president of the United States, commending him on his work with underprivileged children born with disfigurements.

Ethan studied his hands. Did he really have the ability to wield a scalpel, the power to change people's lives? Children's lives?

Could that ability and power, all that training and instinct, be subdued by amnesia?

According to the letters and articles, Dr. Ethan Hunter was not only a brilliant surgeon, but a renowned humanitarian. But if he was such a great guy, why the hell was someone trying to kill him?

One whole side of the office contained dozens of framed newspaper articles written about him, but only one carried a photograph. For some reason he couldn't define, Ethan had been reluctant to do more than glance at the picture earlier. He knew it was a photo of him. In spite of the battered condition of his face now, he'd recognized the features. The brown eyes, the dark hair, the angular jaw and chin were the same ones he'd seen in the mirror in Grace's car.

And yet...

The man in the picture was him and it wasn't.

He couldn't explain it any better than that. He didn't feel connected in any way with the image in the photo, and the moment he'd seen it earlier, a dark haze had descended over him. Try as he might, he hadn't been able to compel himself to take that picture from the wall and study it more closely.

He removed it now and carried it with him to the desk, snapping on a brass lamp as he sat down. Placing the picture before him, he fought off a wave of dizziness as he forced himself to look down at his likeness, to study and absorb his own features.

In the photograph, he was standing in front of a white, one-story building with a lush, tropical backdrop. An older, shorter man with a thin, black mustache was in the picture, too, and Ethan's arm was draped over the man's shoulder. They both wore khaki pants and white shirts, both were smiling for the camera, but there was something about Ethan's expression...

Something about the other man's eyes...

He was frightened, Ethan thought suddenly. In spite of the smile and the reassuring arm Ethan had thrown over his shoulder, the mustached man looked scared half to death.

Shaken, Ethan forced himself to read the accompanying article concerning the reopening of the clinic in the Mexican jungle after a half dozen or so *banditos* had destroyed the place once they'd raided it for drugs. The other man in the picture was a Dr. Javier Salizar, a pediatrician who worked full-time at the clinic and who had been on duty the night the *banditos* attacked.

Fortunately, there had been no overnight patients at the hospital. Dr. Salizar had been all alone, and he'd been forced to flee into the jungle and hide until the terrorists had gathered what they wanted and left, burning the clinic to the ground in their wake.

According to the article, Ethan had provided his own personal funds to restore the clinic, and had used his own hands to help rebuild it. He'd spent months of his time getting the clinic operational once again, and the people in the surrounding villages revered him almost like a god.

Ethan didn't understand why, but the article deeply disturbed him. He sensed something bad had happened at that clinic. Something had made him flee, like Dr. Salizar, into the jungle, but not because he had been pursued by *banditos*.

In his dream, Ethan hadn't seen the men chasing him, but he had known just the same that they wore uniforms. They carried guns. He had almost been killed by the Mexican authorities, but Ethan had no idea why.

All he knew was that in some dark and dangerous way, he was tied to that clinic. To that jungle. And the killers that had pursued him in Mexico had followed him here to Houston. To his home.

Hands trembling, Ethan put the picture away and rifled through the paperwork on top of the desk. He turned on the laptop computer and perused the directories, but the files meant nothing. The case studies, medical notations, and patient consultations may as well have been written in a foreign language. Nothing clicked for him. Nothing at all.

Why didn't anything in this office trigger a memory? Why couldn't he remember being a doctor?

Almost frantically, Ethan searched through the desk. At the bottom of a drawer, a gold frame caught his eye. It had been stuffed facedown under a stack of folders. He pulled it out and stared down at a picture of a woman.

This was no snapshot or newspaper clipping, but an elegant studio shot with lighting that complimented the woman's ebony eyes and her full, ruby lips. Thick, glossy black hair had been pulled back to reveal a face as beautiful as it was flawless.

Movie-star glamorous, the woman stood in front of a grand piano, wearing a strapless black evening gown and opera-length, black gloves. Her body was thin, but incredibly shapely. The word that came instantly to mind was statuesque.

She wasn't smiling for the camera, but her lips were parted seductively and her eyes were heavy-lidded and sensual. At the bottom of the picture, scrawled in red ink, were the words: *To my husband, with much love and gratitude, Pilar.*

So this was Ethan's wife. He knew instinctively

she'd had the picture made especially for him, and he'd put it away in a drawer facedown.

...the acid...your car...

Ethan stared at the photograph for a very long time, wondering how long they'd been married and what had gone wrong between them. She was an exquisite woman on the surface, but somehow her utter perfection left him cold.

Did I do this to you? he wondered. *Did I make you into this...work of art?*

A work of art without a soul, something told him.

He thought of Grace suddenly, of the unevenness of her features, the short, red hair, the lips that were neither lush nor thin, but in his mind, just right. Her light blue eyes held more life, more mystery, than this woman's ever could.

Disturbed by his thoughts, Ethan put the picture away and closed the drawer. It wasn't fair to give a woman he didn't remember unfavorable attributes in order to justify his attraction to Grace. And that was exactly what he'd been doing.

Had he also tried to justify his affair with Amy Cole? Had there been other women in his marriage?

What kind of husband would treat his wife in such a manner?

What kind of doctor would be pursued through the Mexican jungle by the *policía?*

Ethan wondered if he really wanted to know the answer to any of those questions.

GRACE CLOSED AND locked the door of her hotel room, then slung her jacket toward a chair. Flopping down on the bed, she kicked off her shoes, leaned back against the headboard, then removed her cell phone from her purse and punched in a number she knew by heart.

In spite of the late hour, a woman with a throaty voice answered on the first ring. "Hello?"

"It's Grace."

There was a brief pause before the woman asked, "Are you all right?"

"Amy's dead, Myra."

"Yes, I know."

"What the hell happened tonight?" Grace exploded. "What went wrong?"

"Everything. God, it's all a mess. Hunter wasn't supposed to come back to Houston for at least another two weeks. We would have had plenty of time to set up a sting, but now..." Myra Temple trailed off while she lit up a cigarette. Grace heard her exhale angrily. "As it is, we've rushed the whole operation. We're down here without proper backup or support, and we screwed up. It happens."

"Yes, but this particular screwup cost a woman her life," Grace said angrily. Myra seemed more concerned about the potential damage to the operation than about Amy's death, but that should have come as no surprise. The woman was coldly and consummately professional. Nothing got in her way, and until tonight, Grace had thought she was becoming exactly like her mentor. She'd thought she had the guts to do whatever had to be done to bring a killer to justice.

But after tonight...

"Amy should have been under surveillance. Why wasn't she?"

"She was," Myra snapped. "But somehow she

managed to slip through. My guess is that after speaking with us yesterday, she panicked. She had second thoughts about what she'd done, and so she got in touch with Dr. Hunter, probably by cell phone, and warned him that the Feds would be waiting for him when he landed here in Houston. Then she devised a way to get out of her apartment without us knowing.''

"How?" Grace demanded.

"Maybe she donned a wig and borrowed her neighbor's car. How the hell should I know? It doesn't help matters that these idiots in the field office down here don't know their butts from a hole in the ground. We can't count on much help in that regard. In any case, Amy appears to have been a lot smarter than I gave her credit for.'' Myra's tone was a mixture of disgust and admiration.

"So how did Eth—Dr. Hunter manage to get away from us? You were watching the airport yourself.''

A loud silence. "He didn't land at Bush Intercontinental Airport,'' Myra finally said testily, clearly annoyed by Grace's veiled criticism. "I guarantee you, I would have recognized him if he had. We're checking all the private airfields in the area now, but he undoubtedly chartered a plane. Sometime during the flight, he contacted Amy again, and they made plans to meet at the clinic.''

Something in her tone made Grace's heart thud against her chest. "Myra, you don't think—''

"What?''

Grace tensed. Her hand clutched the tiny cell phone. "You don't think *he* killed Amy, do you? Because he found out she talked to us?''

Another pause. "It's possible, but I don't think so.

I think he was followed, probably all the way from Mexico, and ambushed at the clinic. I think you and I both know who killed Amy Cole, Grace.''

Grace closed her eyes, dredging up a name from the past. A face from her nightmares. Trevor Reardon. A man who had changed Grace's life forever.

''By the way,'' Myra said softly. ''That was a brilliant stroke on your part—pretending to be Amy's sister.''

More like an act of desperation, Grace thought. Aloud she said, ''Actually, it was Amy's idea. She introduced me to one of her neighbors as her sister. Then she later told me she didn't have any family, but no one in Houston knew that about her because she didn't like to talk about her past.''

When Grace had arrived at the clinic earlier to learn that Amy was dead and Ethan Hunter had been severely beaten, she knew she had to come up with a reason that would put her in close contact with him. And if everything Amy had told her about him was true, Grace was fairly certain Ethan would be wary of the authorities. She couldn't tell him the truth because he would never trust her, never agree to cooperate with her, and so she'd impulsively devised the cover of being Amy's grieving sister. A woman who wanted to find the killer just as badly as Ethan did.

Grace wondered if the ruse had worked, or if like her, he had suspicions.

She ran her fingers through her bangs. ''Look, there's another contingency we hadn't counted on. Dr. Hunter now claims he has amnesia.''

''Yes, I know,'' Myra said. ''According to his

chart, he's suffering some short-term memory loss due to a rather mild concussion.''

Grace should have known Myra would have done her homework thoroughly. She'd probably been over Ethan's hospital room with a vacuum.

''I'm afraid it's a little more severe than that,'' Grace said. ''He claims he doesn't remember Amy. Or even his own name, for that matter.''

She heard Myra suck in her breath sharply. ''You mean he doesn't remember *anything?*''

''That's what he says.''

Grace could almost hear the wheels turning in Myra's brain. After a few moments, she said, ''Do you think he's faking?''

Grace thought about the darkness and confusion in Ethan's eyes earlier, the desperation that had flashed across his features. Had that been a reaction to what had happened to him in the clinic? Or because he genuinely couldn't remember?

Grace found herself wanting to believe him and that scared her. It was imperative she remain objective. Dispassionate. A consummate professional.

She wondered suddenly what Myra would think if she knew how attracted Grace was to Dr. Ethan Hunter. Would she pull her off the case?

''Well, so what do you think?'' Myra's impatient tone brought Grace out of her reverie, and she realized she'd lapsed into silence for a few seconds too long.

She took a deep breath, willing her tone to remain even. ''I thought he might be faking at first. I mean, it seemed a little too coincidental, if Amy did tip him off that we'd be waiting for him. But after spending some time with him tonight, I'm inclined to believe him. He seems genuinely distressed.''

Myra's tone was pensive. "So maybe this doesn't have to change anything. Let's think about it for a minute. Whether he's faking or not, your cover should hold up. If Amy told you the truth and she really had no family, there won't be anyone coming out of the woodwork to dispute your claim. And if he *does* have amnesia, it could even work to our advantage. Make him easier to control.''

An image of Ethan's bruised and battered face materialized in Grace's mind, and something fluttered in her stomach. Was it pity? Guilt?

Maybe it was just plain old fear, she thought, although for her, that could be the most dangerous emotion of all.

"You aren't having second thoughts about using him, are you?" Myra asked casually, but Grace was immediately on her guard. Was she being tested?

She gripped the phone with grim determination. "Not at all. Ethan Hunter is a means to an end, nothing more.''

"Good," Myra said, satisfied. "Because we're getting close, Grace. Can you feel it?''

Grace's stomach knotted with excitement. Or was it dread? "Yes.''

"This amnesia thing could be a blessing in disguise, exactly what we need to gain Hunter's cooperation. But we still have to be careful," Myra warned. "Don't do or say anything that will tip him off. I don't have to remind you that one false move and this whole thing could still blow up in our faces.''

"Don't worry.'' Cradling the phone against her

shoulder, Grace removed the SIG-Sauer from her purse and released the magazine, pulling back the slide to make sure the gun was unloaded. Then methodically she reloaded the weapon and looked through the sights, relieved to see that her hand was steady, her nerves steeled. "I've waited a long time for this."

"I know you have," Myra said. "But just remember, this can't become a personal vendetta. Once you allow your emotions to get in the way, you become a walking dead woman."

"I understand. You don't have to worry about me. You taught me well."

"I hope so," Myra said softly. "I hope so..."

After they ended the call, Grace poured herself a whiskey over ice and walked out to the tiny balcony of her room. It was still hot. At Ethan's house, the lush tropical foliage, both inside and out, had at least given the illusion of coolness, but here, the heat clung to the concrete and mortar like a desperate lover.

Grace lifted the glass to the back of her neck, letting the cool condensation slide against her skin as the events of the night and remnants of her former life played themselves out in her mind. Funny how one tragic moment, one careless decision could change a person's life forever, could mold you into someone you didn't even recognize anymore.

But tonight she'd glimpsed a bit of the old Grace. Tonight she'd remembered what it was like to be attracted to a man. She'd *felt* something, standing outside with Ethan.

Downing half the contents of her glass, Grace shuddered as the liquid caught fire in her throat and

stomach. Myra's warning seemed to reach out from
the darkness and taunt her.

*Once you allow your emotions to get in the way,
you become a walking dead woman.*

Chapter Four

The sun streaming in through the tall windows in the third-story master suite awakened Ethan the next morning. He'd tossed and turned for hours the night before, sleeping sporadically, dreaming about running through the jungle and then falling. As in most nightmares, he never remembered hitting the ground but instead would awaken abruptly in a cold sweat, his heart pounding, adrenaline still rushing through his veins.

He sat up now and looked around, slowly letting the events of last evening filter back in. He'd hoped that by morning his memory would have returned, but his mind was still pretty much a blank. He still had no idea who Ethan Hunter really was, what he might have done, or why someone wanted to kill him. All he knew for sure was that he had to somehow keep it together. He had to remain sharp until he could find out what the hell was going on.

His body aching, he pulled himself out of bed and headed for the shower. Like the bedroom, the master bath was huge and luxurious, with lush, green carpeting, intricate tile mosaics, a step-up marble bathtub, and a shower stall that could easily accommodate two.

Turning on the water in the shower, Ethan stood staring at his reflection in the mirror over the double vanity. The bruises on his face were still prominent, but the swelling had gone down, and the pain wasn't quite so severe. He almost looked human this morning, although his face was still one he didn't recognize.

Stripping away the last of his clothing, he examined the appendectomy scar on his lower right side. The wound was surprisingly large, about four inches long, and still tender to the touch. Ethan stared at the scar, trying to remember the surgery, but nothing came to him. Nothing but the fleeting memory of being pursued through the jungle. The echoing sound of gunfire. The lingering unease that Dr. Ethan Hunter was a man he wasn't sure he wanted to get to know.

Ignoring the twinges of pain from the cuts and bruises, he stepped under the hot water, washing briskly, trying to elude the questions whirling inside his head by concentrating on the mundane. Showering. Getting dressed. Finding something to eat.

Back in the bedroom, he gazed at the clothing hanging in the massive walk-in closet. The expensive suits and custom-made shirts were as unfamiliar to him as the face he'd studied in the bathroom mirror.

Finally, randomly, he grabbed something casual, a pair of charcoal pants and a cotton knit pullover. The pants were loose in the waist, and he wondered if he'd lost weight after his surgery. The shirt fit fine, but the shoes he pulled from the closet were a little snug. He started to find another pair, but then froze when he heard a noise. Somewhere downstairs a door opened and closed.

It occurred to Ethan that Rosa might have come back, but she'd said last night that today was her day off. She planned to spend the time with her daughter. So who was downstairs then?

Ethan scanned the room for a weapon. His eyes lit on the nightstand next to the bed, and he crossed the floor to search through the drawers. If he kept a gun in the house, he reasoned that would be the logical place for it, but his search was fruitless.

Removing the shade from the heavy brass lamp on the nightstand, Ethan jerked the plug from the wall and picked up the base. As a weapon, it was cumbersome at best, but he didn't have time to look for anything else. Whoever was in the house might even now be slipping up the stairs to ambush him.

Heart thumping, his senses on full alert, Ethan left the bedroom, making his way toward the stairs. He paused on the landing, peering over the railing into the jungle-like living room below him. Nothing moved. No sound came to him.

In sock feet, he slipped silently down the stairs, his gaze searching every nook and corner of the room. There were any number of places an intruder could hide, but the most obvious place seemed to be the study. The door was ajar, and Ethan was almost certain he'd closed it last night before going to bed.

He crossed the room and flattened himself against the wall outside the study, listening. From inside, he could detect shuffling sounds, as if someone was going through his papers.

Nerves pumped, Ethan glanced inside. And tensed.

A woman stood before an open safe, busily removing what looked to be bundles of cash. He recognized her immediately from the picture he'd found in the desk last night. The intruder was his wife.

She didn't see him at first. Ethan watched her for several seconds as she stood at the safe. The red suit she wore was so short and so tight that she didn't appear to be armed, but the thought crossed Ethan's mind that she was probably extremely dangerous anyway. A woman scorned could be deadly.

He set the brass lamp on the floor, then stepped into the room. Her head jerked toward the door, her hand flying to her heart when she saw him. She blinked once, then twice before she finally managed to get her shock under control. "Ethan!" Her voice was lyrical and very feminine, traced with a Spanish accent. "I didn't know you were home."

Ethan glanced at the bundles of cash. "I can see that."

She made no move to close the safe door, nor to hide the money she'd stacked on top of his desk. Instead she took one of the bundles and brazenly thumbed through the bills. "I heard you were in the hospital." Glancing up, her gaze flicked over his bruised features. Something flashed in her eyes, an emotion Ethan couldn't define. "You look and sound terrible," she said.

"Thanks." He returned her perusal, taking a long moment to study her features, and decided that the photograph in his desk, as spectacular as it was, didn't do her justice. She was even more beautiful in person. The deep V-neck of her jacket revealed a magnificent cleavage while the impossibly short skirt highlighted impossibly long legs.

But what drew Ethan's attention more than her grace and sultry beauty was the fact that she appeared to be stealing him blind.

As if reading his mind, she glanced down at the money and shrugged. "It's not like you don't owe me."

When he didn't protest, she gave him an odd glance, then turned back to the safe. Her hair cascaded down her back, almost to her waist, gleaming like ebony when she tossed it over her shoulder.

"What are you doing here anyway?" she asked, her voice muffled as she reached inside the safe. "Bob said you'd been beaten up pretty badly. He thought you'd be in the hospital for several more days." She withdrew another packet of bills, then turned to face him, her dark eyes challenging.

"Bob who?" Ethan asked, without thinking.

She arched a perfect black brow. "Bob Kendall. Your ex-partner, remember? Who else would I be talking about?"

Ethan was immediately on his guard. Kendall was his ex-partner? If the hostility in the man's eyes last night had been any indication, the arrangement had ended badly. Ethan wondered what had gone wrong, in his business and in his marriage.

He stared at his wife, trying to dredge up a memory, some leftover emotion, but nothing came to him. Nothing but a faint uneasiness as he watched her.

"When did you talk to Bob?" he asked.

Something that might have been guilt flashed over her features. She began stuffing the money into a large black tote bag. "He called me last night. He was at the hospital when you were brought in, and he thought I'd want to know what happened."

Ethan remembered what Rosa had told him last evening, that Pilar had called here at the house because Kendall had told her Ethan was returning. Why? he wondered. There had been none of her clothing in the closet upstairs, no makeup or feminine toiletries in the bathroom. It was obvious she no longed lived here, so why had she called Rosa to find out when he was returning?

And why wait until he got back to rob his safe? Unless, of course, things hadn't gone according to plan—

Had Pilar and Kendall been behind Ethan's attack last night? Had they somehow arranged for him to go to the clinic before coming home? Had they wanted to kill him?

Ethan studied his wife and wondered why that notion didn't seem preposterous to him. Was it because Pilar Hunter struck him as a woman who would get what she wanted no matter who she had to hurt in the process?

But she was also a woman Ethan had married, must have once loved. He wondered how he could feel nothing, not even anger, toward her now.

Her task completed, she closed the bag and slung the straps over her shoulder. She walked around the desk and started by him, then paused. "Bob told me about Amy. I guess I should say I'm sorry."

Ethan said nothing.

For the first time, he sensed an uncertainty about his wife, as if she didn't know whether to say more or end it here and now. Then she smiled. "I never believed you loved her, you know. Not like you once loved me." Gazing up at him, she lifted a hand to his face.

Ethan resisted the urge to step back from her. Instead he held his ground, letting her place a cool palm against his bruised skin. For one long moment, he stared down at her perfect features, her incredible beauty, and wondered again why he felt nothing.

And she knew. Like a lightning bolt, anger whipped across her features. *"Cabrón,"* she muttered as she turned and brushed by him. Outside the doorway, she glanced back. "You do look terrible, you know. Besides the bruises, I mean. You've lost weight. Your eyes..." she trailed off, studying him.

"What about my eyes?" he asked sharply.

"They're cold. Even colder than I remembered." She shuddered. "You are not the man I married, Ethan. You haven't been for a very long time."

WHEN GRACE ARRIVED at the house a little while later, she was amazed to see how much better Ethan looked. Even though the bruises hadn't faded, the swelling in his face had gone down so that his features were no longer distorted. She could tell more clearly what he looked like, and when he'd first opened the door, she'd caught her breath in surprise.

"I...hope I didn't get you up," she said, her gaze slipping over him. He was dressed, but his hair was mussed and he wasn't wearing any shoes. His casualness made her feel stuffy in her beige pantsuit, silk shell and brown flats.

"I've been up for a while," he said, his voice still

hoarse. He stood back so she could enter. Grace stepped past him into the foyer, then waited while he closed the door and reactivated the alarm.

"Have you remembered anything?" she asked anxiously.

He gave her a look. "You don't waste any time, do you?"

Grace shrugged. "Why should I? Someone out there killed my sister last night, and he may come back to finish you off. Who has time for formalities?"

"I get your point," he said dryly. "And the answer to your question is, no. I haven't remembered anything."

"Nothing at all?"

"Nothing that makes any sense."

Grace glanced up at him, trying to read his expression. "Well, if it's any consolation, you look much better today. Almost like a different man."

"So I've already been told." He turned and started for the stairs.

"By whom?" Grace asked quickly. "Has someone been here this morning?"

He paused on the bottom step, turning to glance over his shoulder. "My wife was here earlier. I caught her taking money out of the safe in the study."

Grace frowned. "What do you mean, you *caught* her?"

"Just that. Apparently she no longer lives here. But I guess she decided to come back and help herself to whatever cash I might have left lying around."

Grace took a moment to assess this new information. So Ethan had met Pilar Hunter face to face. Grace couldn't help wondering how the meeting had gone, or what he'd thought of the woman. What he'd felt for her. From the pictures Grace had seen, Pilar was an incredibly beautiful woman.

Absently, Grace ran a hand down her pantsuit, smoothing invisible wrinkles. "So what was it like seeing her?" she tried to ask casually. "Did she give you any clues about your relationship? About what might have happened between the two of you?"

Ethan paused. "I don't have any idea what happened between us, but I'll tell you one thing. She struck me as a woman perfectly capable of throwing acid on my car. Or in my face, for that matter."

The bluntness of his words threw Grace for a moment. "Do you think she may have had something to do with Amy's death?"

"I wouldn't rule out the possibility," he said grimly. He turned and started up the stairs. "Come on up. We can talk about this later. I've located the kitchen, and I'm cooking breakfast."

Grace followed him up the stairs and through the living room. The parrot, fully awake and preening on his perch, let out a loud squawk when he saw her.

"Don't even start," she muttered.

"What?" Ethan said over his shoulder.

"I said that's a good start. Learning your way around the house, I mean."

He gave her a quizzical look, then led her through a dining room with a high ceiling and a magnificent stained glass window, into the kitchen, with its stainless steel appliances, satillo tile floor, and wall of atrium doors that gave a broad view of a backyard pool and waterfall.

Ethan walked over to the range and dished up a

plate of bacon and eggs, then added a pile of buttered toast. "Have you eaten? There's plenty for both of us."

Grace eyed the food longingly. She'd started the day with her usual meal, one half of a grapefruit and a cup of coffee. If she ate bacon and eggs, she'd have to add at least half an hour to her daily workout in the gym, not to mention an extra mile or two to her run. For a moment, she considered that it might be worth it. She hadn't had a piece of bacon in ages.

Willpower, she reminded herself. She had to remain sharp both physically and mentally. "Just a glass of orange juice for me."

He poured them both a glass of juice from a pitcher he removed from the refrigerator, then carried his food to the breakfast table. Grace followed him. He took the seat facing the atrium doors and outside, while Grace sat across from him, with a clear view of the kitchen door. She kept her purse on her lap.

For a few moments, neither of them said anything. Ethan ate ravenously, as if he hadn't had a solid meal in days. Grace tried not to stare at him, but his looks had changed so dramatically overnight, she couldn't help studying his features.

When he caught her watching him, she said, "I can't get over the changes in your appearance. It's amazing."

He shrugged. "There was a lot of room for improvement. I looked pretty horrible last night."

"I didn't mean it like that," Grace said. "You must be a really fast healer, that's all."

"Maybe." A shadow flickered over his features, and Grace wondered what he was thinking. If he was remembering something. She couldn't help wondering what he'd been like before all this happened. Would he have been the kind of man she would have wanted to spend time with? Doubtful, if everything Amy had told her was true.

"Were you able to get some sleep last night?" she asked him.

He grimaced. "Some. I'm still not used to this place. It...doesn't feel like home to me, but I guess that's to be expected, considering."

Grace nodded. "It'll take time. I gather you've done some exploring this morning."

"I've been over this place from top to bottom. Nothing triggered a memory. But at least I did find the kitchen. And a gym downstairs. I want to start working out as soon as possible. Build back my strength."

Grace's gaze dropped to his broad shoulders and chest, the muscular arms bulging beneath the short sleeves of his shirt. She remembered the strength in those arms last night when he'd grabbed her, the hardness of his chest when he'd held her against him. If he was out of shape, she could only imagine what he would be like at his peak. "You don't want to rush it," she said. "Amy said you'd had surgery recently. An appendectomy, I believe."

"That's what I've been told, but I don't remember the surgery, either. Although I do have a scar on my side." Again his features momentarily darkened, as if he'd suddenly remembered something he had no intention of sharing. Grace wondered what he was keeping from her.

"Tell me more about your meeting with Pilar," she said.

The cloud over his features changed, but didn't fade. "Not much to tell. Like I said, I found her in the study taking money out of the safe."

"Did she say why she was doing that?"

Ethan pushed aside his plate as if his appetite had suddenly deserted him. He glanced up. "She seemed to think I owed her."

"Because of Amy?"

He shrugged.

"I've seen pictures of Pilar." Grace paused. "She's a very beautiful woman."

"Yes, she certainly is."

"Did you, you know, *feel* anything when you saw her?"

One dark brow rose at the question. "You mean attraction?"

"I'm just trying to figure out what your relationship with her is," Grace said, almost defensively.

"Like I said earlier, apparently we're separated. She wasn't here long enough for me to find out much of anything, but she did mention Amy. She knew about the shooting."

Grace glanced at him in surprise. "What did she say?"

He shrugged. "Let me put it this way. I don't think Amy's death came exactly as a blow."

Something that might have been sympathy crossed his features, and Grace lowered her eyes. Even though her deception was necessary, it didn't make it any easier. "How did she find out about Amy's death?"

"Do you remember Rosa mentioning a man named

Kendall? She said that Pilar had called to find out what time I would be home, because Dr. Kendall had told her I was arriving last night. Kendall was at the hospital when I was brought in. He was in my room when I came to. Evidently he called Pilar and told her what happened.''

Grace thought about that for a moment. "Do you know anything about this Kendall?"

"Only that he's my ex-partner."

Grace paused. "Do you think Pilar and Dr. Kendall might have something going on?"

Ethan's expression didn't waver. "I wondered about that. I've also wondered why Pilar waited until I got back to come here and take money from the safe. According to the police detective I spoke with last night, I was in Mexico for weeks, recovering from the surgery. She could have come over here at any time and taken that money. Why wait until I got back?"

Grace frowned. "What are you getting at?"

"Well, just think about it for a minute." He toyed with the juice glass. "Why would she wait until now to take that money out of the safe?"

"Maybe she didn't need it until now."

"Exactly," Ethan said. "Because maybe all along she thought there would be a lot more where that came from." His gaze went past Grace to focus on the backyard. She didn't turn, but she could hear the faint tinkling of the waterfall cascading into the pool, and she wondered if he was thinking about the jungle. Why did he seem to have such an aversion to it?

"After Pilar left this morning, I went through the safe myself," Ethan finally said. "I found a life insurance policy for five million dollars that named her as the beneficiary. I'd be willing to bet that's a lot more than she took out of the safe.''

''So what exactly are you saying, Ethan? That Pilar was behind what happened to you last night? You think she tried to have you killed?''

His gaze met Grace's. ''I don't know why that surprises you. You said yourself last night this whole thing may be a *Fatal Attraction* in reverse. Don't you think a woman is capable of murder?''

Grace thought about the killer she wanted to bring to justice, felt the weight of her own gun in her purse. ''Yes,'' she said grimly. ''I know there are women who are very capable of killing. Who might even take pleasure from it. But as I also told you last night, from the things Amy told me, I don't think Pilar is the one who wants you dead. Or at least, I don't think she's the one who tried to have you killed.''

Her distinction was not lost on Ethan. His gaze on her cooled. ''You were pretty clear in that regard. You think I did something to set last night's events in motion. You think someone is trying to kill me because of something I did in Mexico. Something illegal.''

His voice was hard, unyielding, but Grace sensed an undercurrent of anguish. A hint of desperation in his tone. She shrugged. ''Look, I'm just going by Amy's letters—''

''Amy's *letters*,'' he said, shoving back his chair and standing. ''Amy *said*.'' He strode to the atrium doors and stood staring out into the sunlit garden. ''I know she was your sister, and I'm sorry she's dead, but I don't remember her, and from what you told me last night, you didn't know her that well, either. What if everything she told you about me was a lie? What if she was setting me up somehow?''

Grace turned in her chair to stare at him. ''You don't really believe that.''

''Why is it so hard to believe?'' His jaw hardened as he turned to face her. ''Why is it so easy for you to believe that I was involved in something that got her killed? You don't know me. What do you really know about me?''

Before Grace could answer, he walked back over to the table and stood staring down at her. The look in his eyes made her shiver. ''And it suddenly occurs to me,'' he said slowly, ''that I don't know anything about you, either.''

''Of course, you do,'' Grace said, ignoring the tiny spark of panic that flared inside her. She stood, trying to take away his advantage, trying to regain control of the situation as she met his gaze and they squared off.

His eyes narrowed on her. ''What do I know about you? Your name? That you're Amy's sister? I know those things because *you* told me.''

Grace moistened her lips. ''What are you driving at?''

''Maybe I've been a little too trusting. Maybe I should have asked a few more questions last night.''

''Ask them now,'' Grace said, her voice growing cold. ''I'll tell you anything you want to know.''

The silence in the kitchen was deafening. When he spoke, his voice was almost too calm. ''Who do you work for?''

Grace's heart thumped against her chest. She fingered the gold clasp of her purse. "Don't you mean *where* do I work? I work for a legal firm."

"You're a lawyer?"

She shook her head. "I went to law school, but I never took the bar exam. I'm more of a…researcher."

"What does that mean?"

"It means I spend a lot of time behind a computer and doing legwork for my superiors. There's a lot of grunt work involved in what I do."

He paused again. "You don't have an accent," he accused. "How long have you lived in Houston?"

She answered without hesitation. "Not long. I transferred down here from Washington, D.C."

"What did you do there?"

"Same thing."

"Why did you move to Houston?"

"To be near my sister." That was the first outright lie she'd told him all morning, but Grace knew there would be plenty of others. She'd say and do whatever she had to in order to gain his trust. That was the way she'd been trained. The way she lived her life. She couldn't afford to get an attack of conscience now simply because a man with a battered face and a hidden past was awakening feelings inside her she had thought were long dead.

"What about your family?" he asked. "Where are they?"

"My parents have been dead for years." Without warning, the old memory came storming back. Grace thought she had buried it, along with her emotions, someplace safe, someplace impenetrable, but all of a sudden it was back, the explosion in her mind as shattering as the one that night had been.

In the beat of a heart, she was a teenager again, running down the street toward the sirens. Seeing the fire licking red-orange against the night sky. Hearing the screams of the people trapped inside the white frame house. Her mother and father. And at an upstairs window, beating against the panes, her hair in flames, Grace's sister. Her beautiful, beautiful sister...

"Everyone is gone," she whispered. Ethan touched her hand, and Grace jumped, forgetting for a moment where she was. Who she was supposed to be. She stared up at him, fighting back the scream that tore at her throat. The horror that had made her who and what she was.

"I'm sorry," he said. His eyes, cold and suspicious before, were now clouded with guilt. It was hard for Grace to witness that guilt, knowing what she knew.

He's not innocent, she told herself. *Don't be fooled.*

She opened her purse and withdrew her wallet, showing him her driver's license, her social security card, and then fishing out a business card that contained the name and address of a downtown law firm. The business cards had been printed overnight. The address and phone number had been supplied by the field office here in Houston.

"You can call them if you like," she said, handing the card to Ethan. The call would be forwarded to either Myra or a support operative who would bear out Grace's story. If Ethan actually went by the office, the receptionist would refer him to one of the partners who had been briefed and would know how to field the inquiry. "But I am who I say I am. My name is Grace Donovan, and I am looking for my sister's killer."

He nodded, as if he'd seen something in her face that had convinced him. He sat down at the table, looking as if the remainder of his strength had suddenly drained away. "Did you bring Amy's letters with you today?"

Grace sat down beside him. She could smell the faint scent of soap and shampoo, and wondered if, like her, he'd spent a long time in the shower that morning, trying to scrub away the past. Or what he feared might be there.

"No, but I brought this." She pulled a newspaper clipping from her purse, and placed it face up before him. The article was accompanied by a picture of a blond man who looked to be in his early thirties.

Grace stared long and hard at that picture, then turned away, shuddering. "I found that clipping in Amy's apartment one day. When I asked her, she denied knowing anything about it, but I could tell she was upset. Frightened. She'd cut this picture out of the paper for a reason, but she wouldn't tell me why."

Ethan picked up the clipping and scanned the article. "Trevor Reardon," he read, then glanced up. "It says he's on the FBI's Ten Most Wanted List."

Grace nodded. "He was convicted on three counts of first-degree murder and sentenced to life in prison without parole. He escaped several months ago and has been underground ever since."

"So what does this have to do with me?" Ethan asked.

"You don't recognize him? Look closely." As he examined the picture of Trevor Reardon, Grace studied Ethan's features, looking for a flicker, any telltale sign of recognition.

After several seconds, he handed the clipping back to her. "I don't recognize him. Am I supposed to?"

"Are you sure?" Grace asked anxiously.

"As far as I know, I've never seen this man before." Ethan's voice was edged with impatience. "And I don't think I like what you're implying."

"I'm not implying anything—"

"The hell you're not. What connection do you think I have to a convicted murderer? Just what kind of man do you think I am?"

"I don't know," she said softly, her gaze meeting his in defiance. "Isn't that what we're both trying to find out?"

For a long moment, his gaze held hers, then he glanced away. Running both hands through his hair, he stared at the ceiling. "What connection do you think I have to this Trevor Reardon?" he asked again.

Grace paused. "I think you may have given him a new face."

Chapter Five

Ethan stared at her as if she'd taken leave of her senses. Then, as the full meaning of her words sank in, he stared at her in horror. "Why would I do that?" He was a doctor, for God's sake. A humanitarian, according to the articles and awards in his office. Why would he knowingly give a murderer a new face, a new life?

Something that almost looked like sympathy flashed across Grace's face before she could subdue it. In the blink of an eye, however, the mask was back in place. She stared at him dispassionately. "It's possible you were somehow coerced."

"But that's not what you think, is it?"

She hesitated, her gaze resting briefly on the picture of Trevor Reardon's face, then lifting to Ethan's. Any trace of sympathy she might have felt earlier had vanished. "No. I think you did it for money," she said bluntly.

"But why would I?" he demanded. "Look at this place. These clothes. It's obvious I already have money."

When Grace said nothing, he grabbed her hand and stood, drawing her to her feet. "Come with me."

"What? Where?" Her voice sounded almost panicky. She grabbed her purse and slung the strap over her shoulder.

Without another word, Ethan pulled her out of the kitchen, through the dining room and living room toward the study. The parrot gave a weak little squawk as they hurried passed him, but Ethan ignored him.

Inside the study, he walked to the middle of the room and gestured to all the framed awards and citations on the walls. "Look at all this stuff." He walked over and took one of the framed letters down, then held it out to Grace. "Do you know what this is? It's a letter from the president of the United States commending me on my work in Mexico. This one is from a senator, this one from our ambassador to Mexico." He went on and on, until he'd taken a half dozen or so frames from the wall and piled them in Grace's arms.

Apparently unimpressed, she stacked them on his desk.

Ethan knew his movements were almost frantic as he removed another frame from the wall, but he couldn't help himself. He had to convince her, and himself, that what she was thinking was ludicrous. "Why would somebody who has done all this work for underprivileged children, received all these accolades, risk losing everything by changing a murderer's face?"

"Because all that philanthropy takes a great deal of money, and you also have very expensive tastes." Grace made a sweeping gesture with her hand. "You can't buy all this with citations and awards and letters from the president. Plus, you have the perfect cover. Your clinic in Mexico is remote, practically inaccessible, from what Amy said, and perfectly legitimate.''

"Except for the fact that, according to you, I operate on criminals on the side," he said bitterly. "I give them new faces so they're free to go out into the world to rape, murder, and steal at will."

Grace's gaze didn't quite meet his. "Reardon probably found out about you from someone in prison. When he escaped, he made his way across the border and somehow found your clinic in the jungle. I think he gave you a great deal of money, probably millions, to give him a new face."

"*Millions?*" Ethan frowned. "The article said he'd been in prison for over six years. Where would he get that kind of money?"

"At the time he was caught, it was estimated that he'd amassed a fortune worth well over thirty million dollars. It was never found."

Ethan stared at her in surprise. "So who is this guy anyway?"

Grace paused. "He's an ex-Navy SEAL and an explosives expert who sold his services to the highest bidder. He became a mercenary, an assassin, sometimes a terrorist. It didn't much matter to him what the job entailed so long as the price was right. He enjoyed killing and he was good at it. It was all a game to him, one he made a lot of money from. The first time he escaped prison, he went after the FBI agent who had captured him. Reardon firebombed the agent's house and wired all the doors to explode when the people trapped inside or the rescuers on the outside tried to open them. There was no way in or out. The agent, his wife and a daughter all died in the fire.''

Her expression remained coldly dispassionate, but Ethan sensed she wasn't quite as calm as she appeared. There were lights inside her eyes. Tiny flares of rage when she spoke. Was she thinking of her sister?

"After that, he remained free for several years," Grace said. "He was a master of disguises, always staying one step ahead of the authorities. He may even have gone out of the country for a while. But then he made one very serious mistake. The only one in the agent's family who hadn't been killed in the fire was a teenage girl who'd sneaked out of the house that night. Reardon came back to get her.''

"Why?" Ethan asked. "How could the girl hurt him?"

"Because she could identify him, for one thing. And because she was a loose end. From everything I've learned about Reardon, he doesn't like loose ends. He's almost obsessive about it.''

"So what happened when he came back for the girl?"

"There was another agent, a woman. She was the murdered agent's partner. She'd made it her life's work to track down Reardon and send him back to prison. She knew he'd eventually come after the girl, and when he did, she got him.''

Ethan didn't much like the sound of that. "You mean she used the girl as bait?"

Grace shrugged. "That's one way of putting it. But she also saved the girl's life. To her, the end justified the means." Grace picked up one of the framed citations and studied it closely.

Ethan used the opportunity to study her. She seemed as focused as ever this morning, her voice steady, her expression still as determined as he remembered it.

But what he hadn't remembered was how the blue of her eyes lightened or darkened depending on her emotions, or how the tint of her lip gloss reminded him of lush, ripe strawberries. What he hadn't remembered was the scent of her perfume, so subtle it seemed hardly more than imagination, or the way her modestly cut jacket only hinted at the womanly curves beneath. Ethan hadn't remembered any of those things—or was it that he had just been working very hard to forget them?

"How do you know so much about this Reardon?" he asked her.

They both glanced up at the same time, their gazes locking. Ethan's gaze was drawn to her lips when she spoke. "A lot of the information is in the article I showed you, plus, after I found that clipping in Amy's apartment, I did some research. I wanted to know why Reardon's picture seemed to frighten her so much."

"You think Amy knew what was going on in the Mexican clinic?"

"I think she at least suspected, and that's why she was so afraid." Grace set aside the frame she'd been holding. "Amy had been to the clinic with you on at least one occasion. She even alluded to the fact that she'd seen a man down there, a patient, whose face was covered in bandages. She didn't know who he was, but she found his presence at the clinic strange because most of your patients down there are children. I think she came back here and somehow started putting two and two together.''

Ethan walked over and stared at the picture of him and Dr. Salizar in front of the Mexican Clinic. If everything Grace said was true, no wonder Salizar looked so frightened. Ethan wondered if the clinic had really been burned to the ground by *banditos,* or if one of his former patients had come back looking for him.

He turned to Grace. ''So you think Reardon killed Amy because she was on to him?''

''No. I think Amy was a bonus. I think you were the target because you may be the only person in the world who has seen Trevor Reardon's new face.''

In spite of himself, Ethan felt chilled by her words. ''And now I can't identify him because I don't remember him.''

''That's the ironic part,'' Grace said. ''He could be anyone. Your next-door neighbor. The mailman. Anyone. If Trevor Reardon wants you dead, the only way you can survive is to somehow find him first.''

''You mean use myself as bait,'' Ethan said, marveling at her coolness. ''Like the FBI agent used the girl.''

Grace shrugged. ''It makes sense. You're a loose end. Sooner or later, Reardon will come after you.''

''And when he does?''

She shrugged again. ''When he does, we have to be ready for him.''

He looked at her and just shook his head. ''Has it ever once occurred to you that you and I are hardly trained to capture a murderer, let alone an ex-Navy

SEAL who has a penchant for explosives?'' For a moment, Ethan thought she was actually going to smile at his words. She almost seemed to be enjoying herself, and he said angrily, ''For God's sake, this isn't a game, Grace. I'm a plastic surgeon without a memory, and you're a—what did you call it—a researcher for a law firm? What in the hell makes you think we can pull this off?''

''Have you got a better plan?'' she demanded. ''You certainly can't go to the police.''

Ethan closed his eyes briefly, remembering the jungle, the fear, the certainty that the men who pursued him *were* the police. Had the Mexican authorities been on to him? Was that why he'd been running?

If what Grace suspected was true, if Ethan had in fact aided and abetted criminals by selling them new faces, then he would more than likely be looking at a stiff sentence of his own if he were to go to the police. And maybe, if he had done all the things Grace thought he had, prison was exactly where he should be.

But there was still some doubt in Ethan's mind, still some lingering suspicion that Grace Donovan hadn't told him everything. That she had left out something very important, and until he could figure out the whole story, he wasn't about to throw himself on the mercy of the court.

''Maybe I can't go to the police,'' he said. ''But I still don't understand what's stopping you.''

''I thought I explained myself last night.''

''But it still doesn't make sense. I don't want to seem cruel, but you can't help your sister by getting yourself killed. If I'm Trevor Reardon's target, then I don't want you anywhere near me."

"Don't be ridiculous," Grace said, frowning. "You can't do this alone. You need me. I can watch your back. We can watch each other's back for that matter, because I'm not giving up on this. Reardon killed my sister, and I'm going to make damned sure he pays. If you won't help me, I'll go after him on my own."

And she would do it, Ethan thought. He could see the determination in her eyes, in the defiant way she held her chin and jaw. She would go after Reardon alone, and then Ethan would have *her* death on his conscience.

The thought of her getting hurt or killed made him almost physically sick. "You don't know what you're getting yourself into," he said.

She lifted her chin. "Yes, I do. I'm not helpless. Believe me, I can take care of myself."

"Against an assassin-turned-terrorist?"

Her gaze flickered but didn't waver. "He's a man. He has weaknesses. We know two things about him. He's dangerous and he's compulsive. He won't be able to resist coming back to finish what he started. All we have to do is be ready for him."

She made it sound so easy, but somehow Ethan knew she wasn't being naive. She really believed what she was saying, and her confidence was almost enough to convince him. Almost.

"So what's our first move?" he asked.

Sunlight from the window fired the red highlights in her hair as she tucked a strand behind her ear. "I guess the best way to flush him out is to go about your normal business. If Reardon is after you, then he's probably made a point of knowing your routine.''

"I hope you're not suggesting I see patients today," Ethan said dryly. "I don't think I'm up for that. And I don't think they would be, either."

"No, of course not," Grace said. "But you can always check in with your office, maybe even go by there. After that, we'll play it by ear."

He said suddenly, "Do you have a key to Amy's apartment?"

"No, why?"

"Because you found one clue there already. Maybe there are others."

"You don't think the police will have cordoned off her apartment?"

Ethan shook his head. "Not likely. From what the detective told me last night, they're inclined to believe someone broke into the office looking for drugs, and Amy was shot when she surprised him. The police will be canvassing the neighborhood this morning, looking for witnesses and evidence dropped or stashed by the suspect. They may never feel the need to search Amy's apartment."

Grace mulled that over. "You're probably right. Like I said, I don't have a key, but I can get us in."

That confidence again. Ethan stared at her admiringly. "All right. You can make yourself at home down here while I go up and finish dressing. Then we can get out of here."

UPSTAIRS, ETHAN HURRIED over to the nightstand by the bed and opened the top drawer, removing the stack of bills he'd found in the safe that Pilar had somehow missed. Then he picked up the pistol he'd found in the safe. The gun was small, a high-caliber, custom-made job that almost fit inside Ethan's hand.

He tested the weight of the gun as a strong sense of déjà vu slipped over him. He'd had that same feeling the moment his hand had closed over the weapon in the safe. It was the first thing he'd come across that had seemed familiar to him since waking up in the hospital last evening.

Ethan knew how to use the gun. Not just a gun, but this particular gun. He knew the sights would be accurate, the trigger pull crisp and the recoil minimal. He couldn't even remember his own mother, and yet he knew how to field strip this weapon and reassemble it in a matter of seconds.

Trying not to think about what that might mean, he slammed back the slide to put one bullet in the chamber, flipped on the safety with his thumb, then slipped the pistol into the back waistband of his pants. Next he peeled away several bills from the wad of money and stuffed them in his pocket. The rest he returned to the drawer.

The shoes he'd been wearing the night before were beside the bed where he'd kicked them off. He slid them on, thinking briefly how much better they fit than the ones he'd tried on earlier that morning. His final preparation was to grab a jacket from the closet. It would be hot outside, but he needed something to conceal his gun. No use revealing *all* his secrets to Grace. Not yet at least.

As he walked down the stairs to join her, Ethan couldn't help reflecting on how much better he felt with money in his pocket and a high-powered weapon within his reach.

Just what the hell kind of doctor was he anyway?

THEY DROVE SOUTH on Gessner Road, a long street that was beautiful in some areas and cluttered with shopping centers, convenience stores and apartment buildings in others. The section near Ethan's house was particularly lovely, with its tree-shaded sidewalks and flower-strewn median.

The abundance of towering oaks and loblolly pines was one of the things that had surprised Grace most about Houston. She had expected a dry, sprawling metropolis dotted with oil wells and ugly refineries, but the city was very wooded with houses and glass office buildings almost hidden beneath thick canopies of green.

Out of the corner of her eye, she saw Ethan staring out the window, watching the road signs, trying to familiarize himself with the city. For a moment, she tried to put herself in his place, but it was impossible to imagine what he was going through. To have no recall of who you were, what kind of person you'd been, but to have every reason to suspect the worst. To have been told everything he'd been told that morning—

Grace nudged away the guilt prodding at her conscience. Everything she'd done was necessary. Every lie and deception essential. She wouldn't spend time regretting what couldn't be helped.

Crossing Westheimer, one of the main thoroughfares in Houston, she turned right on Richmond, then pulled into an apartment group called The Pines.

The complex was like a number of others they'd passed along the way—two-story buildings that housed between four and eight "garden" apartments per unit. The grounds were immaculately groomed, with huge pink and white oleander bushes hugging the sides of the buildings while tall pine trees, circled by beds of impatiens and monkey grass, shaded the common grounds between the units.

Grace parked in front of the leasing office, shut off the engine, and turned to Ethan. In spite of the trees, the intense heat and sultry humidity invaded the car. She lowered the windows, but without a breeze, it didn't help much.

"Maybe you'd better let me go in alone," she said. "I don't want to make anyone suspicious."

She saw from his expression that he understood her meaning. Though improved, his bruised appearance was still enough to raise eyebrows. He nodded and watched her open the car door. Grace felt his eyes on her until she disappeared inside the office.

As always, the air conditioning hit her full blast. That was something else Grace had yet to get used to—going from a furnace to a freezer in a matter of seconds. Houstonians seemed to think they could compensate for the soaring temperatures outside by turning their AC to frigid. Even wearing a jacket, Grace found herself shivering.

A woman with frosted blond hair sat reading a book behind a large desk near the doorway. The red-and-blue rhinestones on her T-shirt sparkled in the overhead lighting as she reached up and removed her glasses. "May I help you?"

Grace walked over and stood in front of the desk.

"I hope so. My name is Grace Donovan. One of your tenants is...was...my sister." She broke off and glanced down at her hands. After a split second, she said, "Her name was Amy Cole. She lived in 4C."

The woman's gaze grew anxious. "You said, was."

Grace bit her lip. "She was killed last night."

The woman gasped. Her manicured fingers flew to her fuchsia-stained lips. "I'm so sorry. H-how did it happen?"

Grace released a long, shaky breath. "I can't really go into the details right now. It's...still so fresh. I'm sure you understand."

"Of course." The woman was at a loss. She stared helplessly at Grace. "Is there anything I can do?"

"As a matter of fact, yes. I need to get into Amy's apartment."

A frown flitted across the woman's features. "Did Amy have you listed as the next of kin on her leasing application?"

"I'm not sure," Grace admitted. "I've only lived here in Houston a few weeks." She paused. "You see, the problem is, I have to choose something for them to...for Amy to...wear."

Understanding dawned in the woman's face. Pity deepened in her eyes. She reached inside her drawer and withdrew a key. "This is a master. I'll have to let you in myself. I can't just give you the key."

"I understand," Grace said. "And that's fine. I appreciate your help."

The woman got up and they started for the door. "I can't tell you how sorry I am. Amy was a good tenant. Always on time with her rent. Except for that one incident, there was never any trouble with her.''

Grace paused with her hand on the door knob. ''What incident are you talking about?''

The woman bit her lip, as if worrying about how much to tell the dead woman's sister. ''There was a man, Amy's boyfriend, I guess. I gather he was...married.'' Her gaze flashed to Grace's face. Seeing no signs of resentment, she continued. ''He was at her apartment one night when his wife showed up. I live here in the complex, you know. Right across the parking lot from Amy's apartment. Anyway, the woman created such a disturbance I finally had to call the police.''

''What did she do?''

Another pause. The woman's frown deepened. ''She had a gun. She shot out the tires on her husband's Porsche, and then threatened to use the gun on Amy.''

AMY'S APARTMENT WAS decorated in soothing pastels—green, peach and cream. The colors reminded Grace of warm breezes and flower-scented afternoons. Of youth and innocence and everything she'd lost one cold Saturday night.

The apartments Grace had occupied since that night fourteen years ago, when she'd lost her whole family, were places where she slept and sometimes ate. They were never home. Not like this.

For the first time since she'd heard about Amy's death, Grace let herself feel the impact of the loss. She hadn't known Amy well. They'd spoken on only two occasions, once here in Amy's apartment. But

Grace had sensed something about the young woman, a loneliness that had touched a chord deep within Grace's own darkness.

The door to Amy's apartment opened, and Grace turned. Ethan stepped tentatively inside. "All right if I come in now?"

Nodding, she motioned him in.

Ethan walked into the room, looking around. "Nice place," he murmured.

"Do you recognize it?"

He glanced at her. "Why? Have I been here before?"

Grace started to tell him the story the manager had related to her, but then decided he'd had enough blows for one day. "I thought you might have, considering."

He walked over to a pine bookshelf and picked up a picture, studying it intently.

Grace knew the picture. Amy had told her about it the night they'd first met, when Grace had come here to talk about Ethan. The photograph was of Amy and a boyfriend who had long since gone his own way, but Amy had told Grace that she liked the way the two of them looked together so she'd kept the picture on display. Grace could see why. Blond and fair, dressed all in white, Amy looked radiant, almost ethereal against a snowy Rocky Mountain backdrop.

Grace walked over and stood beside Ethan. "That's Amy," she said softly. Her eyes were drawn to the picture, and for the first time, she detected a similarity between Amy and Pilar Hunter. The resemblance was not so much in their faces but in the perfection of their features.

"Evidently you have a thing for beautiful women," she said.

Ethan glanced up, his eyes locking with hers. "Evidently, I do."

His gaze dropped almost imperceptibly, touching the curves of Grace's body only briefly before lifting to her face. Something dark flickered in his eyes. Something that made Grace's heart pound in awareness.

For a long moment, neither of them said anything, but the attraction between them was electric.

This can't be happening, Grace thought. *Not here. Not now. And especially not with this man.*

She had a job to do. A killer to find. Nothing could get in her way.

And yet, something *was* getting in her way. Clouding her judgment. Threatening her whole way of life.

She knew that he was going to kiss her, but Grace was powerless to stop it. Powerless to fight it. Powerless to do anything more than close her eyes briefly before his lips touched hers.

And it was only a touch. Nothing more than a faint skimming of their lips, but Grace's heart pounded an erratic rhythm inside her breast. When she made no move to resist, he deepened the kiss, almost urgently, and finally Grace heard the warnings that were screaming inside her head. *You can't do this! You're risking everything!*

Besides which, he was a married man.

Immediately, Grace stepped back, glaring at him angrily, trying to convince herself she'd had no part in the kiss. Trying to reassure herself it would never, ever happen again.

She waited for the platitudes and the apologies. The *I'm sorry. It was a mistake. I don't know what came over me* excuse.

Instead he stared down at her, his dark eyes openly defiant, as if he were daring her to deny the blatant sexual chemistry between them.

Without a word, Grace turned and walked out of the room.

Chapter Six

Inside Amy's bedroom, Grace stood leaning against the wall, eyes closed, while she tried to get her heartbeat, her emotions, under control.

What would Myra say if she could see her protégée now—pulse pounding, hands trembling, stomach fluttering like a schoolgirl's? This was so unlike Grace. She never lost control.

She opened her eyes and took several long breaths. All right, so the kiss had been a mistake. No question about that, but there was nothing to be done but put it behind her. Stop thinking about it and get back to work.

Grace knew all about using work to forget. There had been times when her job was all that had kept her going. After all she'd been through, a kiss seemed so inconsequential.

And yet...

It hadn't been just a kiss. That was the problem. It had been an acknowledgment of the attraction—the dangerous kind—that existed between her and Ethan Hunter. The kind of attraction that made people forget who and what they were, and why they shouldn't be together.

But that can't happen, Grace told herself firmly. *It won't happen.* After all the years of indifference—of *celibacy,* for God's sake—it would take more than a man without a memory, a man with a dangerous past, to awaken her sleeping libido.

Grace would make sure of it.

She drew another long breath and glanced around. She knew it was pointless to search Amy's bedroom. Anything helpful or incriminating would have already been removed. So instead, she opened the closet and glanced through Amy's beautiful clothing, selecting a simple black knit dress and a pair of black heels. Opening the jewelry box on Amy's dresser, Grace removed a string of pearls and a pair of matching earrings.

Just as she closed the jewelry box lid, she heard voices from the other room. Grace thought at first Ethan had turned on the stereo or TV, but when she walked to the bedroom door, she saw a man in a powder-blue suit talking with Ethan.

Grace had never met the man, but she knew who he was. As she entered the room, both pairs of male eyes turned on her, and a shiver of apprehension slipped up her spine.

Ethan introduced her to Sergeant Pope with the Houston Police Department, and the detective lifted his grizzled eyebrows as he took her in. "You were at the crime scene last night. I didn't meet you myself, but Webber told me about you. He said you were pretty distraught. Only natural, I guess, considering."

"Yes, Sergeant Webber was very courteous under the circumstances," Grace said. "I appreciated that."

"Refresh my memory," Pope said. "I don't seem to remember what you were doing at the clinic last night."

Grace glanced at Ethan. He was staring at her curiously. Maybe even a little suspiciously, and no wonder. She'd failed to mention to him that she'd been at the crime scene just minutes after he and Amy had been taken away. Any hint of the passion she'd glimpsed in his eyes earlier had vanished.

She turned back to Pope. "Amy and I were supposed to have dinner. She called and said she might be running a little late because she was going by the clinic first. I went to the restaurant and waited for her, but after a while, I got worried. The clinic isn't in the safest area of town, you know, so I decided to go by and check on her." Grace paused, her gaze dropping to the black dress draped across her arm and the pearls and shoes clutched in her hands. "The police were already there when I arrived." Her gaze lifted to Ethan's. "Dr. Hunter and Amy had already been taken away."

"That's what you meant last night when you said the police had talked to you?" Ethan asked.

She nodded. "They told me what had happened, and then Sergeant Webber asked me to go down to the morgue with him and identify Amy's body." Grace shuddered, remembering the coldness of the room, the steel vaults. The dead bodies. She would never get used to that. Never.

The detective glanced at first Grace, then Ethan. "How did the two of you hook up?"

Before Ethan had a chance to answer, Grace said, "I went by the hospital to see how he was doing. When I learned he was checking himself out, I volunteered to drive him home. And then knowing how difficult it would be, he offered to come over here with me today. I thought it was…very considerate."

The suspicion in Ethan's eyes turned to puzzlement. *Who are you?* his expression seemed to be saying. *What the hell do you think you're doing?*

"I hope we haven't done anything wrong, Sergeant." Grace widened her eyes innocently. "Letting ourselves in here, I mean. There wasn't any crime scene tape on the door, or anything."

Pope's gaze narrowed on her. "How *did* you get in? You have a key?"

"The apartment manager let us in. I explained that I needed to get some of Amy's clothes for her to be…buried in. The funeral is tomorrow."

The detective looked surprised. "Tomorrow? That's rushing it a little, isn't it?"

"Not really." Grace shrugged. "Amy and I don't have any family, no out-of-town relatives to wait for. I just want to get it over with as soon as possible. There won't be a problem…getting her body released, will there?"

Again Grace felt Ethan's gaze on her, but this time she kept her attention on Pope. His awful blue suit, greased hair and world-weary expression didn't fool her one bit. He was sharp. As soon as he got back to the station, he would check out her story. Grace had no doubt about that.

"Shouldn't be a problem," he said. "The coroner has already filed his report. Didn't take long to figure out the cause of death.'' When Grace winced, he said, ''Sorry. Sometimes you forget.''

He took a few steps into the room, gazing around. With his back still turned to them, he said, ''So why did you check yourself out of the hospital, Dr. Hunter? You were in pretty bad shape when I left you last night.''

Ethan exchanged a glance with Grace, one that said, *We're going to talk about all this later. Trust me.*

''I wanted to get home, rest in my own bed. I don't like hospitals.''

Pope turned at that. ''Worrisome hang-up for a doctor, wouldn't you say?''

''Not at all,'' Ethan said smoothly. ''I think you'll find most of my colleagues have that same 'hang-up.' You've heard the expression Doctors Make The Worst Patients. I'm afraid it's true.''

He was good, Grace thought. Quick on his feet. Almost frighteningly so. She stared at him with new admiration.

''I came by to see you this morning,'' Pope said. He withdrew a wallet and a passport from the inside pocket of his suit coat. He handed the items to Ethan. ''I wanted to give you these. I'll have someone deliver the luggage and your briefcase to your house later today.''

Ethan gazed at the wallet and passport for several seconds before putting them away in his own jacket pocket. Grace could only guess what he was thinking. A wallet meant information. A passport could mean freedom.

The detective finished his perusal of the room and

turned back to them. He nodded to the clothing in Grace's arms. "Looks like you got what you came for. The mortuary you select will take care of the arrangements with the morgue."

"Thank you." Grace turned to Ethan. "I guess we should be going then. I still have other arrangements to make."

"Right."

They headed for the door, but Pope made no move to follow them. "I'll lock up when I leave," he said pointedly.

They left him standing in the center of the room, studying Amy's apartment with a keenness, an intensity that Grace found particularly unnerving. She hoped to hell he didn't stumble across something one of Myra's operatives might have missed.

OUTSIDE, ETHAN TOOK her arm when she started down the sidewalk toward the parking lot. "Not so fast," he said. "I want to know what was going on back there."

Grace glanced up at him. "What do you mean?"

"For starters, I'd like to know why you didn't tell me about your being at the clinic last night. You led me to believe the police had called you to tell you about Amy."

"No, I didn't," Grace argued. "All I said was that I'd talked to the police. And I did. What difference does it make if I was at the clinic or at home?"

"What were you doing at the clinic?" Ethan's hand was still on her arm. His grip wasn't tight, but Grace knew that if she tried to walk away, he would hold her. He had too many questions right now to let her go.

"Just what I said. Amy and I were supposed to meet. When she didn't show up, I got worried so I went to the clinic looking for her." Grace knew her words were convincing, but she wasn't as certain about her expression. She slipped on her sunglasses, not wanting to reveal too much.

After a moment, he said, "Why didn't you tell me about Amy's funeral?"

"You didn't ask." When he started to protest, she interrupted coolly, "You didn't ask, so I figured you didn't care. Amy didn't mean anything to you."

His gaze darkened as he stared down at her. "How do you know that?"

"Because you wouldn't have kissed me if she had." There, Grace thought. She'd brought up the kiss deliberately so they could get it out in the open, so that she could make her feelings for him very, very clear. She glanced down at his hand on her arm, arched a brow over her sunglasses, and he released her.

"Then you must not have cared about her either," he said.

"How dare you say that to me? She was my sister."

Ethan's gaze darkened. "Are you denying that you kissed me back?"

"I didn't." Grace was surprised to find that her outrage was more instinctive than studied. She wasn't sure she quite understood it.

"We kissed," he said, glaring down at her. "It was a mutual action. And just because I'm not denying it doesn't mean I'm exactly proud of what's happening between us."

Grace hadn't expected that. She stared at him uncertainly. "What do you mean?"

"I'm a married man, Grace."

It was like a slap in the face. Not that Grace had forgotten his marital status. Far from it. But in truth, that was only one of many reasons why she couldn't allow herself to become involved with Ethan Hunter. She supposed she should be glad that he'd suddenly developed scruples.

"All right," she said calmly. "We both agree that it was a mistake. It won't happen again. There's no reason why it should have to affect our working relationship. We're both adults."

Something glinted in his eyes. "You think it'll be that easy?"

"Yes," she said simply. "Because it has to be."

After a moment, he said, "All right. We'll forget about the kiss. We'll pretend it never happened. We'll promise ourselves it won't happen again, but there's something else we need to get straight."

"What?"

His gaze held hers. "I may not have my memory, but I'm not as stupid or as helpless as you seem to think. I don't know why you won't go to the police with what you know, but I'm pretty sure it has nothing to do with Amy."

Grace was glad her eyes were hidden behind the dark glasses. "I don't know what you're talking about. I already explained why I don't want to involve the police."

"Because you don't want to ruin Amy's good

name. Because to the police she's just another statistic. It doesn't wash, Grace.''

Her heart started to pound, whether from his accusations or from the way he said her name, Grace wasn't sure.

He didn't touch her again, but she couldn't have moved if her life depended on it.

His eyes narrowed suspiciously. ''You're talking about catching a cold-blooded murderer. An assassin, you said. It takes a little more than guts to do that.''

''I know that,'' she said almost angrily. ''I'm not as stupid or as helpless as *you* seem to think.''

''Oh, I don't think you're stupid or helpless.'' His gaze deepened on her. ''Far from it. I think you're very, very clever.''

''Don't give me too much credit,'' she muttered. Because this conversation certainly wasn't going the way she'd anticipated.

''You're not telling me everything,'' he accused. ''Don't think I don't know it.''

''I would never make the mistake of underestimating you,'' Grace said truthfully. Especially not now. ''But I've told you everything I know. I've tried to make you understand why this is so important to me. Don't you see? If I had shown up at the clinic a few minutes earlier last night, Amy would still be alive. If I hadn't turned my back on her years ago, she never would have moved to Houston in the first place. She never would have gotten involved with...you. I've always let her down, and now she's dead because of me.'' Grace paused, feeling the old horror rise up inside her as the memories came swarming back. It had taken her a long time to beat back the monsters, to subdue the night terrors that had once threatened her sanity. Amy's death, and the man who had killed her, had brought it all back.

"How can I live with myself if I let her killer go free?" Grace whispered.

Ethan couldn't see her eyes, and Grace thought fleetingly that perhaps she should remove her sunglasses and let him witness the anguish, the sudden tears that were almost as foreign to her as the attraction she felt for him. She wasn't opposed to using her emotions to get what she needed, but this was too much. Too…intense.

"I can tell you've been hurt," Ethan said softly. "When you drift off like that, I can tell you're experiencing grief. But I'm not sure the grief is for Amy."

When Grace said nothing, he took a step toward her, towering over her like a menacing embodiment of her conscience. "I don't know what's going on here," he said. "I don't know what part I played in Amy's death, or why you seem so willing to work with a man you have every reason to despise. But I do know this." He removed her dark glasses, then put a gentle finger beneath her chin and tilted her head back so that he could stare down into her eyes. "Attraction or not, God help you if you're lying to me."

GRACE LET HERSELF into her room that night and reached for the light switch. Her hand froze before she made the connection. Something was different about the room. She could detect a subtle scent that didn't belong there.

Standing motionless, Grace listened to the dark.

Then very quietly, she slipped her hand inside her purse and withdrew her gun, releasing the safety as her gaze searched the darkness. A breeze touched her face, and she realized suddenly that the sliding glass door was open. She started across the room toward it just as a voice said from the balcony, "It's only me, Grace. Put away your gun."

Grace let the weapon drop to her side, but she didn't put it away as she stepped out on the balcony to join Myra Temple. The woman sat in darkness, the only substance to her shadowy form the arcing glow of her cigarette as she lifted it to her mouth. In the silence that followed, Grace could hear the tiny crackle as the flames ate away at the paper holding the tobacco.

"How did it go today?" Myra asked. Her voice, husky from years of smoking, was one men dreamed of.

Grace replaced the gun in her purse before answering. "I think he'll cooperate."

"How much did you tell him?"

"Almost everything. The truth is almost always more convincing than lies. I've heard you say that dozens of times."

The cigarette lifted again. "He still thinks you're Amy's sister, though. You didn't tell him the truth about that."

"No." Because a man who had managed to stay one step ahead of the law wasn't likely to throw in his lot with an FBI agent. Not a man as resourceful and wealthy as Ethan Hunter.

She thought about their last conversation, the threat he'd given her, and in spite of the heat, Grace shivered. "You have someone watching the house to-night?" she asked.

"Huddleston and Smith have the first watch, but they'll be relieved after midnight, just like last night."

Grace nodded, satisfied. She wondered suddenly what Ethan was doing all alone in that house. Or was he alone? Had Pilar decided to pay him another visit?

Against her will, Grace conjured up an image of Ethan's wife—the lithe body, the glossy hair, the incredible face. What a handsome couple they would make. In her mind's eye, Grace could see the two of them together, in each other's arms. Naked. Kissing. Making love.

She thought about the way Ethan had looked at her today in Amy's apartment, the brief kiss they had shared, and the image changed. She could see herself in his arms. Naked. Kissing. Making love.

I'm a married man, Grace.

"So what are you doing sitting out here in the dark?" she asked Myra, trying to dispel the forbidden image in her mind.

She sensed rather than saw Myra's shrug. "Strangely enough, I've been thinking about the past."

"Don't tell me you're getting maudlin." Grace sank into the green plastic lawn chair next to Myra's. "You always told me the past is a dangerous pitfall, one that should be avoided at all costs."

Grace heard the tinkle of ice against glass as Myra lifted a drink to her lips. "I know, but lately it's become harder and harder for me to avoid that particular pitfall. I find myself reflecting at the oddest times. I guess it comes with age."

"No way," Grace said. "You're still a young woman." Still vibrant and beautiful, though there'd been times when Grace could have sworn her mentor ate nails for breakfast. Grace wasn't the only one in the Bureau who had thought so. Myra Temple was almost legendary.

Myra sighed, an uncharacteristic sound for her. "I may not be old in the real world, but forty-three can be ancient in our world, Grace."

She had a point. Grace fell silent for a moment, contemplating her own life. In twelve years, she would be Myra's age. Would she then *want* to look back, to reflect as Myra had put it? Somehow Grace couldn't imagine it.

Myra picked up a tiny whiskey bottle—the kind stocked in the room bar—from beside her chair and set it on the plastic table between them. The seal on the bottle was broken, but Grace knew Myra's own drink contained no alcohol. She was very disciplined in that regard. The empty bottle was to make a point.

"All right, so I had one drink last night," Grace admitted, wishing she didn't sound so defensive. Wishing she didn't have a reason to be. "But that's all. It won't happen again. You can take the bar key with you if it makes you feel any better."

Myra tossed her cigarette butt over the balcony to the asphalt parking lot below them. Tiny sparks rained down in the darkness. "That won't be necessary. I know you remember how bad it was for you back then. But you're strong now, Grace. Stronger than me in a lot of ways."

Grace didn't think that was possible. Myra was unparalleled. She would never consider drinking alone in the middle of the night, much less making love to a man whose secrets just might be even darker than her own.

"Do you remember the first time we met?" Myra asked suddenly. "You were only seventeen, but I sensed that resilience in you even then. I hated the fact that your father always seemed hell-bent on breaking you."

Don't, Grace thought. *Don't take me back there.*

She closed her eyes, letting the hot breeze blow across her face, willing away the melancholy that seemed to have gripped both her and Myra.

Beside her, Myra shifted restlessly in her chair. "You came by the office to see your father that day. He'd just learned I was to be his new partner. He wasn't too pleased to discover I was a woman."

"Some things never change," Grace said. "The Bureau is still a man's world."

"True enough," Myra said. "But you're becoming a damned fine agent, Grace. You've earned a lot of respect."

"So have you. You paved the way for women like me. I'll always be grateful." For that and so much more, but Grace left the words unspoken. Over the years, she and Myra had developed an internal method of communicating. They'd been through a lot together, but Grace couldn't help wondering if this was to be their final assignment. When Trevor Reardon was no longer their nemesis, who or what would then become their raison d'être?

Myra stood and stretched. "By the way, we lifted some fresh prints from Hunter's clinic last night after the police left. I'll let you know as soon as I hear back from the lab.''

Grace got up and walked her to the door. In the light from the corridor, Myra suddenly looked much older than her years. It made Grace uneasy, watching her.

Grace remained at the door until the agent disappeared around a corner. After a moment, Grace heard the ping of the elevator and the sound of the doors sliding open and then shut again. Only then did she close and lock her door. But she didn't turn on the light. She stood in the darkness as the memories came flooding back.

Putting her hands to her ears, she tried to shut them out, but Myra's pensiveness tonight had inadvertently opened a Pandora's box. In her mind, Grace saw the house where she'd grown up bursting into flames. She heard her mother's terrified cries, her father's anguished shouts, and her sister's tormented screams.

Grace closed her eyes, trembling. It had taken her years to get those images out of her head. Years of therapy and cold indifference before she no longer saw her sister, her hair in flames, at every window. Years of single-minded devotion to her career to block out the argument she and Jessica had had just hours before her sister's death.

Like a roller coaster out of control, Grace's mind whipped around the perilous corners of her past, plunged downward into the murky depths of her memory. Faces flew past her. Scenes blurred by her. She wished she could stop them—she would do anything to stop them—but it was too late for that. Too late to do anything but huddle in the darkness and remember.

There had been a man. Grace had sensed from the first that he was different, someone special, but she hadn't learned until later just how extraordinary he was. When she'd first met him at the library during the Christmas break of her senior year in high school, all she'd known was that he was a dashing older man, probably at least thirty, and more sophisticated and worldly than she could ever have imagined.

She'd also thought that he was the most handsome man she'd ever seen. When he looked up from the book he was reading and smiled at her, Grace knew instantly he was the one. The two of them had a connection, some special bond that had drawn her to him. His eyes were blue, his hair golden brown, and even in the dead of winter, he was suntanned, as if he'd just come from the slopes of some exotic ski resort.

Grace grew so nervous, just watching him, that she dropped the book she was holding. His smile broadened, as if he knew he was the source of her anxiety and was pleased by the knowledge. Grace turned and all but ran from the room.

The next day, she saw him again at the library. This time, her nerves in check, she took a seat two tables away from his, facing him. Every time she looked up from her book, she found his gaze on her, and Grace's insides quivered in delicious anticipation.

On the third day, he approached her. He stood over her table, hands planted on the surface as he bent down to whisper in her ear. Grace could smell the intoxicating scent of his cologne, could see the faint shadow of his beard, and her heart went wild. This was no boy, but a *man*.

"Do you want to get out of here?" he whispered, his voice deep and knowing.

Grace could only nod. He removed the book from her hands, then pulled her to her feet. Clasping her hand in his, he led her outside to the parking area, to an expensive sports car that made Grace catch her breath.

"This is your car?"

He dangled the keys before her. "Would you like to drive it?"

Grace had her license but her father rarely let her behind the wheel of the family sedan. His career in the FBI had made him overly protective of his family, and Grace's nature had made her openly rebellious. The two of them often clashed. She wondered fleetingly what her father would think if he could see her now.

In spite of her defiant nature, the image subdued Grace a little. This man was a total stranger after all. She shook her head. "I'd better not."

"Oh, come on," he said in that dark and silky voice. "You know you want to. For once in your life, live dangerously."

The challenge was irresistible. Grace took the keys from his fingers, and he opened the door for her. So gallant and so unlike the boys she'd dated. She slid behind the wheel and waited until he climbed into the passenger side before starting the car.

The engine roared to life, the sound thrumming through Grace's veins like a shot of pure adrenaline. So this was power, she thought.

The man put his hand over hers on the stick shift, helping her find the right gear. His touch made her shiver. Grace glanced at him warily. "Where are we going?"

"Anywhere you want to go, Grace."

That stopped her for a minute. Her excitement cooled. "How do you know my name?"

He smiled, pulling a card from his pocket and holding it up to her. It was her library card. "You dropped it that first day," he said, "when you were running away from me."

"I wasn't running away from you," Grace protested, not wanting him to think of her as a child.

"Maybe you should have." His smile turned mysterious. "I'm a dangerous man, Grace."

"I know."

Their gazes met and held for the longest moment, then he reached over and grasped the back of her neck, pulling her toward him. His mouth found hers and almost instantly, Grace felt his tongue plunge inside.

She knew she should pull away. This man was way too old and way too experienced for her, and he was a stranger. A stranger who kissed her like no boy had ever kissed her. Who made her feel the way no one had ever made her feel. Who whispered to her things no one had ever told her.

"You're very beautiful," he murmured. "You have no idea how special you are to me, Grace."

Something warm unfurled inside her, some womanly need that made her cling to him, that made her groan against his mouth, that made her want him in ways she'd hardly dared dream about.

She drove them to his apartment a few blocks from where she lived, and they talked a little, trying to get to know one another, trying to ease the almost unbearable tension between them. But all the while they both knew the inevitable would happen—*had* to happen—before she left him that night.

They met again the next night, and the next. Grace was barely allowed to date boys her own age, so she knew bringing him home to meet her parents, especially her father, was out of the question. She started sneaking out of her room at night, begging her younger sister, Jessie, to cover for her.

Unlike Grace, Jessie had never been rebellious. She had always worked very hard to please their father, and lying to him went against her nature. Grace understood that, but her sister's conscience didn't matter enough to Grace to make her want to stop seeing *him*.

On the night of the fire, Jessie had been especially troubled by Grace's deception. She even threatened to tell their parents and take her own punishment for the duplicity if Grace left the house again without their permission.

Grace lashed out at her, calling her a Goody Two-shoes. "Why don't you mind your own business for once," she snapped before climbing out the window and slipping away into the darkness to meet her lover.

That night, he seemed different. Before, he'd always been dark and intense, even moody at times, but Grace had found those qualities deeply compelling. Tonight, however, he was almost ebullient, laughing and smiling, whispering to her that he had a secret.

It was only…afterward that Grace learned what his secret was.

"Would you like to know my real name?" he asked, drawing her fingers to his lips and kissing each one of them.

Grace gazed up at him in confusion. "Your name is Jonathan Price."

He laughed out loud. "Jonathan Price is a fictional character, you little idiot. I got it from a novel."

Grace didn't much care for the insult. She pulled away from him.

He didn't even seem to notice. "I go by many names, but the one you may have heard of is Trevor Reardon."

He laughed again when he saw the horror dawn on her face.

"That isn't funny," she said, shaken. Nothing about him was the least bit amusing. In fact, he was beginning to scare her. Grace jumped up, pulling on her clothes while he lay on the bed, smiling that taunting little smile. "Trevor Reardon is in prison," she said.

"So you have heard of me." He propped himself on his elbow. "I didn't think your old man could resist bragging about the coup he pulled off when he captured me. But didn't he also tell you that I'd escaped from prison a few weeks ago? Didn't he warn you I might come back for revenge?"

Her father *had* been acting strangely lately, even more protective than usual, making the whole family promise to be home by dark every day. Maybe that's why Jessie had been so frightened when Grace had started sneaking out of the house at night. Maybe she'd known something Grace hadn't.

Dressed by this time, Grace started backing toward

the door. She didn't believe him, *couldn't* believe him, and yet…

What if he was telling her the truth?

What if he was Trevor Reardon?

She put a hand to her mouth, trying to swallow back a rising tide of nausea. "Who are you?" she whispered. "Why are you doing this to me?"

"It's all been a game," he said. "And you've been so much fun." He got out of bed and stood naked before her. "But playtime's over, Grace. It's time to get to work."

Her hand on the door knob, she said weakly, "If I scream someone will hear me. The police will come."

"Oh, I wouldn't wait for the police if I were you. Your family may need you, even as we speak."

She saw the truth in his eyes. Knew that he had done something unspeakable to her family while she lay in his arms.

Grace turned and fled the apartment. He didn't try to follow her, but she could hear his laughter echoing in the darkness all around her.

Five blocks away from her house, she heard the sirens. Two blocks away, she saw the flames. When she reached the driveway, she heard the screams.

Oh, God, oh, God, oh, God, was all she could think as she rushed toward the burning house. Someone grabbed her and held her back. She struggled to free herself, and it was then that she looked up and saw Jessie at their bedroom window. Sweet little Jessie pounding at the double panes, screaming in terror and agony as her clothing and hair caught fire.

And somewhere in the darkness, Grace could hear Trevor Reardon, still laughing.…

As the memories all but consumed her, Grace slumped against the wall of her hotel room, weak and dizzy. Even after all these years, the thought of his mouth on her, his hands touching her sent her flying to the bathroom. She lay spent and trembling on the floor moments later, the memories still closing in on her like a crushing weight. She willed them away, but they resisted. They weren't through with her yet. There was still more to be endured, other horrors to relive.

Groaning, Grace rolled to her side, feeling the cool tile against her cheek.

After that night, the guilt and grief over her family's deaths had almost killed her, but Trevor Reardon hadn't been finished with her. Dressed as one of the cops standing guard at the church, he attended the funeral service for her family three days later. Grace knew this because he called her afterward and described in detail the clothing she'd had on, right down to the tiny pearls she'd worn in her ears.

The knowledge that he had been that close to her again very nearly drove Grace over the edge. If it hadn't been for Myra Temple, Grace wasn't sure she would have survived.

But Myra helped her through the worst of those days. She forced Grace from the pit of despair she'd crawled into. Made her stop drinking. Made her realize that Reardon would win again if Grace let him.

So with Myra's help, Grace went on to college and eventually graduated from law school. After a while, she could even pretend she led a normal life. At times, she even managed to forget that a killer was out there somewhere, still waiting for her.

But Myra never forgot.

On the night Grace graduated from law school, Reardon was waiting for her in her apartment. He grabbed her, threw her on her bed, and, knife to her throat, told her exactly what he was going to do to her.

But then Myra came bursting into Grace's bedroom, and the agents with her had quickly subdued Reardon. Myra calmly walked over to him, and with a hand that was completely steady, put a gun to his head. For a moment, Grace thought she would pull the trigger. Wanted her to pull the trigger.

But then Myra lowered the weapon, Reardon was taken away, and Grace collapsed in the agent's arms. Grace promised herself that the tears she shed that night would be her last. That she would never again allow herself to be vulnerable. To be a target.

Within a month, she made the life-altering decision to follow in her father's footsteps at the FBI. When she was accepted so quickly, she suspected that Myra had pulled some strings, but Grace didn't care. She was completely focused. She knew exactly what she wanted from life. While Trevor Reardon was confined to a maximum security prison some seven hundred miles away, Grace began and completed the rigorous training at Quantico, Virginia.

She became an agent as dedicated and single-minded as any who had served before her. If she was lonely at night, she tried not to think about it. If she had difficulty making friends, she told herself she didn't have time for relationships anyway. If she shied away from serious involvements, she knew that was the way it had to be. There was no room in her life for anything but justice.

For Grace, her emotional isolation had become a normal way of life.

But then three months ago, news had come to her of Trevor Reardon's second escape. She hadn't been surprised. Or frightened. In fact, there had been a certain sense of inevitability about it all. She'd always known he would come back for her. She was the one loose end that would torment him.

But it would be different now, Grace thought, lying in the bright glare of the bathroom light. This time, she would be ready for him. This time, she was the hunter.

And when they met again face to face, she and Reardon, this time, only one of them would walk away.

Chapter Seven

The aroma of frying chorizo awakened Ethan the next morning. He sat up in bed, wondering at his ability to identify the scent of the spicy Mexican sausage when he still had no recall of his past life.

The enticing smell drew a rumble from his stomach, reminding him that he'd skipped dinner the previous evening. He got up from bed and hurriedly showered and shaved. Staring at himself in the mirror, he noticed that the bruises were fading, the swelling had gone away, and the cut was starting to heal.

He studied his features dispassionately. Ethan supposed his appearance would be considered above average by most standards, but to him, there was still something disturbing about his face. Something that wasn't quite right.

Not wanting to dwell on the possibilities, he left the bathroom and hurriedly dressed, letting the spicy aroma lead him downstairs and into the kitchen.

Rosa stood at the range, stirring the cooked chorizo into a batch of fluffy scrambled eggs. She turned when she heard Ethan enter the room.

"*Buenos días,* Dr. Hunter." She gave him a critical

once-over. "You're looking much better this morning."

"Thanks. I feel better." He walked over to the breakfast table and sat down at the place she had set for him.

"I made your favorite today. Chorizo and eggs."

"Smells great." Ethan watched as she dished up a plate of the sausage and eggs, then brought it to him. She waited while he sampled a bite, then beamed when he almost choked on the peppery food.

"A little extra Tabasco sauce this morning," she explained. "It'll get your blood flowing, speed up your recovery."

Ethan's blood was flowing all right. He felt as if it were about to explode out the top of his head. "Do you think I could have a glass of orange juice?" he managed to gasp.

Rosa stood with her hands on her hips, watching him. "Since when do you like orange juice?"

"Since I found a pitcher in the refrigerator yesterday."

"That was for me," Rosa said accusingly. "You don't like orange juice, not even fresh squeezed. You drink *jugo de tomate*."

Tomato juice didn't sound the least bit appealing to Ethan, but if it would put out the flames dancing on his tongue, he was willing to give it a shot.

"All right, tomato juice then."

Rosa still hesitated. "That cut on your head, Dr. Hunter. It still makes you strange, no?"

"Strange is a good word for it," he muttered.

Rosa turned and hurried over to the refrigerator. She brought him back a tall glass of chilled tomato juice. Ethan took a quick drink, then another. It wasn't half bad.

He set down the glass and glanced up at Rosa. "You were right. *Jugo de tomate* hits the spot."

She nodded in satisfaction, then circled the air with her finger near her ear. *"Extraño."* She started to turn away, then stopped. She stared down at him, her dark eyes clouding. "I read in the paper about Amy Cole. Dr. Hunter, why didn't you tell me what had happened to you the other night?"

"I didn't want to worry you, Rosa."

She bit her lip, twisting her hands in her white apron. "That poor child. I only met her once, when she came here to the house looking for you, but she was very nice to me."

Ethan nodded, not wanting to encourage a line of conversation to which he had nothing to contribute. He didn't remember Amy. He didn't remember anything about her, only the sound of her scream before she'd died.

He glanced down at his plate, willing away the image.

Rosa must have mistaken his silence for grief. She murmured something comforting in Spanish, then turned and went back to her work.

Ethan took a few more bites of his food, then shoved his plate away. At the thought of Amy, his appetite had deserted him. After several minutes of strained silence, he said, "By the way, how's your daughter and her baby?"

Rosa turned at that, her look one of astonishment.

"What's the matter?" Ethan asked in alarm. "Did I say something wrong?"

Rosa's amazement turned to discomfort. Her dark brows knitted into a frown. "No. It's just that…why do you want to know about my daughter, Dr. Hunter? It's been a long time since you ask about her."

"It…has?"

Rosa hesitated. "We don't talk about our personal lives to each other. That was the agreement we had when I first came to work for you. You said it would be better that way."

"Better for whom?"

Her shrug seemed ominous somehow. She came back over to the table and stood staring down at him. "Dr. Hunter, are you sure you're okay? Maybe you should go back to the hospital." She pronounced it "ohs-pee-tahl."

"Don't worry about me." Ethan tried to shrug away her concern. "I told you it might take several days for the effects of the concussion to wear off."

"I know, but it's not just that." Rosa paused again. "You don't act the same. You don't talk the same. You don't even look the same…" She trailed off, one hand creeping to her chest as if she had the sudden urge to cross herself.

Ethan frowned. "I still have a lot of bruising on my face, and my voice is still a bit hoarse." He wondered why his tone suddenly sounded so defensive.

"Maybe," Rosa agreed, but she didn't look convinced. "I still think you should go back to the hospital."

Ethan tried to smile reassuringly. "Just give me a few more days. I'll be back up to speed in no time."

Rosa muttered something he couldn't understand as she turned back to the stove.

Ethan got up and carried his plate and glass to the sink. "Do we have a phone book around here somewhere?"

"In the cabinet next to the door," she said, watching him. Ethan thought she was probably dying to ask him who he wanted to call. In spite of the agreement about their private lives, he could see the curiosity— or was that suspicion?—simmering in the black depths of her eyes.

He retrieved the Yellow Pages directory from the shelf, and carried the two heavy volumes back to his place at the table. Thumbing through the A-L volume, he located the page he wanted, then quickly scanned the entries underneath Guns. He memorized the name and address of a store on the Katy Freeway that looked promising, but he had no idea how to find it. All he knew was that his house was somewhere off Memorial Drive.

Checking the map at the front of the book, he discovered that the Katy Freeway was the name of the feeder road that ran alongside Interstate 10, and that the gun shop was not far from where he lived. He was fairly certain he could find it.

Closing the book, he put both volumes back in their places and turned to Rosa. Her expression was still dubious.

If you only knew the whole story, Ethan thought. Aloud, he said, "Do you happen to know where my car keys are?"

"No. But I know where you keep your spares." She opened a drawer, pulled out a key, and tossed it to him. Ethan decided the Porsche emblem on the key ring was a good omen.

He pocketed the key. "By the way, I think it would be a good idea to get the alarm code changed. I'd like for you to contact the security company as soon as possible."

Following the covered walkway to the garage, Ethan opened the side door and pressed the lighted button on the wall to activate the automatic garage door opener. The heavy door slowly lifted, letting in sunlight, and Ethan, getting his first look at the Porsche, whistled softly.

Black and sleek, with a mirrorlike finish that was almost blinding, the sports car looked ready and able for action. But almost equally impressive was the vintage candy-apple red Corvette that sat alongside the Porsche, and the white 1964 T-Bird that was parked next to the Vette.

Ethan took a moment to admire all three cars before climbing into the Porsche and backing it out of the garage. Shifting into gear, he gave the car gas, then heard the satisfactory burn of rubber as he headed down the driveway.

A Porsche, a Corvette, and a Thunderbird, he thought admiringly. For the first time since he'd awakened in the hospital, he considered the possibilities—and the privileges—that came with being Dr. Ethan Hunter. Maybe there were certain aspects of his personality that he could admire after all. He apparently had fantastic taste in cars.

And in women.

If the picture he'd seen of Amy Cole yesterday was any indication, she'd been as beautiful as his wife, Pilar, but for some reason Ethan couldn't explain, neither woman seemed real to him. They were almost too perfect, as if he had chosen them—or created them—to be admired rather than loved. In spite of their great beauty, both women left him cold.

Ethan supposed he could attribute his lack of an emotional response to his amnesia, but how would that explain the exact opposite reaction he had to Grace? Her imperfections—the cleft in her chin, the freckles across her nose, the tiny mole beneath her right eyebrow—were infinitely more appealing and more seductive than flawless features could ever be.

She was a real woman and she would know real passion. Ethan was sure of it. He'd glimpsed that passion in her eyes yesterday, before he'd kissed her. Before she'd fled Amy's living room in a vain attempt to run away from their attraction.

But the chemistry had still been there when she'd come back. Still there when he'd gazed into her eyes outside the apartment, and later, when she'd dropped him off at his house that evening.

It had still been there when he'd fallen asleep last night, thinking about her...

In the space of two short days, Grace Donovan had gotten under his skin in a way he knew no other woman had before her. But a relationship with her was impossible, for any number of reasons. He had no memory. He had no idea what he might have done in his past. And the one thing that did seem certain was that he was a married man. He may have had an affair with Amy Cole, but he wouldn't do that to Grace.

What about Pilar? a little voice taunted him. *Aren't you the least bit concerned about your wife's feelings?*

Ethan tried, he really tried to feel something for his estranged wife, but nothing came to him. Nothing but an uneasy feeling that Pilar might have been behind his attack two nights ago, that she might have been the one who had wanted Amy dead.

He glanced in the rearview mirror. The streets weren't crowded this time of day, and Ethan had noticed a white sedan pull out of the neighborhood behind him and trail several car lengths away. But just when Ethan began to think he was being followed, the sedan signalled and turned into the parking area of a large office building.

Just to be on the safe side, Ethan circled the block. When he came back around, the car was still in the parking lot and no one was inside.

A few moments later, Ethan pulled into the shopping center off the Katy Freeway. The gun shop was located between a dry cleaners and a sporting goods store. He parked at the far end of the lot, near the sporting goods store, then removed the unloaded gun from the front seat of the car and slipped it into his jacket pocket.

At this time of morning—a few minutes after ten— stores had just opened. There was no one inside the gun shop except for a clerk who stood behind the counter, polishing the glass. He buzzed Ethan in, and when he entered the store, he could hear another worker in the back, moving inventory.

"Mornin'," the clerk at the counter greeted. He was a tall, lanky man of about fifty, dressed in a white western shirt with pearl buttons and Wrangler jeans that rode low on lean hips. "What can I do you for?"

The store was filled with weapons of varying

makes and caliber. Ethan wondered why he didn't feel the least bit intimidated by all that firepower. The thought crossed his mind again that he was no ordinary doctor. Far from it, if what Grace had told him was true.

He stepped up to the counter and pulled the gun from his pocket, laying it carefully on the glass counter. The clerk whistled softly, much as Ethan had done when he'd first seen the Porsche.

"Ain't that a little beauty? What's your askin' price?"

"I'm not here to sell it. I wondered if you could tell me something about it. My father-in-law left it to me when he died," Ethan improvised. "I think it's custom-made."

"Oh, it's custom all right." The clerk picked up the weapon and studied it almost reverently. "It's a 1911 Colt revolver that's been specially modified. See these night sights? Those set your father-in-law back a pretty penny."

Ethan watched the clerk handle the weapon with an expertise that seemed oddly familiar. "Do you have any idea where he might have gotten these modifications?"

The clerk sighted an invisible target, squinting one eye as he took aim. "There's a gun shop over in Arkansas that does this kind of work. They modify weapons of this caliber—guns that can easily be concealed—for police SWAT teams, the FBI Hostage Rescue Units, and even for some of the elite units of the military."

That caught Ethan's attention. "Elite units of the military? You mean like the Navy SEALs?"

The clerk palmed the weapon and tested its weight. "Was your father-in-law a military man?"

"Not in recent years."

"You mean that you know about." The clerk gave him a conspiratorial wink. "Some of those guys are mighty secretive, you know. They don't talk about their work."

Ethan paused. "This gun shop in Arkansas would probably keep records of their custom orders, right?"

The clerk scratched his head. "More than likely. But if it was ordered through a police department or the military, they wouldn't have a record of the individual the gun was issued to. They might be able to track down the particular law enforcement body or branch of the service that owned the weapon, but I doubt they'd be able to give you that information. And even if they did, it wouldn't do you any good."

"Why's that?"

"See this?" With his index finger, the clerk traced along the side of the gun barrel. "The identification number has been filed away."

Ethan took the gun from the clerk's hand, holding the weapon to the light. He could barely detect the faint imperfection in the barrel where the number had been removed. Someone had gone to a great deal of trouble to conceal his handiwork. The metal had been polished until the scratches in the finish were all but invisible.

The clerk's eyes narrowed with what might have been suspicion. "Looks like your father-in-law—or someone—wanted to make sure this piece couldn't be traced back to him."

"Well, thanks for your help." Ethan gathered up

the weapon, said his goodbye, then hurried out of the shop. He was glad he'd had the foresight to park away from the store. He'd seen the suspicion in the clerk's eyes, and wondered if the man might even now be calling the police. But if he was, he'd have to come outside to get the license plate number from Ethan's car.

Sliding behind the wheel, Ethan quickly started the Porsche and backed out of the space. No one had come out of the gun shop, and he couldn't see anyone at the window. Still, he headed down the street in the wrong direction just to avoid driving by the store.

And all the while, the gun was almost a living, breathing entity in the seat beside him.

He's an ex-Navy SEAL and an explosives expert who sold his services to the highest bidder. He became a mercenary, an assassin, sometimes a terrorist.

Was it possible he had somehow come into possession of Trevor Reardon's weapon? Had Ethan brought it back to the States with him, put it in his safe for—what? Protection? Because he knew Reardon might someday come after him?

Ethan lifted a hand to wipe the sudden beads of sweat from his brow. That had to be it. That had to be the reason he was in possession of such a weapon.

Because the other explanation that came to mind was almost too terrifying to contemplate.

''HE'S NOT HOME?'' Grace repeated. ''Where did he go?''

The housekeeper shrugged, giving Grace a cool appraisal. ''He had errands.''

''He didn't give you any indication where he was

going?" Damn, Grace thought. Why would he just leave like that? He'd known she was coming over this morning. Why hadn't he waited for her?

And why the hell hadn't someone called her to warn her that he was roaming around out there somewhere, making a target of himself?

Rosa eyed her with open disapproval. "I don't ask where he goes. It's none of my business," she said pointedly.

Grace could tell Rosa didn't like her, and therefore, didn't trust her. Grace had run up against the problem before. She sometimes came across as too abrupt, too impatient, too hard. Women didn't like that. Neither did some men, for that matter.

She forced a softness in her tone. "Look, I don't mean to be such a nuisance, but I need to tell Dr. Hunter about the funeral this afternoon."

"Funeral?"

Grace bit her lip and nodded. "You heard about Amy Cole? Dr. Hunter's assistant?"

Rosa crossed herself. "Yes. Such a shame. So young and so *bella*."

Grace nodded. "Amy was my sister, Rosa. I came to tell Dr. Hunter about the memorial service this afternoon."

Rosa's expression changed dramatically. The wariness and suspicion vanished, leaving her features set in gentle lines of compassion. *"Lo siento."* She reached for Grace's hand and pulled her inside. "Please. Come in out of the heat."

She led Grace upstairs, saying over her shoulder, "I'll fix you something cool to drink. Then you can tell me about your sister."

Her soothing tone made Grace want to do exactly
that. For the first time in years, she found herself
wanting to tell someone about Jessie, about her goodness and purity, and about her unfailing conscience.
Jessie had been one of those people who had truly
been a blessing to this world, while Grace—

The parrot's harsh squawk brought her abruptly
back to the present. She glanced across the room,
where the magnificent yellow-and-blue bird strutted
with supreme confidence on his perch.

When he saw Grace watching him, he flapped his
wings and screeched, "They're not real! They're not
real! They're not real!"

"Shut up, Simon, you stupid bird!" Rosa scolded.
To Grace she said apologetically, "He's a terrible
creature. He picks up everything he hears on the *tele-
visión.*"

Grace wondered which programs he'd been watching. Jerry Springer? Howard Stern, maybe?

She followed Rosa into the kitchen and watched
while the housekeeper prepared two glasses of iced
tea. They both sat down at the breakfast table—Rosa
obviously having dispensed with any formalities—
and sipped their drinks.

After a moment, she said, "You came to tell Dr.
Hunter about the funeral?"

Grace nodded. "It's at four o'clock this afternoon
at the Chapel Hill Funeral Home. I...thought he
might like to be there."

Rosa looked as if she wanted to comment but kept
silent.

Grace took another sip of her tea. "How long have
you worked for Dr. Hunter?"

Rosa shrugged. "A long time."

"You must know him pretty well." Grace studied the older woman's face.

"Dr. Hunter is not an easy man to know. He's very..." Rosa struggled for the right word. "*Complicado*. Complex. There are some who consider him a saint."

"Are you one of them?"

A slight hesitation. "He's no saint. He has his faults, quite a few of them. But he is, in many ways, a very good man."

"You're referring to the work he does at his clinics here and in Mexico."

Rosa nodded. "Especially the one in *Méjico*. The children who come there would break your heart. Many of them have been horribly disfigured since birth. They've become outcasts in their own villages. They've never known anything but ridicule."

Grace wondered how he could possibly be the same man who changed criminals' faces for money. Was Ethan some sort of Dr. Jekyll and Mr. Hyde, a man with two very distinct personalities? The notion made her shiver. "How did you meet Dr. Hunter?"

Rosa shrugged, but her expression suddenly became very sad. "It was a long time ago, in Mexico City. When my daughter was young, I worked in a *barra* in a very bad part of town. Marta and I had a little one-room *apartamento* on the second floor, little better than a hovel, but it was all I could afford. Sometimes when I worked late, Marta would get lonely. She would sneak downstairs to be near me. I didn't want her to. She was already starting to look like a woman, and she was so beautiful that men were already starting to notice her. One night a fight broke out, a drunken brawl. In the confusion, a man grabbed Marta and pulled her outside. He tried to—'' Rosa's eyes closed briefly, as if the memory had become too painful to relive. Grace understood that feeling all too well.

''What happened?'' she asked gently.

Rosa shuddered. ''Marta fought him off as best she could and started screaming. He pulled a knife and cut her. The whole side of her face was...mutilated.''

''I'm sorry.''

Rosa shrugged away Grace's pity. ''She was horribly scarred. People would stare at her on the streets, and children would run away from her. Marta withdrew completely into herself. She was very...ashamed of her face. Years passed, and then one day I heard about Dr. Hunter. That was before he had his clinic in the jungle. He use to come to Mexico City twice a year and work in one of the hospitals. People there spoke of him as a god. It was said the handsome young doctor could perform miracles, that he could transform the most hideous monster into an angel. Marta was no monster. She was a badly scarred and frightened child. But Dr. Hunter was my only hope.''

''Was he able to help her?'' Grace asked, caught up in the story in spite of herself.

''Eventually. Marta was frightened of him at first— frightened of every man who came near her—but Dr. Hunter spoke to her so gently that she soon forgot her fears. He told her it might take several operations, but when he was finished, she would be beautiful again.

And she was.'' A tear trickled down Rosa's cheek, and she quickly brushed it away.

Grace was more affected by the story than she wanted to admit. It was hard enough to do what had to be done, but when she thought of Rosa's daughter and of all the children Ethan had helped, Grace couldn't help asking herself if ridding the world of a man like Trevor Reardon was an equal exchange for depriving it of a doctor as talented as Ethan.

Not daring to ponder the question, Grace rose. ''I'd better be going. I still have a million things to do.''

Rosa nodded sympathetically and stood, too. Just as she started for the kitchen door to show Grace out, the phone rang.

Grace held up her hand. ''Go ahead and get that. I can let myself out.''

In the living room, she couldn't resist stopping by the parrot's cage. The two of them had formed some kind of strange bond, Grace decided. A sort of mutual disrespect for one another. Besides which, she needed something to take her mind off Rosa's story and the doubts it had created for her.

''So your name is Simon, huh? As in Simon Says?''

The bird cocked his head and stared at her.

Grace cocked her head and stared back. ''Well, why don't you say it, Simon? I know you're dying to.''

Simon blinked, but remained silent.

After a moment, Grace crooned, ''They're not real, they're not real, they're not real. Come on, what do you say, Simon?''

The bird fluffed his wings importantly and

squawked, "I say we get rid of the bastard once and for all."

SINCE AMY COLE had no family, Grace, in keeping with her cover, had taken care of all the funeral arrangements. She'd kept the service simple, ordering an elegant spray of white roses to rest atop the mahogany casket while a framed picture of Amy, the one from her apartment, was displayed on a nearby pedestal.

The small chapel was surprisingly crowded. Grace glanced around the room, trying to sort out who was who. Several people clustered around the apartment manager from Amy's complex, and Grace decided that most of them were probably Amy's neighbors. Some of the others were undoubtedly from work. But aside from the manager, Grace didn't recognize any of the mourners.

She glanced at her watch, wondering what was keeping Ethan. He'd been incommunicado with her all day, and although he'd been under surveillance for most of that time, Grace had yet to be given a report on his movements.

When ten more minutes had gone by and he still hadn't shown, she began to worry. Could something have happened? Had Reardon somehow managed to slip through the trap they'd set for him?

A sour taste rose in Grace's mouth at the thought. She wanted Reardon, but at what price? Two days ago, she would have said any price, but that was before she'd met Ethan. Before she'd allowed him to get to her.

Now she wasn't sure what she would do if the choice came down to Reardon or Ethan.

You're a fool, a little voice whispered inside her. *You don't know this man. You don't owe him anything.*

True, but in the last two days, he'd awakened something inside Grace she had thought forever dead. Feelings. Attraction.

Need.

She closed her eyes briefly as a wave of doubt rolled over her. She didn't want to need anyone. She couldn't afford to. Need was synonymous with vulnerability. Weakness. And Grace had to remain strong. She had to remain focused. If she didn't, she might not be able to save herself or Ethan.

But what if Reardon does manage to penetrate the screen? that same voice taunted her.

Grace told herself it was impossible. The plan would work.

But would it? Hadn't this operation already been full of surprises? Amy Cole was never supposed to die. In fact, she shouldn't have been anywhere near the clinic that night. Her cooperation with the FBI had been critical in formulating the plan to capture Trevor Reardon, but because Grace hadn't been honest, Amy had gotten scared. If Myra's hunch was right, Amy had gone to the clinic to warn Ethan that the Feds were on to him. And she'd gotten herself killed in the process.

Grace blamed herself for that. Though she wasn't a mind reader, she should have interpreted the signs. Amy was crazy in love with Ethan. When she suddenly realized what her cooperation with the authorities would mean for him—and for herself—she'd panicked. Grace should have seen it coming, but she'd never been the best judge of what love could do to you. What it could *make* you do.

In fact, she had been the very worst judge.

Not wanting to start an avalanche of memories, she turned her attention back to the crowd. A man had come in and gone straight to Amy's picture. He stood staring at it for a long moment, then walked over to the casket, running his fingers along the smooth surface of the lid. He began to sob quietly.

Uneasy, Grace watched him. Who was he? How had he known Amy? She'd told Grace she had no family or close friends, other than Ethan, but this man had obviously been deeply affected by her death.

Someone touched Grace's arm and she whirled. The chaplain, Bible clutched to his chest, stood at her side. He looked to be in his mid-forties, tall and thin with arrow-straight posture. His cheekbones were classically high, giving what would have been an otherwise plain face an almost regal look. His lips were thin, his nose a bit broad and his dark brown hair was streaked with gray. Grace thought he had the kindest eyes she'd ever seen, but even as that notion flitted through her mind, trepidation swept over her. Had she met him before?

He held out his hand to her, and Grace reluctantly took it. His handshake was warm and firm, not in the least offensive, but a shiver racked her just the same. As soon as she deemed it appropriate, she withdrew her hand from his.

The chaplain smiled. "You're Amy's sister, I understand."

Grace hesitated. Lying in the service of her country was one thing, but deliberately deceiving a man of God something else. "We weren't close," she said carefully.

"That often happens in families. A rift occurs, time passes, and before anyone can imagine, it's too late. But take comfort in the knowledge that it never is really too late. You will see your sister again."

Grace's gaze fastened on the man's clerical collar. She realized suddenly why he seemed so familiar to her, why he made her so uneasy. She had not been around a clergyman since her family's funeral, but now she had a vivid recall of that day, of the minister from their church holding her hand, offering her comfort in the knowledge that she and her family would someday be reunited in the hereafter.

It was only later that Grace had decided her only comfort would come here on earth, when she put Trevor Reardon away forever.

The man at the coffin was still crying. The chaplain smiled sadly. "If you'll excuse me…"

Grace watched him approach the casket and put a gentle hand on the man's shoulder. The chaplain spoke to the weeping man softly, and after a bit, his sobs subsided. He turned and walked away from the casket, his gaze brushing Grace's before he seated himself at the back of the chapel.

It was nearing on four o'clock. Rosa came in and nodded to Grace before finding a seat near the front. The group of people from Amy's apartment complex settled near the middle. Others scattered about the remaining pews. Just as the chaplain took the podium, two last-minute arrivals started everyone whispering among themselves.

Grace recognized the woman at once. Pilar Hunter had looked exquisitely beautiful in the pictures Grace had seen of her, but in person, the woman was breathtaking.

Unlike almost everyone else in the chapel, she'd refused to wear black, choosing instead a sleeveless dress in dusky blue linen that did incredible things to her dark hair and eyes. The hemline was short, her heels high, and her bare legs went on forever. Grace couldn't help glancing down at her own attire—a simple silk jersey dress that she had once thought flattering. For the first time that afternoon, she was almost glad Ethan hadn't shown up.

The man with Pilar took her elbow and guided her toward a pew. They settled directly behind Grace, and she caught a strong whiff of Pilar's perfume—a heavy, exotic scent that seemed to capture the essence of the woman herself.

As the chaplain started the service, Grace became increasingly aware of Pilar's presence, as if the woman was staring at the back of Grace's head. She remembered what Ethan had said about his wife, that she seemed like a woman capable of throwing acid on his car or in his face. Grace understood what he meant. In the brief glimpse she'd had of Pilar, Grace had sensed an undercurrent of suppressed violence that was almost as tangible as her perfume.

I say we just kill the bastard and be done with it.

Could she and Myra have been wrong? Grace wondered suddenly. What if Trevor Reardon hadn't been behind the attack in Ethan's clinic? What if someone else wanted him dead?

Grace tried to put the notion out of her head. She couldn't afford to get sidetracked or to let down her guard. That was exactly what Reardon would want. For all she knew, he might be in this very room now, watching her from a distance and laughing. Laughing...

Grace looked up and her gaze met the chaplain's. He smiled at her and nodded almost imperceptibly before he bowed his head to pray for Amy Cole's immortal soul.

Chapter Eight

Ethan stared at the pile of shoes on his bedroom floor as a headache beat a painful staccato inside his brain.

What the hell was going on here?

Why didn't any of these shoes fit him?

His movements almost frantic, Ethan tried on another pair, and then another. Every shoe in his closet was too small for him. The only pair that fit him were the ones he'd been wearing the night he woke up in the hospital, the ones he'd been wearing ever since.

The loafers had been fine with casual clothes, but today, getting dressed for Amy's funeral, he'd found a black suit, white shirt, and somber tie in the closet. When he'd brought out the appropriate shoes, he'd discovered they were too small for him, as was every other pair of shoes in the closet.

He didn't understand why. Granted, the clothes he'd been wearing were loose, but that could be explained by weight loss following surgery. And he knew he'd had the appendectomy because he had the scar to prove it. The dreams of being shot, of falling off a cliff were just that—drug-induced visions. The memory loss was due to the blow to his head. His wariness of the authorities—well, Grace had explained that to him as well.

Clearly, everything that had happened to him had a logical, if disturbing, explanation.

Except for the fact that none of his shoes fit.

Ethan picked up the black dress shoe and studied it. Why would he—why would *anyone*—buy dozens of pairs of expensive shoes in the wrong size? It made no sense—

Without warning, the pain in his head became razor-sharp, blinding. Dropping the shoe, Ethan put his hands to his head, pressing tightly as he squeezed his eyes closed.

An image shot through him. He could see someone running for his life through a jungle. He could smell the dank scent of the vegetation, feel the cloying heat, hear the sounds of pursuit behind him. He *knew* the man's fear. But the man's face was not the one Ethan stared at in the mirror.

And yet…

The man in the vision was him and it wasn't.

Unlike the picture that Ethan had seen of himself downstairs in the study, he felt connected to the man running through the jungle. He knew him in a way he did not know the stranger staring back at him from the mirror.

But…why?

Why was he having another man's visions?

Why did none of the shoes in his closet fit him?

Why was he in possession of a gun that may well have been issued to someone in one of the special forces of the military? Someone like an elite Navy SEAL? Someone like Trevor Reardon?

Why did a plastic surgeon know how to use a weapon like that?

An explanation came with another blinding flash of light.

Pain exploded inside Ethan's head, and for a moment, he thought he was going to be sick.

WHEN THE SERVICE was over, Grace looked up to find Ethan standing in the doorway of the chapel. As his gaze met hers, she felt a physical jolt. It was almost as if a bolt of pure adrenaline had ping-ponged between them.

He looked pale, Grace thought with sudden anxiety. Shaken. What had happened to him?

She got up and started toward him, but was waylaid several times by well-wishers—first by the apartment manager, then by a neighbor, and then by Rosa, whose initial frost toward Grace had thawed. The housekeeper squeezed Grace's hand comfortingly, then, her glance moving over Grace's shoulder, she pursed her lips in stern disapproval.

Grace followed her gaze to find Pilar and her escort on a collision course with Ethan. Wondering if an unpleasant scene was about to erupt, Grace glanced around the room. Most of the mourners had filed out of the chapel by this time. The grieving man remained seated, his head bowed in silent prayer, while the chaplain stood at his podium, waiting for everyone to leave. The late afternoon sun shining through the stained glass window behind the clergyman gave him an almost angelic appearance. The image should have been comforting, but for some reason it was not.

Hoping to abort a possible spectacle, Grace walked

over to stand beside Ethan. Their gazes met again, but neither of them said anything.

Pilar stared at her coolly. Even this close, Grace couldn't find a single imperfection in the woman's complexion.

"So you're Amy Cole's sister." Her voice, light and musical, was as attractive as the rest of her, and the Spanish accent gave her a hint of mystery. "I'm Pilar. Ethan's wife." The slight emphasis on the last word made Grace wonder again about Ethan and Pilar's relationship.

"How do you do?" Grace extended her hand, but the woman's fingertips barely brushed against her palm.

Pilar stared at her critically. "You don't look anything like her, you know."

Grace assumed the comment was meant to cut. "My sister was very beautiful," she said.

Pilar raised her narrow shoulders in an elegant shrug. "In a trampish sort of way."

For the first time, Ethan stirred to life beside Grace. "For God's sake, she's dead. Can't you show a little respect?"

Pilar's dark brows rose in mild outrage. "The same respect she showed for our marriage vows?"

"Why did you come here?" Ethan demanded. He turned to the man standing next to Pilar. "Why did you let her come?"

The man laughed softly. "You don't 'let' Pilar do anything. You should know that better than anyone." He turned to Grace and put out his hand. "By the way, I'm Bob Kendall. I'm very sorry about your sister."

So this was Ethan's ex-partner. Unlike Pilar's, his handshake was firm, and his fingers lingered against Grace's for just a moment too long.

She instantly disliked him. He was too smooth, and his gray eyes were too insincere.

He said to Ethan, "Are you feeling all right, buddy? You look a little pale."

"I'm fine," Ethan said tersely.

"Still, it might not hurt to give Mancetti a call. I don't imagine she was too happy to learn you'd checked yourself out of the hospital."

Ethan didn't answer. Instead he turned to Grace, muttering, "When can we get out of here?"

She shrugged, feeling Pilar's dark eyes scouring her. "Now. I've made arrangements for a private burial."

Ethan nodded. His eyes were shadowed. Haunted. Was it Amy's funeral that had gotten to him? Had he finally remembered her? Remembered that…he cared for her?

Ethan turned toward the door, but Pilar caught his arm. "You can't just walk off like this. We're not through, Ethan."

He stared down at her for a long moment, then very deliberately removed her hand from his arm. "You could have fooled me."

OUTSIDE, THE SUNLIGHT, even at five o'clock, was still brutal. Ethan pulled a pair of dark glasses from the inside of his suit coat and slipped them on. He hadn't been able to rid himself of the headache. A handful of aspirin had dulled the pain, but the confusion whirling inside him was still as strong as ever.

Beside him, Grace tried to match her steps to his, but he had a good eight inches on her. He slowed, then stopped altogether in the shade of a huge water oak. The lower limbs were so heavy, they'd been braced to keep from snapping. Spanish moss dripped silvery green from the gnarled branches, giving the tree a forlorn, almost ghostly appearance. In the distance, the cars in the parking lot wavered in the rising heat from the pavement. Their inconsistency seemed surreal and out of place, but the eeriness matched Ethan's mood.

Grace said a little breathlessly, "What happened to you? I was beginning to worry."

He gazed down at her. "Were you?"

"Of course. You know as well as I do the danger you're in."

"Do I?"

A brief frown flitted across her features. "What happened, Ethan? Why were you so late getting to the service?"

The way she said his name, in a voice that was just the tiniest bit husky, made him want more than ever to discount his earlier thoughts. But the question was like a mantra inside his head.

Who am I? Who the hell am I?

He studied Grace's features, thinking how lovely she looked today, and how very calm she seemed for having just come from her sister's funeral. Her mood was somber, as was the black dress she wore, but there was something about her eyes—an alertness, an intensity—that mystified him and made him believe he wasn't the only one who had secrets.

He took her arm and drew her deeper into the

shadow of the oak tree. "What if I told you, I'm not the man you think I am?"

Her eyes instantly deepened. "What do you mean?"

He paused, wondering what to say, how to tell her his suspicions. *I may not be Dr. Ethan Hunter. In fact, I may be...*

He couldn't even finish the thought. His heart began to beat wildly against his chest. Ethan was sure he'd never felt so alone, so out of control, so lost as he did at that moment.

And Grace. God help him, he was still drawn to her. Still attracted to her. Still *wanted* her. In some perverse way, more than ever because he knew if what he feared was true, he could never have her.

In fact, it might even come down to the basic choice of his life...or hers.

She was still staring up at him, her incredible blue eyes deep and intense. He wondered what she was thinking, if she had even an inkling of what he was feeling.

She touched his arm. The action made Ethan almost groan out loud.

"Have you remembered something?"

"No. But what if I told you—" He wanted to tell her about the shoes, and possibly the gun, but a movement at the entrance of the chapel drew his attention. A man came out of the building and paused, looking around. Ethan dimly recognized him from the funeral service. He'd been seated at the back, weeping quietly, when Ethan had arrived.

Ethan glanced at him, then turned his gaze back to

Grace. But out of the corner of his eye, he saw the man start toward them.

"Do you know who that man is?" he asked Grace suddenly.

She turned, following his gaze, and Ethan saw her tense. "No. I saw him inside, though. He was pretty torn up."

Ethan watched as the man approached them. He had the kind of face that made it hard to judge his age, but something about the way he walked, the way he dressed—casually in khaki pants and a button-down collar shirt—gave Ethan the impression that he was fairly young, no more than late thirties. The receding hairline was probably premature, as were the lines around his eyes and mouth.

As he neared them, Ethan heard Grace catch her breath. He thought that her gasp was not because she suddenly recognized the man, but because of the look of unadulterated fury on his face. Ethan saw Grace's hand slip inside her purse, but before he could wonder about her intentions, the man stepped up to him. He was shorter than Ethan by only an inch or so, but their builds were similar. They stood almost chest to chest.

"Dr. Ethan Hunter?"

"Yes?"

Without warning, the man hauled off and punched Ethan square in the face. Pain flashed white-hot over his already bruised flesh, and as Ethan staggered back a step, red-hot anger shot through him. Almost instinctively, he lunged at the man, but Grace jumped between them.

"Stop it!" she ordered, putting a hand on each of

their chests with surprising strength and authority. She turned to the stranger. ''Why did you do that?'' she demanded.

The man's gaze was still furious. ''He had it coming!''

Ethan said coldly, ''The hell I did. I don't even know who you are.''

The man glared at him. ''Of course, you wouldn't remember me. Why should you? I was nobody important, just the man Amy was going to marry, that's all. Until you came along.''

Grace must have sensed the anger welling inside him again, for she gave him a shove. ''Calm down,'' she said. ''This is not the place for violence.''

The man looked immediately contrite. His blue eyes flooded with tears. ''No, you're right. Amy wouldn't have wanted that.''

He took a few steps away from Grace and Ethan, as if struggling to gather his composure. But he continued to glare at Ethan. ''We did meet once. I guess you don't remember. I came to Amy's apartment to beg her to come back to me, but…it was too late. You'd already seduced her away from me.''

The raw pain in the man's eyes made Ethan's stomach knot. He didn't know whether he was really Dr. Ethan Hunter or not, but at that moment, the one thing he was certain of was that he didn't much care for Dr. Hunter or the way he treated people.

Grace said softly, ''I didn't know Amy was ever engaged. She never mentioned it.''

''That's odd,'' the man said, wiping at his eyes. ''Because she never mentioned having a sister, either.''

GRACE COULD FEEL Ethan's gaze on her, but she kept her eyes trained on the man before her. Something about him seemed very pitiful to her. He was not unattractive, but the way he dressed, the receding hairline, the ordinary features must have made him feel like a moth to Amy's butterfly. No wonder he harbored such animosity toward Ethan. He was the epitome of everything this man was not.

Grace said carefully, "Amy and I were estranged for several years. We hadn't spoken with each other until very recently."

"I guess that explains why she never wanted to talk about her family." The man stuck out his hand. "My name's Danny Medford."

"Grace Donovan. You already know Dr. Hunter," she said with irony.

He shot Ethan a killing glance before turning back to Grace. "I don't suppose it would be possible—" He broke off, looking ill at ease.

"What?" Grace prompted.

Danny looked at her hopefully. "Do you think we could get together sometime? You know, to talk about Amy?"

He seemed a nice enough guy, but Grace had no wish to perpetuate the deception, to contribute in any way to the man's pain. However, with Ethan looking on, she had little choice but to keep up the farce. "I'd like that. Maybe in a few weeks when it isn't so painful to talk about her."

He nodded, smiling wistfully as he fished a card from his shirt pocket and handed it to her. "That's my work number. I'm there at all hours. Feel free to call anytime."

Medford Engineering, the card read. Grace slipped it in her purse and smiled. "It's been nice meeting you, Danny."

"Likewise." He turned to Ethan. "I wouldn't be surprised if you and I meet again someday."

There was no mistaking the threat in the man's words, but Ethan merely shrugged. "I'll be ready next time."

After the man had disappeared into the parking lot, Ethan fished a handkerchief from his pocket and wiped away the trickle of blood at the corner of his mouth.

"Yet another of Dr. Hunter's enemies," he said enigmatically, watching the man's battered Toyota sedan pull out of the parking lot. "They seem to be coming out of the woodwork."

"He seems harmless enough."

Ethan lifted a brow as he daubed at his lip. "Easy for you to say."

Grace almost smiled. "I meant comparatively speaking. The enemy we really have to worry about is Trevor Reardon."

"I wonder." Ethan's eyes grew dark and distant, as if he'd gone someplace in his mind that Grace had no wish to follow. Or had he gone to a place she'd already been to?

There was still blood on his lip. She took the handkerchief from his hand. "Here, let me."

She blotted the droplet of blood as gently as she could, but Ethan winced at her touch. He took her hand and pulled it away. For a moment they stood that way, her hand in his, eyes locked, until Grace's stomach began to flutter wildly.

She was accustomed to butterflies. She got them the first day of every new assignment, every time she had to draw her weapon, or when she faced danger. But this was different, because the greater threat was coming, not from Ethan, but from within herself.

She shivered, watching him. So much about him she didn't know, but the one thing that was all too real was her attraction to him. Her feelings for him. She couldn't explain them. They made no sense. But the emotions raging inside her were so real and so intense, that if he were to kiss her at that moment, Grace knew she would have no willpower to resist.

What few relationships she'd had over the years had been with men who had no expectations of a future with her. There could be no future with Ethan, either, and yet Grace found herself yearning for something she'd never wanted before. The hollowness inside her heart made her feel lost and lonely in a way she hadn't felt in a long, long time.

She almost hated Ethan for that. Hated him for making her lose confidence in her ability to do what needed to be done. For making her want him.

Grace closed her eyes, letting the heat of the day wash over her. The humidity curled the fine hairs at the back of her neck, and she could feel the silk of her dress clinging to her body. She had a sudden image of cool water lapping at her toes. Of a fragrant breeze rippling through her hair. Of a man lying naked beside her, whispering in her ear...

When she opened her eyes, Ethan was staring down at her so intently, Grace thought he must have read her mind. She caught her breath.

"What are we going to do about this, Grace?"

She didn't try to misconstrue his meaning. The sparks between them were all too obvious. "There's nothing to be done. We just have to…ignore it, I guess."

"You think that's possible?" His eyes darkened, so much so that Grace had to glance away. She had to find a way to subdue the power he had over her.

"It has to be, because as you pointed out yesterday, you're a married man. Just because you can't remember your wife doesn't mean you don't still have feelings for her. You might even still love her."

He almost laughed. "Do you really believe that?"

Grace remembered the coldness in Pilar's expression, the emptiness in her eyes, and she shuddered. "I don't think you still love her. Maybe you never did, but it doesn't change the fact that you are still married to her. I don't take that lightly, Ethan."

"I wish I could say the same." Grace didn't think he was trying to be facetious. His eyes were too haunted for that.

"And that brings us back to Amy," she said quietly. "I don't want to be another one of your conquests. I won't be."

"I don't even remember Amy," he said. "Everything you've told me about her…it doesn't even seem real. It's like…someone else had the affair with her. Someone else married Pilar. It wasn't me. I'm not that man."

Grace wished she knew what to say to him, but she didn't. She wished suddenly that what he was telling her was true—that he wasn't Dr. Ethan Hunter, but someone entirely different. Someone free and honorable. Someone with whom she just might have a second shot at life.

But reality and fantasy were two different concepts, and no one knew that better than Grace.

"Ethan—"

"I'm *not* that man, Grace."

He could almost convince her when he looked at her that way. When he skimmed his knuckles along the side of her cheek, brushed back the hair from her face with a touch so gentle, Grace could have wept. She closed her eyes briefly, wanting him to kiss her with every fiber of her being, and knowing all the while that if he did, there would be no chance for her then. Everything in her world would be lost.

She took a step back from him. "Losing memories doesn't change who you are. What you've done."

"What I've done." The shadow in his eyes deepened. He raked his fingers through his hair, turning away from her. "There's nothing that will ever change that."

"No, but there is such a thing as redemption. Restitution."

His gaze came back to meet hers. "And how do you propose I pay for my sins?" he asked grimly.

Grace shrugged. "Helping me bring a man like Trevor Reardon to justice is a good place to start."

Ethan's expression hardened. Something that Grace couldn't quite define flashed in his eyes. "That sounds so naive, but somehow you don't strike me as the Pollyanna type. I may not remember who I am or what I've done, but I don't think I'm the only one here with secrets."

Grace's heartbeat quickened. "What do you mean?"

He gazed down at her, studying her. "I don't know who you are any more than I know who I am. We're strangers, and yet...we seem to have some kind of...connection. Even you can't deny that."

"Maybe our connection is Amy," Grace tried to say calmly.

He shook his head. "I don't think so. I can't help but wonder if you're holding something back from me."

"Like what?"

He hesitated. His gaze grew even more pensive. "Did we know each other before?"

"No." Grace's heart pounded like a piston. He was getting too close. His suspicions were mounting by the minute, and she didn't know what to do to stop them. If he found out who she was...how she was using him...

God help you if you're lying to me.

"I told you before," she said. "We'd never met until that night outside the hospital."

"Then what is this connection we have?" he asked almost urgently.

Grace shrugged. "Attraction. Chemistry. Call it what you like, but that's all it is."

"Why do I feel as if it's something more?" Ethan grabbed her forearms and pulled her toward him. "Why do I feel as if I know you better than I could ever know the woman who claims to be my wife? Why do I know how your lips would taste if I kissed you right now? How your body would feel beneath mine if we—"

"Please don't," Grace said breathlessly. She put her hands to his chest, but it was a meaningless gesture. She wasn't going to push him away. It took every ounce of her strength not to pull him closer.

"You feel it, too. I can see it your eyes."

"Please—"

He drew her so close, their lips were only a heartbeat apart. "You want me to kiss you," he said almost accusingly. "Almost as much as I want to."

"Ethan—"

The space between them evaporated. "Tell me to stop," he murmured against her mouth.

Grace said nothing. Instead she closed her eyes and waited for the inevitable to happen. Waited for her life to come tumbling down around her. When it didn't, her relief—or was it disappointment?—was so intense, her head spun dizzily. She opened her eyes and gazed up at him.

Something glimmered in his eyes, something that looked almost like triumph. He dropped his hands from her shoulders and backed away. "I told you it wouldn't be easy," he said, in a tone that sounded more like a threat than a warning.

GRACE LAY IN bed that night, wide awake and listening to the street noises outside her hotel. The room was dimly illuminated by streetlights and neon signs that caused shadows to leap and cavort across the walls and ceiling, like demons celebrating some dark victory.

Earlier, she'd opened the curtains so that she could see the balcony outside the sliding glass doors. Airplane lights twinkled in the night sky, and between the slats of the balcony railing, she could see the faint movement of pine boughs stirring in the breeze. She would have liked to open the doors, letting in the breeze and the scent of evergreen, but she never slept with the windows open. Her doors and windows were always closed and always locked.

Grace stared out into the darkness and thought about Ethan, wondering what he was doing tonight. His house was under surveillance and secured by a state-of-the-art alarm system that even an FBI agent couldn't find fault with. There was no reason for Grace to worry, and yet she *was* worried. She couldn't shake the uneasiness that had invaded her thoughts since she'd left Ethan at the chapel this afternoon.

I'm not that man, Grace.

What had he meant by that? What had he meant when he'd said, *What if I told you I'm not the man you think I am?*

Was it wishful thinking on his part? The denial of a man with no memory learning things about himself that were more than just unpleasant?

No wonder he was so confused. The man who altered criminals' faces for money was a direct contradiction to the man Rosa had told Grace about earlier. A man who could transform hideous monsters into angels. A man who changed children's lives forever.

Was Ethan Hunter a saint with a badly tarnished halo, or a Dr. Jekyll and Mr. Hyde—a man with two entirely different sides to his personality?

Grace shivered in the gloom, considering all the possibilities but trying not to dwell on the one thing Ethan had said that perhaps troubled her the most.

Why do I feel as if I know you better than I could

ever know the woman who claims to be my wife? Why do I know how your lips would taste if I kissed you right now? How your body would feel beneath mine if we—

Grace sucked in a long breath, trying to remember her objectives, but the situation had taken a turn she couldn't have anticipated. It had seemed so easy when she and Myra had first devised the plan. Come to Houston. Set up surveillance and a cover for Grace. Wait for Dr. Ethan Hunter to arrive from Mexico and then approach him. Convince him to cooperate so that Trevor Reardon could be drawn out into the open.

But then everything had gone wrong. It had all happened too quickly. Ethan had come back from Mexico weeks earlier than planned, before complete backup and support were in place. And then Amy Cole had died. The entire operation had had to be hastily revised, and now everything hinged on Grace's ability to perpetuate her deception. To remain close to Ethan.

But what happened when it was all over? Originally, Grace hadn't stopped to consider what would happen to Ethan once Reardon was safely behind bars again. Or dead.

But Ethan had his own sins to answer for, and leniency would depend on the extent of his cooperation. Grace hadn't thought to be involved in anything beyond Reardon's capture, but now she realized how difficult it would be to walk away, to never look back, to betray a man she was deeply attracted to.

For a moment, she considered calling Myra and asking for advice, but somehow Grace thought this was beyond the older agent's field of expertise. She didn't think Myra had ever been torn like this. Grace couldn't even imagine Myra Temple falling in love.

She couldn't imagine herself falling in love, either. Though it was true she was attracted to Ethan, that they shared a connection she couldn't begin to explain, it certainly wasn't love. It couldn't be love because Grace was immune to that emotion. She'd promised herself a long time ago that she would never again be vulnerable, and love made you vulnerable. It made you weak. It made you forget who you were and what you had to do.

Grace knew exactly who she was. She was a federal agent on the trail of a ruthless killer. And she knew what she was. A woman who would do anything to bring down the man who had nearly destroyed her.

Ethan Hunter could not be allowed to get in her way. She would use him and she would betray him. And in the end, she would walk away from him.

SOMETIME AFTER TWO in the morning, Grace managed to doze off. But her dreams were filled with distorted images from her past and her present. She saw Trevor Reardon smiling down at her, but before she had time to draw her weapon, his face turned into Ethan's. And he was still smiling. Still taunting her.

Grace hovered in that nether realm of dream and reality. She knew she was still sleeping, but she was powerless to control the images playing themselves out in her mind.

In her dream, the phone was ringing. As if watching a movie, she saw herself pick up the receiver and lift it to her ear. "Hello?"

There was no response, but she could tell someone was on the other end. She caught her breath, waiting, while a fine sense of dread seeped over her. "Who's there?"

Silence.

Then a deep, seductive voice said in her ear, "I liked what you were wearing at the funeral today, Grace. Black becomes you."

They were almost the exact words Trevor Reardon had spoken to her fourteen years ago, after her family's funeral. Fear exploded inside Grace, and she gasped in horror.

Wake up! It's only a dream! she tried to warn herself.

Some part of her knew that it was a nightmare, but Grace was powerless to break free of it. She tried to fight her way to consciousness, but it was as if invisible hands were holding her down, pulling her more deeply into sleep.

It all seemed so frighteningly real. Grace heard herself say, "Where are you?"

And that sensuous voice replying, "Closer than you think."

"How close?"

Another pause, then, "You still favor pearls, I see."

There was something about his voice, something that triggered a flash of insight. Grace struggled through the layers of sleep, trying to cling to that elusive revelation that had come to her in the dream.

Something about his voice...

Yes! That was it! She'd heard that same voice recently, only...somehow it had been different, distorted. She hadn't recognized it because he'd disguised it.

As the cobwebs of sleep began to clear, Grace lay beneath the covers, trembling. The dream lingered. The fear it generated made her head swim, and she couldn't think straight. For a moment, Grace considered fixing herself a drink to steady her nerves, but that wouldn't help. It never had before.

She glanced at the nightstand beside the bed, wondering what time it was. In the glow of the clock face, she saw the tiny pearl studs she'd worn to Amy's funeral yesterday.

Forcing herself to get up, Grace crossed the room to the window and stared out into the gloom. Dawn was breaking over the city, and she could see a fleet of low-lying clouds moving in from the coast. The castoff glow of the sun, still hidden below the horizon, tinted the edges with a golden pink that gradually deepened to violet.

It was that strange time of morning, before the sun came up, when the shadows outside deepened and the night terrors had yet to flee.

Grace's first instinct was to run. To pack her bags and leave the city as fast as she could. And that impulse surprised her. She'd thought about this operation long and hard, even before she'd learned Reardon had escaped from prison a second time. She used to daydream about meeting him face to face. She used to picture his features on the targets she destroyed with her pistol at Quantico and wonder what it would be like to look him in the eye the exact moment she put a bullet through his heart.

Reardon's face would be different now, but some-

how Grace had thought she would know him anywhere. She'd wanted to believe that the evil inside
his soul would radiate from his body like an oily,
black aura, but no one she'd met recently had aroused
that kind of suspicion in her. She'd even considered
the possibility that Reardon was hundreds, perhaps
thousands of miles away, and that whoever had killed
Amy and had tried to kill Ethan was someone else.
Pilar or Kendall or even, as the police thought, a
stranger looking for drugs.

But Grace had no more doubts. She was sure now
that she'd heard Reardon's voice recently, but she
couldn't think where. At Amy's funeral? She'd talked
to a lot of people there she hadn't known, men and
women who claimed to be friends and acquaintances
of Amy's. Had one of them been Trevor Reardon?
Had she been that close to him? Had he...touched
her?

Grace shuddered in revulsion. Obviously, Reardon
had managed to disguise his voice well enough to fool
her for a while, but there was a quality about it that
couldn't be altered. In her sleep, Grace had remembered that quality.

Was he out there somewhere? Was he watching her
even now? Was he finding her in the crosshairs of a
high-powered weapon, laughing all the while at her
foolishness? Her weakness?

Grace's insides quivered with fear and dread, but
she forced herself to remain at the window. She was
safe for the time being. Reardon wouldn't shoot her
here. Not from a distance. He enjoyed killing too
much. For him, death was a personal experience. An

intimate one. He would want to enjoy it to its fullest potential.

When he came for her this time, Grace knew it would be more for pleasure than revenge.

Chapter Nine

"Buenos días," Rosa greeted the next morning. She stood back so Grace could enter.

"Good morning, Rosa. Is Ethan in?"

"He's upstairs in his study."

She led Grace up the stairway and through the living room, then tapping on the study door, she opened it a crack and announced Grace's arrival.

Ethan was sitting behind his desk, studying a legal document that was several pages thick. When Grace entered the room, he looked up. "Morning. Or is it still morning?"

"Barely." Grace glanced at her watch. "It's just after eleven."

Ethan's eyes looked a bit unfocused, and his lower face was shadowed with beard. Grace wondered if he'd been to bed at all last night, or if like her, his sleep had been plagued with nightmares. Self-doubts.

He glanced at Rosa still hovering in the doorway. "You can leave whenever you need to. Don't worry about me. I'll manage just fine."

Rosa's dark eyes darted from Ethan to Grace, but this morning she didn't appear to be as disapproving.

Grace wondered if she'd managed to win the house-keeper over, but if she had, it was a hollow victory because it had been won by deception.

Rosa shrugged. "*Adiós* then. I'll see you in a few days."

After she'd gone, Grace turned back to Ethan. "Where's she going?"

"Her grandson is sick, and her daughter needs help so I gave her some time off. Under the circumstances, I thought it a good idea to get her out of the house for a few days." His ominous words reminded Grace all too clearly of the dream she'd had last night.

"As a matter of fact," Ethan said, "I've been thinking about your safety as well. I want to talk to you about something."

He seemed different this morning, and Grace's first thought was that he'd gotten his memory back. "What about?"

"I realized this morning that I've never even been to your apartment. I don't even know where you live."

Grace frowned. "So?"

"So...how safe is it? Do you have a security system? A gated entry? A guard who patrols the grounds?" Ethan sat forward suddenly, his dark eyes intense. "If Reardon is watching my every move as you seem to think, then he knows you and I are working together. He knows you're Amy's sister. He may even know where you live."

There was no doubt in Grace's mind that Trevor Reardon knew where she was. Not after last night. "We can't do anything about that," she said, evading

Ethan's questions. "But believe me, I take every pre-
caution. You don't have to worry about me."

"But I do worry." His eyes deepened, and Grace
could have sworn his gaze dropped to her mouth. She
couldn't help remembering the way his lips had felt
against hers. "What precautions do you take? Do you
own a gun?"

She forced herself to hold his gaze. If she looked
away, she would be admitting her discomfort. "Why
do you ask?"

He shrugged. "It's a logical question. How are you
going to catch Reardon if you don't have a weapon?"

Grace hesitated. "All right, yes, I have a gun. And
before you ask, yes, I do know how to use it."

"Why does that not surprise me?" he muttered.

"I've also taken some self-defense courses." She
wasn't sure why she added that except perhaps to let
him know that if push came to shove, she could more
than hold her own—against Reardon or anyone else.

"Somehow I think it may take more than a karate
chop to bring down an assassin-turned-terrorist," he
said dryly.

Grace almost allowed herself a smile. "That's what
the gun is for."

Their gazes met. Something that might have been
admiration glimmered in his eyes. "Still, I think
you'd be safer, maybe we'd both be safer, if you
moved in here with me. The security system is first
rate, and besides—what was it you said the other day?
You watch my back and I'll watch yours? It would
be easier to do that if we were both in the same location."

She wasn't sure why his words surprised her so

much. Maybe because when she'd hinted the same thing that first night, he'd made it all too clear that he had no intention of inviting her to stay in his home. Now, he was acting as if the idea was his and that it made all the sense in the world.

Grace knew she should leap at the chance to move in with him. Her main function in this whole operation was to get as close—and stay as close—as she could to Ethan so that when Reardon came after him, she would be ready. But now she had to wonder if proximity to Ethan would be such a good idea. Would she be able to remain alert and focused, or would her attraction to him make her careless? Reckless?

A shiver of awareness slipped over her.

"What's wrong?" he asked. "You know as well as I do it makes sense for us to stick together."

"Yes, I know, but—"

"But what?" His gaze became even more penetrating. "Are you afraid to move in here? Are you afraid of me?"

"No. Of course not," she said almost too quickly. "I'm not afraid of you."

"Then who are you afraid of? Reardon? Yourself, maybe?"

Grace felt a prickle of anger at his assumption. "Contrary to what you seem to think, I'm not the least bit worried that I won't be able to constrain myself in your presence."

Amusement flashed in his eyes. "Then what's the problem?"

"A little thing called appearances," she said. "What will your neighbors think if I move in here with you? You're still married, Ethan."

"Not anymore." He picked up the blue-backed legal document from his desk and handed it to her.

"What is this?" she asked doubtfully.

"A courier delivered it this morning. It's a final divorce decree." Something very subtle changed in his voice. "As of today, I'm a free man, Grace."

She took the document and skimmed the front page. "I don't know whether to offer my congratulations or my condolences," she tried to say lightly.

One dark brow arched. "You've met Pilar."

When Grace said nothing, he sat back in his chair and his eyes grew pensive. "It's strange to have proof of the ending of a marriage I don't even remember. But I guess this explains why Pilar was so eager to clean out the cash from the safe. A little something extra added to the settlement."

Grace handed the document back to him. "Have you heard from her?"

"No, and I don't expect to. Unless I see her tonight."

"Tonight?"

He paused. "A woman called me this morning. She said her name was Alina Torres. She talked for five minutes straight before I finally figured out she's Hun...my secretary."

"What did she want?" Grace asked.

"She reminded me that I have an invitation to some sort of charity benefit tonight at the Huntington Hotel. The proceeds will go directly into a building fund for a new children's wing at St. Mary's Hospital. According to Alina, I'd previously sent my regrets because I hadn't planned to be in town, but now that I'm back, she thought it would be a good idea for me to go. It seems I'm being presented with some sort of citation.''

Grace's frown deepened. "Do you want to go?"

"Not particularly. But I've been thinking about what you said the other day. That the best way to draw out Reardon, or whoever wants to kill me, is to go about my normal business. The event tonight is written up in the paper today. If Reardon is keeping tabs on my activities, then he's bound to see it."

Ethan handed Grace a folded newspaper, and she read the headline.

Gala to Honor Dr. Ethan Hunter's Work with Underprivileged Children

He was right, she thought. A public event like this was just the sort of thing that would appeal to Reardon's macabre sense of humor. Still, she felt compelled to warn Ethan. "It could be dangerous. It would be very easy for Reardon to slip in with the crowd unnoticed. Especially since we don't even know what he looks like anymore."

"Isn't that the idea?" Ethan scowled. "I'm supposed to be a target, right?"

Yes. And the end justifies the means, Grace tried to tell herself. But even so, her first inclination was to try and talk him out of going. To somehow convince him to stay here, inside his fortress, where the locks and alarms just might keep him safe.

Out there, he *would* be a target. Bait for Reardon. And there was no guarantee Grace would be able to protect him. She wasn't even sure she could protect herself against Reardon.

She drew a long breath. "Is there any way you can get me an invitation?"

"I'm way ahead of you," he said. "Alina is sending over a ticket today, but you won't be seated on the dais with me."

"That's fine. It's better if I'm in the back, so I can keep an eye on the entire room."

He studied her for a moment, then his gaze dropped to the purse in her lap. "You'll be armed, I take it?"

She nodded. "Under the circumstances, I wouldn't leave home without it."

Their gazes held for what seemed an eternity, but in reality was hardly more than a second or two. But in the space of a heartbeat, Grace saw something in Ethan's eyes that she knew was mirrored in her own. Excitement. Anticipation. The thrill of the hunt.

They were suddenly two kindred spirits embarking on a perilous journey together. A journey that would be fraught with danger, intrigue and, because of the danger, passion.

Passion heightened by the knowledge that for them, tomorrow and regret might never come.

HE LIKED WHAT she was wearing. Her gown was midnight-blue, shot through with silver threads that shimmered in the light. She'd fastened a glittering clip in her hair that helped to glamorize the simple style, and her lips were tinted a dark, enticing red.

Ethan and Grace stood in the regal ballroom of the Huntington Hotel, their images reflected by the dozens of gilt-framed mirrors lining the walls. Overhead, twinkling chandeliers cast a rich ambience over the hall, while the tinkle of champagne glasses and the sound of muted laughter further enhanced the mood.

Ivory candles flickered on round tables covered with fine linen and set with gold-rimmed china, sparkling crystal and silverware polished to a gleaming finish.

Ethan, gazing at Grace, thought that she had been created for candlelight. The soft, dancing light brought out the drama of her features, deepening the blue of her eyes and igniting the red highlights in her hair.

She met his gaze briefly, then turned away, but not before he'd seen the desire in her eyes, in the tantalizing way she parted her deep red lips. Ever since she'd met him earlier at his house before coming here, the sparks had been flying between them.

Ethan's gaze slipped over her, moving from those lips to the pale skin of her throat, and then lower, to the lush curves outlined by the silky fabric of her gown.

Impulsively, he leaned toward her and whispered against her ear, "If you're carrying a concealed weapon in that dress, you're incredibly creative. And I mean that as a compliment."

He saw her smile, and realized, with something of a shock, that he'd never seen her do so before. She was always so serious, so…intense. Was she that way in every facet of her life?

Grace held up a glittering evening bag. "Don't worry. I told you I'd come prepared."

"And you were so right." His gaze moved over her again, and he wondered if he'd ever been as aware of a woman's allure as he was Grace's tonight.

Don't, a little voice warned him. *Don't get involved in something you can't finish. You don't even know who the hell you are.*

The tuxedo he'd pulled from the closet earlier fit him well enough, but like all the other clothing he'd worn, it wasn't a perfect fit. Nothing in Ethan Hunter's life was a perfect fit, except maybe for the way he felt about Grace.

He'd known from the first there was something special about her, something…intriguing about her, but her appeal was far more than just the physical attraction he felt for her. He'd meant what he said yesterday. They were connected to each other. He just didn't know how or why.

He touched her arm and felt her tense. "Would you like some champagne?"

Grace's gaze focused on the tray of sparkling wine as a waiter hovered nearby. "Maybe later. I want to keep a clear head tonight." All around them, people were starting to find their seats. Grace nodded toward the dais at the front of the room. "I think they're waiting for you."

"Wish me luck."

For a split second, he considered leaning down and kissing her, but then thought better of it. But when he would have turned away, she caught his arm at the last moment. Her blue eyes deepened on him. "You don't have to do this. We can find another way to get Reardon."

He stared down at her. "I thought this is what you wanted, Grace." To catch Reardon at any price. And after that—what was it she'd told him that first night? She didn't give a damn what happened to Ethan.

Her eyes were very blue and very mysterious in the candlelight. Ethan couldn't quite define the emotion he saw simmering just beneath the surface, but the possibilities tightened the nerves in his stomach.

"Just be careful," she murmured. Then she turned and walked away.

GRACE SAT AT a table near the back of the mirrored ballroom with a group of doctors and hospital administrators. She absently listened to the conversation around her as she scanned the crowded hall, looking, not just for Reardon, but for the agents she knew Myra would have in place tonight.

As for Myra, Grace had spotted her earlier, looking wonderful in a black sequined gown that would probably cause Vince Connelly, their section chief back in Washington, to have a heart attack when he got her expense account.

Grace didn't know where Myra was seated, but as her gaze continued to scour the room, someone else caught her attention. Pilar, on Bob Kendall's arm, made an entrance that could only be called spectacular. Dressed in a strapless red evening gown, Ethan's ex-wife had every male head in the room turning to stare at her admiringly.

The man beside Grace muttered something she couldn't understand. He'd introduced himself earlier as an administrator at a local hospital, and Grace had told him that she was a "friend of a friend" who had wangled an invitation for the event.

She turned to him now and asked, "I'm sorry. What did you say?"

He shrugged and lifted his champagne glass to his

lips. "Pilar Hunter and Robert Kendall are the last two people I'd expect to see at an event honoring Ethan Hunter."

"Do you know them?" Grace tried to act no more than mildly curious.

"Only by reputation," the man said. "And rumor."

"Rumor?"

"Bob Kendall used to be Ethan's business partner. The two of them started a practice right after completing their residency. After a while, Ethan became somewhat of a celebrity. He started believing his own press and decided he no longer needed a partner. Most of the assets were in his name, and he had the hot reputation. Kendall had been content to work in the background and let Ethan have all the glory, but when Kendall was forced to go it alone, he discovered that most of his patients weren't willing to follow him. He was all but ruined. It's taken him a long time to even come close to where he was before."

Grace listened to the story with interest. "So what is Dr. Kendall's connection with Pilar?"

The man beside her smiled knowingly. "I suspect she's become his consolation prize. And not a bad one at that, I must say."

FROM HIS PLACE on the dais, Ethan examined the crowd, wondering how many of his enemies had bothered to show up tonight. Or should he say, Ethan Hunter's enemies?

What would the people in the audience say if he stood up suddenly and proclaimed that he wasn't who they thought he was? That he, in fact, had no idea who he was.

But even if he really *was* Ethan Hunter, he was still a fraud. A doctor who used the cover of his good deeds in order to take blood money from criminals. A man willing to risk everything for the sake of greed.

Ethan let his gaze move to Grace. She sat near the back of the room, but he could see her face in the candlelight. She was talking with the man seated to her right, and for a moment, Ethan felt a terrible envy well up inside him. He wanted to be the man near her. He wanted to be the one draping his arm across the back of her chair so that he could lean toward her and talk to her in low tones that no one else could hear.

He wanted to whisper things to her that he'd never told anyone else.

But how could he be sure he hadn't? How could he know how many women had come before her? How many he'd claimed to love?

Ethan stared at her, letting a dozen different emotions wash over him. He told himself he had no right to feel that way about her, because if he was Ethan Hunter, he didn't want to drag her down with him. And if he was someone else…someone who had been pursued through the jungle by the Mexican authorities…

He stopped himself, not wanting to dwell on the mysteries hidden somewhere in his mind. Not wanting to consider how, if he wasn't Ethan Hunter, he had come to have the man's face.

But whoever the hell he was, Grace Donovan should remain off-limits, he thought gloomily, even though he knew she was no innocent in all this. Earlier, when he'd left her to take his place on the dais, he'd turned to see her talking to a woman in a black evening gown. The conversation had been brief and by all appearances casual, two women bumping into each other and then lingering for a moment to make small talk, to perhaps compliment one another on their gowns.

But Ethan had sensed something else was going on. An uneasiness had come over him as he stood watching them. Then the older one had looked up and caught his eye. She'd smiled briefly, as if acknowledging his interest, before saying something to Grace. The two women parted, and Grace hadn't looked back as she'd walked across the room to find her table. But Ethan was almost certain the dark-haired woman had said something to Grace about him, and that she'd known he was watching her.

Now, as she sat talking to the man beside her, she seemed just as determined to avoid Ethan's stare. He watched her for a long time, all through dinner and afterward, until, with something of a start, he heard his name being called. He looked up to find that a man had taken the podium. He introduced himself as Dr. Frank Melburne, then proceeded to introduce to the audience everyone else on the dais.

The names were a jumble to Ethan. He didn't bother to memorize them as he surveyed the crowded room, searching for the face of a killer.

Melburne spoke for several minutes, elaborating on the need for a new children's wing at St. Mary's, and how Ethan's work with underprivileged children, both here and in Mexico, should be an inspiration to all of them. He held up the framed citation that was being presented to Ethan, then concluded by saying, "And now I'd like to present the man of the hour, Dr. Ethan Hunter. Ethan?"

Ethan got up and walked to the microphone. He had anticipated being asked to say something tonight, but he hadn't prepared a speech. What the hell was he supposed to say? He didn't remember any of his deeds, good or bad. He didn't even know who he was—only that he was a man hunted by a killer.

Ethan stood at the podium, gazing out at the audience. Here I am, Reardon, he thought. *Where the hell are you?*

"I'm very honored to be here tonight," he finally said, his gaze lingering for one split second on Grace. "But what if I were to tell all of you that I'm not the man you think I am?"

WHAT IS HE DOING? Grace wondered uneasily. She watched Ethan from a distance, realizing that if Reardon were going to make a move tonight, it would be now. Ethan was an open target, and Reardon would relish an audience. She tensed, her gaze darting around the room as she fingered the gold clasp of her evening bag.

From the podium, Ethan said, "I'm not the man you think I am because I don't deserve this award. I'm sure there are any number of my colleagues here tonight who are much more deserving than I."

"What a surprise," the man beside Grace muttered. "Humility is not something one expects from Ethan Hunter."

Grace ignored the comment, focusing her attention

on the room instead, watching for any sudden move, for anyone who looked the least bit suspect. A rustle near the center of the room drew her attention, but for a moment, she couldn't tell what was going on. Then Pilar, her red dress glowing like a beacon, stood and lifted her champagne glass toward the dais.

"False modesty doesn't become you, Ethan." Her clear, lyrical voice rang out over the ballroom. "Why don't you say what you really think about all these people? What you've told me dozens of times in the past? There's not a man or woman in this room—" she swung her glass around, sloshing champagne over the rim "—who can touch your skill as a surgeon. What do you call all of them? Oh, yes. Meat cutters. But you...you're different, aren't you, Ethan? A genius who can change a mortal woman into a goddess. I'm proof of that, aren't I?"

She stood in the center of the room, spreading her arms as if inviting the whole world to look upon her beauty, to worship it. She didn't appear to be carrying a weapon, but Grace slipped open her purse, her hand closing around the SIG-Sauer pistol.

Pilar slowly lowered her arms. "But what do you do once you've created perfection? What is left then but to...destroy it?"

The room grew almost unbearably silent as everyone stared at Pilar. Grace found she couldn't tear her own gaze away. Something about the woman seemed almost...pathetic.

Out of the corner of Grace's eye, she could see Ethan still at the podium. He made no move to leave the dais or to silence his ex-wife. Like everyone else, his attention seemed to be riveted on her.

A man wearing a dark suit and an ear piece that immediately identified him as one of Myra's agents moved in toward Pilar. Before he could reach her, Bob Kendall jumped up and grabbed her arm. For a moment, the two of them almost scuffled, and then he said something to her that no one else could hear. Pilar resisted, then seemed to melt into Kendall. He put his arm around her and led her from the room.

Grace remained standing, adrenaline pumping through her veins. She combed the room, and saw Myra at the back near one of the colonnaded entrances, talking to Joe Huddleston, an agent Grace had known since Quantico. Huddleston turned and followed Pilar and Kendall out of the room. The agent who had been heading toward Pilar quietly faded into the background.

The room erupted into a cacophony of coughs and excited murmurs. Ethan remained at the podium. After a moment, he said, "Now that my fan club has left, we can get back to the business at hand."

Everyone remained stunned. Then there was a smattering of nervous laughter that took a few seconds to build. When everyone grew quiet again, the tension seemed to be somewhat relieved, and Ethan said with a shrug, "No matter what I say now, it's going to be anticlimactic, so let me just conclude by telling you how grateful—and how unworthy—I am to be receiving this honor."

Dr. Melburne, who had been standing behind Ethan on the dais, took his cue. He stepped forward, handing the citation to Ethan and shaking his hand before quickly retreating into the background, as if not wanting to diminish the honoree's glory.

Ethan turned to say something to Melburne, then bent to retrieve a paper he'd knocked from the podium. For an instant, Melburne stood framed in the spotlight, his expression one of shock as his hand went to his chest.

When he brought his hand away, Grace could see his fingers were dripping with blood. A crimson bloom spread across the front of his shirt as he fell backward onto the stage.

Chapter Ten

When he saw Dr. Melburne fall, Ethan automatically went into a crouch as he whipped the gun from underneath his jacket. As the ballroom exploded in pandemonium, Ethan's gaze probed the room, trying to locate Grace, but it was impossible. People were screaming and mauling each other to get to the exits.

Gun still drawn, Ethan knelt beside Melburne and spread open the man's jacket. The entire front of his shirt was red, and blood gurgled from his mouth. Ethan glanced up at the row of stunned doctors on the dais. They seemed incapable of moving.

"Someone help this man," Ethan shouted. "Hurry!"

The command spurred them into action. Two of the doctors crawled along the dais to where Melburne lay and began working on him. Ethan saw one of the others barking orders into a cell phone, presumably calling 911.

Taking one last look at the fallen man, Ethan jumped from the dais into the mob scene on the main floor of the ballroom. He still couldn't see Grace, but he knew he had to find her before Reardon did. She could be in every bit as much danger as Ethan.

THE MOMENT GRACE saw the blood on Melburne's fingers, she drew her weapon. A woman at the table screamed while the man who sat next to Grace gazed at her in shock. "What the hell—"

"I'm a federal agent," Grace said. "All of you get down and stay down."

Whether they believed her or not, they didn't hesitate to follow her orders. They all hit the floor, scrambling for a position beneath the table.

Grace glanced around. The room was in chaos as men and women either tried to flee or were scuttling beneath the tables. She couldn't locate Myra, Huddleston or any of the other agents. Turning back to the dais, she saw Ethan leap to the floor and then plunge into the terrified throng.

What the hell was he doing? He should be trying to find cover. That bullet had been meant for him. If he hadn't bent to retrieve the paper—

Grace shuddered. Weapon at her side, she started through the crowd toward the dais. The majority of the exodus was taking place at the back, where the colonnaded exits were located. Grace made her way to one side, hugging the wall as she tried to catch another glimpse of Ethan. If he'd been hit... If she had let him get hit...

To Grace's right, a closed door was skillfully hidden between two of the mirrors. Until she was almost upon it, the door looked like one of the intricately carved wall panels. Cautiously, Grace opened the panel and glanced down a long corridor. It appeared to be some sort of service hall with swinging doors that led to the kitchen and work areas.

Near one end of the corridor, a man in a white waiter's uniform cowered in a corner, his hands still clutching a circular tray of dirty dishes.

Grace started toward him. "I'm a federal agent," she said. "Don't move."

The man's expression was one of shock. He muttered something she couldn't understand. As Grace neared him, she saw that he was a middle-aged Hispanic with a swarthy complexion and dark, piercing eyes. A thin, black mustache traced the line of his upper lip, and a tiny gold hoop glinted from his left earlobe.

His eyes were wide with fright, and his hands trembled so badly, the crystal and cutlery made a jingling sound on the tray.

"Don't shoot, *por favor*." His tone was pleading, his voice heavily accented as he stared at the gun in Grace's hand.

She took another step toward him. "Just stay calm," she advised. "*¿Habla usted inglés?*"

"*Sí. Un poquito.*"

"Are you alone here? Have you seen anyone else in this hallway?"

His dark eyes lifted to hers. He nodded.

"Where? *¿Dónde?*"

He pointed down the hallway behind her. Grace glanced over her shoulder.

She sensed more than saw the man move toward her. She whirled back around, but as she did so, he slammed the tray into her stomach as hard as he could. The breath flew from her lungs, and Grace stumbled backward, falling against the wall and sliding to the floor. The man took off running toward the end of the hallway. He looked back only once before disappearing around a corner, but in that split second, Grace could have sworn she saw recognition flash across his features.

''Stop!'' she commanded, but her gun had slipped out of her hand when she fell. She scrambled toward it, but the man was gone.

Fighting for breath, Grace pulled herself up from the floor and started after him. The adrenaline rushing through her veins was almost like a drug high. Her head spun dizzily, but she didn't hesitate.

Why had he run from her?

The most logical explanation was that he was an illegal alien who didn't want to be deported, but as Grace rounded the corner where she had last seen him, another thought came to her.

If he was nothing more than an illegal alien, why had she glimpsed a look of recognition on his face?

BY THIS TIME, hotel security had descended on the uproar in the ballroom. HPD would be close behind, and Ethan decided it probably wasn't a good idea to be seen with a loaded gun. He slipped the weapon beneath his jacket, into the waistband of his pants, as he hunted through the crowd. Where the hell was Grace?

Out of the corner of his eye, he caught a flash of midnight-blue, but when he turned, all he saw was his own reflection in one of the mirrors lining the side wall of the ballroom. Then one of the panels in the wall moved, and he realized it was a door that someone had just gone through. Ethan started across the room.

It seemed to take forever to tear his way through the hysterical crowd, but Ethan finally reached the side of the ballroom and located the door. He opened it and peered cautiously inside. Broken crystal and china lay strewn on the floor where a tray had been dropped.

Ethan started to back out of the hall, but then he noticed something else on the floor. An earring sparkling among the shards of broken glass. Grace's earring.

Drawing his gun, Ethan listened for a moment, then started down the corridor toward the sound of a closing door.

GRACE SHOVED OPEN a swinging door, and stepped into a damp, humid room with dim lighting.

The area was cavernous and eerie in its silence. Laundry bags hung from an overhead conveyor, and she stood motionless, searching for movement, the telltale swing of one of the bags as someone brushed by it.

Nothing moved. There wasn't so much as a whisper of sound.

As silently as she could, Grace reached down and removed her high heels. Then in stocking feet, she moved along the rows of laundry bags, searching for Reardon.

As she neared the end of one of the long aisles, the hair on the back of her neck rose. A breath of air touched her skin, as if someone had moved behind her.

Heart racing, Grace spun.

FOR A LONG moment, they stood staring at each other. Neither of them lowered their weapons as they faced off. Grace's gaze went to the gun in his hand, and one brow lifted ever so slightly. Then she raised a finger to her lips, warning Ethan to be silent. She motioned for him to take the right side of the room while she turned to search the left.

He hesitated. Something told him he wasn't used to following orders, that he was the one who was usually in control of a situation like this. But under the circumstances, he couldn't find fault with Grace's logic. Split up. Circle the room. Force Reardon, or whomever she had cornered, out into the open.

Ethan made his way through the mountain of laundry bags stacked in bins along the side of the room. There were any number of hiding places, and flushing out their quarry might not be so easy. But just as the thought occurred to him, Ethan caught sight of something in one of the bins. A flash of black among all the white linen.

He eased forward, until he was directly in front of the bin. The black he'd seen was the arm of someone's tuxedo jacket, but he didn't think it belonged to Reardon. Someone was still wearing the jacket, and a crimson stain was spreading slowly over the soiled laundry hiding the body.

Silently, Ethan unearthed the victim. He didn't recognize the man, but he knew the ear piece the man still wore indicated a cop of some kind. Obviously, he and Grace weren't the only ones on Reardon's trail.

He wondered who the victim was, but he didn't take time to search for his ID. The bullet hole through the man's neck was enough for Ethan.

He had to find Grace.

THE ECHO OF her heartbeat sounded deafening to Grace. She wondered if Reardon could hear it. Wondered if he was taking pleasure from it.

The damp humidity in the laundry room was almost stifling. Grace found she had a hard time breathing. Sweat trickled down the side of her face, but she didn't waste a motion on swiping it away. She couldn't let down her guard for even a second.

At the far end of the room, away from the entrance where she'd come in, a sound finally came to Grace. At first, she wondered if it might be Ethan, but then as she stood listening, she identified the creak and rumble of an elevator car sliding down the cable.

Grace whirled and took off toward the sound. She didn't bother now to try and conceal her movements. If Reardon made it inside the elevator before she could get to him—

She fought her way out of the suspended laundry bags just in time to see the heavy metal doors sliding closed. Grace lunged toward the elevator, jamming the button with the heel of her hand so hard, pain ripped all the way up to her elbow. Ignoring the pain, she tried to pry open the doors, but it was no use. The car began to ascend.

ETHAN EMERGED from the forest of laundry in time to see Grace pound the elevator door in frustration.

When she heard him approach, she looked around, wild-eyed and desperate.

"The stairs," she said hoarsely. "Come on. We have to find him."

She didn't wait to see if Ethan followed her, but turned and raced through the door, retracing their steps down the corridor to a door marked Stairs.

He wondered why he didn't try to reason with her, why he didn't try to stop her from pursuing a cold-blooded killer. She was in danger, but it never occurred to Ethan to grab Grace and hold her back. She was too competent. Too coldly determined, and besides. She had a gun. If he tried to stop her now, she might just use it on him.

Ethan caught her on the stairs and overtook her. She wouldn't care for that, he thought fleetingly, but he was still a man, still had enough of the protective instinct to want to go first and blaze the trail. If he couldn't take out Trevor Reardon, Ethan could at least do enough damage so that Grace would have a chance.

They burst through the stairwell door on the second level. Two uniformed maids stood in the hallway chatting beside their carts. They looked up in surprise and then in terror when they saw the weapons.

"The service elevator," Ethan said. "Where is it?"

Neither of them said anything, but one of them pointed to the far end of the corridor. Grace darted past Ethan, and he swore, wishing she'd stay behind him.

They were only halfway down the hall when they heard the elevator doors swish open. Grace gasped in dismay and lunged forward, throwing herself at the elevator and managing just barely to get her fingers between the doors.

Ethan put his hands above hers, and as the doors yielded to their pressure, both Grace and Ethan jumped back and raised their weapons.

The doors slid open, but the car was empty except for a white, blood-stained waiter's coat lying on the floor.

GRACE SPUN, HER gaze frantically searching the hall. But she knew Reardon hadn't gotten off on this floor because he'd never been in the elevator to begin with. She'd let herself fall for the oldest trick in the book.

She whirled back to the elevator and started to step inside, but Ethan caught her arm. She flung off his hand. "What are you doing? He's still in the laundry. We have to get back down there."

Ethan put away his gun. "He's gone, Grace."

"You don't know that," she said angrily. "He may still be down there. You don't have to come with me, but I'm going back. I'll search every inch of that place, look in every laundry bag down there if I have to, but I'll find him. He won't get away. I won't let him—" She stopped herself as she realized how she must sound to Ethan. How she must look. Like a woman completely out of control.

And that's exactly how she felt. Reardon had thwarted her again. Made her act without thinking.

Grace forced herself to step out of the elevator, to take a long, deep breath. Ethan was still staring down at her, and the look on his face was not one Grace thought she could easily forget. His eyes were dark and narrowed, his mouth set in a grim, forbidding line. She found herself shivering and wondering about the outcome when and if Ethan Hunter and Trevor Reardon ever came face to face.

Ethan wasn't like any doctor she'd ever known before, that was for damn sure.

She said almost calmly, "Where did you get the gun?"

He shrugged, but his gaze darkened. "I found it in the safe at the house. I thought it might be useful tonight."

Grace was tempted to give him the old lecture about weapons in the hands of amateurs, but she was suddenly too weary. And besides, she had a feeling Ethan Hunter could handle a gun as effectively as he could wield a scalpel. She was the last person to underestimate him.

She slipped her own gun back inside her purse. "I guess you're right. Reardon's probably long gone by now."

"He left a calling card in the laundry," Ethan said. "Or at least someone did. There's a man with a bullet through his neck down there. I think he's a cop."

"My God," Grace whispered. Was he one of Myra's agents? Someone Grace knew?

She turned back to the elevator. "We'd better get back down there. Maybe you can help him."

Ethan caught her arm. "Nobody can help him, Grace. He's dead."

She hesitated. "We still have to call someone. We can't just leave him down there."

"I know exactly what we have to do."

Grace glanced up at him. Something in his voice alarmed her. "What do you mean?"

Ethan's expression turned grim. "We were fools to think we could do this alone. Reardon is a killer. A master criminal who has escaped from prison twice. And now at least three people are dead because he's after me. First Amy, then Melburne, and now the man downstairs. How many more people have to die because of me?"

The guilt in his eyes was not an easy thing to witness. Grace said urgently, "This isn't your fault. You didn't kill those people."

"That's not what you said the first night I met you." His voice hardened with disgust. "You said I had a part in Amy's death. And if everything you suspect is true, you were right."

Grace stared helplessly at Ethan. She didn't know what to say to him.

He put his hands on her shoulders, gazing down into her eyes. For the longest moment, they stayed that way as a myriad of emotions flashed across his face. Then he said, "I can't risk your life to save my own skin, Grace. I won't. I'm calling Pope and telling him everything. I'm going to end this tonight. I don't care what happens to me, but we have to get the police involved. Now."

His words blew Grace away. She couldn't believe he was willing to subject himself to a police investigation, to face a prison sentence in order to keep her safe from Reardon.

How long had it been since someone had cared about her that much? Since she had allowed anyone to care about her?

Until that moment, Grace hadn't realized just how

lonely she'd been all these years. How empty her life had become.

Now that knowledge was almost like a physical ache inside her.

She closed her eyes briefly, making a decision that she knew might cost her everything. When she spoke, she heard her voice quiver with emotion. "You don't have to call anyone," she told Ethan. "I am the police."

Chapter Eleven

Back at Ethan's house, Grace stood at the second-story window, staring out. From her vantage, she could see over the brick wall surrounding the grounds to the street beyond where an unmarked car was parked at the curb. The neighborhood sparkled with lights, but the dark sedan blended into the shadows cast by the water oaks lining the sidewalk.

In the opposite direction, where two streets intersected and formed a tiny parklike area in the median, a man stood smoking in the dark. Grace could see the glowing tip of his cigarette lift and fall.

Though from this distance, she couldn't see his radio or his weapon, she knew he would have both, and that he would remain in constant communication with Myra and with the man in the car. After tonight, the operation had suddenly become personal to every agent and support personnel working the case. Joe Huddleston, a well-liked and respected agent assigned to the field office here in Houston, had been killed. Murdered in cold blood, his body stuffed down a laundry chute at the hotel like so much dirty linen.

Grace had known Joe for years. They'd gone

through training together at Quantico. He was one of the few agents in the FBI who knew her entire story. And now he was dead. Because of Reardon.

For a moment, Grace's hatred threatened to consume her, but she forced herself to stand back, take a breath, look at everything logically. There would be time enough later to mourn Joe's death. For now, she had to remain focused.

Could she be absolutely sure that Reardon was responsible for Joe's death? Was Reardon the man she'd seen in the corridor of the hotel? If so, his disguise—whether temporary or permanent—had been nothing short of miraculous.

Grace's mind went back over the events of the evening. The last time she'd seen Huddleston was when he'd followed Pilar and Kendall out of the ballroom. Was it possible that Pilar's little scene had been a diversion? Was she or Kendall—or perhaps both of them—responsible for the shot that had been meant for Ethan tonight? Had they killed Joe Huddleston?

Grace knew that Myra had someone working on that angle even now, but the older agent was still concentrating most of her efforts on Reardon.

When Grace had contacted her earlier, before leaving the hotel, and told her what she planned to do, Myra had been against it. "You can't tell him the truth, Grace. What if he runs?"

"I don't think he will," Grace had argued. "And besides, I don't have a choice. If I don't tell him the truth, he's going to the police. The last thing we need is to get HPD involved any more than they already are."

She'd finally managed to placate Myra, but Grace knew Ethan wouldn't be quite as easy to appease. She wouldn't soon forget the look on his face when she'd told him she was the police. A federal agent, she'd barely managed to get out before the hotel security and several HPD officers had descended upon them in the corridor.

Grace wasn't sure why, but Ethan hadn't said anything to the authorities about what she'd told him. Instead, he'd let her take the lead, and when it had come time for him to give a statement, he hadn't said or done anything to give her away. That action, as much as anything else, made Grace realize how much he had come to trust her. How much she owed him.

And now it was time to pay the piper, she thought, turning away from the window. Ethan, who had gone straight to the kitchen to mix himself a drink when they'd gotten home, would want an explanation, and she had better be convincing. For more reasons than one.

Across the room, Simon moved restlessly on his perch. Grace drifted over to him and stood staring at him for a moment.

"What did you mean yesterday when you said, 'I say we just the kill the bastard and be done with it'?" she asked him.

The bird tilted his head and squawked, "They're not real."

"Forget about that," Grace said impatiently. "We're way beyond that now."

The bird strutted along his perch. "Book him, Dano!"

For God's sake, Grace thought. The bird was a walking, talking advertisement for daytime TV.

"Who do you think I am, Jack Lord?" she muttered.

"That's a good question," Ethan said. She turned to find him standing behind her, a drink in each hand. "Who are you, Grace?"

She moistened her lips. "I told you earlier. I'm a federal agent."

"FBI."

She nodded. "That's right."

"Is your name really Grace Donovan?"

"Yes."

"And I'm supposed to believe this new story? Accept your word for everything?"

"I can show you my ID and my badge if you like."

"Don't bother. I'm sure they can be faked just like business cards. And sisters." He offered her one of the drinks. When Grace declined, he said bitterly, "Oh, that's right. You're still on the job, aren't you?"

"Look." She ran her fingers through her bangs, wondering how she could possibly explain her motives in a way that would make him understand. Make him forgive her. "I'm sorry I didn't tell you the truth from the start. But I couldn't. It wasn't my call to make."

His gaze narrowed on her. "So you were just following orders?"

She hesitated. It would be easy to blame everything on her superiors, but the truth was, the deception had been her idea. Hers and hers alone.

She drew a long breath and released it. "Maybe I should start from the first."

"Maybe you should," he agreed. He downed one of the drinks and set the empty glass aside before turning back to her. "I'm listening."

Grace turned and walked back to the windows that looked out upon the street. The surveillance was still in place, but she wondered why that knowledge didn't alleviate the uneasiness growing inside her. After she told Ethan the truth, would he allow her to stay? Would he accept her protection?

"Three days before Amy Cole was murdered, she walked into the Federal Building here in Houston and asked to speak to an FBI agent. She said it was urgent. The man she eventually talked to was Joe Huddleston."

She sensed rather than saw Ethan's surprise. "The agent who was killed tonight?"

Grace nodded. "Joe and I went through training at Quantico together. We'd kept in touch over the years. He knew that my superior in Washington was coordinating efforts to locate Trevor Reardon. After he talked to Amy, he got in touch with us immediately."

"What did Amy tell him?" Ethan came to stand beside her at the window.

"She said that her employer, Dr. Ethan Hunter, the renowned plastic surgeon, was using his clinic in Mexico to operate on criminals' faces for money."

"What proof did she offer?"

Grace paused. "None. All she had were suspicions."

He made a sudden, angry movement that startled Grace. "Are you telling me you have no proof that anything illegal went down? This whole thing has been based on one woman's suspicions?"

"I know how that must make you feel, but—"

"Oh, I don't think you do," he said coldly. "I don't think you have any idea how I feel at this moment."

"You have every right to be angry," Grace said, wishing his eyes didn't look quite so dark and quite so deadly. "But let me finish before you start jumping to conclusions yourself."

He let that one pass. He turned back and stared out the window with a brooding frown.

"Amy showed Joe Huddleston a picture she'd clipped from the newspaper of Trevor Reardon. It was the same one I showed you. She said that she was almost certain she'd seen Reardon talking with Dr. Hunter...with you...a few months ago at the Mexican clinic."

Ethan glanced at her, his gaze still hard. "Go on."

"Like I said before, Joe knew my superior, Myra Temple, was coordinating the Bureau's efforts to track down Reardon. After Amy left, he called me and told me what had happened. When I briefed Myra, she agreed that we needed to come down here and talk to Amy ourselves, see if her story held water. We didn't discount the possibility that she could have been delusional, or that she was a rejected mistress out for revenge. We wanted to consider every possibility.

"And after talking with her, both Myra and I believed her. We both thought she was on to something. Myra and I started working with the field office here in Houston to set up a surveillance and possibly a sting if it was necessary to get your cooperation."

He spared her a brief glance. "Just what were you willing to do to *get* my cooperation?"

Grace shrugged. "Whatever it took."

A look she couldn't define flashed across his face. "I accused you once of being cold, remember?"

"Yes. And you were right." She forced herself to shrug. "I am cold. Ruthless. I'll do whatever it takes to catch Trevor Reardon."

Ethan's gaze hardened on her. "Why does it mean so much to you?"

Grace tried to suppress a shudder. She wanted to be honest with Ethan, but there were some things she'd never told anyone. Some things she still couldn't talk about. "He's a killer. A cold-blooded murderer. I don't want anyone else to die because of him."

"And that's all it is?" Ethan's voice had a strange quality that Grace had never heard before.

She shivered again. "Isn't that enough?"

He fell silent for a moment, contemplating everything she'd told him. Then he said, "What went wrong? Why is Amy Cole dead?"

Grace released a long breath. "After talking with her, we didn't expect you back in the country for at least two weeks. We thought we had plenty of time to set everything up, get everyone in place so that no one would get hurt. But evidently Amy got cold feet. She may even have found out about your impending divorce and then had second thoughts about what she'd done to you.

"When she found out you were coming back early, I think she got in touch with you and warned you that the Feds would be waiting for you. We had the airport staked out, along with your house and Amy's apartment. We thought we had it all covered, at least as best we could with such short notice, but then you chartered a plane and flew into a private airfield. We think you somehow contacted Amy, either by cell phone or through a neighbor, and the two of you made plans to meet at the clinic, possibly to get rid of incriminating evidence. Amy somehow managed to slip through our surveillance, and then hours later, she turned up dead.''

Grace glanced up and saw Ethan's reflection in the window. He was staring at her, and the look on his face...the expression in his eyes unnerved her.

''That still doesn't tell me what happened to her,'' he said slowly. ''Unless you're implying that I killed her.''

Grace spun toward him. ''No, that's not what I think. That's not what any of us think. Trevor Reardon followed you, probably all the way from Mexico. He ambushed you at the clinic and made it look like you'd stumbled upon a robbery, an addict looking for drugs. I never thought you killed Amy,'' Grace repeated. Somehow she had to make him believe that. She had to at least give him that.

''How did you know to go to the clinic?'' he asked.

Grace shrugged. ''That was purely a hunch. What I told you before was true—I was supposed to meet Amy that night. When she didn't show and I found out she'd slipped out of her apartment unseen, I knew I had to find her. I knew she could be in danger. So I went to the clinic, almost as a last measure. When I found out what had happened, I knew I couldn't tell the police who I really was. The homicide was their jurisdiction, and if they found out Amy had been working with the FBI, we would have had to bring them in on the case. It would have tipped off Reardon that we were on to him, and so I told them I was Amy's sister.''

Ethan cocked a dark brow, staring down at her. ''You didn't think she might have a real sister who would come forward and dispute you?''

''I knew she didn't. She'd already told me she had

no one, and that she didn't like to talk about her past. I felt the cover would be reasonably secure.''

"And so then you decided to approach me." Ethan turned back to the window. "I still don't understand why you didn't tell me the truth. Wouldn't that have been simpler?''

"Maybe," Grace agreed. "But I couldn't take that chance. I had no reason to believe you'd be willing to cooperate. Why would you?''

"I don't know," he said flippantly. "To save my life, maybe? Because it would have been the decent thing to do?''

Grace said nothing.

After a moment, Ethan said, "I guess my amnesia was a bonus for you then.''

She didn't bother to deny it. "It made you vulnerable. You couldn't go to the police without incriminating yourself. And without a memory, without knowing who wanted you dead, you couldn't protect yourself, either. I made sure you had to turn to me.''

He winced at that. "Tell me something, Grace. How far were you willing to go to get my cooperation?''

"I already told you. Whatever was necessary.''

"Did that include this?" He turned suddenly and grabbed her shoulders, forcing her to face him. His eyes were dark and turbulent, his expression like an icy mask. When he kissed her, Grace's first instinct was to push him away, to somehow try and regain control of the situation.

But a split second later, she felt the ice inside him begin to melt. She knew, instinctively, what he wanted at that moment. What he needed.

She kissed him back with every ounce of her

strength. With every fiber of her being. With every emotion that raged through her mind and body and soul.

When he finally pulled away, they both stood shaken by the experience. Grace's knees trembled weakly, but she forced herself to remain steady, to stare up at him as openly and honestly as she dared.

"That was never a lie," she finally whispered. "The way I feel about you is something I never counted on."

His hands were still on her shoulders. He stared down at her for a long time, his breathing ragged. "How do you feel?"

Grace's heart pounded against her chest. It had been a long time since she'd had a conversation like this. Since she had felt this exposed. "It's like you said once. We're connected somehow. I don't understand it, but…it's more than just attraction. It's as if…"

"We're meant for each other," he said.

Grace closed her eyes. "But I *can't* feel that way. I can't let my emotions get in my way. I can't forget who I am or what I have to do. And I can't forget who you are, either."

"Who I am." His hands dropped from her shoulders and he turned and walked away from her.

Grace hesitated, unsure whether or not to follow him. But he didn't go far. He walked to the center of the room and stood looking around, as if he suddenly realized he didn't belong there.

For a long moment, neither of them said anything, then he turned to her. His gaze was shadowed with an emotion that made Grace's breath quicken. "I'm not the man you think I am."

"You've said that before." She moved across the room toward him. "And I think I understand why you feel that way. It's like there're two sides of you. One man operates on criminals' faces for money, while the other can change monsters into angels. That man can give children without hope a whole new life. That's the man you really are, Ethan. That's the man you remember. The other one doesn't seem real to you because you don't want to be him."

Uncertainty flickered in his eyes. Then his gaze darkened again. "That's a rather whimsical explanation for an FBI agent, Grace. I don't think you buy it any more than I do."

"You're wrong. I do believe it." On impulse, Grace put a hand on his sleeve, felt him tense at her touch. "I know there's something fine and decent about you. I know there's goodness in you, just like there's darkness." She paused, searching for the right words. "Who knows what brings that darkness to the surface, but I think we all have the capacity for it. I think there's darkness in all of us."

His brow lifted at that. "Even you?"

She gave a bitter little laugh. "Maybe even especially me. I'm not sure I'm in any position to judge you, no matter what you've done."

He didn't seem to hear her. He'd turned away and walked back over to the window to stare out. After a bit, he said, "It's been a long day and I'm beat. We can talk about this in the morning, decide what to do then."

Grace had brought a bag over earlier before they'd gone to the Huntington, but after her confession, she wasn't sure he'd let her stay. But it appeared now that he'd accepted her presence, and for the time being at least, wasn't going to ask her to leave. Grace was glad. She would hate to have to force the issue now.

"That's probably a good idea," she agreed. "We could both use some rest. I'll see you in the morning."

She waited for him to turn and acknowledge her leaving, but he remained at the window, his back to her. He didn't even say good-night, and after a moment, Grace turned and left the room.

A FEDERAL AGENT. A cop.

Ethan should have known. And maybe a part of him had known. He couldn't say her revelation had come as that much of a shock. He'd always known there was something Grace wasn't telling him. That there was more to her than a grieving sister.

No wonder she had seemed so confident in her ability to deal with Trevor Reardon. She was trained to deal with the likes of him.

Ethan thought about that for a moment. How did that make him feel? he wondered. Knowing that Grace was an agent who had not only been sent here to find Reardon, but to also protect Ethan in the process. How did he feel about his life being put in a woman's hands? In Grace's hands?

He tried to muster up the requisite resentment, but it wasn't in him. There were too many other things about the situation that troubled him more. The fact that she had lied to him, deceived him into believing she was Amy's sister. The fact that those lies had seemed so easy for Grace.

He'd been a means to an end for her. It was as simple as that.

Oh, he knew she was attracted to him. She couldn't

hide it and she hadn't bothered to deny it. But her desire to find Trevor Reardon far exceeded her desire for Ethan, and that fact bothered him the most. She was a consummate professional before she was a woman, and Ethan knew that situation wasn't likely to change any time soon. At least not for him.

He remembered the way her eyes had burned with an inner fire when she'd first told him about Reardon, and an uneasiness Ethan couldn't explain swept over him.

What was it about Reardon that made Grace so passionate in her hatred of him, that made her almost careless in her pursuit of him?

What had made this assignment so personal for her?

Ethan knew the answer even before the question had completely formed in his mind, and a sick feeling rose in his throat as he stood staring out into the darkness.

GRACE STOOD WRAPPED in a towel at the bathroom mirror as she blow-dried her short hair. Afterward, she gazed at her reflection for a long time, wondering if she had done the right thing by telling Ethan as much as she had. But she hadn't really had a choice. Once he'd decided to go to the police with the story, she'd had to tell him the truth, and trust that he would continue to cooperate with her.

But why should he? She'd lied to him, deceived him at every possible turn. Why would he want anything more to do with her?

The end may have justified the means, but right now, Grace was having a hard time dealing with her conscience. She had deliberately put Ethan's life on the line in order to capture Reardon, and she hadn't even had the decency to tell him why. At least not completely.

Her past was something Grace had never told anyone. She couldn't even talk about it with Myra. What Trevor Reardon had done to her and her family was too personal, and Grace had never gotten over the guilt, let alone the shame.

She hadn't told Ethan because she hadn't wanted to see the disgust in his eyes over what she had done.

Grace didn't want to see it in her own eyes, either. She turned away from the mirror and walked into the guest bedroom where she'd left her suitcase earlier. Digging through the contents, she pulled out a pair of white silk pajamas and put them on. As she was turning down the bed, the door behind her opened.

Grace grabbed her gun from the top of the nightstand, going instantly into a crouch while, with a two-handed grip, she swung the weapon toward the door.

Ethan stood just inside the room, his gaze going first to the gun in her hand, then to her face. He wore jeans, no shirt, and his dark hair glinted with moisture, as if he'd just come from the shower. Grace's hand trembled on the weapon as she stared at him, her awareness of him surging over her in a crest of heat.

As he walked into the room, she hesitated, then slowly lowered the weapon. She placed it on the nightstand behind her.

Ethan came over and stood in front of her. He didn't touch her, but his nearness made Grace's breath quicken. The look on his face made her heart pound inside her. She was tempted to put her hands on his bare chest, to feel the hardness beneath her fingers.

"You're her, aren't you?"

Grace stared up at him as a shock wave rolled over her. "What are you talking about?"

"The FBI agent's daughter you told me about. The only one in his family who didn't get killed in the fire. The one Trevor Reardon came back for. You're her."

She turned away, but he put his hands on her arms, forcing her to face him. She didn't want to. She didn't want to see the look in his eyes.

"Why didn't you tell me?" he demanded.

"I couldn't. After all these years, it's still too…painful." And she still couldn't look at him.

He put one hand under her chin, tilting her head up so that she had no choice but to meet his gaze. What she saw in his eyes wasn't disgust. It was another emotion that took Grace's breath away.

"What happened that night?" he asked softly.

"Please." Her eyes closed briefly. "I can't talk about it. I've never talked about it."

"Don't you think it's time you did?"

"It's too personal." She put trembling fingertips to her lips. "I don't think I *can* tell you. I don't think I want you to know."

"You said earlier that you weren't in any position to judge me. That goes both ways, Grace."

When she looked up at him, his eyes were so dark and so haunted, she thought for a moment she was staring at her own reflection. She took a step back from him, and he let her go.

He walked to the window to stare out into the darkness. "I think I may be exactly the person you need to talk to." There was something about his voice that was different.

Grace shivered, staring as his profile. After a moment, she said, "My father was the agent who arrested Reardon. The FBI had been after him for a long time, years. After he left the military, he became a killer for hire, an assassin at first, taking out government officials in foreign countries and certain high-powered businessmen for money. Then he fell in with some zealots in the Middle East and discovered they were willing to pay big bucks to someone with his expertise to carry out their dirty work. The notoriety appealed to Reardon, as did the money. And the killings."

She paused, trying to get her thoughts in order. Trying to dispel the tormented images twisting and turning in her mind. "My father tracked him for over two years and was finally able to arrest him. But before Reardon could stand trial, he escaped. I'd heard my father mention his name at the time of the arrest, but he never told us about Reardon's escape. I guess he didn't want to worry us, and I don't think he really believed Reardon would come after him. He thought Reardon would flee the country, but my father underestimated Reardon's obsession with order, with tying up loose ends."

Ethan glanced at her then, but he still said nothing.

Grace took a long breath and continued. "He got into our house one day when everyone was gone and planted a bomb. He rigged all the doors and windows with explosive devices that were wired in to the main timer. When he detonated the bomb, the other devices were then triggered to explode if anyone tried to open the doors or windows from the inside or the out. It was an unbelievably intricate design and one he'd used before, on an Italian businessman's home several years before that. When the bomb exploded, the whole house erupted into flames. My mother and father were on the ground level, but my sister was trapped upstairs. I saw her at the window. Her hair and clothes were on fire—''

Grace broke off abruptly as the images bombarded her. Ethan had turned to face her, but he didn't move toward her. ''I can't imagine what that must have been like for you.''

Grace shrugged. ''No one can. I arrived right after the first bomb exploded, but the fire spread so fast, they didn't have a chance. The booby-trapped doors and windows were almost overkill.''

''Where were you?'' Ethan finally asked. It was the question Grace had been dreading.

She squeezed her eyes shut as if she could somehow stop the screams inside her head. ''I was with him. I was with Trevor Reardon.'' She put her hands to her face and turned her back to Ethan.

The room was so quiet, Grace could hear the blood pounding in her ears. She sensed Ethan's shock, the deep revulsion he must feel for what she'd just told him.

After a moment of stunned silence, she felt his hands on her wrists, pulling her hands away from her face. ''Tell me the rest,'' he commanded softly.

Grace shuddered. ''I'd met him a few days before the fire. I realized afterward that he'd sought me out. It was all part of his game, the ultimate way to get back at my father, and I was so gullible. So *stupid*. I fell for everything he told me because I wanted to believe an older, sophisticated man could find me special and desirable. He seduced me,'' she said, trying to swallow past the nausea that rose in her throat. "But I let him. I *wanted* it."

When she would have turned away, Ethan clung to her hands. "How old were you?"

"Old enough to know better."

"How old?"

She drew a long breath. "Seventeen."

"You were a kid, Grace. You were no match for Reardon."

"But I should have known," she said in anguish. "I should have known who he was, what he planned to do. I should have been able to stop him."

A tear slid down her face, the drop of moisture as foreign to her as the look of compassion in Ethan's eyes. Releasing one of her hands, he wiped the tear away with his fingertip, the gesture so gentle and so caring that Grace felt more tears, deeper tears rising inside her. With sheer force of will, she blinked them back.

"You've carried this guilt inside you all these years," Ethan said, staring down at her. "Don't you think it's time to let it go? Don't you think it's time to forgive yourself for having once been young and naive?"

"I didn't just go out and skip school," she said almost angrily. "I didn't stay out past my curfew. My whole family was killed while I—"

"There was nothing you could have done to stop Reardon. Deep down inside, you have to know that. He would have done what he did whether you had been with him or not. The only difference was, you stayed alive. And I think that's what you haven't been able to forgive yourself for."

Grace bowed her head, overcome with emotion.

She couldn't say a word, couldn't deny or acknowledge what he was saying. All she could do was let him reach for her gently and draw her into the warm circle of his arms.

A part of her wanted to resist, because she knew she was vulnerable tonight in a way she hadn't been in years. She needed Ethan's arms around her more desperately than she would ever have thought possible. And that scared her. Terrified her.

Neither of them said anything for a very long time. They stood motionless, Ethan's arms around her while Grace battled the demons inside her that had threatened to destroy her for years.

After a while, the demons didn't seem quite so powerful. The images inside her mind weren't quite so strong. Grace lifted her face to Ethan's. "I've never told anyone what happened back then. There are those in the Bureau who know. Myra Temple, the woman who saved my life when Reardon came back for me, and Joe Huddleston. A few others who knew because they were around when it happened. But I've never been able to tell anyone else. I've never trusted anyone enough."

Something flashed in Ethan's eyes, an emotion so dark, Grace shivered. "I hope you've done the right thing telling me."

She pulled back a little to stare up at him. "I don't understand."

He hesitated. "I hope I'm worthy of your trust."

Grace knew instantly what he meant. He was no longer thinking about what she'd told him, but about his own past. About the things he'd done. The demons he now had to battle.

She reached up and touched his face with her fingertips. "I meant what I said earlier. I know there's goodness in you. And now you know about the darkness in me. Does it change the way you feel?"

He almost smiled at that. "If anything, it only strengthens the bond between us. It makes me want you even more."

The fire in his eyes was suddenly an emotion Grace did recognize. Passion. The powerful kind. The reckless kind. The kind that matched the slow heat building inside her.

With a sense of inevitability that was almost stunning, Grace watched as he lowered his head toward hers. Their gazes clung for a long, scorching moment before his lips touched hers. Grace's eyes drifted closed as a shudder ripped through her. Ethan's kiss was powerful, electric, breathtaking. An explosion of desire that made her knees grow weak and her heartbeat thunder.

This was not attraction, she thought weakly. This was not chemistry. This was…destiny. This was a moment that had to be, no matter what the consequences.

She wrapped her arms around his neck and threaded her fingers through his hair. Ethan's own hands splayed against her back, holding her closely for a moment before starting to move over her in slow, deliberate strokes. Her back, her hips, her breasts, and then upward to cup her face. He broke the kiss to whisper against her mouth, "God, Grace…"

She couldn't have put it more eloquently herself. She pulled him to her, kissing him with an urgency that left them both gasping for breath. He pushed her back on the bed and moved over her, his fingers ripping loose the buttons on her pajamas so they could lay skin to skin. Heartbeat to heartbeat.

Grace shivered as his body molded to hers, as his mouth ground into hers. She accepted the assault, welcomed it. Wanted more of it.

They rolled over, and Grace was suddenly on top, staring down at him. His eyes were heavy-lidded and seductive, his mouth a sensuous invitation. She kissed the scar above his brow, his temple, then skimmed along the side of his face to tease his earlobe with her tongue.

He groaned and shuddered as she pressed her body into his and moved against him. After a few moments, he rolled them again, and now he was back on top, back in charge, and Grace was pliant beneath him. And then he did to her exactly what she had done to him.

The teasing became almost unbearable. The buildup almost the release. Grace's fingers moved to the buttons at the front of his jeans, but to her surprise, his hand closed over hers, stopping her.

His lips hovered over hers, a breathless heartbeat away. Then he lifted himself, so that for a moment they were staring into each other's eyes. His gaze was still clouded with passion, intense with longing, but another emotion simmered just beneath the surface. An emotion that made Grace almost gasp when she saw it.

Regret. Maybe even guilt.

She lay staring up at him, helpless with her own desire.

"I can't do this," he said.

A rush of humiliation swept over her. "What?"

He lifted himself off her and sat on the edge of the

bed, his back to her. He put his hands to his face and scrubbed. "I can't do this to you."

Grace sat up, too, wrapping her pajama top around her and drawing her knees up to her chest. She rested her cheek on her knees, saying nothing. Embarrassment heated her skin, but it was a remorse that wasn't pure because even in the face of rejection, she still wanted him. Her body still quivered with need.

"I told you before that I'm not the man you think I am." He turned his head slightly, so that she could see a little of his profile. "I deliberately let you misunderstand what I meant. You think there're two sides to my personality—a good one and a dark one. And now that I've lost my memory, the good one is winning out. But you're wrong, Grace. Dead wrong."

He turned on the bed to face her, and Grace lifted her head to stare at him. "What do you mean?"

"I'm not Ethan Hunter."

Grace sat up, forgetting about the torn-away buttons on her top. The silk parted, and for just an instant, she saw Ethan's gaze waver. Then he glanced away, running a hand through his dark hair. "I'm not Dr. Ethan Hunter," he repeated.

Grace said breathlessly, "If you're not Ethan Hunter, then who are you?"

He shrugged. "I don't know. I don't even know *what* I am. What I may have done. When I woke up in the hospital a few days ago, the only thing I could remember at first was running through the jungle, being pursued by men with guns. Those men were the Mexican police, and they shot me. Here." He touched a spot on his side hidden by his jeans. "I fell from a cliff. When I came to in the hospital and found out who I was—or who I thought I was—I convinced myself that the whole episode was just a dream. The scar on my side was from the appendectomy I'd supposedly had recently. And everything else started to fall into place. I remembered then that I'd been in a clinic, that a man wearing a ski mask had been standing over me with a gun. I remembered Amy walking in, and then the fight I had with the gunman. He knocked me unconscious, and I assumed that's how I got the amnesia."

Grace stared at him in shock, not knowing where he was going with his story, but sensing it might be a place she didn't want to follow. "That's what everyone assumed. I don't understand, Ethan. Why do you think you're not Dr. Hunter?"

"Because I don't think the skills of a surgeon, especially one as talented as I'm supposed to be, would be something I would forget."

Grace frowned. "You can't know that for sure."

"Then how do you explain the other things that I didn't forget. Like how to use a weapon." To demonstrate his point, he picked up Grace's gun from the nightstand, ejected the clip, pulled back the slide to remove the bullet from the chamber, and then slammed home the magazine once again. He stared at the weapon for a moment, then laid it aside with a visible shudder.

"A lot of people know how to use a gun."

He stared at her. "So you're saying you don't think it's strange that I remember how to do what I just did with your gun, but I wouldn't have the faintest idea what to do with a scalpel if you handed me one right now."

Grace shrugged. "Amnesia is a tricky thing. I'm just saying that from what you've told me so far—"

"There's more," he said darkly. He got up and started to pace the room. "The man I dream about in the jungle—I know his fear. I know he's me. But his face isn't the one I see when I look in the mirror."

A cold chill slipped over Grace. "But maybe it is just a dream."

"Maybe. But how do you explain the fact that there are dozens of pairs of shoes in my closet, and not a single one fits me. They're all too small by at least half a size."

Grace couldn't explain that. The chill inside her deepened. "Are you sure? You tried them all on?"

"Every last one of them. The clothes aren't a perfect fit, either, but I attributed that to a weight loss following surgery. But I can't explain the shoes. Can you?"

Grace wrapped her pajama top more tightly around her. "There has to be a logical explanation."

"And then there's the gun," Ethan said, as if he hadn't heard her. "I found the pistol you saw earlier in the safe downstairs. I knew the moment I saw it that the gun belonged to me. I knew exactly what it would feel like to shoot it, the accuracy of the aim, the pull of the trigger. Everything. I took it to a gun shop here in town and found out that it was probably customized by a place in Arkansas that does special orders for police SWAT teams, the FBI, and some of the elite forces of the military. Like the Navy SEALs, for instance."

"The Navy SEALs—" Grace broke off, gasping. She stared at Ethan in open shock. "My God. What are you saying?"

He stopped pacing and turned to watch her for a

long moment before moving toward the bed. Grace had to fight the urge to retreat.

He placed his hands on the bed and leaned toward her, his eyes those of a stranger. "I'm saying that I don't know who I am. I don't know how to explain everything that's happened to me, the dreams I have, the shoes that don't fit, the gun that was custom-made for me. Even the connection you and I seem to have."

He paused, his gaze intensifying on her until Grace's breath became suspended somewhere in her throat. "What I'm saying is that for all I know, I could be the man you're looking for. I could be Trevor Reardon."

Chapter Twelve

Grace put a hand to her mouth to hold back the scream that tore at her throat. She stared at the space where Ethan had stood only moments before, and nausea rose in her stomach like a tidal wave.

He wasn't Trevor Reardon. She knew it couldn't be true, and yet the moment Ethan had said the words, the doubts had begun to mount inside her. She hadn't been able to hold back her horrified gasp, and when Ethan had seen her face, he'd turned and strode from the room, slamming the door behind him.

The sound still echoed in the silent room. His words still rang in her ears. Grace shook her head, trying to dispel the almost hypnotic effect his words had had on her. She couldn't move, couldn't think, couldn't reason.

Weakly she reached for her purse on the nightstand. Taking out her cell phone, she dialed Myra's number. The throaty voice answered on the second ring.

Without preamble, Grace said, "Did you hear back from the fingerprints you sent to the lab?"

If Myra had been sleeping, she gave no indication

of it. She sounded wide awake and fully alert. "The ones we lifted from Dr. Hunter's clinic?" Grace heard Myra's lighter click open as she lit up a cigarette. "Strange that you should be calling about that."

Grace was instantly alarmed. "Why?"

Myra hesitated. "Actually, we lifted several sets of prints from Dr. Hunter's office, some from around the desk area that we were pretty certain were his. But just as a control, we also took some from the water glass in his hospital room." She paused to take a long drag on her cigarette. Grace wanted to scream in frustration. "When we ran all the prints through the computer, we found that the ones from the glass were flagged."

Grace sat on the edge of the bed, frowning. "Flagged? By whom?"

"I don't know yet."

"Wait a minute," Grace said. "Are you saying the prints from the glass didn't match any of the prints in Dr. Hunter's office?"

"No, they did. Only, the prints that were a match didn't belong to Dr. Hunter."

Grace gripped the phone until her knuckles hurt. "Myra, are you saying the man in this house with me isn't Ethan Hunter?"

There was another long pause. Then Myra said slowly, "It's possible."

Grace's breath rushed from her lungs in a long, painful swish. "Just when the hell were you going to tell me?"

"As soon as I had all the facts. Listen, Grace, I just got this information myself a little while ago. I didn't know what to make of it. I've been trying to find out what I could from the Information Division, but they haven't been exactly forthcoming. It's all hush-hush. I don't understand what it all means yet, but Connelly said the lab is suddenly crawling with agents.''

"FBI?"

"He doesn't think so."

"Then who?"

"We don't know, but if that man isn't Ethan Hunter, then someone else is looking for him. And not only that, they want to make damned sure they know when and if someone else finds him. That's why the prints were flagged, and now Connelly is catching hell.''

"What has he told them?"

"Nothing yet, and he won't until he finds out just exactly who and what we're up against." Myra paused again. "It may be time to pull you out, Grace.''

Grace's heart was thumping so hard against her chest she thought her ribcage might explode. But she had never been one to walk away from an assignment until it was finished. And this one was far from over.

She drew a long breath, trying to calm her racing pulse. "If we pull out now, the whole operation craters. We may never find Reardon. I don't want to run that risk. Until we find out what's going on, I think I should stay put.''

"This could get very sticky," Myra warned.

"I'm aware of that."

After a moment, Myra said, "Maybe you're right. Whoever he is, he had us fooled. He may be able to fool Trevor Reardon as well.''

Grace's mind was a whirlwind of chaotic thoughts. After hanging up the phone, she paced the room nervously. Never had she been so unsure of a situation before, so out of control of an operation as she was at that moment.

Who was he? her mind screamed. Who the hell was he?

Spinning toward the nightstand, Grace grabbed her gun and gripped it in one hand while crossing the floor to lock her bedroom door. And all the while she kept telling herself that what she was thinking, what Ethan had suggested was crazy. He couldn't be Trevor Reardon. She would have known, for God's sake. He couldn't have fooled her again. Not so completely.

Her legs shaking with nerves, Grace sat down in a chair facing the bedroom door. She propped her feet on the edge of the bed and put the gun in her lap. There would be no sleep for her tonight, but just to be on the safe side, she wouldn't lie down. She would remain in this chair, awake and vigilant, until morning came and with it, hopefully answers.

YOU'RE SO BEAUTIFUL. Do you have an idea how special you are to me, Grace?

Trevor Reardon's voice awakened Grace with a start. She gasped and grabbed her gun, aiming at first one spot in the room and then the next.

It took her a long, terrified moment to realize she was alone in the room and she'd been dreaming.

Reardon's voice, whispering in her ear, came back to her and a shiver of dread tore up Grace's spine. The dream had seemed so real. She had heard his voice so clearly, that indefinable quality that had haunted her for years.

Grace thought she'd only dozed off for a few seconds, but when she glanced at the clock on the bedside table, she realized she'd been asleep for almost an hour. It was nearly three o'clock in the morning and the moon was up. The sterling light danced along the fringes of the room, deepening the shadows in the corners.

The moon glow was what alerted Grace first. Earlier, she'd turned on the lamp on the nightstand, but now it was off. And the faintest scent of men's cologne lingered in the air.

Grace's heart boomeranged against her chest. Ethan hadn't been wearing cologne earlier. He'd come straight to her room from the shower, his hair still damp and smelling of shampoo, his skin scented only with soap.

But the smell of cologne on the air was unmistakable.

Slowly, Grace got up from the chair, her weapon drawn. The first thing she did was search the bathroom, then she crossed the bedroom to the door. It was still locked, and for a moment, she told herself she was imagining things.

But that whisper came back to her. *You're so beautiful. Do you have any idea how special you are to me, Grace?*

And she knew without a doubt it had been no dream. Reardon—or someone—had been in this room with her. He'd managed to pick the lock on her bedroom door, but that was no surprise. The flimsy bolt wouldn't keep out a determined ten-year-old, let alone a criminal mastermind.

No, the surprising part was how easily he'd been able to slip through the surveillance surrounding the house, and then disable the alarm without detection. Unless, of course, he'd been in the house all along.

Grace closed her eyes, terror stealing over her. She gripped the pistol, forcing herself to open the bedroom door and move out into the hallway. But with every step she took, she heard Ethan's warning. *I'm saying that I don't know who I am, Grace. I don't know how to explain everything that's happened to me, the dreams I have, the shoes that don't fit, the gun that was custom-made for me. Even the connection you and I seem to have.*

Grace was on the stairs now, moving stealthily downward. The living room below was silent. Eerie. The shadows ghostly in the moonlight.

She came to the bottom of the stairs and moved into the living room.

What I'm saying is that for all I know, I could be the man you're looking for.

Slowly, Grace crossed the living room toward the study. A thin line of light glowed at the bottom of the closed door. Someone was inside.

I could be Trevor Reardon.

Grace paused outside the door, catching her breath and steeling her nerves. Then she reached out and swung the door inward.

Ethan sat behind the desk, his face dimly illuminated by a lamp that had been angled away from him. He looked up when Grace entered, seemingly unconcerned by the gun she had pointed at him, and smiled. A smile that was as charming as it was inherently evil.

Chapter Thirteen

The man seated behind the desk was Ethan, and he wasn't.

Grace couldn't quite believe her eyes. She blinked once, then again, but the face before her didn't change.

She saw almost immediately that the faces weren't identical, but there was a very strong resemblance. This man, Dr. Hunter she presumed, was a little smoother around the edges. Polished to a high gloss of sophistication, while the Ethan she knew was tougher, more dangerous looking.

However, as Dr. Hunter rose and came around the desk to stand in front of her, Grace thought her initial assessment of him might have been wrong. The glint of greed and deadly determination in his eyes was unmistakable.

"Where's Ethan?" She kept the gun leveled on him.

Dr. Hunter cocked a dark brow, very reminiscent of the man she knew as Ethan. "You mean my look-alike? Don't worry, he's safe. For the time being, at least."

Grace wondered what that meant. Her hand trembled slightly on the gun, but she used all of her resolve to steady it. "Where is he?" Her tone hardened with threat. "I want to see him."

"You will," Dr. Hunter said. "But I've a few things here I have to take care of first."

"I don't think you're in any position to bargain," Grace said coldly. "In case you hadn't noticed, I'm the one with the gun here."

"Oh, I couldn't help but notice," Hunter said smoothly. Then his voice hardened. "But in case you hadn't noticed, we aren't exactly alone."

And with that, a man stepped through the door behind Grace and put a gun barrel to her head. "Drop the gun, *por favor,*" he said with a heavy Spanish accent.

When Grace hesitated, Dr. Hunter said, "Better do as he says. For all his gentle appearance, Javier can be quite vicious. Besides which, you can't possibly take us both out."

He was right about that. When Grace lowered her weapon, the man behind her reached down and took it from her hand. Then he tossed it to Dr. Hunter.

The man called Javier walked slowly around Grace, still keeping the weapon drawn on her. When he was in front of her, she stared at him, recognizing the dark hair, the coal eyes, the thin, black mustache. He was the man she'd seen in the corridor outside the ballroom of the Huntington Hotel, the man she had pursued into the laundry room, and possibly the man who had murdered Special Agent Huddleston.

"You already know who I am," Dr. Hunter was saying. "This is a colleague of mine, Dr. Javier Salizar. He runs the clinic in Mexico when I'm not around. It's been a mutually advantageous arrangement over the years, but now that I'm bowing out, he'll be free to use the clinic to continue the small but very powerful drug cartel he's building.''

Salizar made an abrupt movement with his gun, one that had Grace's heart pounding in alarm.

Dr. Hunter put up a hand, as if to restrain his colleague. He said something in rapid Spanish, then to Grace he said, ''But I still don't know your name.''

She saw no reason not to tell him. ''Grace Donovan.''

''FBI, I presume?''

She shrugged.

''Well, at least you're not denying it,'' he said. ''Not that it matters. Now that you've seen me, I'm sure you realize I can't let you go.''

''Is that why you killed Huddleston?'' When Hunter glanced at her blankly, she said, ''The agent at the Huntington Hotel.''

''Ah.'' Hunter steepled his fingers beneath his chin. ''He saw me at the hotel while he was shadowing Pilar and Bob. I couldn't let him go after that.''

Grace glanced at the gun in Salizar's hand, then at Dr. Hunter, assessing her situation. Unfortunately, she didn't see a way out. Not yet at least. ''How did you get in here?''

''Past your surveillance, you mean? It was pathetically easy. We were back here before you arrived from the Huntington.''

''But Ethan told me he changed the alarm code.''

''So he did, but I almost always have a backup plan. Once when I came back from Mexico, my loving wife had changed the code so that I couldn't get into my own house. After that, I had the security company program in an override code that only I knew. Pilar never pulled that stunt again.''

The smile vanished from his face, leaving in its place a cruel sneer that made Grace shiver. If she had underestimated Dr. Hunter's capabilities before, she would not do so now.

''Why did you give him your face?'' she asked suddenly.

The charming smile was back in place. He shrugged nonchalantly. ''Because I knew Reardon would come after me. And if not him, then some other criminal whose face I've changed. They're all extremely grateful at first, but then they get to thinking. Paranoia sets in. Their plastic surgeon is the only one who can identify them. Sooner or later, one of them was bound to come after me.''

Grace frowned. ''So you created yourself a double? How did you think you could pull that off? Eventually someone would catch on.''

''Not if the double was dead,'' Dr. Hunter said with another shrug. ''I had it all planned out very carefully. Or so I thought,'' he added ironically. ''I brought him back to Houston, dumped him in my clinic, and then one of Dr. Salizar's American associates was to shoot him in the face before he came to and make the whole thing look like robbery. Only, your friend decided to wake up before he was supposed to, and he managed to save himself. Imagine my surprise when I found out what had happened, that my look-alike was still alive and poking around in my life, digging up secrets I didn't want exposed.''

"An autopsy would have revealed he wasn't you," Grace said. "You couldn't change blood types, fingerprints, DNA."

"There was no reason to," Dr. Hunter said almost impatiently. "With both Amy and him dead in the clinic, there would have been no reason to suspect he wasn't me. Especially since I'd made sure my passport and ID were on him, along with my wedding ring. There would have been no need for anything other than the most rudimentary autopsy, and I'd taken care of the blood type by changing my medical records at the hospital before I went out of the country. I thought of everything."

Not everything, Grace thought. She wondered if she should tell him about the fingerprints, about the fact that the FBI were on to him. But if cornered, he might become even more desperate, and Grace wasn't willing to admit yet that she couldn't somehow find a way out of this.

"Who is he?" she tried to ask without emotion. "Where did you find him?"

Dr. Hunter smiled. "That's the beauty of it. He's no one anybody would ever come looking for, except maybe for the police. He was affiliated with one of Dr. Salizar's rival drug cartels, and the Mexican authorities shot him while he was trying to escape capture."

Affiliated with a drug cartel? A sour taste rose to Grace's mouth. *He's no one anybody would come looking for, except maybe the police.*

Not Trevor Reardon, she thought weakly, but someone perhaps just as dark.

"Apparently, he fell off a cliff, and some of the

locals found him and brought him to me," Dr. Hunter said. "I'll spare you the details, but suffice to say, his face was badly damaged, and he had a severe head trauma which resulted in acute amnesia. When he woke up, he didn't remember who he was or how he'd gotten to the clinic. He remained heavily sedated at the clinic while I came back here. He couldn't remember his past before he arrived at the clinic, and the drugs ensured he wouldn't remember his time there. We were spared a lot of questions that way. I even brought his gun back here with me so there would be no way to identify him. Once his wounds had healed sufficiently, I went back to Mexico and began the reconstruction on his face. He didn't remember anything about his former life, so I gave him a new one."

She lifted her chin, staring Hunter straight in the eyes. "I'm a federal agent," she said. "This house in under surveillance. The minute you fire one of those guns, the place will be crawling with FBI."

"You mean the three men watching the house? Javier's American *amigo* has taken care of them for us."

The sick feeling inside Grace deepened. Three more agents dead? God—

Dr. Hunter turned to Salizar and spoke rapidly in Spanish, something about the American Salizar had apparently hired for the job. As best Grace could tell, there'd been a last minute change in plans, and in spite of Hunter's cool demeanor, he was worried about the new man.

When Hunter turned back to Grace, she said, "What are you going to do with me?"

He shrugged. "Oh, I have plans for you. Lofty plans, you might say."

Dr. Salizar had moved behind her, and now Grace saw Dr. Hunter nod to him over her shoulder. She whirled, automatically putting up a hand to defend herself, but she was too late. The butt of the gun caught her square in the back of the head.

With a blinding flash of pain, Grace pitched face forward to the floor.

WHEN SHE AWAKENED, the pain was a dull roar in her head. She lay facedown in what she first thought must be a van or a truck, but the rumble of engines below her and the sway and dip as they hit air pockets told her they were airborne.

She struggled to rise, but her head swam sickeningly, and when she tried to move, she realized her hands were bound behind her. With an effort, she rolled to her side, then managed to sit up, gazing around.

Ethan was directly in front of her, leaning against the wall of the plane, his hands behind him and his eyes closed. One side of his face was covered in blood, and Grace's heart lurched in terror. For one heart-stopping moment, she was positive he was dead. He was so still and his face was deathly pale.

But then very slowly he opened his eyes and focused on her. A look of intense relief flooded over his features, and Grace realized he must have been conscious for some time now, and wondering the same thing about her.

"Are you all right?" he whispered, throwing a glance toward the front of the plane.

Grace nodded, unsure of her voice. "Are you?"

"I will be, as soon as I get these ropes loose."

His brow wrinkled in concentration as he strained at the bindings. Grace glanced around, assessing their situation. They were in the rear of the plane. Luggage and crates of supplies were stacked near the back, and directly opposite, a door opened to the front. Grace could see two or three rows of seat backs, and beyond that, a curtain that closed off the cockpit.

The cargo door was on the wall nearest her, but without parachutes, the exit wouldn't do them much good.

She glanced back at Ethan. "What happened?" she whispered.

"They were waiting for me when I came back downstairs. They were in the house when we got back from the hotel."

"Yes, I know. The agents watching the house are dead."

Ethan's eyes flickered briefly as he struggled with the ropes.

"Where are they taking us?" Grace asked, working at her own bindings. Her wrists grew raw from the effort.

"I heard them mention Mexico. Hunter still thinks he can pull this off."

Grace glanced up. "You've seen him then?"

Ethan's gaze met hers, and something dark flashed in his eyes. "I've seen him."

Grace wondered what he was thinking, what it must have felt like to come face to face with his reflection. She tried to temper the rush of emotion she felt for him by reminding herself of what Hunter had told her—that the man she knew as Ethan had been involved with a drug cartel in Mexico.

But looking at him now, Grace couldn't bring herself to believe it. Didn't want to believe it. If he never got his memory back, would that side of him disappear forever?

Could he live with that? And could she?

Maybe it was all a moot point anyway if they couldn't find a way out of their current predicament.

As if reading her mind, Ethan said, "He still thinks he can get rid of me and have everyone believe he's dead."

"It's been him all along," Grace said. "Not Reardon. Hunter hired someone to kill both you and Amy so that everyone would think he was dead."

"Not a bad plan," Ethan said dryly.

"Except for the fact that the FBI knows you and he are not one and the same man."

Ethan's movements ceased. He looked up at her. "What?"

"We lifted some prints from the water glass in your hospital room and ran them through the national database. My superior knows that you're not Dr. Hunter."

"Who am I?" A look Grace couldn't identify crossed over his features. Fear. Dread. Hope. Uncertainty.

What could she tell him that would alleviate his worry? "You aren't Trevor Reardon," she said.

"Then who am I?"

"I…don't know yet."

His gaze on her hardened. "How long have you known this? From the first?"

Grace shook her head. "No. No. I just found out tonight. I didn't have a chance to tell you—"

Before she could finish, a shadow blackened the doorway to the front of the plane, and Grace looked up to find Dr. Hunter staring down at her. It was still so uncanny to see how much he looked like Ethan.

Grace glanced at Ethan. His gaze was riveted to Dr. Hunter. She couldn't imagine what this must be like for him. For the first time that night, she wondered what he'd looked like before the surgery.

"You're both awake, I see." Dr. Hunter moved into the cargo area, and Dr. Salizar followed him. Salizar carried a gun in his hand, and another gun—Grace's—was stuck in the front waistband of his khaki trousers.

Hunter walked over to one of the crates, opened it, and extracted three parachutes. He handed one of the chutes to Salizar, then buckled himself into the other.

"Go tell your amigo it's time to set the automatic pilot," he told Salizar. "I hope to God you're right about him, Javier. I hope he can be trusted."

Salizar handed Hunter one of the guns. "Don't worry. Julio vouched for him."

"That makes me feel so much better," Hunter muttered.

A fine dread slipped over Grace as she realized his intent. He, Salizar, and the pilot would parachute from the plane, leaving Ethan and Grace tied up inside.

She glanced at Ethan, but his gaze was still on Hunter. "Who am I?" he asked suddenly.

Hunter arched a brow at Grace. "You didn't tell him?"

Grace felt Ethan's gaze on her and she turned to

him quickly. "He didn't tell me who you are. I swear it."

Hunter laughed. "I didn't give you a name, but I did give you a few details. But don't worry," he said to Ethan. "You two will have an hour, maybe two before the fuel runs out. Or before you crash into a mountain."

Grace said almost desperately, "You'll never get away with this. The FBI knows Ethan isn't you. They have his fingerprints."

That stopped Hunter for a moment. He stood gazing down at Grace, a frown playing between his brows. "Well, that is unfortunate, but it can't be helped. I guess instead of playing dead, I'll just have to disappear somewhere and live out the rest of my life on my Swiss and Cayman Island bank accounts. Which is exactly what I intended to do anyway."

"But now you'll be a hunted man," Grace said. "You're a murderer. The FBI will track you to the ends of the earth, not to mention Trevor Reardon."

A man came through the door behind Hunter. He wore a red baseball cap pulled down low over his features. In one hand, he carried a parachute; in the other, one of Salizar's guns.

Hunter said over his shoulder, "Where's Javier?"

"He'll be along in a minute." The man kept his head bowed, as if studying the parachute in his hand.

"Is everything all set in the cockpit?" Hunter asked him.

The man nodded, then walked over to the cargo door, threw back the catch, and slid the door open.

A rush of wind streamed inside, the fury catching Grace off guard. For a moment, she was afraid the force might pull her through the opening. She worked even harder at the ropes around her wrist. When she glanced at Ethan, she could tell he was doing the same thing. His gaze on her seemed to say, "Hang in there. We'll get out of this somehow."

Grace desperately wanted to believe him, but even if they got free of the ropes, Hunter, Salizar, and the pilot were all armed.

Hunter finished buckling his parachute and turned back to Grace. "You can stop worrying about Reardon," he shouted over the roar of wind through the opening. "His cleverness has been greatly overrated. I've managed to stay one step ahead of him so far, and where I'm going now, he'll never find me."

"Is that so?" The man wearing the red cap looked up, and for a moment, Grace stared at him in puzzlement. Then, as if in slow motion, he lifted his hand and removed the cap from his head, revealing a receding hairline.

Dr. Hunter swung around, reaching for his weapon. But Danny Medford had a gun leveled at Hunter's chest, and Grace saw horror and recognition dawn on the doctor's face.

"Reardon!"

It didn't register with Grace what Medford's sudden appearance meant at first, but then, as the realization hit her, she turned to stare at him, terror spiraling through.

"You're—" She couldn't even say his name. Before she could hardly catch her breath, he fired the gun, and a stunned look crossed over Dr. Hunter's features. Then he slumped to the floor.

Reardon bent down and with a knife, cut away the

straps of Hunter's parachute. Then he tossed the blade aside, and rolled the body out the open cargo door.

Grace's heart pounded inside her. She turned to stare at Ethan. She could tell from his expression he was as shocked as she was. And he was still working to free himself from his ropes.

Reardon walked over to Grace and stood grinning down at her. For the first time, Grace saw behind his new face and the contacts he wore, to the evil that couldn't be masked. "What's the matter, Grace? Don't you recognize me?"

Fourteen years ago, he had been the handsomest man Grace had ever seen. Now his features were almost plain, his good looks sacrificed for his freedom.

He knelt, caressing her face with the barrel of his gun—her gun, she recognized. Obviously, he'd killed Dr. Salizar and taken the gun from him.

Reardon put his hand around Grace's neck, and her skin crawled at his touch. Her stomach rolled sickeningly. When she would have jerked away, he said, "You're so beautiful. Do you have any idea how special you are to me?"

Grace felt the bile rising in her throat. On the other side of the plane, she could see Ethan openly struggling at his ropes. Reardon noticed him, too, and nodded in Ethan's direction. "I see the clone wants to come to your rescue."

Ethan looked up, his gaze meeting Reardon's. The look on Ethan's face chilled Grace to the bone. He was a match for Reardon. She had no doubt of it.

Reardon must have sensed it, too, for he stood abruptly and disappeared through the door to the front of the plane. When he came back moments later, he had Salizar's chute. He tossed it out the door. Grace saw the wind whip it away in a blur.

The only parachute left on board was Reardon's. He came back to stand over Grace, and for a moment, she thought the end had come. He was going to finish her off.

Ethan said, "You touch her, and I'll kill you."

Reardon cocked his head, staring at Ethan. "Do you know who I am?"

Ethan almost smiled. "Yes. And that's going to make killing you all the more pleasurable."

A look that might have been admiration flashed in Reardon's eyes. Or was it fear?

Then he laughed, a sound that took Grace straight back to that night fourteen years ago. She closed her eyes as the horror swept over her.

"I admire your nerve, my friend, but you are hardly in any position to make threats." He turned to Grace. "And you. Imagine my surprise when I followed Hunter to the clinic that night and saw you there. After all these years, we finally meet again, Grace. I believe it's destiny, don't you?"

When Grace didn't answer, he said, "You've made everything very convenient for me. I can take care of you and Dr. Hunter in one fell swoop, and you—" He turned back to Ethan. "You've seen my new face, so I'm afraid it's *adiós* for you as well. The only thing left for me to do," he said, walking over to the open door and preparing to strap on his parachute, "is to look up my old friend, Myra."

Grace strained at her ropes. She couldn't let Reardon get away. She couldn't let him get to Myra. As she struggled furiously with the bindings, something caught her eye. A flash of metal. The knife Reardon had tossed aside.

"Oh, and one last thing," he said, turning back to Grace. "That last night you and I spent together. I called your father when you'd gone into the bathroom. You didn't know that, did you? The last thing on his mind before he died was the knowledge that his precious daughter was with me. I wanted you to know that before you die."

Fury swept over Grace in a blinding flash. She lunged at Reardon, but before she could reach him, before he even had time to sense her intention, Ethan was on him. Somehow he'd gotten loose from his ropes, and now the force of his attack almost sent both him and Reardon plunging out the open door. Reardon dropped the parachute, and Grace saw it slip over the side of the door.

Both men fell to the floor of the plane, the gun in Reardon's hand whipping upward before Ethan could grab his wrist. Then he slammed Reardon's hand against the floor of the plane, and the gun went flying.

The fight was ugly. The men were evenly matched, one as deadly and cold-blooded as the other.

Grace scooted sideways, turning so she could get one hand around the knife. Twisting it awkwardly, she began to saw at the ropes around her wrist.

Her heart almost stopping, Grace saw Reardon roll toward the open doorway, pulling Ethan with him. With a vicious kick, Reardon sent Ethan half over the edge. Ethan clung to the metal frame around the opening, but the wind force almost ripped him away. Grace could see the strain on his face, the sheer force of his willpower as he began to pull himself inside.

Reardon stood poised in the open doorway, clinging to an overhead support to brace himself against the rush of wind as he stared down at Ethan.

Desperately, Grace hacked at the ropes around her wrist, felt the sting of pain as the blade found skin. Then she was free. In one fluid movement, she rolled on the floor and grabbed the gun just as Reardon lifted his foot to kick Ethan loose from the door.

Grace screamed Reardon's name over the rush of wind and when he turned to her, she saw his eyes widen in surprise at the gun in her hand. Without hesitation, Grace pulled the trigger. The force of the bullet, combined with the wind velocity, knocked Reardon from the plane. Grace heard him scream and saw the scarlet bloom on his chest before he disappeared into the darkness.

In a flash, she was on her knees in front of the doorway. She grabbed Ethan's arms and helped pull him inside. They lay panting on the floor of the plane for a long moment before Grace scrambled back to the opening, peering out into the darkness.

"He's dead, Grace. You got him," Ethan said.

Grace turned back, her gaze uncertain. "I hope you're right. God, I hope you're right."

They stared at each other, letting the adrenaline rush carry the emotions through their bloodstream. Then Grace said, "I don't suppose you knew how to fly a plane before your amnesia?"

Ethan's gaze darkened for a moment, and then he said, almost grimly, "I think I might have."

Chapter Fourteen

They were on the ground at an airfield just across the border from Brownsville, Texas. Grace was in the police magistrate's office, talking with Myra on the telephone and filling her in on all the details.

Myra listened, and then when Grace was finished, said, "After all these years, you finally got him. How does it feel?"

Grace hadn't had time to deal with her emotions. She supposed what she felt most strongly at that moment was uncertainty, about her future and about Ethan's. She said almost urgently, "What's happening on your end? Have you found out anything else about the fingerprints?"

A long hesitation, then Myra said, "Turns out, the agency who flagged his prints is the DEA, Grace. Evidently they've been looking for him for a long time, and now they're demanding that we turn him over to them."

Grace sucked in a long breath. "Are you sure? There could have been a mistake. A computer glitch."

"There's no mistake. You've got to bring him in, Grace. You don't have a choice."

ETHAN COULD TELL from the look on Grace's face that the call hadn't gone well. "You talked to your superior?"

She nodded. She started to say something else, then turned to stare across the street at a seedy-looking bar that blasted tejano music.

"Let's take a walk," she suggested. "It's a little noisy around here."

They strolled along the cobblestone sidewalk until they reached the edge of town. The night seemed darker over the desert, with only a few stars and the moon to soften the gloom. In a few hours, it would be dawn, but right now, daylight still seemed a long way off.

Without looking at her, Ethan said, "I'm going back to the jungle, Grace. Back to that clinic. I have to find out who I am. I have to know...what I've done."

"Ethan—"

He took her arms, turning her to face him. He stared down into her eyes, feeling the connection with her as he had never felt it before. Maybe because he was about to sever it.

"That call you just made. What you found out wasn't good, was it?"

He saw the denial flicker over her features, then she closed her eyes briefly. "It doesn't matter."

"Yes, it does." His grip tightened on her arms. "You're a cop, Grace. An FBI agent sworn to uphold the law. How can you say who I am and what I've done doesn't matter?''

She gazed up at him. "Going back to the jungle may be the most dangerous place for you. If you come back with me—''

"You'll see that they go easy on me?" He shook his head. "I'm not above the law, Grace. If I've done something wrong, something…bad, then I'll take my punishment for it. But not until I find out the truth for myself. Not until I know the whole story. Can you understand that?''

What he was asking of her went against everything she stood for, everything she believed in. A wave of guilt rolled over Ethan for what he was about to do, but there was no other way.

He took a step back from her, and he saw her bewilderment in the moonlight. Then her disbelief.

He took another step away from her, backing into the desert as he leveled the gun on her.

"It's the only way, Grace. I can't ask you to give up everything for me. I won't. So don't try to follow me.'' It was more of a plea than a warning, but for one split second, he sensed her resistance.

"This isn't goodbye,'' he promised.

"Then why do I feel like it is?" she said, before turning and walking away.

GRACE SAT IN the cubicle Myra had confiscated at the Houston office and tried to ignore the tension that fairly sizzled in the room. Two huge men wearing black suits and identical scowls stood on either side of Grace while Myra sat across a metal desk from her. When Grace had first entered the office, less than twenty-four hours after her flight back from the border, Myra had introduced the two men as her counterparts at the DEA. Which meant they had considerable clout.

Myra folded her arms on the top of the desk and said, "Please tell Agents Mackelroy and Delaney what you told me, Grace."

Grace glanced up at first one man, and then the other. She shrugged. "He got away."

Mackelroy, the larger of the two men, came around to perch on the edge of Myra's desk. "How?"

"He pulled a gun on me."

She could see the disbelief in the man's eyes before he flashed a glance at his partner. Mackelroy said, "Tell us exactly what happened."

Grace complied, leaving out only the part she deemed too personal for them to hear. Some of what had gone down between her and Ethan was none of their damned business.

Mackelroy leaned toward Grace, his gaze intense. "Do you have any idea where he is now? It's imperative that we find him."

Grace met his gaze. "Why do you want him so badly? Who is he?"

The two men exchanged another glance. Then Mackelroy said almost urgently, "His name is Tony Stark. He's one of our agents. For the last two years, he's been under deep cover, infiltrating one of the drug cartels down in Mexico."

For a moment, Grace thought she hadn't heard him correctly. She stared at him, stunned. Then she said slowly, "He's a DEA agent?"

Mackelroy nodded. "The last we heard, he'd been

arrested by some local authorities who were working
for a rival cartel. Somehow he managed to escape,
and then he just disappeared. We assumed he was
dead, but then his fingerprints turned up in the computer. The rest you know.''

Grace felt as if she had just been sucker punched.
She couldn't breathe, much less talk.

Myra said throatily, ''Of course, we'd like to cooperate as much as we can, but Grace has told you
everything. Stark is down in Mexico somewhere,
wandering around without a memory. If he were one
of my agents, I wouldn't waste time in getting down
there to find him.''

BY THE END of the week, Grace was back home in
Washington. She'd filed the last of her reports and
attended one final debriefing before leaving the J. Ed-
gar Hoover Building in a downpour.

She stood at the window of her apartment, and
stared out at the city. It was Friday, past eight o'clock,
and the city was coming alive. The streets were still
clogged with government workers and officials wend-
ing their way southward, to the suburbs in Maryland
and Virginia. The ones who lived in the city were
finding little pockets of shelter in the hundreds of bars
and bistros scattered throughout Washington.

The rain had stopped a little while ago, and a
breeze drifted in from the Potomac River. The heat
of the day gave way to a crisp coolness of evening,
and the sky deepened to violet.

Grace had never felt more at loose ends after wrapping up a case, because this had been no ordinary
case. Trevor Reardon was dead, and for the first time

in fourteen years, she felt the weight of her guilt begin to ease. She knew she could let go of the past now, say goodbye to a family she would never stop missing.

But in some strange way, the emptiness inside her had deepened. The lonely years of her life stretched before her, and Grace suddenly realized how much she'd given up to her dedication. A home. A family. A man she could love.

A future that made her want to get up in the mornings.

Ethan had done this to her, Grace thought without bitterness. Ethan had made her realize what she was missing, what her sacrifices had cost her. He had reminded her that she had once been capable of love. Might still be.

She closed her eyes briefly, resting her forehead against the cool glass. She wondered where he was now, if he was safe, if he had been found by the DEA and told who he was. What he was.

She had known all along there was goodness in him.

Grace turned when the doorbell sounded and reluctantly left her place at the window to answer it, figuring it was Myra trying to talk her out of the resignation Grace had tendered after her last debriefing. But it was time for a change. Time to try her hand at being a lawyer, which was what she'd always wanted to be.

She pulled back the door. "I'm not changing my mind, Myra—"

Ethan stood on the other side, dressed in jeans and a dark cotton shirt, a raincoat slung over his shoulder.

His dark hair glistened with moisture as he gazed down at her uncertainly.

"I wasn't sure this was the right place," he finally said.

Grace stepped back to let him enter. "How did you find me?"

"Some of my friends at the DEA office in Houston helped track you down."

Grace's heart quickened. "Then you know?"

"A couple of agents were waiting for me at Hunter's clinic down in Mexico. I guess they somehow figured out I'd be going there to find some answers." He gave Grace a pointed look, and she quickly turned away.

"It would seem a logical place to start searching for you," she said, leading him into the living room. She glanced around at the dismal atmosphere of her home. Come Monday morning, she was going to start redecorating, Grace decided. A new career, a new apartment, a whole new life.

Where would Ethan fit into her plans? she wondered. Or would he want to?

She motioned toward the sofa, but they both remained standing. "I've been wondering about you, you know. Where you were. How you were doing. There're a lot of things we've left unsaid, Ethan."

He smiled, and Grace caught her breath. He looked different all of a sudden. Like a new man. "My name is Tony."

She smiled, too, her heart pounding inside her. "I know, but that'll take some getting used to."

He watched her move toward the window. She

stood with her back to the glow of city lights, and the way she looked almost took his breath away.

He walked over to stand beside her, and they both turned to stare out at the glistening night. "I don't have my memory back," he finally said. "Not all of it, but bits and pieces are starting to come back. And I've been told quite a lot." He turned to her. "I've seen pictures of myself, the way I looked before. Unless I agree to more surgery, I guess I'm stuck with this face."

"It's a nice face," Grace said softly.

"You don't think of...*him* when you look at me? You don't feel revulsion?"

She reached up and touched his cheek very briefly with her fingertips. "I see you. No one else. It doesn't matter what you look like. Appearances are only skin deep. It's who you are that counts."

He gazed down at her, resisting the urge to touch the fiery strands of her hair, to let the softness sift through his fingers.

She turned back to the window, but he could see that she was watching his reflection. After a moment, she said, "It must seem so strange, finding out about yourself like that. You must have had a million questions."

His gaze met hers in the window. "There was one question in particular I was anxious to find the answer to."

She faced him. Her eyes were very clear and very blue. He thought she had never looked more beautiful. "What question was that?"

He did touch her then, lifting his hand to smooth back her hair, letting his fingers slip through the silkiness. He saw her eyes close briefly. "Can't you guess?"

She took a breath. "Are you married?"

He grinned. "That's the one."

"And?" she asked impatiently, folding her arms across her breasts. She put up a good front, but Tony was gratified to see the flash of uncertainty in her eyes.

"I'm not married," he said softly. "Never have been."

"And never will be?" she challenged, the doubt in her eyes changing to a teasing glint.

"I wouldn't say that." He raised his other hand and threaded his fingers through her hair, then kissed her. Her lips quivered beneath his, and Tony thought in wonder what an incredible woman she was. A woman who could face a cold-blooded killer without showing fear, but one who trembled at his kiss.

He pulled back, staring into her eyes. "The connection is still there, Grace. Do you feel it?"

"Yes." She smiled. "Oh, yes."

"The question now is, what are we going to do about it?"

She looked up at him slyly. "You could kiss me again." After he complied, she said, "We have some unfinished business, you and I."

Her boldness thrilled him. "We've got all night. There's nowhere in the world I have to be."

She slipped her arms around his neck. "As a matter of fact, I find myself in the same situation. I'm not an FBI agent anymore," she told him. "I resigned today."

He lifted his brows at that, but instead of asking

her why, he said, "I'm not a DEA agent anymore, either. I wouldn't be much good in the field without a memory."

Grace sighed deeply, but it wasn't an unhappy sound. More one of relief. "So what are we going to do?"

He wrapped his arms around her, pulling her close. "I don't know, but we have the rest of our lives to figure it out. I do know one thing. I want to get to know you, Grace. I want to know everything about you. The last few days don't seem real somehow. I want to spend time with you without looking over my shoulder. Without wondering if this moment will be our last."

"Wow," Grace breathed. "You want all that? And here I thought we were just going to spend the night together."

"That's a start," he said seriously. "Believe me, that'll be one hell of a start."

PROTECTIVE INSTINCTS
Debra Webb

This book is dedicated to my husband,
Nonie Webb, who has trusted me
from day one and has allowed me to
follow my dream. Forever would never
be long enough to spend with you.

Prologue

"Now who's in control, Ned?"

The razor-sharp edge of the dagger she held glistened in the light. He tried to speak…to beg, to tell her he would do anything she asked, but he couldn't. He could only mumble through the scrunched-up panties she'd forced into his mouth. Why had he let her into his apartment? He should have realized something was wrong…but she'd distracted him.

"Oh, that's right," she said, her voice condescending, as she trailed the metallic tip down the center of his chest. A crawling shiver followed its path. "You can't talk right now, can you?" She smiled a sick, sinister smile he'd never seen on her before.

He needed desperately to swallow. He tried, gagging reflexively on the nylon choking him. His eyes burned. He was a grown man and he was going to cry. Why the hell was she doing this?

A sheen of sweat coated his skin. His heart pounded harder, making his chest ache, as she walked all the way around him. Please, please, he prayed, let this be just another of her games. He didn't want to die like this, naked and tied to a chair. He didn't want to die at all.

"If they found you like this," she continued, her tone casual, as if tying up a man at gunpoint and then waving a dagger in his face was an everyday affair, "maybe they'd recognize you for the pervert you are." She checked the rope binding his wrists behind his back. He groaned and tried to pull away.

Ned closed his eyes and fought another sting of tears. Surely she couldn't mean to—

"Look at me, *Dr.* Harrison," she ordered.

He opened his eyes. She stood in front of him now, the tip of the blade pressed against the flesh directly over his heart. It thundered savagely. So hard he could scarcely draw a breath.

What had he done to her that was so bad? She'd enjoyed the sex just as much as he had. And, as he always did, he'd ended the brief affair on an upbeat note and she hadn't complained. Why now?

"All those women, Ned." She shook her head in disapproval. "You're a user," she snarled. "You strike when your prey is the most vulnerable. You're nothing but scum."

He whimpered, the sound small and desperate. No! He wanted to scream. He was a great man. He'd achieved far more in his psychiatric practice than he'd ever dreamed possible. How could this happen now? They'd all been willing. He hadn't forced any of them. They'd liked it…wanted it…

The tip of the blade pierced his flesh. He felt the warm blood bloom, then ooze down his chest. Felt the tears spill from his eyes. Something like a sob escaped his aching throat. This couldn't be happening to him. Not now.

She laughed, the sound brittle and harsh. "You bastard. You're not a man, you're a wimp. A real man wouldn't have to prey on vulnerable women. A *real man* wouldn't cry when faced with the truth." She poked him a little harder, drawing blood again. A muffled cry emerged from him. "You're sick. That's what you are. What's next for you—little girls waiting at the bus stop?"

He stilled. The realization hit him like a mallet between the eyes. Damn. So that was what this was all about. She was pissed off because— Dear God, could it be that simple? He snorted, then laughed as best he could with those frigging panties shoved halfway down his throat. What a stupid bitch. What the hell had she expected?

Fury darkened her face. "Are you laughing at me?"

He tried to control himself, but he just couldn't stop. If he hadn't been tied to the chair, he would have doubled over with the laughter bubbling up inside him.

"You son of a bitch."

He laughed, then coughed, almost choking. This was all about one stupid little slut.

"Go to hell!" she snarled, her eyes wild.

She lunged, jamming the dagger into his chest.

His body jerked as his startled gaze collided with hers.

She looked as surprised as he was.

Shaking her head, she backed away from him.

He blinked, then stared down at his chest. The jewel-handled weapon was buried to the hilt.

Shit.

He looked up at her one last time as the narrow focus of death closed in around him.

Chapter One

Elizabeth Young imagined that Dr. Ned Harrison was every bit as good-looking in death as he'd been in life. The navy-blue pinstripe suit and red power tie had probably been his favorites. The white linen that draped his coffin, along with the six tall candles surrounding it, made an impressive display. But the most effective ploy was the huge choir assembled behind the distinguished-looking priest. The choir's grand entrance, as well as the blessing, had been nothing short of awe-inspiring. And Elizabeth wasn't even Catholic.

It was the perfect send-off for such a highly regarded, nationally renowned psychiatrist. The brooding medieval architecture of the Holy Trinity Church lent a dramatic atmosphere for his final public appearance.

No one who knew him, least of all Elizabeth, would be at all surprised to find Ned's picture on the social page of tomorrow's issue of the *New York Times*.

The city would mourn the loss of a brilliant doctor,

and a great number of its female inhabitants would mourn him for completely different reasons.

Elizabeth surveyed the crowd around her as the priest continued to chant mass in solemn, hushed tones. More than half those present were women under forty, fashionably dressed, all beautiful and probably all wealthy.

Though Elizabeth was neither rich nor glamorous, she would bet her next month's earnings that the one thing all the females in this room had in common was that they had slept with the deceased.

Including Elizabeth.

She shifted on the hard wooden pew, knowing full well there was no getting comfortable physically or mentally. What on earth had possessed her to come to Ned's funeral mass? She glanced around at the other women, all facing forward in somber attention, and wondered what *their* reasons for putting in an appearance might be. Maybe rather than mourning or merely showing their respect, they'd all come for the same reason she had—to make absolutely certain that he was really dead.

Of course the visit the homicide detectives had paid her had pretty much driven the point home. The two men had been fairly cordial at first, but the questions had soon turned openly accusing, as had their attitudes. Elizabeth shuddered at the memory of one detective in particular. She hoped she wouldn't have to go through that again. She had a new life here....

Another shudder quaked through her. She'd almost allowed him to ruin everything. How could she have been so foolish?

"Can you believe she wore that dress to a funeral?"

Elizabeth turned her attention to the woman sitting next to her, her one trusted friend. "What?" she whispered.

Gloria Weston angled her head to the right in a gesture that made Elizabeth want to hunker down out of sight. "Over there. The blonde in the devil-red dress," Gloria elucidated beneath her breath.

Elizabeth strained to look without actually moving her head. She frowned. "Do you know her?" The woman looked vaguely familiar to Elizabeth, but she couldn't quite place her.

Gloria shook her head. "She looks like that model who had all that trouble last year. I don't know. She's probably just another one of Ned's hussies."

Elizabeth cocked an eyebrow. "What does that make us?" she murmured.

Gloria snorted softly. Fortunately no one seemed to notice the rude sound. "Fools," she retorted. "Just like the rest of them."

Elizabeth didn't want to think about that—or the telephone call she'd gotten from Ned late Friday afternoon. The slimeball. He'd called two or three times last week, begging her to have dinner with him. "Just to talk," he'd assured her. "I'm not ready to let you go," he'd added in that charismatic voice of his. What a jerk. She knew what he wanted all right, and she had no intention of falling into that trap again.

No way.

But on Friday she'd gone to the restaurant, anyway. He'd made her an offer she couldn't refuse. Her pulse quickened at the thought of the videotape. It was the only reason she'd gone. And then he hadn't shown up. She'd wanted to kill him. Who'd have thought that a few days later she'd be attending his funeral? It was eerie. She shivered. What if the detectives had found…?

No. She resisted the urge to shake her head. She wouldn't think about that. They would definitely have mentioned that little fact.

"Look." Gloria nodded toward another woman who sat two rows up. This one had coal-black hair cut in one of those sleek, face-hugging styles. She sported a dress that defied any description Elizabeth might have attempted. "That's Vanessa Bumbalough," Gloria said, one hand over her mouth to muffle the words.

The name didn't ring a bell. The woman sat next to a man who resembled the late John Lennon in profile. He hadn't bothered to remove his sunglasses. Elizabeth's brow furrowed in question as she leaned fractionally closer to her friend. "Who's Vanessa Whatever-you-said?"

The man sitting directly behind them cleared his throat. Elizabeth cringed. Gloria ignored him. "She's a new phenomenal fashion designer. She's been all over the papers lately. Don't you ever read?" Gloria made an impatient face. "Apparently her designs stole the show at this season's big fashion debut. The whole industry's up in arms. She's hot, hot, hot."

Ned wouldn't have chosen her otherwise, Elizabeth mused. The man had a reputation to maintain, after all. She winced at the idea of just how gullible she herself had been. How could she have thought that Ned Harrison was really interested in her? She wasn't beautiful in the classic sense of the word, though she wasn't exactly chopped liver, either. She possessed no real social graces, and couldn't tolerate contact lenses, leaving her no alternative but to wear glasses. Even worse, she'd done the unthinkable by giving up a prestigious job at a ritzy interior design firm and taking what most would consider blue-collar work in a city where one's profession was the single most qualifying factor for being a part of the *in* crowd.

Screw the in crowd. Elizabeth was happy just as she was. Well, for the most part, anyway.

She glanced at her friend. Gloria was one of the city's beautiful people. Petite, a head of fiery-red corkscrew curls, pixie features. Not to mention she had one of those awe-inspiring power jobs on Wall Street. Wherever Gloria was, everyone always flocked to her and wanted to know the inside scoop. People loved her. She was a smooth operator, as street-smart as she was business-savvy, and a real sweetheart, especially if she liked you. She was the first friend Elizabeth had made when she arrived in the city. She'd met her at one of Brian's, her ex-fiancé's, infamous parties. Gloria had been there for Elizabeth ever since…through everything. The breakup with Brian, leaving the firm and having to find a new, low-rent place to live. Elizabeth owed her. Big time.

Ned ''the Casanova Shrink'' Harrison had almost cost her that friendship. And he definitely was not worth it.

Then again, he hadn't deserved to be murdered, either. Elizabeth didn't like the trickle of guilt she experienced on the heels of that thought. It was true that she'd felt just a little glee upon reading of his abrupt demise in Sunday's paper, but then she'd caught herself. That she'd spoken with him only hours before his unfortunate date with destiny was definitely unnerving. What if he'd actually shown up for their dinner date and laid on the charm? What if she'd fallen under his spell one last time?

Last being the operative word. She shivered as her mind conjured up the murder scene the newspaper had described in grim detail.

Dying in such a humiliating manner was overkill, she reasoned, no pun intended. Sure, there'd been a moment or two when she could have killed him herself, but the truth was she was an adult. It wasn't like Dr. Harrison had taken advantage of a helpless child. She'd made a conscious decision to enter into a sexual relationship with him. As had, she presumed, the rest of those assembled here today. She scanned the seated crowd of women who could easily inspire an issue of *Vogue* or *Glamour*. The mass ended and the priest began the eulogy. His opening remarks bemoaned the great man New York City had lost. Elizabeth wondered for a few moments if the kindly Father would have waxed so eloquently if he'd had a loved one who'd been one of Ned's conquests.

"Look," Gloria murmured, then inclined her head toward the aisle that separated the rows of pews. "Remember her from the party the other night?"

Elizabeth peeked past her friend to the woman in question as she scooted in at the end of a row. The rustle of silk and lightweight wool accompanied the efforts of those already seated to accommodate the newcomer. The woman was tall, impossibly thin and, of course, beautiful. Supermodel material. Elizabeth did remember her. If memory served, she was an actress. Soaps, that was it. She'd just landed some bit part in a soap. Elizabeth nodded in response to her friend's expectant expression.

She remembered the party, too. She hated those kinds of parties, but Gloria dragged her to them, anyway. Hardly a weekend night went by without some sort of party Gloria insisted they simply could not miss. Luckily they'd only run into Brian a few times. But no matter where they went, the crowd was always the same: a little too wild for Elizabeth's liking. Gloria called her a party pooper, when the truth was, Elizabeth was simply a homebody. She wasn't into the party scene the way Gloria and her other friends were.

Besides, it had been only ten months since she and Brian parted ways. That was entirely too long in Gloria's opinion for Elizabeth to still be afraid to go out on a limb with someone new. But Elizabeth didn't see it that way. In spite of her mother's desertion, she'd been raised in a small town where people mated for life, not for one night. Although, she'd be the first to admit that Brian had not been the love of her life. Rather, he'd been a means to an end. She just hadn't seen it until it was too late. She had regrets, but only a couple. Moving to New York had been the right thing to do. Breaking out on her own with the only real skills she possessed was also the right thing to do, even if it had been scarier than hell at first. But she'd survived.

She'd survived Ned Harrison, too, hadn't she? How could Gloria have expected her to look for a new love when Elizabeth had gotten so tangled up in Ned's web of deceit?

Elizabeth shook off the disturbing thoughts. She was a survivor. That was what her daddy had always said, and her daddy had been a very smart man.

Moistening her lips to conceal the tiny smile thoughts of her father evoked, Elizabeth straightened and focused her attention on the priest's words. She was here. She might as well pay attention. She darted a look at her friend. Gloria appeared to have finally settled in now that she'd scrutinized the crowd. A mixture of affection and respect bloomed in Elizabeth's chest. Gloria was in a league of her own. It seemed impossible that Ned, the heartless bastard, had fooled her. Well, maybe even Gloria had her vulnerable spot.

Lord knew, Ned Harrison was an expert at finding those spots.

Elizabeth drew in a heavy breath. They'd both survived Ned—but would she survive his murder?

SPECIAL AGENT Collin MacBride paid little attention to the priest's words as he continued his evaluation of the attendees. The group was a veritable cast of who's who from the city's high society and the up-and-coming. Mostly women. No surprise there.

Mac watched one woman in particular. Elizabeth Young. He shifted slightly so that he could see her better. Tall, slender. She wore a black dress, though not the kind one expected to see at a funeral.

Then again, none of the women present were dressed in proper mourning attire. Things had definitely changed since his days as an altar boy. He saw enough long, shapely legs and silk fabric here to feel as if he was watching a fashion runway loaded with Victoria's Secret models, rather than a knave filled for a funeral service. Amid the variations of in-vogue sameness was Elizabeth Young. Oh, she wore the little black dress rightly enough, yet she was decidedly different.

Tall, even wearing flat-heeled shoes, she didn't walk with the same confident glide as the others. No nail polish, very little makeup. He'd gotten a pretty good look at her when she first entered the church. He'd been standing in the shadows near the massive double doors. She and her friend, one Gloria Weston, had hurried to find a seat as if they feared they might miss the opening act of the hottest new Broadway play.

Elizabeth Young wore glasses, the small, gold-wire-rimmed kind. Oddly enough, there was something appealing about the prim look they gave her, along with her neatly braided hair. He cocked an eyebrow at the direction his meandering thoughts had taken. He'd definitely gone too many hours without sleep. Anytime he looked at a possible suspect and found her appealing in some way, he needed to recharge his batteries. Years of training and field experience weren't supposed to just fly out the window. Where was his usual control? Down the toilet, obviously, with his patience for bumbling homicide detectives. He gritted his teeth when he considered how badly they'd screwed up.

Next to him, Luke Driver edged a bit closer and in a low voice said, "She doesn't really look like the type who could bury a knife into a man's chest."

Mac glanced at his brand-new partner, a kid fresh from the Farm. Luke had a lot to learn that only experience would teach him. "They usually don't," he returned, putting forth a concerted effort not to show his impatience. What the hell did he think? That a killer walked around with an identifying mark stamped on his forehead?

Driver shrugged, too cocky to be embarrassed. "I mean, she just doesn't look like the type who screws around with some guy, then sticks him."

Still waters ran deep more often than not, Mac considered, but said, "Harrison's murder was an emotional kill, an act of passion. You saw the videotape. Miss Young is certainly capable of the necessary emotion."

"Man, is she," Driver muttered wistfully.

Mac clenched his jaw as the images he'd watched on that videotape quickly played in the private theater of his mind. Oh, yeah, Elizabeth Young was definitely passionate. His pulse quickened as his mind focused on one particularly vivid image of her nude body. Streaks of gold highlighted her lush brown mane of hair as it glided over her skin with her rhythmic movements atop her lover. Small, firm breasts jutting forward, begging to be tasted. She might not have that high-class walk down pat, but she damn sure had the art of sex down to a science. Mac's groin tightened before he could stop his reaction.

Mentally cursing himself, he looked away from her then. Elizabeth Young wasn't just a suspect; she was the prime suspect in this high-profile murder investigation. The last thing he needed was a genuine case of pure lust. The facts were all he needed. And he had several of those.

Ned Harrison had had a dinner appointment with Elizabeth Young at seven o'clock on Friday night. By nine he was dead. The homicide detectives had found the very private, definitely X-rated videotape of Harrison and Elizabeth Young hidden in his bedroom. There was no way to determine when it had been made. Other tapes had been found, as well, more than two dozen. Ned had been a busy man. All the tapes except Elizabeth's had been safely tucked away in his walk-in closet, right behind his wall of Armani and Donna Karan suits. Each had been labeled with a name and date—all except Elizabeth's.

Mac didn't know yet what made hers different. But he would find out. *That* she could count on. It was an absolute miracle the detectives hadn't given away that ace in the hole. At least they'd had sense enough to keep the tapes to themselves when conducting their hasty interviews and spilling their guts to the media.

As if that fiasco wasn't enough, the so-called rush-rush forensics report that should have been ready yesterday was stuck in a political bottleneck. He'd had to fight like hell to get jurisdiction over this case. It was Wednesday already and he hadn't even been allowed to interview any witnesses or suspects. Hell, he hadn't even gotten the detective's report until this morning. He hated delays; he hated screwups even more. One brash detective had already royally screwed up by pushing Miss Young until she went on the defensive—the absolute wrong thing to do. What did they teach these guys in detective school?

Mac folded his arms over his chest and seethed.

Now, five days after the man's murder, he'd finally gotten the word to proceed as lead on the case. If he could just get his hands on the damned autopsy report, he'd be in business.

Yep, he hated delays, hated not knowing the facts. Simple things, like whether or not Harrison had had sex before he died or if he'd been drinking. The only two things he did know at this point were the approximate time of death and the apparent cause of death. Brannigan, the shoot-first-ask-questions-later detective from the NYPD working on the case in supposed cooperation with Mac, was running down the history of the dagger. Was it a part of Harrison's personal collection? Or had the killer brought it with her or him?

Mac had a gut feeling that it belonged to Harrison. He owned an extensive collection of antique swords and daggers. Too bad one of his toys had been used against him.

Some hobby, Mac mused. He imagined that the weapons gave the guy a sense of power. He wondered how powerful he'd felt when one was jammed between his ribs?

Mac hadn't liked Ned Harrison. He liked him even less now that he was dead. It blew Mac's ongoing case all to hell. Mac, as a member of a special task force, had been watching Harrison for weeks, hoping for a break in the case concerning illegal Internet activities of a group known only as the Gentlemen's Association. Harrison was the first of the group they'd been able to pinpoint and identify. Now he was dead, leaving Mac back at square one. The Bureau wasn't

very happy about that, which only added to the mael-
strom of the past five days.

It was definitely possible that Harrison's death was
a well-planned hit designed to look like a crime of
passion. The head of the Gentlemen's Association
might have learned that Harrison had been compromised. But Mac couldn't see how anyone could know
that the feds were on to Harrison. Mac had been too
careful. It made more sense that it was just what it
appeared to be. But before he scrapped Harrison as a
lead and moved on, leaving the final mop-up details
to the local homicide detectives, Mac intended to be
sure there was nothing else to be garnered about this
association from Harrison's life or his death.

He'd gleaned every bit of information about the
man that his past offered. Harrison had risen above
his orphaned beginnings. Both he and his only sibling,
a twin brother, had done well for themselves despite
a bad beginning. His brother's death four years ago
had left Harrison alone in the world since he'd opted
not to marry and have a family of his own. But men
like Harrison were too selfish to give enough of themselves to have any kind of real family.

"Our lady is on the move," Driver warned beneath
his breath.

Mac jerked to attention, his gaze seeking Elizabeth
Young. She was working her way to the end of the
row, muttering *excuse me*s to those seated between
her and the aisle. Now just where the hell was she
going? Heads turned as she dashed down the aisle,
past Mac and into the vestibule.

He glanced at Driver, giving him an unspoken
command to stay put. Mac slipped quietly into the

large entry hall. He watched, remaining still and silent, as Elizabeth Young pushed up her glasses and swiped her eyes, then wrapped her arms around her middle. She was trembling. Had her heinous deed finally pinged her conscience? Or maybe she was considering everything the cops had openly accused her of in the past two days.

Without making a sound, he stepped closer and instinctively offered her the crisply starched handkerchief from his coat pocket. He never could tolerate a weeping female. "Are you all right?"

Elizabeth stared at the white handkerchief for several seconds before she reluctantly accepted it. "Thank you," she murmured without looking at him. "I'm okay."

Another step disappeared between them. "Did you know him well?"

Her head shot up at that question. She looked straight into his eyes, then blinked. "What?"

He inched closer. "Dr. Harrison," he offered, coming closer still. Close enough to watch the pupils of her eyes dilate when she realized she was alone with a stranger who was suddenly in her personal space.

"I mean," he explained carefully, keeping his voice low, soft, "you're so upset, I thought maybe you were family or maybe his girlfriend."

Her fingers clenched the white cotton. She didn't even breathe—at least, not that Mac could see. She looked like a deer caught in the headlights of an oncoming car, frightened but too shocked to react.

She shook her head finally, the movement strained. "No. I...I'm...a former patient."

Mac nodded, then shrugged one shoulder. "I suppose losing your therapist can be overwhelming."

Her gaze narrowed at the hint of sarcasm in his voice. Dammit. He hadn't meant to let it slip out. She looked him up and down for the first time. "I'm sorry, I didn't get your name."

Mac smiled, the one the ladies always told him they liked. All confidence and charm. If Miss Young liked it, she showed no outward indication. "Collin MacBride." He started to offer his hand but decided against it, since he was more than a little certain the offer wouldn't be well received.

She was clearly suspicious now. She pushed her glasses higher on her nose and asked, "Were *you* one of his patients, too?"

Smart lady, Mac admitted. She was watching closely for any signs of lying. She might look like the naive librarian who needed to get laid, but she hadn't fallen off the turnip truck just yesterday. "No," he confessed. "Just a friend."

She shoved the handkerchief back at him without having used it. "Thank you, Mr. MacBride, but I should get back."

"Wait." He stopped her before she could escape. She looked back at him from the entryway to the knave, reluctance slowing her. He cranked up the wattage of his smile. "You didn't tell me your name."

Something flickered in those amber eyes, fear, anger, both maybe. "No," she said, her voice tight with something like disdain. "I didn't."

She left him staring after her. The all-natural, almost tomboyish gait made his gut clench.

Mac's smile widened. Let the games begin. She had until tomorrow morning and then she was his.

However smart she thought herself to be, whatever cover-up skills she'd learned since the last time she'd stabbed a man in the chest, it wouldn't be enough. Mac would not give up until he knew everything she'd seen, said and done where Ned Harrison was concerned.

Elizabeth Young had herself a new shadow.

SAD...SO SAD.

We want to weep, but the tears won't come.

We miss him already.

It's all their fault. All those pretty bitches.

One of them...no, no, all of them stole him away. They made him weak. Made him want things he shouldn't. Now he is lost. And we are sad.

They will pay.

They all will pay.

Chapter Two

She'd had more than enough time for the shock to
fade and the reality of Harrison's death to steep her
conscience, Mac decided. That was assuming she had
a conscience. Considering the bout of tears she'd suffered at the funeral, he was relatively certain she still
had one. Driver had been right in that respect. Mac
really didn't see her as a cold-blooded killer. But jealousy could drive people to do things they normally
wouldn't. Or maybe she'd found out what Harrison
was doing with his vidcotaped sessions. That would
piss anybody off.

It was 8 a.m. and Mac had opted to leave Driver
back at 26 Federal Plaza to work on yanking Brann-
nigan's chain regarding the origin of the murder
weapon. Quite honestly, Mac preferred questioning a
suspect alone the first go-around.

He'd arrived at Elizabeth Young's small Leonia
apartment at 7 a.m. sharp. On the Jersey side of the
Hudson, the apartment was actually the attic-turned-
living-space portion of an older home owned by an
elderly woman who lived alone and no longer needed
the additional space. According to the landlady, who

acted as a sort of answering service, Miss Young had already left for the job site this morning. Another two steps in the wrong direction for Mac. The most effective interviews were conducted on the suspect's home turf where they were the most comfortable. Who'd have thought she'd be up and at 'em so damned early?

Mac checked the street and number he'd jotted on his notepad again. Almost there. He drove past some of the city's finest cast-iron architecture with the ornate facades and oversize windows until he reached the SoHo address the landlady had given him. He parked in a nearby alley and walked to the entrance of the four-story building. One second turned to five as he studied the top-floor windows before going inside. When he entered the lobby, he found scaffolding and indications of ongoing plaster repair on the walls and ceiling. An ancient warehouse turned residential lofts, eight in number and with price tags to match the upscale address, no doubt.

He boarded the old-style freight elevator and set it into motion. Though in a state of refurbishment, the building, as well as the location, was a far cry from Elizabeth Young's own current home address.

He already knew her poignant Cinderella story. Her defense attorney would use that saga to sway sympathy from the jury when the time came. Small-town girl falls in love with big-city boy and follows her heart in hopes of making all her dreams come true. Then, as dreams have a way of doing, they'd crashed down around her. The love of her life had turned out to be a lying, cheating, smooth-talking womanizer.

Poor Elizabeth had suddenly found herself on her own in the big, bad city.

The elevator came to a stop, groaning loudly in protest. Somehow, though, Mac thought with a twinge of respect that annoyed the hell out of him, she'd managed to land on her feet. She'd found an affordable, yet tolerable place with reasonable rent, and she'd fallen back on the trade she'd learned from her father—painting. Not the artsy kind, but the plain old, elbow-grease-required, interior-redecorating sort.

In the past eight months she'd built up a solid reputation and enough business to merit hiring a helper. Mac walked down the corridor toward the open door on the right. There were two large lofts on each floor, one on either side of the centrally located elevator. Since the other door was closed, it made sense to go for the open one first.

He supposed her helper was about somewhere. She'd picked herself a real winner there, too. Mac wondered if she had any idea the con artist she'd hired had a rap sheet as long as his arm. But then, her own rap sheet was nothing to scoff at—which was another thing they had to discuss. According to Detective Brannigan, she didn't like to talk about her past. Mac felt fairly certain she wouldn't care for any of his questions, especially after the report he'd read this morning.

The preliminary report from the medical examiner stated that Harrison had had sex just prior to his death. The only substantial clue as to the identity of the person with whom he'd had sex was a single pubic hair that didn't belong to the deceased. Well, that and a few healthy scratches on his neck that were only a couple of hours old at the time of death. DNA testing was already under way. All they needed was a comparison sample to try for a match.

Miss Young wasn't going to like that, either.

Mac paused in the open doorway and surveyed the scene before him. Beaumont Devers, better known as Boomer to his friends, stood on a ladder applying long brush strokes of white paint to the wall around the expansive windows. According to his file, he was just over six feet in height and a wiry 140 pounds. His twenty-second birthday had come and gone a month ago, but his crime-ridden teenage years had left their mark on his thin face. A white scar, which stood out despite his fair complexion, stretched downward from his hairline through his right eyebrow, leaving it with a permanent part. He'd buzzed his blond hair to the point of baldness. A number of nasty-looking tattoos adorned any visible flesh below his neck. The tattered jeans and black T-shirt completed the untrustworthy picture.

Mac couldn't imagine what Elizabeth saw in the kid, unless it was a kindredness of spirit. And there was no time like the present to ask. His gaze slid across the empty room to her location facing the wall farthest from him. She rolled the paint onto the wall with broad, even strokes in a sort of zigzag pattern, carefully covering the newly replastered surface with a fresh coat of pristine white paint. Her hair was secured high on the back of her head in a long ponytail. The kind little girls wore when they jumped rope. She wore baggy overalls and a plain white T-shirt. A red shop cloth, stained with a bit of white paint, hung from her right rear pocket.

The image was incredibly innocent-looking and tugged hard on his protective instincts. Another image, one from the videotape, abruptly appeared before his eyes. He blinked, shattering the illusion, but not before it had its usual effect. Even with her head thrown back in ecstasy, she looked somehow vulnerable, innocent.

A muscle pulsed in his jaw. Looks could be deceiving, he reminded that idiotic part of him that stupidly found her appealing. He was halfway across the room, his leather soft-soled shoes silent on the dirty hardwood floor, before she sensed someone's presence and turned around.

"Miss Young," he said as if she should have expected him. "I hope this isn't a bad time."

She looked startled, then annoyed. There was a tiny splatter of white paint on the lower edge of one lens of her glasses, and those amber eyes beneath widened in surprise. Mac heard the ladder creak as Boomer turned to see what the intrusion was about. To his credit he kept his mouth shut. Mac hoped he stayed smart that way.

Elizabeth stared, dumbfounded, at the man standing before her. She remembered him without effort. What was his name? Something MacBride. He wasn't the kind of man one forgot easily. Tall, good-looking, exuding a charm and confidence that any woman would find attractive. What was he doing here? She frowned. The bigger question was why was her heart suddenly pounding as if she'd never been this close to a handsome man before?

New York City was full of handsome guys. But this was the first time a total stranger had affected her so…so deeply. She squared her shoulders and ignored her silly reaction. Nerves, that was all it could be. She'd had a hell of a week so far. Enough to shred anyone's composure.

"We met at the funeral," he offered, apparently taking her silence as a sign that she didn't recognize him.

He extended one broad hand and smiled that cocky, oh-so-masculine smile that was a perfect complement to his polished appearance. The dark-blue suit screamed tailor-made, the white shirt was spotless and crisply starched, and the tie burgundy and probably Cardin. The black leather loafers, no doubt of Italian craftsmanship, were the only deviation from his cutting-edge attire. For stealth, she decided. That was how he'd sneaked up on her the way he had. Those damned soft-soled shoes hadn't made a sound.

Get it together, Elizabeth, she ordered herself, then promptly passed the paint roller and handle to her left hand so that she could swipe her right on the leg of her coverall before accepting his. Be cool. He was probably just an insurance salesman. Didn't those guys always hang out at funerals?

The jolt of electricity that passed between them as their palms touched startled her all over again. She jerked her hand back and instantly went on the defensive. "Do you make a habit of looking up all the women you hit on at funerals, Mr. MacBride?"

One side of that full mouth hitched up a little higher. "Only on occasion, Miss Young."

She resisted the urge to rub her still-sizzling palm against her leg again. He was looking at her—no, not just looking, studying her and seemingly contented not to say anything else. Who was this guy? When she could bear the scrutiny of those piercing blue eyes no longer, she said, "So what's the occasion?"

He reached into his interior coat pocket and pulled out a black leather case. Her frown deepened with growing confusion—and then suddenly she knew. He was a cop. Damn. Why hadn't she thought of that? Just what she needed—more questions she couldn't answer.

He displayed his credentials for her perusal, then tucked them back into his pocket. "*Agent* Mac-Bride," he clarified for her benefit in case she hadn't read the fine print on his Federal Bureau of Investigation ID. "I'm looking into the murder of Dr. Ned Harrison. Your landlady said you'd be here."

Ice slid through her veins, followed by a draining sensation that almost buckled her knees. "I've already answered the detectives' questions. I don't know anything else." Dammit, why did her voice have to sound so shaky?

The paint roller felt suddenly too heavy to hold. She swiveled stiffly and placed it in the pan. Her thoughts raced around in her head like a competitor at the Daytona 500 as she straightened. She'd have to talk to Mrs. Polk about giving out her whereabouts to strangers. But that wouldn't have stopped this man, she rationalized, if he'd shown his official ID. Mrs. Polk had no recourse but to answer his questions. What did he want with Elizabeth? She'd told the others everything she knew. There was nothing else that needed telling. Not if she could help it, anyway.

"I just need to clear up a few discrepancies," he offered nonchalantly. "Routine procedure."

Déjà vu hit like a blow to her midsection. The blood on her hands, her ex-brother-in-law screaming in pain. The police handcuffing her and forcing her into the patrol car. Routine procedure often included unjust incarceration. She couldn't afford to miss any more work. The developer would refuse to pay her the remainder of her contract if she failed to finish on time. She had to have these two lofts finished by the end of next week.

She moistened her lips and adopted an outer calm she in no way felt. "All right. I don't know how I can help you, Agent MacBride, but I'll do what I can."

Boomer was watching, his mounting uneasiness radiating clear across the room. She wanted to say something to reassure him, but at the moment she could only stare into the eyes focused so intently on her. Those haunting memories from the past she'd worked so hard to put behind her kept clawing at her shaky bravado.

"According to Harrison's appointment book, you were scheduled to have dinner with him at seven o'clock the evening he was murdered."

It wasn't a question. He already knew the answer. So did the detectives who'd interrogated her on two different occasions. But he wanted to analyze her answer. She could see it in his overconfident expression. He checked his facts carefully, made his own measured evaluations. He would never take anyone else's word for anything.

Judging by the set of his broad shoulders and the intensity of his gaze, he already knew more about her than she wanted him to know. Far more than the other detectives had bothered to glean. He'd read her file, made calls, had her pegged as a suspect. Had known exactly who she was when he approached her in the church. Dammit, she didn't need this right now. Didn't want to go through this kind of life-shattering, emotion-twisting investigation again.

Why had she lost control during the service? She'd never convince anyone that it had nothing to do with Ned's death and everything to do with fear for herself. Selfish she knew, but the truth. It must have looked as if she'd been overcome by grief—or guilt. And the tape. Hell. What if he'd found the tape? The other two men hadn't mentioned it. Maybe Ned had thrown it away or locked it up somewhere.

"Miss Young?" he prodded.

"That's right," she heard herself say, her voice sounding as if it came from someone else. "But Ned—Dr. Harrison—never showed up at the restaurant."

MacBride slipped his hands into his trouser pockets and inclined his head, his relentless gaze never deviating from hers. "The maître d' confirmed that Harrison never arrived. Where did you go when you left around eight?"

Breathe, she instructed. *In and out.* "Like I told the other gentlemen," she explained, her impatience showing a little, "I went home." She tried not to sound curt, but it was hard not to. She hadn't done anything wrong and she hated being made to feel as if she had. How could this man or anyone else see her as a suspect? Just because of a broken dinner date she hadn't even wanted to accept? Ned, the bastard, had screwed her one last time before getting his, hadn't he?

No, she decided on second thought, that wasn't it. MacBride was basing his theory on her past. *You could never outrun it,* she reminded herself in a moment of inner clarity. *The past always caught up to you.*

He took a step closer. She drew back a step. "Can anyone vouch for your whereabouts?" His tone was calm, but she could feel the fierce determination beneath the innocuous words. "It would be very beneficial if someone could corroborate your statement."

"What's up, Elizabeth?" Boomer planted his long lanky form right between them. She hadn't even heard him climb down from the ladder.

"Who's the suit?" He glowered at MacBride with obvious disdain.

"It's all right, Boomer," she said quickly in hopes of heading off any trouble for the kid. He was loyal to a fault, always her protector, especially when they worked in rougher neighborhoods, which she'd had to do a lot of in the first few months of getting her business off the ground. But he needed to stand clear of this one. "Agent MacBride is with the FBI. He has some questions about Dr. Harrison's death."

Boomer didn't look impressed. He folded his skinny arms over his chest and continued to blatantly size up the agent. "Just let me know if he gives you any trouble. He don't look too friendly to me." He gave their guest one final glare before stalking back to his work.

Elizabeth almost sagged with relief. Things were bad enough without Boomer getting involved. From the unyielding expression on MacBride's face, she was pretty sure he felt nothing that even remotely resembled relief. Indifference or disapproval quite possibly, but definitely not relief.

"The answer to your question is no," she said pointedly. "I don't have anyone who can verify my whereabouts. I'm sure that was in the detectives' report. My landlady was out that night."

Of course he had known that, but rather than comment, he jerked his dark head in Boomer's direction. "Do you know your assistant has a record a mile long?"

Oh, yes. Condescension, as well as disapproval. He not only knew it all, he was above it all. A blast of indignation melted some of the ice paralyzing her from the inside out. "I'm not as naive as you apparently think, Agent MacBride," she replied sharply, her voice too low for Boomer to hear. "I did a thorough background check before I hired him."

One dark eyebrow climbed upward a notch. "You don't mind that he's had a half-dozen drug charges, including possession with intent to sell? Or that he's done time in one of our less-friendly prison facilities?"

Rather than bank her temper, she allowed it to shore up her courage. "Everyone deserves a second chance."

He nodded knowingly, something new, primal, in his eyes. "Ah, yes. How could I have forgotten? You would be a heavy supporter of second chances, wouldn't you?"

Elizabeth looked at him then, really looked at him. She no longer saw the cocky, handsome man in the thousand-dollar suit, who was perfect from the thick black hair he wore in that short, spiky style that drove women crazy all the way down to the expensive leather shoes. What she saw, instead, was a man who'd had his whole life handed to him on a silver platter. Money, the best schools, probably had never worked a day in his life until he'd signed on with the Bureau. And now he shone like a new penny, chasing bad guys and making the world a safer place. A hero...who didn't know the first thing about what it was like to be down on his luck.

Guys like him didn't need second chances. His world was perfect. He probably worked murder cases just to keep life interesting.

"I'm not ashamed of my past, Agent MacBride," she informed him hotly. "I did what I had to do."

"I see."

She didn't miss the effort it took for him to keep a patronizing smile off his face. "Sure you do." He had no idea what her life had been like, and he sure as hell didn't know how she felt. "How could you possibly have a clue?"

"Of course the drugs weren't really *yours*," he offered, a bitter edge to his words that was impossible to miss. "But then, are they ever when an addict gets caught?" He smiled then, and it wasn't pleasant. "And taking a butcher knife to your brother-in-law was certainly a clear case of self-defense. Am I right, Miss Young?"

A new burst of fury flamed inside her. She would not justify herself to him. She'd done this song and dance twice already. He shouldn't even be here. He knew *nothing* about her. "Golly, mister," she tossed back. "You must be psychic. How else could you read my mind so well? Or maybe you've got a crystal ball in your pocket."

He leaned toward her, the briefest flicker of anger in his eyes before he reined it in. The man was a master at concealing his emotions and thoughts. He'd likely spent a lifetime building that level of control.

"Did Harrison do something that made you take that dagger to him?" he murmured harshly, his breath hot on her face. "Were you about to be dumped *again?*"

Maybe he wasn't so good at restraining his emotions. He was angry—she didn't have to see it in his eyes because she heard it in his voice. She resisted the urge to flee and held her ground. "I told you I went home when he didn't show," she repeated, emphasizing each word and praying he wouldn't see the lie in her eyes. Before good sense stopped her, she added, "And, for your information, I stopped seeing him weeks ago."

He leaned closer still. Her breath caught. His nostrils flared, a feral gleam in his eyes. "As a patient or as a lover?"

She shivered in response to his cold, lethal tone. How could he know that unless he'd seen the tape? Her heart banged painfully against her sternum. No one knew. No one but Gloria, and she would never tell. Elizabeth grabbed back control. Maybe he was guessing. "We weren't—" She started to deny the notion, but he cut her off with a slow shake of his head.

"Don't lie to me, Elizabeth," he warned, the use

of her first name only adding to the unbearable tension. "I saw the videotape."

She stumbled back a couple of steps, barely missing her freshly painted wall in her effort to get away from those words—the very words she hadn't wanted to hear. Oh, God. Ned had promised to give her the tape. That night. He was going to give it to her at dinner. He'd said he was sorry. He hadn't meant to hurt her—he'd really liked her. He'd sworn that he'd make it up to her. He'd lied. He'd refused to give her the tape, and then...

She blinked back the tears brimming. She'd believed him one last time and he'd lied to her. And now this man knew. He'd seen her...

As if he actually could read her mind, that relentless gaze traveled slowly down her body, and in spite of everything, heat kindled in its wake. Damn her traitorous body! Her pulse reacted as he retraced his path, then looked directly into her eyes once more. "You can't hide from me, Elizabeth. I'm very good at what I do. You don't want me for an enemy."

"I'd like you to leave now, Agent MacBride," she told him, her voice oddly devoid of emotion and far steadier than she'd believed possible. She had to think. Had to talk to Gloria. Probably needed a lawyer.

"All right. Have it your way." He reached into his pocket.

She gasped.

A grin tugged at one corner of his mouth. "Don't worry, Elizabeth. I've never shot a suspect who didn't shoot at me first."

The urge to slap that smug expression from his face

was almost more than she could restrain. He handed her a business card. "I'll see you in my office at five. Today. Don't be late."

Before she could argue, he turned and strode away. She watched, stunned, until he'd left the loft, then she stared down at the card. Her hand trembled.

This couldn't be happening. Not again.

Her heart thundered violently in her chest, making it ache.

Dizziness swamped her. Her body flooded with adrenaline.

She couldn't breathe. Oh, God. A panic attack.

The trembling that had started in her hands quaked through her suddenly unsteady legs. She closed her eyes, took a long, deep breath and let it out to the count of ten, then repeated it.

This was supposed to be behind her. She hadn't lost control over a threatening panic attack since... since her third session with Ned. At least he'd been good for something.

Then he'd seduced her. Elizabeth forced her eyes open and banished those painful memories. She had to move, had to walk off this excess adrenaline.

Back and forth. Back and forth. From one end of the loft to the other. Boomer probably thought she'd lost her mind, but he didn't say anything—just did his job. *Breathe. In...hold...out. Again.*

Ned had taken advantage of her, used her. And now he was dead. She couldn't change that. The trouble was, it looked as if he was taking her down with him. Why hadn't she stayed until he'd given her the tape? She should have done whatever he asked, anything for the tape. But no, she'd stormed off, knowing she'd have no choice but to go crawling back when he called again. She'd been angry. She'd had no way of knowing she'd never see him alive again.

MAC HESITATED a moment after pulling back out onto the empty street. His gaze drifted up to the fourth floor where he'd left Elizabeth. He pounded the steering wheel with the heel of his hand. He'd done a bang-up job of recovering the ground the detectives had lost. He called himself every kind of fool. Cool, he was supposed to have played it cool. Give her space, let her tell her story. Gently guide her.

Dammit.

If he could have kicked himself in the ass, he would have. His body hummed with adrenaline. He gritted his teeth and denied the other sensation the sparring had elicited. It was that very reaction that had made him push harder than he'd intended, to go over the line. He'd shaken her but good. The hell of it was, he was just as rattled as she was.

Perfect. Just perfect.

He blew out a disgusted breath.

By five o'clock when she arrived at his office, and she would come, she would most likely have an attorney with her, and then he'd get nowhere even faster. He'd have to try to regain some of the ground he'd lost, attorney present or not.

Mac glanced in the direction of a dark sedan parked on the opposite side of the street in a neighboring alley. But just in case she decided to cut her losses and make a run for it, someone would be watching.

His cell phone rang at the same time that a horn blared behind him. Mac pressed the accelerator and started forward while fishing in his coat pocket for his phone. He flipped it open.

"MacBride."

"You're going to love this."

It was Driver. "What've you got?"

"We traced the dagger to an antique shop over on West Fifty-fifth."

"Yeah." Mac knew there was more. He could hear it in his partner's voice. Anticipation spiked.

"It was purchased as a gift for Harrison," Driver told him, dragging out the moment, "by a Miss Elizabeth Young."

Some of Mac's tension eased instantly at the news that at least one loose end was tied up. "Good work." He glanced at his watch and ignored an uncharacteristic twinge of regret that followed directly on the heels of the relief. She'd already lied to him, so he shouldn't be surprised by this latest development. But he was. She'd gotten to him on some level. He didn't like it. Not in the least. "See you in thirty," he told his partner.

Mac closed the phone and dropped it back into his pocket. A satisfied smile slid across his face. This would definitely work to his advantage. He couldn't wait to see how Elizabeth planned to talk her way out of this one. He shook his head as he thought of the pretty lady who could win herself an Oscar for her portrayal of innocence and suffering. She would use the hardships of her past as a smoke screen. But she hadn't fooled him at all. Well, maybe he'd been thrown off balance for a moment or two, he admitted.

Not now, though. Now he was focused and fully back on track. She wouldn't be able to tap-dance her way out of this one.

"Gotcha," he muttered.

Chapter Three

Elizabeth waited impatiently in Chico's Cantina. One-fifteen. Gloria was late. She let go an unsteady breath and fiddled with the straw in her cola. She had to get hold of herself. She couldn't let MacBride get to her this way. He'd been worse than those two detectives put together. Something was different about him. More intimidating. A subtle ruthlessness that frightened her. He wouldn't give up until he knew everything.

She hadn't done anything wrong. Sure, there'd been moments when Ned's actions had made her want to kill him, but she hadn't. Thinking about it wasn't against the law. Likely dozens of women, especially former patients, had probably thought about it more than once.

Maybe one of them had actually done it.

Elizabeth went rigid. Could one of the women who'd come to his funeral have been his killer? Was that why MacBride was there?

He suspected *her.* That was why he'd been there. Something frigid seeped into her bones. He'd discovered the dinner date and the videotape of her and Ned together, and he'd put it all together and come up with murder. She sipped her cola to wet her desperately dry throat. How long would it be before he found out about the two big arguments they'd had? Very public arguments in the lobby of Ned's office building—and at that party. She'd slapped him during the second one. He'd grabbed her by the shoulders and shaken her and she'd slapped him again.

And she'd…God, she'd told him he'd be sorry. Had anyone heard her say it? It had been a threat, there was no way to interpret the words any other way, but she hadn't really meant it. Everyone said things like that in the heat of anger. She wouldn't be the first or the last—except maybe where Ned Harrison was concerned.

Had she been the last person to threaten him out loud? In front of dozens of witnesses?

But she hadn't killed him.

Dammit.

Elizabeth pressed a hand to her lips and closed her eyes long enough to pull herself together. The evidence would be stacked against her. She was an outsider. Despite having lived here almost two years, she was still an outsider. It would be much easier and certainly less messy to pin the rap on her. She could barely afford her rent at the moment. A high-dollar attorney was out of the question. And if she was stuck in a jail cell, she'd lose her contract on the rest of the lofts and any prospects of future income.

She had no family who could help. Her sister, Peg, would sympathize, but it was all she could do to keep a roof over her three kids' heads. Too bad that scumbag she'd been married to hadn't had any life insur-

ance. Then when he'd careened off a bridge and into
a river while intoxicated, at least he would have been
worth something. Instead, her sister'd had a tough
time scraping together the money to bury the worth-
less bastard.

Elizabeth swiped her eyes and forced herself to
think calmly. She wasn't guilty. Surely the real murderer had left some sort of evidence. She knew Ned
had been with someone else. It was why he hadn't
shown up at the restaurant for their dinner date. Had
that woman returned later and killed him, or was it
someone else entirely? Maybe she'd even been hiding
in the apartment while Elizabeth was there. There was
no way to know. She'd thought he was alone when
she confronted him. But someone had definitely been
there shortly before her abrupt arrival. She'd seen the
tousled sheets, smelled the musky scent of sex.

The son of a bitch.

She drew in a deep breath and again focused on
calming her racing heart and jangled nerves. When
she'd left Ned Harrison he had been very much alive.
But MacBride would never believe that. If she admitted that she'd gone to his apartment, he would use
it against her. Besides, she was pretty sure no one had
seen her. Why give the authorities any more ammu-
nition than necessary? She'd be a fool not to recognize that she was at the top of the suspect list already.

She couldn't tell MacBride anything and risk being
charged with Ned's murder. The truth didn't always
set you free. Elizabeth knew that better than anyone.

The bell above the door jingled, drawing her back
to the here and now. Gloria stood just inside the entrance and scanned the small cantina. Elizabeth waved

and her friend rushed over, a briefcase-size purse hanging on one shoulder, a folded newspaper tucked under the opposite arm.

"Sorry I'm late." She dropped into the seat across from Elizabeth. "Last-minute BS on a conference call that shouldn't have lasted more than five minutes." She beamed a smile and lifted one eyebrow triumphantly. "But I saved the account. Everyone, including Murphy, was suitably impressed."

Murphy was Gloria's boss. She continually surprised the man. He knew how good she was and how hard she worked; she'd worked for him for three years now. But somehow she always managed to amaze even him with one more unexpected coup. Gloria insisted it was the luck of the Irish. But Elizabeth knew differently. Her friend was smart and relentless, and had a sixth sense about market maneuvers.

Wriggling out of her elegant suit jacket, Gloria called out her drink order to the passing waitress.

Elizabeth smiled for the first time that day. One of the things she liked most about Chico's was that everyone was treated the same. It didn't matter if you arrived wearing a power suit or baggy denim overalls. People from all walks of life frequented the place. Elizabeth could look around now and point out the stock traders like her friend, the computer geeks, the starving artists and the electricians and plumbers who were much like herself. No one, particularly the cantina staff, seemed to pay any attention to the differences.

"Sounds like your day was better than mine," Elizabeth commented thinly, thoughts of MacBride's visit drawing the black clouds back over her head.

Gloria studied her closely as the waitress plunked her diet soda before her. "What happened?"

Elizabeth clutched her hands together in her lap and swore she would not get emotional. She had to stay calm. "An FBI agent paid me a visit today."

Surprise claimed her friend's features. "An *FBI* agent?"

Elizabeth nodded. "You remember after the funeral yesterday I told you about the good-looking guy who'd been so nice to me? You know, he gave me his handkerchief, like guys in the old movies we watch?"

A predatory gleam flashed in Gloria's eyes. "Oh, yeah. You said he was really something."

Elizabeth nodded grimly. "He is. He's an FBI agent and he was there watching me."

Disbelief registered. "He told you that?"

Elizabeth shrugged. "In a roundabout way."

Gloria shook her head. "This is insane. How could they suspect you?"

Elizabeth stared at the red-and-white checked tablecloth. God, she didn't want to have to tell Gloria this. The subject was still a little tender between them. But she lifted her gaze back to her friend's and confessed, "He asked me to have dinner with him…the night of his murder."

A beat of silence echoed, blocking out all other sound.

"Ned asked you to have dinner with him?" The color of excitement that had tinged Gloria's cheeks only moments ago faded. "You didn't agree. Not after…"

Her words trailed off. She didn't have to say the rest.

Elizabeth knew.

Dammit, she knew.

She blinked back the tears she'd sworn she wouldn't allow to fall. "He said he'd give me the tape."

"The tape?" A stillness settled over Gloria.

Elizabeth nodded. "He promised he would give it to me if I'd have dinner with him." There was no need to tell her the rest. Ned had hurt them both badly enough. She wasn't about to add insult to injury by telling Gloria that he'd gone on and on about how much he cared for Elizabeth. It had been a lie, anyway.

A line of confusion or maybe irritation creased Gloria's usually smooth brow. "And you believed him?"

"I was afraid," she said, her voice trembling. "I didn't know what he'd do with it if I didn't take it when he offered. There's no telling what he might have done if—"

"You're not the only woman he taped," Gloria said bluntly, her voice painfully hollow as all emotion except one—desperation—visibly drained out of her. "He probably had one on all of us."

"Maybe he destroyed the others," Elizabeth hurried to assure her, but they both knew that wasn't likely.

Gloria snorted a dry laugh as she shook her head, her gaze distant, no longer focused on Elizabeth. "That lowlife bastard. I should have known he couldn't be trusted."

Elizabeth frowned. "How could you have known?"

Gloria gave a start, as if she'd forgotten where she was. She seemed suddenly nervous. "No, no. I...I meant that neither of us should be surprised by anything the cops uncover about him."

"That's true," Elizabeth agreed slowly. She didn't have time to analyze Gloria's sudden edginess before they were interrupted.

"You ladies ready to order now?" the college-age, scantily clad waitress asked as she paused at their table. Actually, *paused* wasn't an adequate description. Her feet were planted firmly on the floor next to their table, but her hips never stopped swaying, the pencil in her hand poised above her pad.

Gloria ordered her usual salad with dressing on the side. Elizabeth ordered the same, since she wasn't very hungry, anyway. When the waitress sashayed off, Gloria, appearing to relax a bit, propped her elbows on the table and focused on Elizabeth.

"All right, so tell me what the fed wanted."

Elizabeth wrapped her arms around herself, feeling cold and far too much like the way she had that day eight years ago when she'd been in a too-similar situation. "That's easy. He wants to prove that I killed Ned."

"But you didn't kill Ned," Gloria countered, the edge back in her voice. "He can't pin anything on you without evidence."

"He knows we were supposed to have dinner together that night." Elizabeth resisted the urge to look away. This was Gloria. Her best friend in the whole world, no matter what had gone down between them where Ned was concerned, Elizabeth could trust Gloria.

"Did you have dinner together?" she asked pointedly, her eyes giving evidence of the hurt hovering just beneath her strained composure.

"I went. For the tape," Elizabeth added emphatically. "He didn't show. I waited about an hour and then I left."

"Someone at the restaurant saw you, I presume."

Elizabeth nodded. She sat up straighter, feeling oddly ill at ease with the tone of Gloria's voice. What was the deal here? Was Gloria upset about Ned's calling her? Elizabeth had thought they were past all this. The cards had been laid out on the table. Both of them had been taken in by the man. After much shouting and more tears, they'd reached an understanding... and put it behind them.

Until now.

Damn him. If Ned had to die, why didn't he just do it the old-fashioned way? A simple heart attack or massive stroke. Or, hell, even a taxi accident. Lord knew, the cabdrivers in this city were more than a little reckless.

"You told the fed that he didn't show and that you went home, right?"

"Yes, but I don't think he believed me."

A new wariness slipped into Gloria's surprisingly unsympathetic expression. "Why wouldn't he believe you?"

Elizabeth's heart threatened to burst from her chest. She wet her lips and forced out the words she didn't want to say. "Because I lied."

Gloria huffed a sound of disbelief. "Damn it, Elizabeth, why did you do that?"

"I was angry, okay?" she tossed back. The people at the next table turned and stared. She took a breath and ordered herself to be calm once more, then began again, quietly, for Gloria's ears only. "I wanted him to know that he should never call me again. I was tired of him hurting us. So I went to his apartment. I banged on the door until he answered." She shook her head. "He was pulling his clothes on, insisting he was running late." She clenched her jaw to slow the emotions mounting all over again. "He was so apologetic. But I knew he was lying."

"What'd you do?"

"I stormed into the apartment, straight to the bedroom. The sheets were tousled." Her gaze locked with Gloria's. "He'd called and pleaded with me to meet him for dinner, then kept me waiting an entire hour while he had a romp in the sack with someone else."

Gloria closed her eyes, shuddered visibly. "Bastard," she hissed. "I'm glad he's dead."

Elizabeth scrubbed her hands over her face. "We argued. I told him never to call me again. And then I demanded the tape." She made a sound, something along the lines of a laugh, but pathetically lacking in humor. "He just laughed at me. He..." She chewed her lower lip to stem the tears threatening. "He was going to use it to blackmail me. He told me I'd get it when he was through with me." She shrugged, still scarcely believing her own stupidity. "I couldn't believe it."

Gloria's breathing had grown as rapid and shallow as Elizabeth's. "Tell me exactly what you did then."

"I slapped him and he...he tried to..." She frowned, trying to remember the exact sequence of events. "He grabbed my arm and I fought to get away. Then I ran out."

"Okay," Gloria said, visibly grappling for her own composure. "You listen to me, Elizabeth. You do exactly what I say. Do you hear me?"

She nodded.

Gloria released a shaky breath. "You stick to your original story. He didn't show, you went home. Don't tell the cops anything else. This is a high-profile case. They'll want to solve it as soon as possible. Pinning the rap on you would be the fastest route." She reached across the table and placed a reassuring hand over Elizabeth's. "What about the tape?"

God, she could just die. "That's the worst part. He wouldn't give it to me...and the cops found it. That FBI agent, MacBride, told me he'd viewed it."

"Damn."

"My sentiments exactly." Elizabeth stared down at their hands. What a mess. She might as well face it. She was doomed.

"Look," Gloria said, drawing Elizabeth's gaze back to hers. "You didn't kill him. They can't prove you did. Having sex with a man doesn't make you guilty of murder."

Elizabeth smiled. Her friend was right. Regardless of how it looked, she was innocent. "True," she agreed. She studied Gloria for a long moment, trying to see what it was that nagged at her. She supposed her friend was just afraid for her...or angry that Ned had once more hurt her. "I really didn't kill him, you know."

Gloria squeezed her hand. "I know you didn't. The cops are just looking for an easy out. If they had any real evidence, they'd arrest you."

Been there, done that, bought the T-shirt, Elizabeth thought grimly. "He brought up Billy and the drug charge." Gloria knew the whole sordid story about Billy, the brother-in-law from hell, and the time Elizabeth had claimed her sister's drug stash to save her from a beating. Elizabeth had never even tried drugs, but she had a possession charge on her record because she'd gone the distance for her only sibling.

"Well," Gloria said after a few seconds of consideration. "That still doesn't make you a murderer."

Elizabeth wrapped her arms around herself again, feeling cold. "No, but it puts me at the top of the suspect list."

Gloria frowned suddenly, as if she'd just remembered something important. "You said this MacBride guy is from the FBI?"

Elizabeth nodded.

"Why would the FBI investigate a simple homicide case?"

Not sure she could answer that one, Elizabeth could only speculate. "They must think his murder is connected to others or—" she spread her hands "—to some other criminal activity where the feds have jurisdiction."

"Or maybe we've just seen too many TV dramas," Gloria teased, acting more like her old self now. "Maybe the cops asked for their help since it's such a high-profile case. The media will be all over every aspect of the investigation.''

''That could be, I suppose.'' Another thought occurred to Elizabeth. She shook her head in frustration. ''It'd be just my luck that they think I'm some sort of serial killer.''

Gloria started to smile, then gasped and pressed her hand to her chest. ''Speaking of murder, I almost forgot.'' She quickly retrieved and opened the newspaper she'd tossed on the bench seat next to her. ''Look at this.''

She pointed to a headline that read *Fashion Designer Found Murdered.* Elizabeth skimmed the brief article. The details were gruesome.

''Remember her?''

Elizabeth glanced from the unnerving article to her friend. ''Should I?''

''Look at the picture.'' She tapped the photo to the left of the article.

Recognition dawned. The long-legged, raven-haired beauty at the funeral. The one with the John Lennon look-alike for an escort. ''Oh, my God.'' She looked up at Gloria. ''She sat a couple rows in front of us at the funeral.''

Gloria nodded. ''The scuttlebutt is that someone in the industry did in the hottest new competition.''

''My God,'' Elizabeth repeated. She stared at the article again. Who gave the press permission to print such grim information? Weren't these sorts of details supposed to be kept hush-hush? The woman's throat had been slashed. ''What kind of person could do that to another human being?''

''Yeah, really.'' Gloria tapped the newspaper.

"That's the murder your FBI agent should be investigating. Not wasting time on some jerk who only got what he deserved."

Elizabeth refolded the paper so she wouldn't have to look at the woman's picture. It was definitely too much right before lunch. "I'll be sure to tell him that at our five-o'clock meeting."

Gloria tensed. "You have to talk to him again today?"

Elizabeth nodded. "At 26 Federal Plaza." Seeing Gloria's gaping expression, she added, "I think he's trying to intimidate me into a confession."

"Don't tell him anything he doesn't need to know," Gloria warned again. "In fact, I'll talk to a friend of mine about a good attorney for you, if you'd like."

A worried sigh escaped Elizabeth. "I hope it doesn't come to that."

When she spoke, Gloria sounded a lot more confident than Elizabeth felt. "I don't think it will. But it would be nice to have the right name to toss around. It might even get the feds off your back."

"Good idea."

The waitress zipped by, pausing only long enough to deposit their salads and ask if they needed anything else, to which they both replied no.

Elizabeth dribbled ranch dressing over her salad, noting that Gloria did not. Her friend was extremely calorie-conscious. Elizabeth supposed it paid to be when you spent twelve hours a day behind a desk. Gloria had made the comment on several occasions that the asses of her female co-workers got wider every day. Gloria had no intention of following that trend. Elizabeth supposed the one good thing about her line of work was that she got plenty of exercise.

She smacked her forehead with the heel of her hand. She'd almost forgotten again. "How's your niece?"

Gloria appeared taken aback by the question. "She's fine. Why do you ask?"

"You mentioned she was having some trouble a couple of months ago, and I keep forgetting to ask how she's doing," Elizabeth explained. Gloria seemed quite put off, which puzzled Elizabeth. The two of them usually talked about everything. Her niece, apparently, was as touchy a subject as Ned.

"You know how it is when you're eighteen and a freshman in college," Gloria said dismissively. "You think nobody knows anything but you. Since her father's death last year, she's sort of withdrawn from everyone, especially her mother. It hasn't been easy, but she's managing."

Elizabeth remembered that terrible night Gloria had called. Her brother-in-law, an NYPD detective, had been killed in the line of duty. His wife and daughter were devastated. Not long after that, Elizabeth's father had died. God, that had been a lousy month.

"I'm glad she's doing better," Elizabeth said, feeling guilty for bringing up the subject, yet knowing she'd feel guilty if she hadn't. "It's tough to lose your father, especially at that age." At any age, Elizabeth thought. She still missed hers. They'd been so close.

Gloria picked at her salad. "She's all my sister has left." Her tone had turned somber. "We have to protect her at all costs."

Elizabeth paused, a forkful of salad halfway to her mouth. Her friend's swift mood changes were immensely disturbing. They were so unlike Gloria. "Of course you have to protect her," Elizabeth agreed gently. "Let me know if there's anything I can do to help."

Gloria smiled, but the expression didn't reach her eyes. "Just keep me up-to-date on what's going on with your fed." Her faint smile widened to a genuine grin. "And remember, if things get too hairy, you can always seduce him."

Elizabeth almost choked on a cherry tomato. "Yeah, right," she muttered when she'd stopped coughing. "I don't think MacBride is seducible." She remembered vividly his steely gaze and precisely controlled responses. He wasn't the kind of man a simple girl like her could get to…even if she wanted to.

"Oh, honey, that's the country girl in you talking," Gloria scolded, the words and the tone so very Gloria. "They're *all* seducible. Trust me."

"I'll bear that in mind," Elizabeth replied. She refused to analyze the warm glow that accompanied the ridiculous suggestion. Gloria had no business putting ideas like that in her head. That was the last thing Elizabeth needed. An affair with another man she couldn't trust. Especially considering this one suspected her of murder.

And had seen her naked having sex with another man.

Elizabeth blushed to the roots of her hair. How would she ever face MacBride this afternoon? She had to find a way to keep him from getting to her….

THE NEWSPAPER didn't do our work justice.

We will have to leave a stronger impression next time.

One pretty bitch down.

One by one we will make them pay.

All of them.

We won't rest until it's done.

Chapter Four

"I'll have to see your ID, sir," the guard posted in the entry hall said as Mac stepped off the elevator.

It wasn't as if he hadn't flashed his ID in the lobby before he boarded the only elevator in the building that went all the way to the top floor. Rather than informing the rookie of that, Mac fished in his pocket for his badge and showed it again.

The youthful cop, whose badge read Ledbetter, flushed. "Sorry, sir, but a reporter managed to get inside last night before the homicide detectives got here and we've all been instructed to double-check IDs."

"No problem," Mac muttered as he ducked beneath the police tape that marked the penthouse apartment off-limits to anyone other that authorized NYPD personnel. He hadn't needed Officer Ledbetter to tell him that the perimeter had been breached sometime shortly after the discovery of the body. The morning's headlines had screamed that loud and clear. It only made bad matters worse that the breach had occurred before the arrival of the crime-scene techs. No telling what the eager reporter had contaminated in his haste to get the story.

Mac paused long enough in the doorway to slip on latex gloves and paper shoe covers. Every detective and agent was taught to carry extras just in case. One never knew when they'd be needed. As he prepped for entering the crime scene, Mac noted that the handles of the elegant double doors that separated the posh Upper Eastside penthouse from the entry hall were sooty with fingerprint powder.

The whish-whish of someone else's paper shoe covers echoed from down the hall. Mac surveyed his surroundings as he made his way in the direction of the sound. A grand dining room and great room flanked the hall on either side a few feet beyond the main doors. A small powder room and guest bedroom lay on the right beyond that, then the hall took a slight turn to the left and opened up into an extravagantly appointed sitting area that bordered a massive master suite.

This was where the murder had taken place.

Mac paused, his gaze landing on the spray of blood fanned over the wall above the headboard. No matter how many crime scenes he'd examined in his ten-year career, the initial sight of spilled blood always rattled him.

The victim would already be in the capable hands of the medical examiner, but telltale signs of the final battle for life she'd waged were clear to all who entered.

Through the floor-to-ceiling windows, which displayed a magnificent Manhattan view, brilliant sunlight poured into the room, gleaming on the plush, sand-colored carpet. Despite the two techs working vigorously, collecting everything from carpet fibers to dust on the glittering chandelier, the room felt vast and empty. The stark white walls framing the room were marred only by the blood that trickled down like garish streamers toward the rumpled bed.

Judging by the spray of blood above the bed, Mac surmised that the victim had been dragged there for the final affront. The tousled condition of the turned-down covers indicated that she'd likely been in bed before or after the intruder arrived. He thought about the undamaged doors, handles and lock assembly he'd viewed while slipping on his gloves and shoe covers, and decided that *intruder* wasn't the right word. Whoever had done this had been allowed in by the victim. Since the front doors were the only means of entry and windows were not likely since they were on the thirtieth floor, he had to assume that the victim knew her killer.

''Agent MacBride?''

Mac turned toward the familiar voice coming from the doorway behind him and bit back a curse. Detective Brannigan. The last person he wanted to see. He hoped like hell the guy wasn't the lead on this investigation, because he was the one who'd bungled the Harrison investigation before it had hardly started.

''Officer Ledbetter told me you were here,'' Brannigan said as he moved into the room. ''I'm the lead on this investigation. What interest do you have in this case?''

Perfect.

Brannigan resented like hell that the Harrison case

had been taken from him, he wasn't going to be happy about Mac's presence here, period.

"Vanessa Bumbalough was one of Harrison's patients. She also attended his funeral." Mac surveyed the enormous room once more, noticing that the techs had paused in their work to listen, apparently, to the exchange.

"That's correct," Brannigan said. The fury that burned in his eyes belied his even tone. "But I can't see how that ties into her murder."

Mac thought about the condition of the room. The overturned bedside table, the twisted bedcovers, the blood. Then he considered the rest of the house—immaculate, every little thing in place. In the lull the techs turned their attention back to their task of collecting any evidence they'd missed on their first sweep, which would have taken place late last night shortly after the discovery of the body.

"Were there any witnesses?" Mac asked rather than responding to Brannigan's comment regarding the victim's connection with Harrison.

The middle-aged detective shook his head, sending his triple chin into a sluggish side-to-side motion. "No one saw or heard anything. The doorman insists that no one other than residents entered the building yesterday. He checked the log."

"I assume there was more than one doorman during the twenty-four hours prior to the body's discovery."

Brannigan shoved his hands into his trouser pockets. "Yeah, there were four and we interviewed all of 'em. Doormen and anyone else who worked on the premises in the last forty-eight hours."

"The other residents?" Mac knew he was pushing his luck now. Brannigan was more than a little ticked off.

"We're working on that right now. It takes time to cover this many apartments."

"Of course."

"We're also talking to the people she worked with," Brannigan went on as if he felt the need to prove himself. "With all the hoopla surrounding her splash onto the fashion scene, it could have been a competitor."

Mac looked around the room again. "Maybe."

In a tone just shy of seething, Brannigan said, "And maybe it was a jealous lover. We're still looking for the guy who accompanied her to Harrison's funeral. From what we've learned, she recently dumped her longtime lover for him. We haven't located the jilted lover, either, but we will."

Mac nodded, affirming the detective's conclusions. "That would be the most logical avenue to follow."

Brannigan shifted his considerable bulk from one foot to the other. "I suppose you want details," he said irritably.

Mac lifted a skeptical eyebrow. "Are there any that weren't in the newspaper this morning?"

Brannigan's retort didn't bear repeating and once more snagged the attention of everyone in the room. He glared at the techs, who immediately returned to the task at hand. "We got that little mystery solved. One of our new guys has a cousin who's a reporter. That won't happen again."

Vanessa Bumbalough had been found in a skimpy

negligee, tied to her bed and her throat slashed. All that information had been in the paper.

"There was one thing," Brannigan said after a moment.

Mac waited, trying not to let his impatience show. Brannigan would give him the details in his own time. There was no telling when he'd see the ME's report. Payback for stealing the Harrison case. But Mac did what he had to do.

"The reporter didn't get a chance to see this," Brannigan explained smugly, "before he was ousted."

"What would 'this' be?" Mac asked when the detective hesitated.

"The victim had also been gagged—with a pair of panties."

Mac tensed, the ME's report on Harrison slamming into his brain, rocketing him into a higher state of alert. Harrison had had a pair of panties shoved into his mouth to silence him.

"Not the fancy, sexy kind, either, mind you," Brannigan added. He rocked back on his heels, seemingly tickled to know something Mac didn't. "They were the cheap nylon kind. The killer shoved them so far back in her throat that she'd surely have choked to death even if he hadn't slit her throat."

Mac absorbed that information, knowing full well that Brannigan had already made the connection with Harrison. "What makes you think the killer is male?" There was more. Mac could feel it. Brannigan's whole demeanor was far too cocky.

The portly detective shrugged nonchalantly. "Well, the ME did mention that he thought the victim had been sexually assaulted. We won't know the full details until we see the preliminary report, of course, but that was his initial conclusion.''

When Mac had gleaned all he could and had tolerated all of Brannigan's gloating he could stomach, he made his way back to the elevator and down to the lobby. He glanced at his watch as he settled behind the wheel of his sedan. He still had time to drop by the morgue and take a look at the body before he returned to his office and prepared for his meeting with Elizabeth Young. He needed to know what kind of struggle the victim had put up. If, as Brannigan suggested, she had been sexually assaulted, he wanted to know details. Had she first submitted, then changed her mind? Or was the act a flat-out rape from the get-go? If she hadn't resisted, that would lend credence to the idea that she knew her attacker.

One thing was certain, if Miss Bumbalough's killer was male and there was a connection to Harrison's murder, then that sure as hell let Elizabeth Young off the hook.

Mac eased his sedan into the flow of traffic and thought about that for a moment. Maybe it wouldn't let her off the hook. Maybe she and the killer were a team. Of course, connecting Harrison's murder with this one, even though the victim was one of his patients and had attended his funeral, was a stretch even with the cheap panties.

It could be coincidence. But Mac's instincts were humming. He had a feeling that, somehow, the two were connected. He mentally ran through the similarities. The victims had been restrained, both had been gagged with cheap panties, and now there was the possibility that both had participated in sexual activity prior to death.

Coincidences? Maybe.

Too soon to tell. But he would find out. Because whether Brannigan liked it or not, Mac wouldn't let it go until he knew for certain the two cases weren't connected.

ELIZABETH STOOD outside the building at 26 Federal Plaza and took a deep, bolstering breath. She had to do this. Had to be calm and collected, as well as strong. She'd left work early this afternoon and stopped at home long enough to change into the one and only suit she owned. A black broomstick skirt and matching single-breasted jacket. It was the only remaining ensemble from her days with Brian and the firm. Everything else she'd burned in a bonfire one night after too much wine with Gloria. She'd learned very quickly that even in a not-so-upscale neighborhood people called the police when they saw suspicious activity.

She'd almost gotten arrested for the act of liberation. Ultimately the cop had felt sorry for her since she'd just been dumped and lost her job on the same day. So he'd ushered her and Gloria back into her apartment and made them swear they would sleep it off before undertaking any other activities. The next morning she'd awakened with the kind of headache one got from drinking cheap wine and with a closet that was considerably barer. She suddenly wished she could go back to that night, or at least the morning after. That was the morning she'd made the decision to go see the shrink Gloria had recommended for the panic attacks she'd suffered with for nearly a year. Which led her to this place.

Elizabeth braced herself for the worst and entered the intimidating building.

After consulting a directory she crossed the cavernous lobby and hesitated at the turnstiles that blocked the elevators which would take her to the twenty-seventh floor.

"I'll need your name and a picture ID, ma'am," the guard informed her brusquely.

She dug out her driver's license and held it up for his inspection. "My name is Elizabeth Young. I have a five-o'clock appointment with Agent Collin MacBride."

The guard checked his list and then nodded for her to pass. Elizabeth thanked him and tucked away her license. Once through the turnstile she had to turn over her purse to a female guard, who rummaged around inside it before sending it through an X-ray machine similar to those at the airport. Elizabeth stepped through the metal detector and waited patiently for her purse to be returned to her.

She exhaled a heavy breath as she pressed the button for the elevator. The doors slid open immediately and the moment she selected the proper floor the doors closed and she was whisked upward.

The blue-carpeted reception area on the twenty-seventh floor was sparsely furnished and rather cold-looking except for the enormous FBI seal decorating the far wall. The seal boasted of pride and demanded respect and managed to undo every scrap of bravado Elizabeth had mustered.

She moistened her lips and held on to the shoulder

strap of her purse. Might as well get this over with. She marched up to the receptionist's desk and said, "Hello, I'm—"

"Miss Young?"

The voice jerked her around as efficiently as if its owner had grabbed her by the arm and pulled.

"I'm Agent Luke Driver," the man said. "We've been waiting for you. If you'll come this way please."

The blood roaring in her ears, Elizabeth allowed Agent Driver to direct her down a long corridor to the sixth office on the right. He opened the door and stood back for her to enter ahead of him.

Elizabeth studied his face for a moment before she did so, but she found no comfort, no assurance that all would come out right. She was on her own here. She should have listened to Gloria and called that attorney. But she couldn't afford a fancy attorney. If she could get this matter straightened out without having to go into hock for a retainer, she would.

Forcing one foot in front of the other, she walked into the office and Driver closed the door behind her. She glanced over her shoulder and wasn't surprised to find that he hadn't followed her inside.

Agent MacBride was not behind his desk, nor was he anywhere in the office. She really was on her own. Thankful for the reprieve, Elizabeth used the time to learn what she could about the man. She read each and every one of the accolades hanging on his walls. Plaque after plaque. Certificate after certificate. There were numerous pictures of him receiving commendations. But there wasn't the least sign of family or loved ones. No pictures on the desk or wall of anyone other than those related to work. Nothing.

Like the man, the office was elegant. She wondered vaguely if all FBI agents had mahogany desks and credenzas, expensive leather upholstered chairs and a view that looked out over the city he served and protected. Somehow she doubted it. These luxuries were probably his personal belongings. They matched his thousand-dollar suits and Italian-made shoes.

She then wondered what kind of house he lived in and just how much an FBI agent was paid. Not this much, she'd bet. Nope. Collin MacBride was exactly what she'd suspected—a rich guy with a need to prove his worth. Once more Elizabeth scanned the many plaques and pictures that attested to his accomplishments. Just what she needed. A refined greyhound with the simple-minded tenacity of a pit bull.

The door opened behind her and she turned to see Agent MacBride step into the office. The air felt suddenly charged, and the size of the room diminished instantly.

"Miss Young, I apologize for keeping you waiting." He skirted his desk and gestured to one of the chairs.

Without preamble she sat. She tried to moisten her lips, but her mouth was too dry to make a difference. The pounding of her heart was almost deafening as she forced herself to focus on the man who walked around his desk to settle into the leather chair behind it.

He was tall, at least six-two. And just as handsome and well dressed as she remembered. He had the build of an athlete, but with a little more bulk to fill out his designer suit. She felt a flare of heat in her midsection, startling her. She blinked, frowned and tried to analyze the reaction. Before she allowed herself to admit the surge of heat for what it was, he spoke again.

"Have you thought about our earlier visit?" he asked in that smooth voice that spoke of breeding and an Ivy League education.

Had she thought about it? Fury seared away all other emotion. What the hell did he think? "Actually," she said, not bothering to keep the fury out of her tone and lying through her teeth, "I haven't had time to think about anything but work. Was there something in particular I should have thought about?"

He smiled, but it was venomous. "Do you recognize this?" He tossed a photograph to her side of the desk.

Gingerly she reached for it. Her breath caught when she recognized the object pictured in the eight-by-ten print.

The dagger.

The one she'd found at the junk store on Fifty-fifth. The one she'd bought Ned as a thank-you for helping her with her panic attacks. The gift she'd given him before she'd recognized him for the monster he was.

"I thought you might," MacBride said smugly.

Her gaze shot to his. "So what if I do?" Her words were flinty with a fear she couldn't name. Somehow some part of her knew this was bad. Very bad. She pitched the photograph back on his desk as if merely holding it would further condemn her.

"That's the murder weapon." He picked up the picture and pretended to study it. "It was buried to the hilt just left of the victim's sternum." He shook his head solemnly. "Slid right between the ribs, punctured a lung and nicked the pericardium." He shrugged then. "He couldn't have lived more than a few minutes. Not even long enough for help to arrive had someone called for it."

The trembling started in Elizabeth's hands, but quickly spread to her entire body. She stared at her fingers as if she could still them by sheer force of will, but she could not. Her stomach roiled and for one beat she was certain she'd be sick.

"Except no one called for help. Whoever plunged this dagger—" he tapped the photo "—into Ned's chest left him there, naked and dying."

Elizabeth lifted her gaze to meet his. "I didn't do it." She struggled to swallow back some of the desperation tightening her throat. "I swear I didn't kill him."

Those blue eyes bored more deeply into hers, that relentlessness she'd recognized yesterday flashing like a neon sign. "All I want from you, Elizabeth, is the truth."

The truth.

God, he knew she'd lied.

How could she hope to fool this man?

Gloria's words echoed in her ears. *Stick with your original story. Don't tell the cops anything else.*

She drew in a ragged breath. "I've already told you everything I know."

Lights pulsed behind her eyes. Nausea burned bitter and hot in her throat. She'd never before had a migraine, but the abrupt chord of pain in her skull now was no ordinary headache.

That unyielding gaze never deviated from hers. He

didn't even blink, just kept watching her. "I don't think you have."

The trembling escalated. Unable to sit there another second, she lurched to her feet. "I've told you everything. This…this harassment is pointless. I can't help you, Agent MacBride."

She whipped around and headed for the door. She had to get out of there. The pain was excruciating, the trembling almost violent. If she didn't leave now, she might not be able to under her own steam. She would not give him the pleasure of seeing her collapse beneath the pressure.

Before she could jerk the door open, he was standing next to her, one broad palm plastered against the slab of wood that stood between her and escape.

"If you think of anything you need to tell me, my cell number is on that card I gave you."

She closed her eyes and struggled to hold herself steady. "I won't think of anything." Forcing her eyes open, she met that blue gaze. "You shouldn't be wasting your time on me, Agent MacBride. You should be out there looking for the killer."

"What is it you're afraid of, Elizabeth?" he asked softly, the gentle tone a vivid contrast to the fierceness in his eyes.

Shaking her head in denial, she glared at him with all the disdain she could marshal. "I'm innocent." She'd meant to hurl the words at him with the fury smoldering inside her, but she'd fallen well short of the mark. All she'd managed to do was sound desperate.

"Then you won't mind submitting to certain tests," he suggested in that same smooth baritone.

Tests? Her mind raced with the possibilities. Had she touched anything? Left prints or some form of DNA that would tighten the noose already around her neck?

She remembered slapping Ned. Maybe she'd scratched him. He'd grabbed her brutally. Shaken her. Had she lost a loose hair on his clothing?

Her heart slammed mercilessly against her rib cage. That was it. She'd watched enough forensics shows to realize what he was up to.

"Elizabeth? Is there a problem?"

Her gaze locked with his once more and she shook her head. "Call my attorney." She rattled off the name of the legal eagle Gloria had given her. "You can discuss it with him." She couldn't take any more. She couldn't do this. Not again. Not alone.

He leaned in closer, fully into her personal space. "I'll call him, Elizabeth, but that's not all I'm going to do."

She swallowed, hard. Grasped the anger that swelled just enough to give her the strength to demand, "Is that a threat?"

He smiled and her foolish heart skipped a beat. This close she could feel the pleasure it gave him to have her trapped so firmly in his net of suspicion. She wanted to pound on that broad chest and rant at him. She wanted to shake him until he realized she was telling the truth. She did not kill Ned Harrison. She was innocent. Why couldn't he see that?

But she couldn't do any of those things. All she could do was stare into those intense eyes and fight the urge to admit defeat.

"No threat," he said on something that could have

been a sigh but sounded more like a chuckle. "Just fair warning." All signs of amusement or gentleness vanished then. That chiseled jaw hardened like granite and his unflinching gaze seemed to go straight through her. "I'll be watching you, Elizabeth," he warned with all the determination and confidence of a fire-and-brimstone preacher. "If you make one mistake, I'll know it." The corners of those firm lips tilted upward, hinted at a smile. "And you will make a mistake. They all do."

For two long beats she stood frozen, staring into those accusing eyes, and then he moved. The instant he backed off she flung open the door and hurried to the elevator.

By the time she reached the street the panic had gripped her in its vicious talons. The pain in her skull all but blinded her.

And she realized, beyond a shadow of a doubt, that he knew.

He knew she was lying.

Chapter Five

Elizabeth had little choice but to work sixteen-hour days for the past two days. She'd fallen seriously behind on her schedule with the funeral and the interrogations related to Ned's murder. Not to mention the worry and guilt slowing her usual pace. She'd never survive as a criminal. She just wasn't cut out for a life of deception.

It was Saturday and she hadn't heard from Agent MacBride since their meeting on Thursday evening. She hoped she never heard from him again. A little shiver chased over her flesh, reminding her that she might not have heard from him, but she'd seen his people watching her. The moment she pulled out onto the street each morning, a dark sedan slid in behind her and followed her to the job site. Boomer, too, had noticed the feds hanging around.

MacBride had warned her he'd be watching.

But what if it wasn't him or his men? What if it was whoever murdered Ned? She shuddered at the thought. Borrowing trouble wasn't going to do her any good. She'd worried enough for several lifetimes during the past week. Besides, Boomer was certain her tail was "fibbies," as he called them. He swore he could spot a federal agent from a mile away—they all looked the same. Same fancy suits, same designer sunglasses and the same superior attitude.

Boomer was right about the attitude, she decided as she put the lid back on the fresh bucket of paint she'd had to open an hour or so ago. MacBride had enough cocky male attitude for a dozen men. That much testosterone in one guy could be a little scary. She shivered again. Only this time it had nothing to do with fear and everything to do with awareness.

Okay. Time to call it a day. Whenever she started fantasizing about the guy attempting to pin a murder rap on her, it was definitely time for a break. It was late. She was tired. She'd have to work tomorrow. Working on Sunday was her least-favorite thing to do, but finishing up this loft was essential. She'd just have to grin and bear it come morning. She glanced at her watch. It was well past ten and she'd obviously gotten punchy. Too little sleep and far too much pressure bore ruthlessly down on her. A decent night's sleep would do wonders for her ability to think straight. The final finishing touches could wait until morning. But she wouldn't ask Boomer to help on Sunday. He likely still had a social life.

"I'll finish up here," she said to Boomer when he noticed her putting away her tools. "You go on ahead and I'll see you on Monday."

A frown creased his brow. "I'll just hang around and walk you out," he offered, ever the protector.

She shook her head. He'd already put in far more hours than his meager salary covered, but he'd insisted on helping her catch up. "No. Really. I'll be okay." She shrugged. "Who's going to bother me with my very own federal agent watching?"

He crossed to the opposite side of the room and peered out the window. "He's still out there, all right." Boomer expelled a couple of inventive curses. "I don't know why you put up with it. They got no right watching you like this."

"It's okay." She ushered him into the dimly lit hallway and pointed to the elevator. "Now go. I'll be fine."

Reluctance slowing his step, Boomer shuffled to the only exit. He hesitated before boarding the antique lift. "Don't let 'em see you sweat, Elizabeth." His gaze settled on hers. "We both know you didn't kill that prick." He pushed open the iron bars that served as a door to the elevator, then paused to look back at her once more before boarding. "But he deserved exactly what he got."

Boomer stepped into the elevator and pulled the bars closed before setting it in to motion. His gaze remained steady on hers until he was out of sight. She shuffled back into the loft, exhaustion clawing at her.

How often had she complained about Ned in front of Boomer? She hadn't told him everything, but she'd gone on and on about how he'd used her, how he'd hurt her.

A new kind of iciness crackled inside her. Surely Boomer hadn't—

No! She refused to believe that. MacBride's innuendo about Boomer's past was playing on her mind, that was all. She knew Boomer. He wouldn't kill another human being any more than she would.

Elizabeth moistened her suddenly dry lips and

made quick work of putting away the tools of her trade. She refused to dwell on a concept as ridiculous as that. The whole idea was just another indicator of how badly she needed a good night's sleep.

Shortly after Boomer's departure, she was ready to go, as well. She glanced out the window to see if the sedan was still there. Yep. Right there in the alley across the street. The driver had backed in so that he could pull out behind her without any real effort. She wondered if they'd been trained to do that very thing to ensure that they didn't lose their surveillance target while turning around. Probably.

As the old lift lowered to the still-under-construction corridor that would eventually serve as a lobby for the building, she couldn't help thinking what a monumental waste of time the surveillance of her movements really was. If the feds expended half as much effort on finding the real murderer as they did on watching her, they might have solved the case by now.

By the time she stormed out of the building, she'd worked up a pretty good head of steam. Instead of climbing into her old beat-up truck, she marched across the street and right up to the sedan parked in the alley.

She banged on the driver's window. ''Why do you keep watching me?'' she demanded, any good sense she'd possessed now lost to exhaustion and fury.

For a few seconds she wasn't sure whoever was on the other side of the tinted glass intended to respond, then the door opened. She fell back a couple of steps. What if Boomer had been wrong? What if this wasn't one of MacBride's henchmen?

Agent MacBride himself emerged from the vehicle. He towered over her with only the car door between them. To her utter chagrin, her gaze swept him. The usual elegant suit jacket was missing. The crisp white shirt he wore beneath remained free of wrinkles and stretched tautly over his incredibly wide shoulders. The top two buttons of his shirt were open and the navy tie hung loose at his throat. His short hair looked as if he'd run his hands through it repeatedly, leaving it tousled in a manner that could only be called sexy. But by far the most unnerving feature was his relentless gaze.

"I told you I'd be watching, Elizabeth."

Damn her treacherous emotions, but she shivered at the sound of his voice. She wrapped her arms around herself and glared up at him, determined not to allow him to see another indication of weakness. "This is ridiculous. Why aren't you chasing the real bad guys, instead of harassing me?"

He eased around the door and shoved it shut behind him, putting his big body mere inches from hers. "We both know why I'm watching you, don't we?"

Anger flamed inside her. "Did you call my attorney?" She definitely had, as much as she'd hated to— the retainer alone had set her back two months' rent, but her landlady had been understanding and offered to allow her to pay the rent a little late. Thank God there were still a few compassionate people around.

"Do I need to call your attorney?" he countered smoothly. "I thought maybe we could settle this between us."

Her breath stilled in her lungs as that fierce gaze settled on her lips. What was he doing? Was this a

new strategy? Had he noticed her attraction to him
physically and decided to play on it? Was he that
desperate to pin this on her? Or maybe he simply
thought she truly was guilty.

"I'm tired, MacBride," she admitted, too exhausted to fight this battle now. "Just leave me alone,
okay? I don't need this crap."

She gave him her back and headed toward her truck
on the other side of the street. Damn him. She was
sick to death of being accused. What was it about her
that made people believe she could commit a crime
so heinous? Even the sheriff back home had initially
believed her sorry-ass brother-in-law, not her. But,
with her prodding, he'd dug more deeply, finally dis-
covering the real truth. She was innocent. Just like
now.

Who knew? Maybe it was a guy thing. Maybe they
had to side with each other, protect the brotherhood
at all costs. If there was a woman anywhere nearby
to blame, that was the preferred route.

"Did he help you do it?"

MacBride's voice stopped her dead in her tracks
midway across the street. She turned slowly, afraid to
ask what he meant by that statement and equally
afraid not to.

"What the hell are you talking about?"

The streetlights were few and far between, but there
was just enough moonlight combined with the yellow
glow of the nearest street lamp to allow her to see the
knowing expression that tipped those sensual lips into
the vaguest hint of a smile.

"Your assistant, Boomer. Did he talk you into it?
Maybe the two of you have something going on and

he got jealous of your relationship with the good doctor. Those younger guys are like that, you know. Is he the one who tied up Harrison?''

White-hot fury exploded inside her. She clenched her hands into fists and shook with the effort to restrain the fury when she spoke. ''This isn't going to work, MacBride.'' She scarcely recognized the icy voice as her own. ''I didn't kill him and neither did Boomer. If you have some kind of evidence that leads you to believe I'm guilty, then arrest me. If not, leave me the hell alone.''

She spun away from that all-consuming blue gaze and started forward again. This just kept getting worse and worse. He was like a dog with a bone. He just wouldn't let it go. All she had to do was reach her truck, climb in, and she was out of there. She would not waste another moment of her time on this man or his silly suppositions.

''But you can't prove you actually went home after being stood up at the restaurant.''

The words were spoken softly, yet there was no denying the determination in his tone. He wasn't going to let this go until he knew everything.

She hesitated once more and summoned the necessary courage to face him yet again. ''That's right.'' She looked straight into those assessing eyes. ''I don't have anyone to vouch for my whereabouts. I can't prove anything. You'll just have to take my word for it.''

Enough already. If he had evidence he would arrest her. But this intimidation had to stop. She'd had all she could take.

''All right.''

Startled, she stared up at him. "You believe me?"

That shadow of a smile again. "I didn't say that. You said I'd have to take your word for it. I can do that if—" he paused "—you're willing to repeat those words during a polygraph."

Fear paralyzed her. She couldn't take a polygraph. He would have proof of her lies then.

"Is there a problem?" He inclined his head and studied her more closely. "If you're telling me the truth, then you have nothing to lose and everything to gain."

"I…I thought polygraphs weren't admissible in court," she retaliated. The blood froze in her veins. This was it. She was done. He had her. He would never in a million years believe her story now. She'd lied. Once labeled a liar, she would be doomed.

"You say you're telling the truth. I'm simply offering you an opportunity to prove it," he said, effectively avoiding her question.

"I'll…I'll have to talk to my attorney," she stammered.

He moved closer—back into her personal space. She couldn't have moved had her life depended on it. The fear had nailed her to the spot. She couldn't move. Couldn't think what to do or say next.

"All I want from you, Elizabeth, is the truth. If you're really innocent as you say you are, then you must know that your uncooperative actions are slowing down this case. You're essentially helping a murderer to continue walking the streets. If you want to clear your name, then help me."

"I…can't help you. I don't know anything."

Mac stared down into those frightened amber eyes

and it was all he could do not to reach out to her, not to comfort her. She was scared to death, and every instinct screamed at him to reach out. These kinds of feelings were totally unacceptable. He gritted his teeth and got himself back under control. She was a suspect, the primary suspect, in a murder investigation. He needed her cooperation. Losing his focus was not an option.

"Did you have sex with Harrison that night? Did you go to his place looking for him when he didn't show up at the restaurant? Did you have a fight? Maybe you didn't mean to kill him. Maybe it was a game that got out of hand. I know about the kinky sex he enjoyed, the games he played."

She shook her head, her whole body tense with the urge to flee. But something, the fear maybe, held her firmly in place, right where he needed her.

"I didn't—"

"Don't lie to me, Elizabeth," he pressed. "You've already lied to me once," he ventured. He'd known from the moment he first laid eyes on her that she was hiding something.

She blinked. "Why would I lie to you? I didn't kill him."

He tried to read the other emotion whirling in those wide, fearful eyes, but he couldn't. "Is it the videotape? Are you afraid that your relationship with Harrison is going to be exposed to the whole world? Is that it?"

She shook her head again. "He…he used me. It was a mistake." She looked away then. "I made a mistake." This time when her eyes met his, they were filled with certainty and fortitude. "But I didn't kill him."

"Are you the one who scratched him when you argued?" Mac went on. "Is it your pubic hair we found on his body?"

The bravado vanished in an instant. "I told you I didn't go to—"

"Why don't I believe that?" he asked, cutting off her denial. His gut told him she was telling the truth about her innocence where the murder was concerned, but there was something more. She was lying about something and he had to know what it was.

She held up her hands, palms out. "Enough." She backed away a step. "You can arrest me or you can let me go home. Which will it be?"

His cell phone vibrated in his chest pocket. "Go home," he told her as he reached for the infuriating cell. "But remember, I'll be watching."

Without responding to his blatant threat, she stormed away. He let go a disgusted breath and flipped open the phone. "Yeah," he barked.

"Mac, we've got another one. Brannigan just called. I'm on my way there now."

Mac's frown deepened. "Where?" He didn't have to ask what. He already knew. There'd been another murder.

"Mercer Street. Willidean Delinsky." Driver rattled off the exact address. "She goes by the name Deana Dell. She's that supermodel who got busted for drugs early last year. You know the one who does the Sass ads."

Sass was a designer perfume that was all the rage with younger women. Mac definitely remembered the model. Blond, glamorous. She'd been at Harrison's funeral wearing a red dress that turned every head in the place. "What's the connection?" He knew there was one, otherwise Brannigan would not have let them in on his turf. Considering her presence at the funeral, she at least knew Harrison on a social level.

"She's one of Harrison's patients. Brannigan found the appointments in her calendar."

Mac swore. "I'll meet you there."

The scene was every bit as gruesome as the one two days earlier involving Vanessa Bumbalough. The modus operandi appeared to be exactly the same. Only this time Mac got to see the victim before her body was removed. She'd been tied to her elegant bed, sexually assaulted and then murdered in the same manner. The spray of blood adorning the wall testified to the violence.

As he stood back and viewed the undisturbed crime scene, his predominant thought was that this was an execution. Someone had demoralized and executed this woman. This was no random act of sexual violence. This murder had purpose and calculation. Again, the home was undisturbed elsewhere. Not a single item looked out of place. Absolutely no signs of forced entry. This building didn't have a doorman but whoever had entered the premises had been allowed to do so by a resident who pressed a simple button and disengaged the lock barring the entrance. Brannigan already had officers canvassing the residents to see if anyone had buzzed in a visitor today.

The ME had put the time of death at six to eight hours ago. Of course this was only an estimate; they wouldn't have more concrete details until after the autopsy. The victim's live-in boyfriend had come home late from the office and discovered the body. Brannigan was still grilling him in the next room. But Mac didn't need to hear any of the interrogation. This had nothing to do with the boyfriend.

This was about Ned Harrison.

He was sure of it. He'd felt that nudge at the Bumbalough crime scene, but now it was more than a nudge. Someone had murdered Ned Harrison and now, whoever that was, appeared bent on killing his patients. But why? What did Vanessa Bumbalough and Deana Dell have to do with anything? Why these two patients? What did they have in common besides Harrison?

Those were the answers he needed.

The possibility that these two women would not be the last abruptly surfaced in the flood of scenarios crashing into his consciousness.

Elizabeth.

She had been Harrison's patient.

A cold hard fist of fear jammed into Mac's gut. She might very well be hiding the answer to all this and not know it. He thought of the videotape of Elizabeth Young and then the ones of the two dead women. Was it simply being a patient of Harrison's that marked these women for death, or was it the videotapes? Each one had likely already been viewed by the Gentleman's Association, whose membership was spread out across the country like a disease building toward an epidemic. It could be any one of those sick bastards. If someone high enough in the association had realized that Harrison was under federal surveillance, his death may have been ordered.

But why the women?

There had to be something more.

And somehow Elizabeth Young was the key. He was certain of it. His protective instincts surged. Whether or not she was guilty of murder, she most likely needed protection.

He motioned for Driver to step into the hallway with him.

Once out of earshot of the crime-scene techs and any of Brannigan's men, he said quietly, "I want you to go straight to Elizabeth Young's apartment and stay there until I relieve you."

Driver frowned. "But what about—"

"Go now." Urgency had tied his gut in knots. He didn't want her alone. "I'll be there as soon as I can."

None too pleased to have to give up a crime scene for a simple stakeout, Driver nodded and headed out without an argument. He had a lot to learn, but he was a good kid.

Relaxing a fraction, Mac returned to the master bedroom where Deana Dell's body was being prepared for removal by the ME. The ordeal to come would serve as further violation and injustice to her physical remains, but it would help identify her murderer.

She and Vanessa Bumbalough were the only witnesses they had.

ELIZABETH CLIMBED out of the tub, quickly dried off and wrapped a clean white towel around her. She felt better already. She'd needed that long, steamy soak.

Deciding a cup of hot cocoa was in order, she padded into the kitchen. As she poured the milk into the pan to warm, she attempted to block all thoughts of Agent MacBride.

But she failed miserably.

If he forced the issue, she would have no choice but to take the stupid polygraph test. It was too late at night to call her attorney, but she knew that if she refused the test, it would be taken as a sign of guilt.

She was screwed if she did and screwed if she didn't.

She shivered when she thought about the way Mac-Bride had looked at her lips. Her fingers instinctively went there, tracing her mouth, her mind struggling with the question of why he would have looked at her that way. As if he wanted to kiss her, as if he was attracted to her. But that was impossible. He only wanted one thing.

To pin a murder rap on her.

All this surveillance crap was nothing but intimidation. Her attorney had confirmed her suspicions, but she hadn't really needed him to. She'd already been down that road.

It was these other feelings that worried her. She hadn't been attracted to a man sexually since Brian. Sure she'd had an affair with Ned, but that had been about pure physical release and nothing more. She'd needed someone in that way to prove it hadn't been her fault that Brian dumped her. Ned had known it and he'd taken advantage of her.

But this was different. This was almost overwhelming. Maybe it was nothing but a combination of all the events that had befallen her in the past year. Maybe she was simply vulnerable. She needed someone to take care of her. She was so damned tired. And

Agent MacBride was strong and had that take-charge mentality down to a science.

She poured her warm milk into a cup and slowly stirred in the cocoa mix. All this time she'd been telling herself she could make it on her own. That she didn't need anyone to support her.

Dammit, she didn't.

She was doing fine. If she hadn't gotten behind on her schedule with all this insanity surrounding Ned's murder, she would be fine, financially and otherwise.

She did not need anyone taking care of her. She was strong and self-reliant. She always had been.

This would pass and she'd be fine again. She sipped her cocoa and wandered into the living room. It wasn't as if it was the first time she'd been faced with seemingly insurmountable obstacles to overcome.

Feeling better already, she set her cocoa on the table next to the sofa and clicked on the television. She might as well catch the news before she hit the sack. Although it was April and the weather was pretty good for this time of year, a sudden winter storm wasn't unheard of. When self-employed, you had to stay on top of anything that might set the work schedule back.

Before she could sit down, her telephone rang. She answered on the second ring.

"Hello."

A beat of silence, then the distinctive click of the party at the other end of the line hanging up.

"Jerk," she muttered. She hated telemarketers. Why the hell would they call so late? And when they did, they always wanted to speak to Mr. Young, assuming the man of the house would be more receptive to their pitch. She'd tried to tell previous callers there was no Mr. Young, but they didn't seem to believe her. Apparently the new way to handle the situation was to simply hang up when a female answered the phone.

"There ought to be a law against it," she hissed.

Then she remembered. The *law* was too busy intimidating innocent people like her.

She was so caught up in her law-bashing session that the knock on the door made her jump.

Taking a deep breath, she forced herself to remain calm. Then anger took over once more. Now he was knocking on her door? Mrs. Polk would not like her having visitors at this hour. The elderly woman didn't want anyone living above her who partied or had late-night guests. Elizabeth couldn't blame her. She was an old woman who supplemented her income by renting out her unused upstairs. She didn't need any additional stress in her life. Hell, who did?

This was ridiculous. She would not have anyone, not even federal agents, knocking on her door at all hours of the night. Too furious to think rationally, she went in search of her robe, then stomped over to the door in her bare feet, unlocked it and jerked it open.

The tiny landing atop the private rear stairs that led to her apartment stood empty. She stared out over the narrow alleyway that separated Mrs. Polk's small frame house from her neighbor's. The moonlight that managed to penetrate the darkness and surrounding trees did little in the way of illumination. Elizabeth blinked and looked again. Nothing. Too dumb-founded to be afraid, she stepped out onto the landing and squinted into the darkness to survey the steep set of stairs leading to the drive where her truck was parked. Nothing. No one.

Had she imagined the knock at her door? There'd been only one. Maybe a passing car backfired.

A shudder passed through her. She was obviously more exhausted than she'd realized.

After closing and locking the door, she had another thought. What if the jerk had called and knocked on her door just to make sure she was home? Maybe MacBride thought she'd slipped out.

Indignation burst inside her. She strode to the front window and stared down at the street. A dark sedan sat at the curb directly across the expanse of pavement from the house.

"Damn you," she muttered, wishing he'd been at the door so she could have told him just what she thought of his mind games.

A smile slid across her face. His cell phone. That was how he'd called from the car. She let the curtain fall back into place and rushed to find her purse. Dumping the contents, she rifled through the mess until she found MacBride's card.

She'd punched in the number and heard the first ring before she allowed herself time to have second thoughts. When she would have hung up, he answered.

"MacBride."

Renewed fury flared inside her. "Look, you pompous jerk, I don't appreciate being harassed in the middle of the night."

"Elizabeth?"

"Don't pretend you don't know what I'm talking

about,'' she went on. ''I can't stop you from watching my house or my job site, but I will not tolerate you calling my house and hanging up, or your knocking on my door and then disappearing. Just leave me alone!''

Before Mac could ask what the hell she was talking about, she hung up. He replayed her words in his mind. Someone had apparently called her and hung up and then knocked on her door and disappeared.

Why the hell would Driver do anything as ridiculous as that? If he'd wanted to ensure the suspect was indeed at home, he should simply have asked when he called, not hung up.

Something dark and foreboding crawled up Mac's spine. He dialed Driver's cell and held his breath until his partner answered.

''Driver.''

The noise in the background made Mac frown. Horns blowing. People arguing. ''Driver, what the hell is going on? Elizabeth Young—''

''I was just about to call you,'' Driver shouted into the phone. ''I've been in a little fender bender. I'm trying to talk the investigating officer into releasing me now.''

Driver wasn't even at Elizabeth's house.

Mac's blood ran cold. Then who the hell made that call? Who knocked on her door?

Chapter Six

Despite driving like a bat from hell and zooming through the Lincoln Tunnel, which would have been impossible had it not been the middle of the night, it still took Mac far longer to reach Leonia and Elizabeth's apartment than he'd have liked. He didn't bother to covertly park on the street, choosing, instead, to roar straight into the driveway and skid to a halt right behind her beat-up old truck.

He was out of his car before it stopped rocking and took the exterior stairs up to her door two at a time. Despite his hurry, he took note of each vehicle within a block of the house on either side of the street. The surrounding homes were still and dark. Mac knew this section of the small town. Low crime, mostly blue-collar workers, all probably tucked in for the night in anticipation of church on Sunday morning.

Sucking in a deep breath to calm the thrashing in his chest, he pounded heavily on the door. He refused to consider that he might be too late already or that…he was overreacting. He shook his head as he let go a ragged breath of fatigue. He shouldn't have left her without surveillance. Every instinct had warned him that something far beneath the surface was going on and that she was the key. For more than forty-eight hours, he or one of his men had watched her every move.

And what had he done tonight? He'd left her on her own.

The door opened just as he raised his fist to pound on it again. Relief, mixed with a kind of vague defeat, gushed through him at the sight of her.

Her hair mussed and her glasses askew, she stared at him for a moment before recognition flared. In the next beat, her eyes widened in surprise, which was quickly followed by unbridled fury.

"What are you trying to do? Wake the whole neighborhood?"

Highly trained agent that he was, he couldn't even respond when faced with the fact that she stood in the doorway wearing a T-shirt that scarcely reached the tops of her thighs. Backlit by the interior light behind her, the gentle curves of her slender figure were clearly silhouetted beneath the thin cotton fabric.

Before he could stop himself, he gazed down the length of her, all the way to her neatly manicured toes. But it was the return trip that ultimately shattered the last of his defenses. Back up those long, toned legs, over a slim torso and small breasts that jutted firmly against the flimsy fabric covering them and on to a slender throat that curved upward into delicate cheeks and full lips. When his gaze at last came back to rest on hers, the look of rage in those amber eyes jerked him from the trance of lust he'd fallen victim to.

"I'm calling the police." With those snapped

words, she executed an about-face and left him standing there like the unwelcome guest he was.

His own temper flaring, Mac crossed the threshold uninvited and slammed the door behind him. "I am the police," he snarled.

The frightened-rabbit expression that captured her pretty face sent him hurtling back into reality. What the hell was wrong with him? He never lost it like this.

Elizabeth couldn't believe her eyes, much less her ears. Maybe it was her, but she didn't think so. MacBride was behaving strangely, and she didn't know whether to run for her life or slap some sense into him. Either way she was reasonably sure he had no intention of backing off.

"What is it you want, Agent MacBride?" She planted her hands on her waist and marched straight up to him, lifting her chin defiantly. How dare he barge into her home in the middle of the night! It was bad enough she'd endured his shenanigans with the phone call and the anonymous knock on the door. "I'm sick and tired of you and your people following me around." When she was toe-to-toe with him, she poked him in the chest with her forefinger. He flinched. That mere touch sent an electrical charge surging through her, but she quickly recovered. "This is blatant harassment."

"You called me, remember?" he growled.

She shivered as the sound of his voice shimmered over her already exposed nerve endings. "Only because you called first and hung up like a kid playing a prank." She huffed a sigh of exasperation. "And let's not forget you knocking on my door and then vanishing like Houdini. What'd you think? That I'd sneaked out the back door to go murder someone else? I don't even have a back door.'' Control snapped. "Why are you doing this?''

As she fought to regain her composure, something changed in his eyes, and that lean, chiseled profile softened just the tiniest bit. "That's just it,'' he said. Even his voice was softer. "I didn't call you and I damn sure didn't knock on your door until just a few seconds ago.''

Mac watched the confusion claim her, lining her smooth brow, parting those luscious lips. "One of your men then,'' she refuted. "I opened the door—'' she gestured to the one he'd slammed only moments before "—and no one was there.'' Her gaze arrowed to his. "You said you'd be watching. I saw the car.''

"I didn't follow you home tonight, nor did any of my men. Can you describe the vehicle you saw?''

She trembled, shook her head in answer to his question, as well as in denial of the possibility that obviously scared the hell out of her.

Someone had been watching her, all right.

"I…I don't understand.''

Mac squeezed his hands into fists and resisted the urge to reach for her. Every moment with her was a battle for control. His immediate instinct was always, always to protect her.

"Is there anyone in your neighborhood who would do this sort of thing as a joke?'' he asked, determined to keep this discussion on track. "A friend who gets off on scaring others, maybe?''

Her head moved jerkily from side to side. "All the neighbors are older, like Mrs. Polk.'' She laughed, but the sound held no humor. "No way could one of them have knocked and gotten down the stairs and out of sight before I opened the door. I mean, I hesitated before opening it, but not that long." She seemed to wilt beneath the weight of the realization that she'd just dismissed the safest, most reasonable possibilities, leaving only one alternative.

Mac crossed to the door, opened it and moved out onto the small landing to survey the situation from her vantage point. He peered over the side and concluded that even jumping over the railing wouldn't have been a big deal for a younger person, an athletic type. He knew he could do it easily. But if her neighbors were around Mrs. Polk's age, seventy or so, there was no way one of them could have taken that leap. He glanced up and down the narrow alley that separated the house from its neighbor. With the numerous overgrown shrubs and small detached garages, there were plenty of places for someone to hide. A quick jump over the rail and simply darting back under the stairs would be sufficient camouflage.

He stepped back inside and closed the door. During his short absence Elizabeth had donned a tattered terry robe. With her arms wrapped around herself, she looked incredibly vulnerable and very much like a frightened little girl in need of a hug.

But she was no little girl. Those full lips were parted slightly as if she was on the verge of asking something but feared the answer. She'd straightened her glasses and thrust her fingers through her hair, leaving the silky mass hanging loosely around her slender shoulders.

Mac bit back a sigh. Beating himself up for noticing every little thing about her would accomplish nothing, but somehow he had to get a grip and pull it together.

Right now was the perfect time to strike. She was vulnerable. But it took every ounce of determination he possessed to force himself to do his job. "It's time to stop playing games, Elizabeth. Tell me what it is you're hiding and we'll get this mystery solved." He stared directly into her eyes. "You won't be safe until this thing is settled. I know it and I think deep down you know it."

The delicate line of her jaw hardened just a fraction. "Are you admitting that you believe me when I say I didn't have anything to do with Ned's—" she blinked rapidly "—with Dr. Harrison's murder?"

He wanted to believe that she was capable of a slick move like this—that the whole phone-call-knock-on-the-door thing was a hoax designed to garner sympathy—but he knew better. No way could she fake that kind of fear. He'd seen it in her eyes when she realized it hadn't been the authorities outside her door or on the other end of that call. She'd been truly frightened. Still, on the off chance that he was a bigger fool than he already suspected…

"No," he told her flatly. "I'm admitting that I believe someone else knows your secret and that maybe that very secret is putting you in the same kind of danger Harrison found himself in."

Bingo. Direct hit. Her breath caught and the stark fear glittered in her eyes once more. Now all he had to do was move in for the kill.

Stepping closer—into her personal space, a move he already knew unsettled her—he pressed, "Tell me the truth, Elizabeth. I can't help you if you don't.'' She tried backing away from him, but he just kept moving nearer until she backed into the sofa and had no choice but to admit defeat. "Do you know where I was when you called tonight?" he asked.

She couldn't breathe, couldn't think, couldn't escape those penetrating blue eyes. *Please,* she wanted to cry, *just leave me alone. I didn't do this awful thing!* But she couldn't speak. She could only stare into those accusing eyes and pray he wouldn't see the truth in her own.

"I was at the scene of a ten fifty-four. Do you know what a ten fifty-four is, Elizabeth?"

He was closer, yet she wasn't sure he'd moved. But something about his savage demeanor made her feel as if he was right on top of her, waiting. Waiting for the truth.

"A homicide," he said in answer to his own question.

Emotion shuddered through her. Another murder. God, she didn't want to know this. Why didn't he just leave? It couldn't have anything to do with her. She blinked back the sheen of tears that threatened to wreck the remnants of her already shredded composure and stared back at him in defiance. "What does that have to do with me?"

"Did you know Deana Dell, the model?" he went on, ignoring her question, his face mere inches from hers. "She was one of Dr. Harrison's patients, too, just like you. Maybe you saw her at the funeral."

The blonde. She knew instantly. In the devil-red dress. A model. Living large and fast. Elizabeth remembered her now. She'd read about her and her trouble with drugs, last year maybe. She'd instantly wondered if the model had been covering up for someone else, too. But at the funeral Elizabeth hadn't gotten a good look at her face. Hadn't recalled who she was then.

And now it no longer mattered.

She was dead.

Homicide.

That meant murder.

Dear God.

Her stomach rolled over.

"That's the second one of Harrison's patients to die since the funeral," he said pointedly. "Don't you find that strangely ironic?"

The room tilted and then started to spin. Nausea boiled up in her throat. She was going to be sick.

Mac stumbled back a step as Elizabeth pushed away from him and ran from the room. Restraining the need to go after her, he took a moment to calm the crazy mixture of emotions raging inside him. But he couldn't take any chances that she might make a run for it. There was a window—no fire escape, though. In four steps he'd crossed the room and entered the small hall. As he reached the closed bathroom door, his concerns were allayed by the sound of her violent retching.

Guilt stabbed him right in the gut as he leaned against the wall next to the door. He'd forced that on her, had pushed her to the edge. Damn. Sympathy wasn't supposed to enter into this. Where was his usual detachment? Why the hell couldn't he maintain a proper distance?

He released a weary breath and refused to consider the answer to either of those questions.

Eventually he heard the toilet flush and the water running in the basin, then a minute or so later she opened the door. "I'd like you to leave now," she announced with a good deal more strength than she looked capable of managing.

"I need some answers first."

She ripped off her glasses and rubbed her eyes, then glared at him. "Don't you ever give up? I'm telling you I don't know anything!"

He stepped nearer to her. Didn't miss the flicker of uncertainty in those amber eyes. "Yes, you do. And I'll keep coming back until you tell me everything."

She pushed her glasses back into place and shoved her hair from her face with trembling fingers. "You're wasting your time, Agent MacBride."

Another thought poked its way through the jumble of theories whirling in his brain. "How did your ex-fiancé take your affair with Dr. Harrison?"

She blinked, taken aback by the question. What was he fishing for now? Didn't the man get it? She didn't know anything relevant to his case. "Brian and I broke up months ago."

Mac shrugged, the move casual, but his expression was anything but casual. "That may be, but he had to be pissed off when he learned he'd been replaced by a hotshot shrink. Wasn't Harrison a friend of his?"

A frown worried her lips. She'd seen Ned at some of the parties she and Brian had attended. She'd even seen Brian talk to Ned from time to time, but then, he talked to everyone. Not once in their nine-month relationship had she heard Brian mention Ned. Ned certainly never mentioned Brian other than in the context of how her breakup with him added to the stress that brought on her panic attacks.

"I don't...think so," she admitted in all honesty. "I suppose you could call them casual acquaintances."

MacBride was watching her so closely that she could almost feel his eyes on her. She tugged the lapels of her robe tighter around her, but it wasn't her body that held his attention, she knew. He was studying her face, analyzing her responses, looking for signs of deception. She knew what he was after. Someone to nail with this murder rap.

"It's late, Agent MacBride," she said, squaring her shoulders and moving slightly away. "I'd like you to go now."

For one long moment she was sure he intended to argue the point, but to her surprise, he didn't.

"I'll be outside all night," he said, instead. "When I go, one of my men will take over. Don't even think about trying to give us the slip."

She nodded, too grateful for the presence now to react to his order.

With one final, lingering look, he turned and made his way back into her living room. She followed, suddenly conscious of her meager furnishings and less-than-spectacular housekeeping skills. She wasn't exactly a slob, but she wasn't neat, either.

At the door he hesitated once more. "This door doesn't have a peephole or a dead bolt. Think about getting both installed. In the meantime, at least ask who's there before you open the door."

Oddly, she was pretty sure his words were well meant. That he cared what happened to her.

Yeah, right.

He only wanted to keep his prime suspect alive and well until he could nail her for murder.

"Thanks for the advice," she retorted, a hint of sarcasm lacing the words.

That sea-blue gaze bored into hers. "I'm serious, Elizabeth. I don't want you to end up dead. You were one of Harrison's patients, too."

With that profound statement, he left.

For several seconds after the door closed, she could only stand there absorbing the impact and ramifications of his words.

Two of Ned's patients had been murdered in the past seventy-two hours. Coincidence? Apparently the FBI didn't think so.

Cold, bony fingers of fear clutched her throat. Maybe MacBride was right. Maybe her life was in danger. Before the thought fully formed in her mind, she turned the button on the knob locking the door. She hurried over to the front window and drew back the curtain. Just as he promised, MacBride backed out onto the street and parked directly in front of the house. A relief so profound slid through her that her knees almost buckled.

Vanessa Bumbalough was dead. Deana Dell was dead.

Who would be next?

Elizabeth half stumbled to the sofa in her haste and snatched up the phone. She punched in Gloria's number and paced the floor as she waited for her friend to answer. *Please, God,* she prayed, *let her be home. And safe.*

When a groggy hello came over the line, Elizabeth blurted, "We have to talk!"

MAC WAITED patiently for Driver to answer his cell phone. "They find anything else?" he asked without preamble.

"Nothing. The MO appears to be exactly the same as the last one. No sign of forced entry, probable sexual assault after being tied to the bed and panties shoved into her mouth. The only signs of struggle are in the bedroom. The techs found dozens of different prints. The lady apparently had a lot of guests. Since she and the Bumbalough woman ran in the same circles, there's no telling how many sets matching the previous scene they'll find."

A lot of nothing leading nowhere. Mac rubbed his eyes and stared up at the light in the window of Elizabeth's apartment. He had a bad feeling about this. A very bad feeling.

"I'm going to keep up the surveillance on Elizabeth Young tonight," he informed his partner. "I'll need relief around 8 a.m. I want you to track down a Brian Novak of Design Horizons and have him meet me at my office at nine."

Driver snorted. "Tomorrow's Sunday, Mac. How can I—"

"I don't care if it's Christmas," Mac shot back. "Death doesn't observe weekends or holidays. Have the guy at my office at nine sharp."

"Will do," Driver replied sheepishly. "Anything else?"

Mac exhaled a weary breath. "That's it. Call me if they find anything new."

He closed his phone and dropped it on the console. It was going to be a long night. Shifting until he found a comfortable spot, he considered the layout around Elizabeth's apartment. She had no security, and the surrounding area was an intruder's wet dream. Everyone went to bed early and likely didn't hear as well as they used to. If someone wanted her, getting to her would be easy. She worked long hours and probably slept like a rock during the few hours of rest she got.

If she was the innocent she insisted she was and the latest turn in this case evolved into what he suspected, she could very well be in grave danger.

Whether she was a suspect, a material witness or simply a woman in jeopardy because she got mixed up with the wrong guy, Mac was duty bound to protect her.

The scary part was, who was going to protect him?

He was plunging headfirst into personal involvement. Something he never did.

But there didn't appear to be a damned thing he could do about it this time. Some part of him was hell-bent on saving the woman, whether he saved himself or not.

ELIZABETH SLEPT maybe two hours the entire night. Even before sunrise she was pacing the floor. At six she'd forced herself to bake her Sunday favorite— blueberry muffins—and she'd made a strong pot of coffee. The way she felt at the moment it would take the entire pot to get her through the day. But she had to work. She simply had no choice.

She pulled on her jeans and a T-shirt, rolled on a clean pair of socks and then slipped on her sneakers. Another cup of coffee and she'd be good to go.

She stilled, her gaze drawn to the front window. How was MacBride faring? she wondered. She moved to the window and peeked around the edge of the curtain. He was still there. The driver's-side window had been lowered to let in the cool morning air. As she watched, he scrubbed a hand over his face. She could just imagine how he felt. Exhausted. Hungry.

"Dammit," she uttered.

No matter how many times she told herself that her most recent problems were entirely his fault, she just couldn't help feeling sorry for him sitting out there in a cold car after having no sleep.

Admitting defeat with a mighty exhale, she filled a thermos with coffee and wrapped a couple of muffins in a napkin. The least she could do was feed him. He had, after all, spent the night watching over her. The thought made her shiver with an awareness she could no longer deny. She was sexually attracted to the man.

What an idiot she was. Outright asking for trouble.

Ignoring the alarm bells jangling in her head, she pulled on a jacket and marched out the door, down the steps and across the street. He'd caught sight of her before her sneakers hit the pavement, and he was climbing out of the car.

"Is everything all right?" he asked, those blue eyes surveying her from head to toe.

Just like last night, she could feel his eyes roaming her body, leaving heat everywhere. And damned if he didn't look fine with a night's growth of beard shadowing that chiseled jaw. "Everything's just peachy," she lied, forcing the forbidden thoughts to the farthest recesses of her mind. "I thought you might be hungry."

Actually he appeared ravenous. But then, she hadn't noticed that look in his eyes until after he'd given her the once-over. She shivered and scolded herself for allowing such a silly notion. Rich guys like MacBride didn't bother with working girls like her. Well, working girls in the sense of blue-collar types. Which was what she was. She'd been born into a blue-collar family and she was damned proud of it.

"Thanks." He reached for the thermos she offered. "I hope this is coffee."

She shrugged one shoulder, attempting to come off as indifferent. "Black. I didn't know if you liked cream or sugar."

"Black is perfect," he said, unscrewing the top while his eyes and full attention never deviated from her.

She pushed a tremulous smile into place. "Muffins," she explained as she thrust the still-warm baked goods at him.

He set the thermos on the roof of his car. The lid that served as a cup was filled with steaming coffee and clutched in his left hand; with his right he reached for the muffins.

Her heart banged against her ribs when his fingers brushed hers. She silently railed at herself once more. "I have to get to the job site," she said, her voice quavering like that of a sophomore hoping to be invited to the prom.

He sipped the hot coffee, then asked, "On Sunday?"

Shoving her hands into her back pockets, she offered another of those careless shrugs. "Sometimes it's necessary." Unlike him, she had to really work for a living. Even so, she didn't have money to throw around on elegant clothes and fancy cars. She stole a glance at the dark sedan he drove. Foreign, pricy, luxurious. She'd bet those leather seats were heated, too. Must be nice, she mused. And here she'd felt sorry for him out here in his sixty-thousand-dollar car. How many ways could she prove herself a fool?

For a time they stood in silence. He consumed the muffins and drank a good portion of the coffee without commenting on the quality or palatability.

Finally he tossed the napkin that had contained the muffins into his fancy car, then screwed the lid back on the thermos and handed it to her. "That was great, thanks."

She accepted the thermos, careful not to allow her fingers to graze his. She was already in enough trouble here. "It was the least I could do," she said before she thought. A flush heated her cheeks. "I mean…you did keep an eye on my place last night and I was pretty shaken up."

Those twin blue laser beams cut right through her pretenses. "You didn't think of anything you needed to tell me?"

Here they were again, right back at square one. "I'm telling you—"

His cell phone buzzed, cutting off the rest of her words. He reached into his breast pocket and pulled out the slim device, quickly opening it. "MacBride."

She looked away, not wanting to intrude. It could

be his girlfriend. Or his wife. Her head turned around so fast it almost gave her whiplash. In search of a wedding ring, she lowered her gaze to his left hand.

No rings whatsoever.

She emitted a little snort of self-disgust and forced her attention to the ground where it belonged. What an absolute idiot she was! He was the enemy. She was a pathetic woman who'd been dumped by her fiancé and taken advantage of by her shrink, to whom she'd paid top dollar to climb inside her head. He had, in turn, used what he'd learned to get inside her pants.

It just didn't get worse than this.

"Give me the address again." The steely tone drew Elizabeth's attention back to him. He listened intently, his face devoid of emotion. "I'm on my way."

She waited, her nerves jangling, as he snapped the phone closed and put it away. His voice had sounded so ominous. Maybe there'd been a break in Ned's case. This whole nightmare couldn't be over soon enough for her.

He lifted his gaze to hers and said the last thing she wanted to hear. "There's been another murder. Cassandra Fowler."

Her heart took off at a gallop, the blood whooshing in her ears as it roared through her body. Even though she didn't recognize the name, he didn't have to say the rest. She already knew.

He glanced away briefly, then zoomed in on her with such ferocity that she almost stumbled back from the force of it. "Another one of your former lover's patients."

Tension thickened between them.

"It's time to come clean, Elizabeth," he said grimly. "Before anyone else has to die."

Chapter Seven

Lucky Strike bustled with activity at noon on Sunday. The cool downtown eatery was on Grand between Broadway and Wooster. Though incredibly hip, it wasn't the kind of place a girl had to worry about dressing up for. A good thing, too, since Elizabeth had walked straight from her job site. She'd felt a panic attack coming on and had needed the long walk. Her private fed had followed in his dark sedan, taking care to keep his distance. As soon as she'd arrived, the waitress had shown her to one of the wooden tables in the back and taken her drink order.

Despite all that had occurred the night before, as well as that morning, Elizabeth had managed to complete the final details on the job this morning. If she could get the second loft on the floor finished by the end of the upcoming week, she'd have it made. For a couple of weeks, anyway.

She fingered the mug of coffee and forced herself to focus on the events of the past week. As much as she didn't want to, she had to consider that something very sinister was happening and somehow it related to Ned and his dirty little secret. Her dirty little secret.

The bastard. Even in death he haunted her.

She repressed a shudder and once again wrapped her mind around the concept of serial murders. Whoever had killed Ned could very well be the one killing his patients, seemingly one by one. This time the shudder would not be repressed, and her whole body shook with it.

Maybe she should have ordered a stiff drink, instead. She felt suddenly cold and alone. She glanced around the lively dining room with its French copper bar, seemingly carefree patrons and attentive staff, but she couldn't shake the feeling.

There was always the off chance that the murders weren't even related, she debated.

"Yeah, right," she muttered. Maybe she could have gone along with that theory after the first woman was murdered. And maybe even the second. But the third...

Three women.

Three of Ned's patients.

In some instances the third time was considered the charm, but in this situation Elizabeth could only conceive that it was a sign. A sign of bad things to come.

She was a woman.

She was one of Ned's patients.

If there was a list with those two common factors, she would be on it.

A shiver crept over her skin. How could this be happening?

She moistened her lips, then clamped down on her lower one to stem the fear welling up in her throat. What had any of those women done to deserve to die?

If her initial conclusion at the funeral was true, then

they had all likely slept with Ned, just as she had. But he was dead; he wasn't killing anyone. He hadn't had a fiancé or even an ex-wife or girlfriend that she or Gloria knew of. Jealousy couldn't be the motivation. Some of his patients probably had husbands or significant others who could have done the killing. With one murder perhaps, but surely three different men wouldn't have decided on the same route of revenge against the former lovers of Dr. Ned Harrison. And why would one man kill his, as well as someone else's, cheating partner?

This couldn't be about scorned lovers.

She stilled. Or maybe it could.

Who said the murderer was a man? It wasn't confirmed yet that the victims had been sexually assaulted.

Maybe some woman who'd secretly been in love with Ned had decided to kill him and all his hussies. The term Gloria had used to describe them brought a wan smile to Elizabeth's lips. The realization that she could very well have hit on the answer chased away any real humor.

Three women were dead. God only knew who might be next.

"There you are."

Elizabeth looked up at the sound of Gloria's voice. The corner of her mouth instantly rose, but the automatic response melted away when her gaze landed on the woman standing next to her friend.

"Elizabeth, this is Annabelle Ford." Gloria ushered the other woman forward. "Annabelle, Elizabeth Young, my best friend."

Annabelle extended her hand and Elizabeth had little choice but to shake it. The woman's touch was warm and firm with confidence, as was her smile. ''It's a pleasure to meet you, Elizabeth. I'm so sorry it has to be under the present circumstances.'' Her voice wasn't unpleasant, just a little gravelly.

Elizabeth studied the tall, thin woman for a long moment, wondering vaguely who exactly Annabelle Ford was and why she was with Gloria. Her light-brown hair was cut in a fashionably short style that framed her somewhat angular face. Brown eyes that appeared both intelligent and sincere assessed her with equal curiosity.

''Nice to meet you, too,'' Elizabeth eventually remembered to say.

''Did you order already?'' Gloria asked as they took seats, one on either side of Elizabeth at the square table.

She shook her head. ''Just my drink.'' She sipped her café mocha once more, noting from the corner of her eye that Annabelle was still scrutinizing her.

When the waitress had taken drink, as well as food, orders all around the table and rushed away to place it, Gloria leaned forward and kicked off the conversation in a quiet tone.

''I don't know what's going on, but after you called I did some thinking.''

Elizabeth had actually called her friend twice in the past twelve hours. Once around midnight after her run-in with MacBride and then again this morning when he got the call that another woman was dead. She and Gloria had decided to push the meeting they'd planned for dinner this evening up to lunch. Neither of them could stand the suspense a moment longer. All that had kept them from meeting that morning was Gloria's overnight company from the party she'd attended and Elizabeth's need to finish up that one loft.

"This can't be coincidence," Gloria went on. She sat back in her seat and shook her head. "My God, three women...all Ned's patients." She inclined her head toward her companion. "That's why I called Annabelle."

Just when Elizabeth was about to ask who Annabelle was, Gloria told her. "Annabelle is—" she swallowed with difficulty "—was Ned's attorney."

"And his confidant," Annabelle put in, that husky voice modulated to a discreet level. "I've known Ned since our college days. We shared a great deal. He was an outstanding man." She fell silent and her gaze grew distant.

For just a second, Elizabeth couldn't help wondering if Annabelle had been one of Ned's lovers, too. When she'd spoken of their relationship, there'd been a smidgen of intimacy about her tone. But Annabelle didn't strike Elizabeth as Ned's type at all. She was really tall, at least six feet. Her slim frame lacked the curves Ned's women usually possessed. Who knew, though? Ned clearly was not a man of high morals, so maybe his standards didn't always dictate the voluptuous type. And admittedly, Elizabeth didn't quite fit that mold, either. Maybe she and Annabelle had something in common.

"She knew Ned better than any of us," Gloria rushed to add. "On the way here, she told me some very startling secrets about our old friend."

That tweaked Elizabeth's attention. She propped

her arms on the table and leaned into the circle, speaking directly to Gloria. "How about this news-flash. Whoever is doing this may have both of us on his list, as well."

"Precisely," her friend agreed. "This is why we have to do something."

Elizabeth gave her a palms-up gesture. "Do what? I spend half my time looking over my shoulder. I'm scared to death someone is already watching me." She leaned closer still. "I told you what happened last night."

"Someone besides the FBI, you mean?"

This query came from Annabelle. Startled that Gloria had shared this with a stranger, Elizabeth could only stare at the woman.

"Don't be angry, Elizabeth," Gloria said. "I had to tell her everything. She can't help us if she doesn't know everything."

Where had she heard that before? Elizabeth mused. Mac had used the same line on her, but for totally different reasons. She shook herself. When had she started calling him Mac? "Yes," she said bluntly in response to Annabelle's query. "I feel like someone besides the FBI is watching me."

Annabelle placed a hand over hers. Elizabeth gritted her teeth against the instinctive reflex to jerk her hand away. "I think you might be right," Annabelle said. She looked from Elizabeth to Gloria and back several times as she spoke, her gaze direct, insistent. All attorney. "Have you ever heard of the Gentlemen's Association?"

Both shook their heads.

Annabelle sighed. "Well, it's not something you're

going to enjoy hearing about, but I feel I must tell you.'' Her gaze took on a kind of desperate quality. ''Ned shared this information in confidence with me, but he's dead now and I'm almost certain it may be crucial to your continued survival.''

Her words frightened Elizabeth. ''What is this Gentlemen's Association?''

Finally releasing her hold on Elizabeth, Annabelle went on, ''The association is a coast-to-coast group of men, all wealthy professionals much like Ned, for whom life has become tragically boring because they have it all.

''They have all the money they could ever wish for, social status, anything they want. So the thrill of the hunt, of the challenge is gone.'' She shook her head sadly. ''I watched this very need eat away at Ned. None of his accomplishments were ever enough. His life lacked the primal kind of excitement that comes from a new conquest. So he joined this association.''

Elizabeth felt her blood turn to ice when the next logical thought occurred to her. ''The videotapes.''

Annabelle nodded. ''They make these tapes, each attempting to outdo the other, and then play them on the Internet via private chat rooms for the entire association's viewing pleasure.''

Gloria's gaze locked with Elizabeth's. ''He did that to us.'' Her words were scarcely a whisper but filled with the same emotions whirling through Elizabeth.

Anger, humiliation. The feelings almost overwhelmed her, but she fought them. She had to hear all of this. Had to find a way to protect herself. And her friend.

"Once you become a member of this association, there is no turning back. The only way out is death."

Elizabeth felt her face drain of color. "You think they killed him?"

Annabelle nodded grimly. "I firmly believe that's the only logical answer. Ned had a weakness, ladies. He became addicted to these darker needs. The more perverse the better. I believe that addiction cost him his life. This association is responsible for what he became."

A frown furrowed its way across Elizabeth's brow. "But what about the women? They don't even know this association exists. Why kill them?"

Annabelle seemed to ponder the question for a moment before responding. "There's always the possibility that the two aren't related. But Ned told me only a few days before he died that he thought someone was watching him. He feared he'd done something to displease those in power." She shrugged. "I have no idea what he'd done or thought he'd done. I only know he was afraid."

"Oh...my...God," Gloria muttered slowly.

Both Elizabeth and Annabelle stared at her.

"That's why the FBI is involved. We should have known it would be something like that."

Sex, videotapes, the Internet. It made sense to Elizabeth. "You could be right."

"Think about it," Annabelle said, picking up the ball and running with it. "If the association thought that Ned's affiliation had been compromised and the FBI had an eye on him, they would certainly want to neutralize the threat. What better way than to execute him?"

Elizabeth shook her head in confusion. "But what about the women?"

Silence reigned for what felt like an eternity.

"They must think one of you knows something." Annabelle gave a decisive nod, warming to her theory. "Obviously they're not certain who knows what, so they've decided to take out all of you, one at a time. Or perhaps the other murders are simply to cast suspicion elsewhere."

"That's crazy!" Elizabeth hadn't meant to sound so vehement. But the whole thing was ludicrous. This was real life. Why would some anonymous association risk killing dozens of women over one jerk they'd already taken out of the picture? "The risk is too great."

"I don't have all the answers," Annabelle admitted with an urgency that struck a chord of dread deep inside Elizabeth. "The only thing I am certain of is that both of you—" she glanced from one to the other "—are in serious danger."

"What do we do?" Gloria directed her question to Annabelle, her tone filled with every bit as much urgency as Annabelle's.

A stillness settled over Elizabeth as realization dawned on her. Annabelle was right. There was no use pretending otherwise. Either one of them could be next. "There's only one thing we can do," she said.

The other two turned to her, their faces expectant, hopeful. Even Annabelle looked as if she feared she might somehow be on that list. Who knew? Maybe she was. When it came to animal attraction and raw sex, type wasn't always an immediate concern.

"We fight back." Elizabeth felt the weight of her own words. She'd been there once, had prayed she'd never have to go back, but here she was, eyeball deep in a battle to prove her innocence. And quite possibly to protect her life. "They already think I'm guilty," she continued solemnly. "All they need is one real piece of evidence. If they can't prove I did it, they'll move on to the next likely suspect." Her gaze slid to Gloria's. "Can you prove where you were that night?"

Gloria's pupils dilated slightly. "I...I—"

Elizabeth cut her off. "The point is, they won't stop until they have someone to prosecute. If not me, then you." She turned to Annabelle. "Or you." She paused, gathering her courage before she said the rest. "The way I see it, the real problem is staying alive until the police either nail someone or we do it for them."

The three simply stared at one another for a minute that became two.

"How could we possibly—"

"That was my thinking." Annabelle interrupted whatever protest Gloria was about to launch. "We can't trust anyone else. We have to work together, just the three of us, and solve this mystery." She pressed a hand to her throat. "Our very lives may depend upon it."

Gloria held up both hands. "Wait. Wait. Wait. How are we supposed to do that?"

Before anyone could answer, the waitress arrived with their order. Elizabeth had pretty much lost her appetite at this point, but she needed energy for work, as well as for what lay ahead where this murder investigation was concerned.

As soon as the waitress had moved on, Annabelle said, "We need the connection between Ned and the association."

Elizabeth laughed. She couldn't help it. It just popped out. She fiddled with her fork to avoid the expectant looks from the other two. "If the FBI couldn't find enough evidence to take them down, which obviously they hadn't, how are we supposed to?" It was her turn to insist on a reality check. She'd been thinking more along the lines of checking out everyone who knew or associated with Ned. People they knew, not some ghostlike organization they couldn't even prove existed.

"My sentiments exactly," Gloria reiterated.

Annabelle sat in silent consideration for a moment before telling one more secret she knew about her dearly departed client Ned Harrison. "The FBI will be searching his computers, at the office and at home, but they won't find anything."

Apprehension inched its way up Elizabeth's spine. "What do you mean? How do you know that?"

"The association's business is conducted in cyberspace, the Bureau will try tracking where Ned has been, but they won't find anything, because he used a special system for his little hobby."

Elizabeth didn't know much about computers, but she did know that, like a telephone, anything a person did on the computer could be traced. Somehow a trail was left. "So where is this system he used?" Elizabeth felt her pulse quicken at the idea of bringing down this association. Her stomach roiled at the thought that the members of the demented group had likely seen her videotape. She tamped down the urge to gag. She didn't even want to think about some of the games Ned had prodded her into playing. God, how could she have been so stupid?

"At his office there's a secret room. It was a part of the original architecture—a bomb or storm shelter of some sort. It's like a vault. But when the building was renovated some forty years ago, it was filled in, or at least that's what the blueprints said." Annabelle smiled knowingly. "Apparently the contractor on the job at the time decided to save himself a little money and just boarded it over. Anyway, Ned discovered it when he had the office remodeled a couple of years ago and decided to make it a vault for his most private files." She sighed as she peered down at her salad. "Eventually he turned it into a media room for his forbidden pleasure."

Elizabeth shivered at her choice of words.

"You've seen it?" Gloria asked, appalled.

"Well, I haven't actually seen it, but he did tell me about it. He had some sort of shield installed so that the room's presence couldn't be detected. It's all quite high tech."

"We have to go there!" Gloria exclaimed, an extra portion of desperation in her voice.

Elizabeth shook her head. "No. We have to go to the authorities." MacBride's image loomed large in her mind. He would know what to do, she was sure of it.

"How do we know we can trust the authorities?" Annabelle said offhandedly. "What if one or more of them belong to the association, as well? After all, they haven't brought the association down in all this time. I happen to know that Ned has been affiliated with the group for more than a year now. What's the holdup?'' Her fierce dark eyes settled on Elizabeth. ''I'll tell you why—because they're *men*.''

''We can't trust men on this issue,'' Gloria said. ''We get the goods on the association and we take it to the press. We could blow the whole thing wide open, then the authorities would have to take action.''

''Not we,'' Annabelle corrected. Again she looked from Gloria to Elizabeth. ''His office is surely being watched. One person slipping past anyone who might be watching will be problematic enough. But all three of us…'' She gave her head a brisk shake. ''It would never work.''

Seemingly endless seconds of tension-filled silence passed as each digested what that meant.

''I would have done this myself as soon as I was notified of Ned's murder, but the police were everywhere,'' Annabelle said. ''I couldn't risk it. I couldn't be sure the man in charge wasn't involved.'' Anger etched fierce lines into the features of Annabelle's face. ''I wanted so to find whoever had done this to him.''

Elizabeth and Gloria exchanged a look of uncertainty.

''Even if I had been able to get into his office I couldn't have managed,'' Annabelle went on. ''I was in an accident a few years ago. My right shoulder and my left arm were severely damaged. I have almost no upper-body strength. The hidden door is extremely heavy and there is no automatic opener. Ned explained that the mechanism would be too easily detected. Therefore the entryway has to be opened and closed manually."

"I'll do it," Gloria offered without hesitation. "I can do it."

Elizabeth shook her head. "No. I'm stronger than you. I'll do it."

"I said," Gloria argued, her Irish temper flaring in those green eyes, "that I would do it."

"I'm accustomed to *manual* labor," Elizabeth pointed out. "I know I can do it. If you get in there and then you can't—"

Gloria heaved a sigh of exasperation. "Fine. You do it."

"Time is of the essence," Annabelle suggested. "We shouldn't waste any. We need to act now."

"Just one question," Elizabeth wondered aloud. "Why did Ned tell you this? Wasn't it dangerous for him to tell anyone?" She watched Annabelle closely as she responded.

"He wanted me to know—" her voice faltered and her eyes grew suspiciously bright "—in case something happened to him."

Well, Elizabeth didn't know this Annabelle from Adam's house cat, but she did know Gloria. She trusted Gloria. And if Gloria thought she was okay, then she must be. Besides, what choice did they have? Annabelle knew far more than the two of them put together. And knowledge was power.

BRIAN NOVAK was not accustomed to being rousted from bed like a common criminal. His money generally bought him a blind eye. But, Mac mused, there was a first time for everything.

"You know, Agent MacBride," Novak said, his hangover obvious in his rusty voice, as well as his disheveled appearance, "my attorney will be calling your superiors first thing tomorrow morning." He reached for the crystal decanter on the sideboard that served as a bar in his spacious great room. "I'm quite certain there is a law against this type of behavior."

Agent Driver had worked half the night and all morning to locate Novak, who'd recently moved into a criminally expensive midtown high-rise. Not one of his colleagues or cronies seemed to have his new address, but Mac had his own ideas about that. Finally Driver had managed to run down the secretary at Novak's design firm. Being young and new to the firm, she had been more easily intimidated and she'd rolled over on her boss like a playful puppy.

Now, at half-past noon, Mac finally had Novak's attention. He'd asked him where he'd been on the Friday night the doctor was murdered.

Novak took a sip of his whiskey and made a sound of approval before smiling at the question. "You think I killed Ned Harrison?"

What Mac really thought was that Novak had a connection to the Gentlemen's Association, but he hadn't wanted to press his luck by bringing up that theory unless it became absolutely necessary. Right now Novak was the only possible thread they had left on that case, and even that connection was thin. Too thin. Unlike with Harrison, they had no hard proof. Even with Harrison the only true evidence they'd managed to gather in months of work was one intercepted telephone conversation. Mac had clung to that link, knowing Harrison would eventually make another mistake.

"Yes," Mac said in answer to Novak's question and to the man's utter surprise. "Actually, I do." Driver stood silently on the other side of the room. He'd learned the first week on the job with Mac not to show any emotion. No matter how startled he might be at what he witnessed.

"Please, gentlemen—" Novak gestured to the sofa and chairs "—make yourselves comfortable. This discussion could prove interesting."

Mac didn't have any hard evidence connecting the murders of the women to Harrison's, but in his gut, he knew they were connected. Harrison's murderer might have been a woman, but a man had killed those women. The preliminaries on the first two victims had confirmed sexual assault. The killer had left behind seminal fluid, which could ultimately identify him. Mac wondered if Brian Novak was that stupid.

He dumped Elizabeth, so he must be. That notion seared Mac's brain like a hot blade. He blinked it away, refused to allow her into his thoughts right now.

Mac took Novak up on his invitation and settled on the sofa. Driver remained standing near the door. That routine was another thing he'd learned. When two agents attended an interview, one always stood to maintain the intimidation factor.

"Do you have an alibi or don't you?" Mac prodded.

"I was at a party," Novak said smugly. "Ned was supposed to be there, as well, but I guess he ran into a snag, so to speak."

The man's treatment of Elizabeth Young aside, there was something Mac didn't like about Novak. Maybe it was that beach-bum tan or the windblown way he wore his blond hair. Could be the earring— or even the blatant way he stared at Mac. From his manner of dress to his posture, the man clearly thought he was God's gift to women. Men, too, Mac decided. He hadn't missed the way Novak had sized up Driver and himself when they arrived. Poor Elizabeth. She hadn't had a chance against a smooth operator like this.

Mac clenched his jaw and attempted again to banish her from his mind. For the hundredth time he marveled at just how much difficulty he was having with this case... with her.

"I'd say he did," Mac replied, not the least bit amused by the man's gallows humor. "Why don't you give me the names of people who can verify your whereabouts?"

Novak drained his glass and set it aside. "Certainly."

As Mac jotted down the information, Novak rattled off more than a dozen names and telephone numbers. When Mac had crossed the "t" on the last one, he lifted his gaze to the other man's. "I don't see Elizabeth Young on your list. Aren't you two involved?"

Mac knew that his question must have confused Driver, for Driver was aware that he knew differently. But this bozo didn't.

The truth was, Mac wanted—no, needed Novak's take on the relationship. What did that make him? A masochist?

"That relationship ended months ago," Novak said

with a practiced laugh. "Your people really need to sharpen their investigative skills."

Mac nodded and made another note on his trusty pad that had absolutely nothing to do with Novak or Elizabeth or this case. "And what exactly was the nature of your former relationship?"

Novak took a deep breath and then slouched back on the couch, allowing his shirt to fall open and offering up his well-defined chest for display. Oh, yeah, this guy was bleeping big time on Mac's *gaydar*.

"Well, let's just say I did Elizabeth a favor." Novak inclined his head. "I gave sweet little Elizabeth the opportunity to grab the brass ring and she went for it. She couldn't wait to get out of that pathetic little dump of a town. I helped her get what she wanted and she made it worth my while."

Mac tensed before he could stop himself. Every muscle in his body jerked with the need to pound the hell out of this bastard.

A knowing smile lifted one side of Novak's mouth as he leaned forward and braced his arms on his knees, his gaze focused intently on Mac. "She's very good."

Fury sent Mac's blood rushing to his head, throbbing there in time with the stampede in his chest. His fingers tightened around the pen as if it were Novak's neck.

"She's always a little hesitant at first," Novak went on, pretending to be oblivious to Mac's reaction. But he knew. He knew and he enjoyed it immensely. "But once you get her started, man, is she hot."

Mac stood, his control slipping away fast. "I'll get back to you as soon as I've checked out your alibi."

Novak pushed lazily to his feet and led Mac to the front door, which he opened.

Mac wanted to kill him. He'd never in his life before wanted to kill a man over a woman, but he wanted to tear Brian Novak limb from limb.

Driver was already heading down the corridor to the elevator, but Mac hesitated in the doorway. "I wouldn't leave town if I were you." His gaze locked with Novak's pale-gray one. "There will be more questions."

Novak leaned against the door frame as if being visited by the FBI was an everyday occurrence. The bastard didn't even have the good sense to be worried.

"Take her, Agent MacBride," Novak said softly, knowingly. "You won't be sorry."

With his pen and pad in his pocket, Mac's fingers curled into tight fists of rage, but somehow he held himself back. "Thanks for your cooperation."

Mac stormed away without a backward glance. As angry as he was, the only thing he could think about was that videotape and the images it held. By the time he reached the elevator, he was as hard as a rock from merely thinking about Elizabeth Young and what Novak suggested.

He stepped into the waiting car and Driver punched the button for the lobby. "Quite a character, huh?"

Mac's only response was a grunt. He couldn't think clearly enough right now for a proper one. Every ounce of blood in his body had raced to his loins.

He had to close his eyes against the truth he wanted to deny.

Novak had seen it. Had rubbed it in.

Mac wanted Elizabeth. He wanted her riding him

slow and easy at first, and then hard and fast, her head thrown back in ecstasy. He wanted her touching him, kissing him. He wanted to feel her lips, her tongue on his skin. And then he wanted to take her with such intensity that she wouldn't even remember a jerk like Brian Novak when it was over.

He wanted her all to himself.

Suspect or not.

Mac shook himself. He'd lost it. That much was clear. "Driver, I want you to take the surveillance on Young tonight."

His partner was about to protest. Mac saw it in his eyes, but one look at the ferocity in Mac's and he snapped his mouth shut.

"Sure," he muttered. "Sure, why not?"

"IT'S THE RIGHT THING to do," Elizabeth told herself under her breath one last time.

Leaving the subway she'd glanced around again. No sign of the guy who'd been watching her. She'd had a hell of a time, but she was pretty sure she'd given the agent the slip. If she'd driven her truck, she'd never have been able to do it. But she'd parked it in an alley and then disappeared in the subway before the guy realized what she was up to. Then she'd ducked into a group of missionaries while he searched for her in the crowd on the platform. He was so certain she'd gotten on the train that he'd climbed aboard for a second to look for her. When he moved farther down the platform, she'd sneaked aboard the car he'd just checked. She'd watched him search for her as the train took off for its next stop.

Then she'd walked the ten blocks over to Avenue

of the Americas and to the row of old brownstones now used as offices, Ned's among them. It was really dark on this part of the street. Trees and architecture all but blocked the meager light from the streetlights. But she knew her way here with her eyes closed. What a joke. Look at what it had gotten her.

Nothing but trouble.

With the spare key Annabelle had given her now tightly clasped in her hand, Elizabeth slipped into an alley and then down the backside of the row of brownstones. She tried without success to calm her racing heart, to quiet her breathing. What if she was being watched this very minute? She swiveled her head from side to side. Nothing.

Keeping close to the wall, she moved toward the rear door that would lead into Ned's office. She supposed Annabelle had a key because she'd been his attorney. Since he had no surviving family, his attorney would be the most likely person to settle his affairs. Annabelle seemed just as scared by the murders as Gloria and Elizabeth were. This kind of action seemed their only recourse when they couldn't know who to trust. Elizabeth ignored the little voice that screamed at her that this was all wrong somehow.

She had to do this. Had to help exonerate herself. If they could prove the Gentlemen's Association was involved in Ned's death, then she would be free and clear. But they needed hard evidence.

Taking a deep breath for courage, she pushed away from the concealing security of the shadowed wall and moved to the door. Though there was no exterior light nearby to worry about, just enough moonlight glimmered down to guide her without giving away her presence. Thank God the police hadn't padlocked his office as they had his apartment. She supposed that made sense since his home—not his office—was the scene of the crime.

She had the key inserted into the lock when she heard it.

A footstep…something…

Before she could turn around, a strong arm snaked around her throat. A punishing hand clamped down on her mouth. The scream she tried to deliver died in her throat.

His angry breath on her cheek sent a shudder of recognition—of dread—through her. She felt his hard body pressed against her backside. Tried to jerk away. Twisted to break free, but he only held her more tightly to him.

His lips close enough to touch her skin, he whispered, ''I knew it was you.''

Chapter Eight

"Open the door, Liz," he ordered, his voice savage and cold.

Even before he'd used that pet name for her, she'd known it was him. An all-too-familiar shudder had quaked through her the instant he touched her...the instant she felt his breath on her skin.

"Let go of me, Brian, or I'll scream!"

He laughed the condescending laugh that punctuated the very essence of his macho mentality. He considered himself above all others, especially her. Why hadn't she seen that when they first met? Why hadn't she picked up on what a jerk he really was?

"So scream," he taunted. "Who's going to hear you?" He reached for the knob, gave it a fierce twist and kicked the door inward. "We're going to talk." Shoving her inside ahead of him, he quickly closed the door behind him.

Elizabeth scrambled to regain the equilibrium she'd lost physically, as well as mentally. Too many possibilities for her to choose just one swirled wildly amid the confusion and irritation clouding her ability to reason. Why was he here? What did they have to talk about?

Brian moved to the long table in the center of the dark interior and switched on one of the brass reading lamps. The dim glow pitched the space into long shadows, but she would have been fine without the light. She had firsthand knowledge of every inch of this room. After all, she'd helped decorate these offices just months ago. How else could she have afforded such an exclusive analyst? She'd worked hard to make Ned's suite of offices into everything he'd wanted. This room was no exception.

Ned's professional library. The walls were lined with book-filled, gleaming mahogany shelves. A single conference-style table, also mahogany, surrounded by upholstered armchairs served as the focal point. Built-in brass reading lamps lined the table, four of them altogether, their dignified appearance disrupted only by the latest technology in telephones sitting square in the middle. The classic reading lamps gave the room a more intimate ambiance than overhead lighting; the telephone with built-in conferencing capabilities was essential equipment.

The far corner of the room was equipped with a small wet bar complete with a dormitory-size fridge, a state-of-the-art coffeemaker and a small marble sink. A Monet print hung next to a shiny brass rack that held mugs and glasses. But the perks didn't stop here. In Ned's office there was another bar, one containing almost any kind of liquor one could want. To most the elegant piece of furniture looked like the matching credenza to his desk, but he had insisted that he needed a means of entertaining certain *special* clients.

She'd learned the hard way just what *special* meant to him.

Ned Harrison hadn't missed a trick. Whatever he wanted, he got. No matter the cost. He'd once lived in the upstairs portion of the brownstone, but fame had sent him in search of more elaborate housing. Now the rooms above his offices served as mere storage. She wondered briefly if it had all been worth it. Had his primal urges been worth dying for? She'd pretty much concluded that his murder had something to do with those very urges—and the Gentlemen's Association.

Who would ever have suspected? On the outside he'd been all charm and grace and appeared to have the world by the tail. All one had to do to join him in his glorious life was be obedient and submissive to his demands. Yet somehow he'd always managed to make her think it was what *she* wanted. It sickened her now to realize how naive she'd been.

"Sit." Dragging her attention back to the present, Brian motioned to one of the chairs.

He loved tossing out those one-word commands as if she were a dog or other well-trained pet. And hadn't she been?

But those days were over. "No thanks," she threw right back at him, folding her arms in defiance.

Those pale-gray eyes, as hard and icy as a frozen lake, gazed relentlessly into hers as he started toward her. She fought the urge to run. She would not let him have his way. Not again. Not ever again.

"I said sit!" He jerked out one of the chairs and clamped a hand on her shoulder with crushing strength, propelling her into the waiting seat.

For the first time since she'd realized it was him, fear slithered around her, tightening her chest. What was his problem? And what was he doing here, anyway?

Before she could demand some answers, he gave another order. "Tell me what it is you think you know." He propped himself on the edge of the table, positioning himself so that he could look down at her. "I don't want to have to hurt you."

If he'd slapped her, she wouldn't have been any more surprised. As cruel and belittling as Brian could be, she'd never feared him in the physical sense until now. With her heart pumping feverishly and dread dampening her skin, she seized back some semblance of control and dredged up an innocent look. "I don't know anything. What're you talking about?"

Her heart beating relentlessly against her sternum, she held her breath and prayed he would let it go at that.

He smiled, the surface convention utterly sinister. She swallowed. Hard. Was this some sort of game? She'd never seen him like this.

And suddenly she knew.

Brian was a part of this. He was probably a card-carrying member of the Gentlemen's Association as well. God knew he had the penchant for perversion.

"I know what you did, Elizabeth," he said softly, the gentler tone laced with a threatening edge. "The truth is, I don't give a damn that Harrison is dead." He made a sound, half growl, half chuckle. "He took too many chances." Brian reached out to graze her cheek with his fingertips. She flinched, earning herself another of those unnerving smiles.

"I know how he felt about you," he told her in that same low tone. His fingers trailed down her throat. "He thought you were special. Didn't want to let you go like he should have.'' His fingers splayed around her throat.

Elizabeth was determined not to let him see her fear. Damn him. ''Don't touch me like that.'' Hard as it was, she maintained eye contact, kept him looking at her so he wouldn't notice her left hand inching its way toward the center of the table.

That evil smile only widened. ''All you have to do is tell me the secret you're keeping and everything will be fine. I know you know—that's why you're here.'' The pressure of his fingers increased ever so slightly, raising goose bumps on her flesh. ''He wanted you, so I let him have you. But it wasn't easy, you know.''

She froze, the thoughts screeching to a halt inside her head. ''What're you saying?''

''Marrying you wasn't going to change who I am,'' he went on mysteriously. ''It would have simply provided the kind of image I needed. Until I found you, there hadn't been anyone I would have allowed that privilege. But I knew you'd never suspect.'' His fingers slid around to cup her neck and draw her closer. ''As naive as you were, you could still bring me to my knees with that sweet mouth and that hot body.''

Fury burned away every other emotion, including the paralyzing fear she'd felt only a second earlier. She tried to jerk away from him. This was insane. Nothing he said made sense.

''But Ned…'' He released her and shrugged. ''He was obsessed with you. Just watching you at the parties turned him on. He had to have you. What could I do? He was my best friend.''

This just couldn't be. She shook her head in denial of what his words meant. ''I rarely even saw the two of you speak. How could he have been your best friend? You didn't even come to his funeral!''

"Our relationship wasn't like that," Brian explained. "It was a private bond." He leaned nearer still, those menacing eyes carrying enough of an arctic blast to form icicles inside her. "Just like the one I know you're keeping from me."

A new thought punched through the pile of others tumbling into her head. "But it was Gloria who introduced me to Ned." She shook her head thoughtfully. "She suggested I see him...professionally." He couldn't be right about any of this. "You didn't have anything to do with it."

Brian stared at her lips now in a way that had once drawn her like a moth to the flame. Abruptly his earlier threat echoed loudly in her ears. He wanted answers—or he would hurt her. She inched her fingers closer to the telephone in the center of the table.

"I'm the one who told Gloria that seeing Ned would be a good idea for you," he said.

His statement stunned her, stole her breath. Gloria—her best friend, the only person in the world she trusted—was involved in this? Any bravado she'd managed collapsed like a house of cards. "I don't believe you," she protested weakly.

He straightened away from her, snapping out of his fixation on her lips. "Well, it's true. I have no reason to lie." He stared down at her once more, impatience registering. "Tell me what you know." When she would have argued, he said, "Careful now, I don't want you to regret anything." Something knowing slid into his expression. "I could always tell the police that I have evidence you killed him."

"I didn't kill him!" How could he say that? Just

when she'd thought nothing else could shock her. It was beyond all question now. He was insane.

"Of course you did," he countered.

Her head moved side to side in denial of his ridiculous accusation. "Why would I kill him? You can't possibly have any evidence."

"Because he wasn't going to let you go, even after you discovered his socially unacceptable appetite and was repulsed by it. He wanted to keep you, anyway. We all knew the troubles the two of you were having." That evil smile stretched his lips once more. "You'd be surprised what can be turned into proof."

The way she'd openly avoided Ned, the argument. God. The dagger.

It had been a gift from her. Had Brian planted it there? Horror gripped her by the throat. Surely he hadn't killed Ned!

"A man should always know when to let go," Brian rambled on. "But he just wouldn't let it go. I warned him that keeping you would be a mistake. The longer the relationship went on, the more likely you were to discover our secret. Others were concerned, as well."

Keeping her? Incredulity momentarily overshadowed the fear. This was the twenty-first century. Men didn't *keep* women. And the only appetite she'd known Ned to have was the insatiable one he had for women. He liked to screw around, especially with those who trusted him on a professional level. One woman would never have been enough for him. He'd been far too smooth to ever get caught. He knew how to make a woman think she needed him—believe it had been her own idea. She stilled. But there had been that one secret—the videotapes...and the Gentlemen's Association.

"I don't know what any of this means," she said, her fingers finally touching the edge of the telephone base. Anticipation propelled adrenaline into her bloodstream. She struggled to keep the tumultuous emotions from her eyes.

"Tell me, Liz." Brian leaned in her direction again. "How did it feel to plunge that dagger into his chest? Was it like the time you stabbed your brother-in-law, or was it all the better knowing you'd sliced straight into his heart?"

"I didn't do it!" The raw, primal sound of her voice startled even her.

"But can you prove it?" he taunted. "Now, tell me what you know."

Her fingers curled around the receiver, and in one swift move she surged upward and slammed it into his skull before he could block the move. He crumpled to the floor.

And didn't move.

A trickle of blood bloomed at his hairline along his temple. Her first instinct was to see if he was dead or alive, but her second overrode it. She ran. Jerked the back door open and ran like hell.

She had only one thing on her mind— finding Gloria.

Brian couldn't have been telling the truth. She refused to believe that Gloria had betrayed her like that. Hadn't they both suffered at Ned's hand? Gloria was just as hurt as she was. They were best friends, for God's sake.

Pushing herself to move faster, Elizabeth bounded onto the sidewalk. Brian could come to any second and chase her down. She felt certain she'd only stunned him. She shuddered at what he might have had planned for her. But why? What did he have to do with any of this?

How could she not have known he and Ned were close?

What did they have in common? Ned was a psychiatrist. Brian was an architect. At least five years separated them in age. Their tastes in clothing, music, in everything, were worlds apart. She couldn't even imagine what they talked about.

The Gentlemen's Association.

The realization struck her like a blow to the abdomen. Brian had to have been a part of it, too. He'd seen the video. Renewed horror rushed through her. How many of *their* lovemaking sessions had he videotaped? Her knees threatened to buckle. Would this nightmare ever end? All these years she'd felt so sorry for her sister living in hell with an on-again-off-again drug habit and an abusive husband. And look at her. She hadn't fared much better.

Elizabeth slammed headlong into a brick wall—or what felt like one.

Kicking and clawing, she wrenched away from the hands grabbing at her, but he was too strong. She couldn't let him get her now. Had to get away. She opened her mouth to scream.

"Stop fighting me!" he ordered.

She went limp as recognition of the voice filtered through her hysteria. Her gaze flew to his face.

MacBride.

"What the hell are you running from?" he demanded sharply.

In the next second Elizabeth realized two things.

She had just committed assault and been caught fleeing the office of a victim in an ongoing murder investigation.

A murder investigation in which she was a prime suspect.

She was screwed.

MacBride shook her just hard enough to get her attention. Those strong fingers gripping her arms sent spears of heat through her. "What happened, Elizabeth? What're you doing here?"

"I...I thought I'd left something in the library." She trembled at the idea of having lied to him yet again. She was tired of lying—especially to him. If he ever found out...

Even in the dim light she saw his eyes narrow. "At Harrison's office?"

MacBride was no fool. He knew exactly where she'd been. Had probably known this was where she was headed the minute his man reported her having given him the slip in the vicinity of midtown.

"Yes." She sucked in a ragged breath and shrugged free of his hold, even though a part of her would have liked nothing better than to wilt in those powerful arms. "I...I helped decorate his office," she stammered, grappling for an acceptable excuse, "and I only just realized my paint chips were missing. I thought maybe I'd left them here."

"The work you did for Harrison was months ago, wasn't it?" That scrutinizing gaze bored straight into her.

She lifted her chin and flat out ignored his innuendo. "I guess I must have left it someplace else."

He cocked his head and eyed her suspiciously.

"That doesn't explain why you were running for your life. Was someone else here, too?"

God almighty. If by some sick twist of fate Brian was dead, she was done for. Even if he was alive and kicking, she didn't want MacBride to talk to him. The last thing she needed was Brian putting ideas about evidence and motives into MacBride's head. She was already at the top of his list.

"While I was searching I...I thought I heard someone outside, maybe a burglar, so I ran." She held her breath as she waited for his reaction.

"I guess we should check it out, then."

Before she could come up with a reasonable excuse not to, he was dragging her back toward the office. At the door her heart leaped into her throat. If Brian opened his big mouth...

"You left the door open?"

The door stood ajar the way she'd left it, but there was no sign of Brian. She blinked and looked again just in case. No Brian. Thank God.

She nodded in answer to MacBride's question. "I was too scared to take the time to lock up." Now that was the truth.

"You have a key?"

The slightest dash of surprise flavored his voice.

"I guess I forgot to give it back after the job was done," she offered, moving to the conference table to lean against it. She couldn't trust her ability to stay vertical at the moment. A mixture of relief and trepidation had turned her muscles rubbery.

She imagined that Brian must have noticed that someone had detained her as she fled. He'd likely slipped away unnoticed in the other direction.

Lucky him.

She was stuck here with MacBride.

She shivered when her eyes took in the whole of him as he stood in the middle of Ned's library surveying the place. Agent MacBride was a hottie, that was undeniable. And there was a definite attraction between them. But she damn sure didn't need any additional complications right now. Not to mention the fact that MacBride thought she was a killer.

Staring down at the floor, she contemplated that reality. She still had trouble accepting that Ned was actually dead—murdered. She shivered again and wrapped her arms around herself. She'd never known anyone who wound up murdered. Setting aside the fact that in some ways he'd deserved a bad end, he'd still been a human being and now he was gone.

Standing there in the library she'd helped choose colors and carpeting for, that bottom line crashed in on her. No force on earth could bring Ned back. His life was over and hers might very well be, too, if MacBride had anything to say about it.

"You're certain there was no one else here besides you?"

Careful not to look directly at him, she nodded. "Just me—until I heard the sound outside. Someone must have been poking around in the alley." She'd let him draw his own conclusions. Could have been a homeless person for all MacBride knew.

He bent down and picked up something from the floor. "I guess I overlooked this the last time I was here." He held the item out for her inspection and she knew instantly what it was. Brian's money clip. A fourteen-carat gold showpiece with the initials BWN. Brian Wayne Novak.

MacBride dropped the item into his jacket pocket.

"I'll just take it in for analysis by the folks in forensics."

If he questioned Brian…

MacBride's slow, deliberate approach abruptly derailed that worrisome thought. She tried not to look at him, but she simply couldn't help herself. The way he moved, fluid, predatory and with the unparalleled grace of a hunter. The fit of that expensive suit, even with his collar unbuttoned and his tie jerked loose, lent a dangerous element. There he was all polished and smart-looking on the outside, but something deeply primal simmered just beneath. She could see it in those blue eyes. She could feel it vibrating all around him like a force field. That short, silky hair looked as if he'd just raked his fingers through it, and his jaw sported a five-o'clock shadow.

Everything about him screamed sex, blatantly challenged any female within sight or smelling distance to come have a taste.

He stopped no more than two feet away, his long-fingered hands propped firmly on his hips, the lapels of his jacket pushed aside. She told herself not to look into those eyes, not to let him draw her in more deeply.

But then he spoke and any hope of denying the urge was lost. "This was not a smart move, Elizabeth," he said quietly, his voice soft and deadly serious. "Coming here makes you look even guiltier than you already do. Didn't you stop to consider that access to this office was too easy? I've had someone watching 24/7 for just this moment. You'd better start talking."

She blinked once, twice, her mind frantically attempting to focus on his words while the part of her that made her female zeroed in on all that marked him male. Her very skin felt electric, ready to combust. "I told you I—"

"I know what you told me, but it was a lie. Just like the other lies you've told me. I'm giving you another chance here. Tell me what you know, and this will be a lot easier on the both of us."

Summoning her scattered resolve, she looked him square in the eye and said the only thing she could. "I don't know what you want from me, Agent Mac-Bride. I've told you everything I know."

"Did you have sex with Harrison the night he was murdered?" he asked casually, unhurriedly. But he gave himself away when he shifted his gaze from hers, a visible concession to the tension mounting between them.

"No," she said adamantly.

"Then you won't mind submitting a sample for DNA comparison to the intimate body hair discovered at the scene."

Mac knew he'd gotten her attention then. He heard the harsh intake of breath, saw the widening of her eyes.

"My attorney—"

"Your attorney can't make this go away, Elizabeth," he cut in smoothly. "Only *I* can. But to do that I need to be able to eliminate the possibility that you were in Harrison's bed that night."

For an instant she wavered, uncertain. He didn't want that moment of increased vulnerability to pass. "Making that elimination would be a major step in the right direction."

"I guess it couldn't hurt," she said stiffly.

He watched her lips as she spoke, knowing it was

a mistake but unable to help himself. There was just something about her mouth, something that drew him, made him want to taste her.

Before he could thwart the impulse, he'd moved closer, his thigh brushing hers as he stood closer than was safe. The resulting charge of the slight contact went straight to his loins.

"See how easy that was?" he offered roughly, fighting hard to stay on track here.

She watched his lips now, her own slightly parted. Was she attracted to him, as well, or was this just one of her maneuvers to distract him?

Her tongue darted out to moisten her lips. Control slipped another notch and he was pretty sure that getting any *harder* would be impossible. But he had her right where he wanted her. He couldn't let the moment go—just yet.

"Tell me why you really came here tonight," he urged, his voice as soft as it was insistent. "Was it Novak's idea or yours?"

Her gaze collided with his. "I'm no fool, Elizabeth. The clip has his initials on it."

"It's…" She shook her head. "It's not what you think."

"How do you know what I think?"

She lifted one shoulder uncertainly. "You think I killed him."

For the first time since he'd met Elizabeth Young, he allowed himself to look at her—the woman, not the suspect. The tomboyish sprinkle of freckles across the bridge of her nose. The way her glasses always needed pushing up or setting straight. The rich amber of her eyes. His fingers itched to tangle in the thick mass of dark hair she always kept pulled back in a braid or ponytail. Long strands had slipped loose now. They clung to her face, appearing even darker against the creaminess of her skin. But it was her mouth that tormented him more than anything else. Wide, full, the bottom lip noticeably heavier than the top.

"You wanted to kill him," he said without thinking.

She chewed that tempting lower lip for a second. "But I didn't."

"Was Novak in on it? Did the two of you plan this together?"

That sent her rushing for cover, but he blocked her path. "He was, wasn't he?"

"I don't know!" She tried to push away the arm that held her back, but only succeeded in shoving him a little further over the edge with her touch.

"Is he involved with the Gentlemen's Association, too?"

Her head came up. She opened her mouth to refute his suggestion, but her face gave her away before she could tell him yet another lie.

"Don't waste your breath, Elizabeth. Your eyes already gave me the answer I suspected." He choked out a laugh. "Do you have any idea how much danger you're in right now?"

The fear and uncertainty vanished with one blink of her long-lashed lids. "From whom? Them or you? You keep pushing me and pushing me like you really believe I'm guilty, but I see the way you look at me. I'm not blind, MacBride."

And that easily he was lost. He took her face in his hands and kissed her. As his mouth swooped down to claim hers, he felt the little hitch in her breath. She tensed but didn't draw away. He took that as permission to plunder the luscious mouth that had been driving him insane for days.

That was the final rational thought Mac managed. She tasted like chocolate and coffee. Café mocha maybe. And she was hot, so damned hot.

He gently lifted her glasses up and off, leaving them on the table so that he could get back to touching her with both hands. His fingers delved into the thick softness of her hair, and he groaned with satisfaction. He'd wanted to touch her like this from the moment he first laid eyes on her. He took the kiss deeper, thrusting his tongue inside her, wanting, needing more.

Still she didn't surrender to the kiss. He was kissing her. She allowed it but didn't respond.

Images of the innately sexual creature on the videotape flooded his head, and a jolt of jealousy went through him. He wanted her like that, wanted her responding to his touch, to his kiss.

He kissed her harder, demanding a reaction.

And that made him just like them.

He tore his mouth from hers, but couldn't draw away completely at first. Had to hover there. This close he could still feel her pull. He licked his lips, tasting her, feeling her quick little puffs of warm breath on his damp skin. The way she smelled, like a rose beneath the warm sun, made him want to pull her to him again.

But he didn't.

He stepped back, at a loss, for a moment, for words. She refused to look at him, kept her gaze somewhere in the vicinity of the third button on his shirt. Right about the same location where the knife had entered Harrison's chest. Another dose of reality slammed into him.

"I'll take you home."

At some point he would need to acknowledge having overstepped his bounds. But not right now.

Right now walking away pretty much took all the strength he possessed.

TRUST WAS SUCH a powerful tool. Who would ever suspect? By the time the victim grew suspicious, it was too late.

Far too late.

One carefully calculated strike was all it took. So easy, so quick. The blade sliced deeply into the creamy smoothness of her throat. The gush of blood flowed like a crimson river, propelled by the final frantic beating of her heart. Her entire body tensed and the scream that would have rent the air wilted impotently behind the panties stuffed in her mouth.

We are so proud of ourselves. It's almost over. We are so very close. Only a few more to go.

And vengeance will be ours.

Chapter Nine

Elizabeth lay in the predawn darkness and thought about the previous night. A part of her had wanted to go to Gloria's place and demand answers. But how could she do that? It would be an outright admission that she didn't trust her friend. A slap in the face. She just couldn't do that. Gloria was the one person she *had* been able to trust. Brian had to be lying. There was no other explanation. Ned had almost ruined their relationship; it would be just like Brian to try to finish it off.

He was jealous that way. A selfish son of a bitch who cared only for himself.

She closed her eyes and exhaled a heavy breath. She'd been so blind. The whole idea of moving to the big city, of working with the masters at a design firm like Design Horizons. It had been her dream since she was twelve, when she realized what one could do with a mere gallon of paint and a yard of fabric. Her father's work as a handyman had ingrained in her a love of houses and their care. As she'd grown older she realized there was a whole world of possibilities out there. And she was good at designing and decorating interiors. Really good, though she'd had no formal education in the field. Her skill came naturally, like breathing. She looked at a room and saw a bare canvas.

But the break with Brian had ended all that. She had no reputation, no contacts of her own, so she'd had to fall back on the sort of work she could do without any of those things—good, honest hard work. Interior painting could be backbreaking. You had to be good, as well as fast, to earn a living wage at it. She was both, but she was a woman, which was an automatic strike against her. She'd had to work cheaply at first, and being choosy about her work location hadn't been an option. Finding Boomer had proved a lucky break. He wasn't afraid of anything, including hard work.

Now her work was pretty steady. The locations were a great deal better and she'd earned the beginnings of an excellent reputation. She could make it.

Just when things had been looking up financially, if not personally, Ned had entered the picture. Sure, she'd seen him around; the kind of parties Brian attended or hosted catered to the rich and socially privileged. Seeing Ned on a professional level had felt right at first. He'd seemed kind. She'd needed that. All her life everyone she'd depended on or needed had deserted her, one way or another. Her mother had walked out on them when Elizabeth was in kindergarten, her father had died last year, and then Brian had dumped her. According to Ned, the panic attacks were caused by years of uncertainty. His counseling had helped.

The affair had been an accident—at least she'd

thought so at the time. Brian's caustic words rever-
berated in her head. It was hard to believe that Ned
would have set out to reel her in like that when he
could have any woman he wanted. The memory of
the videotape slammed into her thoughts like an out-
of-control dump truck on a downhill stretch. Oh,
yeah, she shouldn't be shocked at anything she discovered about him.

She flopped over onto her side. But the part about
Gloria, she simply refused to believe that. Elizabeth
had every intention of chalking up the whole idea to
Brian's cruel selfishness. He'd lost his friend and he
wanted Elizabeth to lose hers. The first time she'd
gotten accolades from a pleased design client, Brian
had found a way to ruin it. Despite all the nasty little
things he'd done, she hadn't realized until the very
end just how selfish he was. Or maybe she hadn't
wanted to see it.

But that was over now and she was left wondering
if Brian was involved in Ned's murder. Had it been
his intent to set Elizabeth up? The fact that whoever
had killed Ned had used the dagger she'd given him
seemed to support that theory. She considered Mac-
Bride's suggestion that she submit to DNA testing.
Shuddering at the implication, she curled into the fetal
position. She didn't kill Ned, so she wasn't really
worried on that score, but what if whoever had attempted to set her up had planted the evidence they'd
discovered? She emitted a harsh spasm of laughter.
*Okay, Elizabeth, exactly how would someone have
gotten any of your pubic hair without your knowledge?*

She thought about her shower or bathroom floor.

Sometimes there were loose hairs scattered about when she got around to housework. Lord knows she didn't bother with it often. She supposed someone could have come into her place while she was at work and Mrs. Polk was off playing bridge or something. It wasn't outside the realm of possibility. Nor was the possibility that Brian had saved a couple of her hairs from their time together, she considered. They'd lived together for several months.

But all that was just too farfetched. That kind of thing only happened in movies.

This wasn't a movie; this was real. Elizabeth hugged her knees more tightly to her chest. MacBride was certain she was involved. He knew she was lying to him. He read her so well. And he kissed like no one had ever kissed her before.

At the unnecessary reminder her skin heated from the inside out. She'd tried so hard to block the memory, but it just wouldn't go away. All night she'd awakened every couple of hours, and her first thought each time was of his kiss, his touch. He'd startled her with the move, although some part of her had known it was coming, and she'd frozen at first, unable to respond on even the most basic level.

Who was she kidding? She always froze—at first. It took a great deal of trust just to dive in, and she simply didn't trust any man that much. She'd trusted her father, but he was gone now, then she'd put her faith in Brian, and look where that had gotten her. Her sister had trusted her husband and she'd paid dearly for it. So had Elizabeth. She'd almost gone to prison after taking that knife to her brother-in-law to stop him from hurting her sister yet again. Hadn't it been another man who'd taken their mother away from them? She'd fallen so desperately for him she'd deserted her husband and two small children, never to be heard from again. According to Ned, it was that abandonment that had set the stage for her current phobia. She wasn't entirely sure that was true, since she'd long ago blocked all thought of her mother from her mind. But maybe it was true.

One thing was certain, she couldn't trust MacBride. He was an FBI agent who considered her a suspect in his current murder investigation. Even if she could muster up the courage to trust him, he would use that trust to prove her guilty. That combined with the undeniable truth that he was one hundred percent male, canceled any hope of her being able to trust him.

No matter how attracted she was to him—and she was definitely attracted—she couldn't let down her guard. Ned had offered some fancy name for her little trust problem, but she didn't necessarily agree with his conclusion. Sure, with a guy she was attracted to she could work up enthusiasm for sex eventually, *eventually* being the key word. She closed her eyes and pressed her forehead to her knees. Brian had called her frigid. They'd fought so many times over her lack of sexual ambition that eventually she'd learned to submit to his needs a little more quickly, but only with conscious effort. Ned had known all the right words to coax her into cooperation. But no one, absolutely no one, had ever made her *want* to jump in with both feet.

Except MacBride.

Oh, she'd gone through the usual routine of freezing up at his first touch. But in mere seconds she'd wanted to throw her arms around him and climb his hard male body. The only thing that had stopped her had been her lack of trust. Yet for the first time in her life, she was certain she could have dived straight in, ignoring the whole trust issue. Just her luck to find the one man who set her on fire with barely a touch and he wanted to charge her with murder!

She uncurled and rolled onto her back to stare at the ceiling, noting the cracks in the old plaster and the fact that the ceiling, as well as the rest of her apartment, needed a fresh coat of paint. She harrumphed. Painters were like hairdressers; they always needed a makeover but were too busy taking care of everybody else to find time to do their own. That was the story of her life. Always wishing for what she couldn't have.

The telephone next to the bed rang, cutting short the self-pity session.

Her heart took a breath-stealing dip. It was scarcely daylight. Who would call her at this hour? Her sister? Something could have happened to one of the kids...

She snatched up the receiver. "Hello."

"Elizabeth?"

She frowned, not immediately recognizing the woman's voice. Something like a moan and then a grating attempt at clearing a throat. "Yes," she answered, trepidation slowing her response.

"Elizabeth, it's Annabelle."

The ache of hopelessness in the woman's voice propelled Elizabeth into a sitting position. Fear ripped through her at her first thought—Gloria. "What's wrong?"

"There's been...another murder," she stammered.

Elizabeth felt herself go numb.

"I heard the call go out on the police scanner," Annabelle explained solemnly. "I checked the address they called out against Ned's patient log."

A tense beat of silence sent Elizabeth's heart into warp speed.

"It's Marissa Landon, it has to be. The officer at the scene reported that the victim was female and that's her address." Another of those moanlike sounds. "Is this ever going to stop? Why can't they do something?"

"I'll call Gloria." Elizabeth scarcely recognized the stone-cold voice as her own. The relief at her friend's safety was there, but the realization that another woman was dead overrode it to a large degree. Thank God it wasn't Gloria. But still, another murder.

"We have to talk," Annabelle urged. "I think there's a new pattern developing here. Did you get to Ned's office yet?"

Elizabeth was already out of bed and searching for clothes. The question stirred the dread that had settled like a rock in her stomach. "We can talk about that when we're all together. Where should we meet?"

"My office." She gave Elizabeth the uptown address. "I'll be waiting."

After disconnecting, Elizabeth punched in Gloria's number and jumped into her clothes as she waited out the rings.

Four murders. It was only Monday. Ned had been dead for just over a week and already four of his patients were dead.

Dear God, who would be next?

MAC WAS AT THE OFFICE when the call came in. He hadn't been able to sleep, so he'd come in to study what he had on the murders that had been dubbed "The Princess Murders," since all of the victims had been New York society elite.

All three of the women were young, all were beautiful and wealthy, but other than that the only true connection among them was that they'd been patients of Ned Harrison's. After the second murder, Brannigan had started checking female victims against Harrison's patient log as a matter of course. Mac hadn't asked for lead on this case, but he'd asked for cooperation; Detective Brannigan seemed happy to give it, since he was more than aware that Mac could take the case if he wanted it.

Each victim had been bound to her bed and gagged with a pair of cheap nylon panties. The ritual was the same each time—she was sexually assaulted and then murdered with a single slash to the throat. No sign of struggle in any room other than the bedroom was evident at any of the scenes. Who was this man that the women would allow him into their homes without question? Did he force his way in with a gun?

At each scene numerous prints were lifted, but it would take forever to cross-check them all. The killer's seminal fluid was left behind in each case. DNA testing and cross-matching with CODIS—the FBI's bank of DNA profiles on convicted offenders—was in the works. Mac had made all the right calls to ensure a speedy response on the DNA results.

But now there was a fourth victim. It wasn't that Mac hadn't anticipated additional victims. He had. Whether Brannigan was ready to admit it or not, he had himself a serial killer. And somehow the killings were connected to Harrison.

The one thing about the latest killing that startled the hell out of Mac was the location. The victim was found in her home less than six blocks from Harrison's office—where both Elizabeth and Novak had been the night before. According to the ME she'd been dead long enough to be in full rigor mortis with some cooling of body temperature, which indicated the victim had been dead twelve to fourteen hours.

Mac glanced at the digital clock on his desk as he got ready to head to the crime scene. It was 7 a.m. now. That would, roughly speaking, put the time of death at sometime between 5 and 7 p.m. the previous night. He'd discovered Elizabeth and evidence of Novak, at Harrison's office at approximately 7:30. He was still furious that the surveillance team monitoring Harrison's office had somehow missed Novak's presence. They'd spotted Elizabeth and called him immediately, but they'd missed Novak entirely. The wily bastard couldn't be that good. Catching someone with motivation to get inside Harrison's office had been the whole point of surveillance versus locking down the damn place. They needed a break in this case. With the proper surveillance he could have pinpointed Novak's exact time of arrival. Hell, maybe he'd just beat it out of the guy.

Mac was still investigating Novak, but there were several things he already knew about the man. He'd been born to wealthy parents who were still movers and shakers in the financial world. His father had been immensely disappointed when his only son chose to go into architecture and design, rather than mergers and takeovers. Novak had never been in any real trouble, other than one petty drug bust in college and a charge four years ago of soliciting prostitution. Like Harrison, Novak had himself a sick little obsession with the seamier side of sex.

Until now Mac hadn't had any evidence to warrant the subpoena of DNA evidence from either Novak or Elizabeth. But things were different now. They had both been in the vicinity of the crime, were guilty of breaking and entering the office of a recent murder victim whose case was ongoing, and the two were definitely hiding something.

One way or another, Mac intended to know what it was.

He would push Elizabeth Young until she broke.

Before he could stop it, the memory of kissing her erupted inside him, yanking the rug right out from under him. Sending his senses reeling all over again. He'd worked hard all morning and most of the night not to think about her in that sense. To forget the insane move he'd made kissing her. But he couldn't seem to keep it pushed away. The taste of her, the smell of her, kept haunting him.

He shook his head as he exited his office and headed for the elevators. He couldn't stop thinking about her when what he needed to be focusing on was the facts.

Fact one: Elizabeth Young was supposed to meet Ned Harrison the night he was murdered.

Fact two: the murder weapon was a gift from Elizabeth.

Fact three: an illicit affair between Elizabeth and

Harrison had ended badly; already several of their mutual friends had given statements to that effect.

Fact four: Elizabeth had a record of drug possession and felony assault.

Fact five: she had no alibi for the night of Harrison's murder.

Finally and the most damning of all: Elizabeth knew he was attracted to her. She'd said as much. *I see the way you look at me.* Which meant he wasn't being objective where she was concerned.

Even in light of all that, he still wanted her.

ELIZABETH SAT adjacent to Gloria in one of the matching wing chairs flanking Annabelle's desk. The office was nice, not quite as luxurious as Ned's, but on that order. She had an uptown address that spoke of money and prestige.

Elizabeth had no idea what kind of attorney Annabelle was, since she hadn't met her until yesterday, but if accommodations were any indicator, she must be doing well for herself. Elizabeth liked that. Any time a woman could flourish in a man's world, she loved it.

"Look at the last names." Annabelle pointed at the list she'd made of the victims, all former patients of Ned's.

"Damn," Gloria breathed the word. "They're in alphabetical order."

Annabelle nodded in confirmation. "Bumbalough, Dell, Fowler and now Landon. I checked the log of patients and there are four more, including the two of you."

Elizabeth's forehead pleated into a frown. "I'm sure Ned had a lot more than eight patients."

"Definitely," Annabelle hastened to agree. "But these are the ones I've pretty much narrowed the list down to, having had a more personal relationship with him."

Elizabeth and Gloria exchanged uncertain glances.

Annabelle sighed. "Yes, I'm aware that Ned sometimes broke the rules with his patients." She folded her hands atop the clean blotter on her desk. "I didn't really have a problem with his less-than-savory involvement with the association and the darker side of sexuality." She paused, her expression intent, thoughtful. "But I fear that this association business and his crossing the line with his patients delved into far more dangerous territory than he intended."

"How did you figure out that he had become sexually involved with—" Elizabeth swallowed tightly "—some of his patients?"

Annabelle leaned back in her chair and fixed her gaze on Elizabeth. "To be perfectly honest with you, I suspected as much months ago."

"What did you do?" Gloria leaned forward a bit in anticipation of her answer.

"I confronted him, of course. Gave him my professional advice whether he wanted to hear it or not."

"But he didn't want your advice," Elizabeth said, knowing how Ned would have reacted to being told what to do by anyone. He was far too arrogant to allow anyone to boss him around.

Annabelle looked down for a moment before saying more. "He was my friend," she said when she again met their gazes. "I didn't agree with what he did, but I couldn't just walk away, either."

Elizabeth blinked back the tears that had blurred her vision. Ned had used them all. When would she ever wake up and stop allowing men to take advantage of her? Furious with herself, she glanced at her watch. Nine-thirty already. Boomer would be wondering where she was. He knew to get started without her, but she couldn't put off going much longer. Getting behind wasn't an option. She needed to fulfill this contract. She needed the money.

"Did you find the hidden door?"

The unexpected question startled Elizabeth back to attention. With the news of another murder, she'd completely forgotten about the previous evening's mission, even though she'd promised Annabelle an update and had expected the question.

She shook her head. "Brian followed me there or stumbled upon me there, and I couldn't do anything."

Annabelle straightened, clearly surprised. "Brian Novak?"

Elizabeth nodded. "He…" She frowned, trying to remember his exact words. "He accused me of killing Ned and then urged me to tell him the secret I knew." Her gaze connected with Annabelle's. "Do you think he was talking about the Gentlemen's Association?"

"Brian was watching Ned's office?" Gloria asked, her voice, as well as her expression, revealing her shock.

"Apparently." Elizabeth couldn't think of any other explanation for why he would have been there at precisely the same time she was. She shuddered inwardly. "He kind of scared me." As furious as it made her that MacBride had her under surveillance, the sight of that nondescript sedan parked outside her place this morning had been reassuring. It hadn't been him, but it was one of his men.

"Jesus," Gloria muttered on a shaky breath. "This just gets more bizarre by the minute."

"If the police don't stop this murderer..." Annabelle allowed her words to trail off. She didn't have to say the rest. They both knew what she meant.

"What're we going to do?" Gloria looked from Annabelle to Elizabeth. "If there're only four others and two of them are us, we have to do something to protect ourselves."

Her friend was right, Elizabeth agreed silently, dread rocking through her. And Gloria was her friend. She wasn't about to put any stock in anything Brian said. She trusted Gloria, to confront her with Brian's accusations would be wrong. "How?"

"Do you have someone you could stay with at night?" This from Annabelle. She looked from one to the other. "I really don't think either of you should be alone, especially at night." She massaged her forehead as if an ache had begun there. "I can't believe the police haven't noticed this already. They're supposed to be trained to see these details. You should have police protection."

Elizabeth suddenly wondered if MacBride had considered this fact. If he had, then why hadn't he warned her? *Because he thinks you're a murderer,* a little voice taunted.

Elizabeth's entire being trembled again.

"I could stay with my sister," Gloria said uncertainly. "She has her husband's gun."

This time the tremble stayed with Elizabeth. "That's a good idea," she said thinly, trying hard to be steady.

"But what about you, Elizabeth? You could stay with us, too," Gloria urged.

Elizabeth shook her head. If the killer was after her, no way would she endanger Gloria's family. She stilled. What if it was her he really wanted? What if all these other murders were nothing but a decoy? She could be the coup de grâce.

Enough, Elizabeth, she railed silently. *Don't make this about you. It's about Ned…somehow.*

"I'll ask Boomer to stay over." That would work. He'd be glad to. And he was tough. She wouldn't have to worry with him around.

"Just be sure you do," Gloria said, her voice still full of apprehension. "I don't think any of us should be alone." She looked at Annabelle. "What about you?"

The attorney waved her hands in a forget-about-it gesture. "I'll be fine. I have friends I can stay with. So you'll be with your sister," she said to Gloria, "and you'll have *Boomer* to protect you?" She frowned. "Who, exactly, is Boomer?"

Elizabeth laughed, the quick burst of humor easing some of the tension. "He's my assistant."

"An ex-con," Gloria added. "She'll be safe with him."

Annabelle looked a little skeptical, but said, "No doubt."

Something else nudged at Elizabeth. "Annabelle, could Ned have been murdered for his money?"

The attorney considered the question for a moment.

"I don't see how. I've started his will through probate. His brother was to inherit everything—"

"His brother?" Gloria asked incredulously. "I didn't know he had any siblings."

Annabelle's expression turned solemn. "Well, he did have a brother, but he died several years ago. No other family left. So in accordance with Ned's wishes his assets will be distributed to various charities."

Well, well, Elizabeth mused. Who would have thought that Casanova Ned would turn into a philanthropist upon his death? Too bad he hadn't shown that kind of compassion in life. She'd never once wondered if he had any family. He just seemed to *be*— as if he'd sprung forth fully grown with no need for any family.

All of them had work to get to, so the meeting broke up and Gloria and Elizabeth walked out together. On the sidewalk Gloria, in vintage Gloria fashion, hailed the first cab that passed. At least a dozen always whizzed by Elizabeth before she could get one's attention.

"Call me tonight," Gloria ordered as she climbed in. "I want to hear Boomer's voice coming across your phone line."

Elizabeth nodded. "Don't worry. I won't take any chances. And you'll be at your sister's."

"Immediately after work," Gloria assured her. The look in her eyes told Elizabeth there wasn't any question. Gloria was obviously as afraid as she was.

When Gloria's taxi had merged with the traffic, Elizabeth walked slowly toward the garage where she'd parked her truck. Others, hurrying to work, brushed past her, and she moved closer to the curb to avoid them. She thought about the woman who'd been murdered last night and tried without success to understand why this was happening. Why would anyone want to kill Ned's patients unless he somehow suspected one of them of being responsible for Ned's death? And that was assuming the murderer was a friend of Ned's.

Is that how Brian fit into all this? Had he killed Ned because of her? She shook her head. Brian didn't care that much about anyone and neither did Ned. Playing sick little games appeared to be what the two had in common. Could their game playing have turned into murder?

She wrapped her arms around herself as that bone-chilling cold that came from deep inside made her tremble. She was on that kill list. If the killer knew about her fight with Ned and the visit to his apartment, he would no doubt consider her a prime suspect. But why kill the others? Maybe he just wanted to be absolutely certain he got the right one.

She'd lived with Brian for months. Surely she would know if he was capable of murder.

A car screeched to a halt at the curb, the abrupt sound jerking Elizabeth back to the here and now. Her heart slammed against the wall of her chest and she started to run.

Surely he wouldn't strike in open daylight on a crowded street. Then recognition flared.

MacBride peered at her from inside the dark sedan. She'd forgotten all about her private watchdog.

"Get in," he ordered.

She waited as a couple of pedestrians pushed past her, rushing for a passing cab. Irritation instantly mounted in her. MacBride had been following her again. "What?" she demanded as she stepped nearer to the curb and the waiting car.

"Get in," he growled, his gaze every bit as fierce as his command.

She leaned down to peer inside the car. Turned toward the passenger window, his left hand on the steering wheel and his right arm braced against the back of the front seat, he looked like a panther poised to lunge at his prey.

"Why?" she asked, uncomfortable with his whole demeanor.

"Get in willingly or I'll arrest you. It's your choice."

The edge in his voice sliced right through her annoyance, changing it to uneasiness. "All right."

Knowing she had no choice, Elizabeth opened the door and slid into the passenger seat. Before she had time to fasten her seat belt, he barreled into the flow of traffic, earning himself squealing tires and impatient honks.

"I'm only going to ask you this once, Elizabeth," he said without glancing her way. "What were you and Novak doing at Harrison's office last night?"

Not that again. "Who says Brian was with me and why do you want to know?"

"I found you there," he said, sparing her a swift but thorough assessment, "around seven-thirty. I have every reason to believe Novak was there, as well."

The money clip. It wouldn't take any time at all to prove it was Brian's. "What difference does it make?'' she asked, exasperated. She was so tired of this. She hadn't done anything illegal.

"Because around that time, just a few blocks away from where I found you, Marissa Landon was being murdered."

Chapter Ten

Mac drove around for almost ten minutes without speaking. Elizabeth's tension escalated with every passing second. She felt certain he planned to take her to his office, but he didn't. Then she figured he planned to take her to the police station to face those two detectives again, Brannigan and the partner whose name she couldn't recall. But he didn't do that, either.

Instead, he just drove, finally stopping in front of a well-maintained, older building located in the vicinity of Ned's office. The recently renovated architecture was ornate with intricate detailing around the windows and porte cochere. For another tension-filled minute he sat without moving, forcing Elizabeth's pulse rate into the danger zone, in spite of her valiant effort to focus on anything but his silence. She mentally listed the various elements of the structures looming just beyond the sidewalk and patches of grass, but every breath she drew was an effort. Her heart pounded so hard she couldn't imagine MacBride not hearing it.

Just when she thought she couldn't take anymore,

he spoke. "You see that center window on the seventh floor?"

Elizabeth looked upward to the floor he'd indicated. She knew where they were, knew what he was trying to do. When her eyes focused on the center window, she answered, the hollow word a mere whisper, "Yes."

"That apartment belonged to Marissa Landon."

As Elizabeth stared at the dark window with its flower box overflowing with a bright spring mixture of blooms, the reality of what Annabelle had told her settled on her like a sopping-wet quilt. Who would water those flowers now? Marissa was dead. Murdered.

"Do you know what arterial spray is?"

A hard knot formed in Elizabeth's stomach. "I don't want to hear this." The shaking that had plagued her in Annabelle's office started again.

"It's usually found near the victim of brutal violence," he went on cruelly. "The perpetrator has to inflict a wound that involves an artery. Like with Marissa. The slashing wound almost completely severed her head from her body. The carotid artery, as well as the jugular, were sliced clean through. Imagine the depth of evil hostility it took to inflict that kind of violence on another human being."

She squeezed her eyes shut and tried to block the gruesome images his words evoked. "Please, just take me back to my truck. I don't know anything."

Without a word he swerved away from the curb and merged into the traffic again. Her body was ice, her senses numb. She fought back the tears and silently screamed at the indignity, the senselessness.

How could she know anyone who would do something so heinous? Surely her suspicions were wrong. Surely Brian couldn't be responsible for that kind of horror. But what if he was, and what if she did know something that would make a difference?

Could she live with herself if even one more person died?

When MacBride parked once more, they were at Ned's office. Elizabeth blinked as confusion jumped into the painful mixture of emotions twisting inside her.

"Why are we here?" Fear raced to the forefront of all else, and she turned to face MacBride. His blue eyes were dark with emotion. "Why did you bring me here?"

"Get out," he ordered. "We're going inside."

She reached for the door handle, but her hand shook so badly it took two attempts to open the door. Her head spun, making her movements awkward, unbalanced. What if MacBride had found the hidden door? What if he knew why she'd come here last night? She glanced quickly from side to side as he ushered her toward the front entrance. Had her being here last night somehow caused that brutal murder? Was Detective Brannigan waiting inside to interrogate her? Her chest ached with the impotent floundering of her heart. She couldn't drag in a deep enough breath. She wanted it to stop—the murders, the suspicions, the fear. She just wanted it to stop.

MacBride used a key to open the front door, then locked it behind them once they were inside. Elizabeth sucked in a shallow breath and tried to calm herself. She couldn't let the panic take over now. She had to stay in control.

The reception area was only dimly lit by the sparse sunlight filtering in through the half-closed shades. The air smelled stale already. The owner was dead, whatever kind of jerk he'd been. Whatever good he'd done in his life, if any, it was over. He was dead and so were four of his patients. And somehow she was a part of it all.

She had to sit down. Elizabeth stumbled toward a chair and collapsed into it. "I don't want to be here," she murmured for all the good it would do. MacBride apparently wanted to punish her, to make her tell him what she knew, which was nothing that would matter. She was certain of it. If she'd thought for one second that anything she'd seen or heard or done would matter...

Except that one thing...

Mac wrestled back the sympathy that rose immediately as she crumpled beneath the weight of fear and guilt. He gritted his teeth, bracing for the charge that would accompany touching her, and took her by the arm to haul her to her feet. "This way, Elizabeth."

She lurched forward, having little choice but to go with him or be dragged behind him.

He took her into Harrison's private office, the one where he saw his patients, and herded her toward the leather chaise longue. He leaned against the edge of the massive desk and crossed his arms over his chest, cranking up the intimidation as he glared down at her.

She sat like a statue except for the fine trembling she couldn't hide. Before he could stop his traitorous eyes, he'd taken in every last detail of the way she looked today. She wore faded jeans and, unlike the overalls she usually donned for work, the jeans fit snugly, hugging her slender figure. The blouse was of soft cotton, short-sleeved and buttoning up the front. One sneaker was about to come untied. But it was the way she wore her hair that unsettled him the most. It hung unrestrained over her shoulders, a cape of rich brown velvet. Her amber eyes stared up at him from behind those delicately rimmed glasses. She was scared to death, sick with dread at what she feared lay ahead.

By God, he intended to have some answers! Five people were dead. One might damn well have deserved a bad end, but the others were victims in the truest sense of the word. Whatever Elizabeth knew, whether she considered it relevant or not, he would have it before they left this room.

"What do you want from me?" she asked, her voice unsteady.

"Is this where you spent all those hours with him?" The question was issued sharply, and Mac wanted to bite off his tongue when he recognized the emotion behind it. Jealousy. Dammit all to hell. He was jealous of a dead man's relationship with the woman who could very well be his killer. He clenched his fists and fought the ridiculous feelings.

"Yes," she replied softly. Her fingers twisted together as she wrung her hands nervously. "Always right here," she volunteered to his surprise. "The first time I came he—" her eyes took on a distant look "—he insisted that comfort was of primary importance. I needed to relax and speak freely, knowing that anything I said or did in this office would never go any further.''

Silence screamed for three beats as Mac realized how telling her final statement really was.

"But he lied to you, didn't he?"

She nodded. "His sessions were helpful at first. The panic attacks went away." She took a steadying breath and looked up at him. "But then he took our relationship to another level. He knew I needed more work to make it financially, so he offered to let me decorate his office. He was very kind to me." She blinked as if attempting to reason out the unreasonable. Her voice sounded machinelike, flat and emotionless. "That's when he…" She lapsed into silence, unable or unwilling to go on.

"He seduced you," Mac said from between gritted teeth.

She moved her head in what he took for a nod. "I didn't mean for it to happen. But he knew all the right things to say and…I needed to hear them." She stared at her clasped hands for a time. "It was a mistake. I should have seen through his machinations."

The blast of fury that roared through Mac forced him to his feet. Harrison had used her, just as he had all the others. But for Elizabeth it was different. The playing field hadn't been level—she was too naive to have any clue about the kind of world she'd allowed herself to be lured into. She wasn't like the others. Another jolt of anger shook him when he considered that he was falling for that same sad Cinderella story he'd predicted she would use to rationalize her actions.

He'd taken the bait, hook, line and sinker.

"So you killed him." He hurled the accusation at her, even though, at this point, he was pretty sure she was innocent—of murder, anyway.

Her head came up and her face flushed. "No! How do I get that through to you, MacBride? I didn't kill him!"

His name on her lips sent something like desire curling through him, which only increased his fury. "But you know something about his death, don't you." He moved nearer to her, towered over her to achieve the effect he desired. It worked. She retreated as far as her position on the chaise would allow.

"I don't know…" She shook her head, her brow lining in confusion. "I don't know who killed him."

"You went to his place that night, didn't you?" Mac outlined the scenario that had been forming in the back of his mind. Her startled gaze connected with his. "He stood you up and you were angry." She looked away guiltily and he knew he'd hit the mark. "Did you have a fight? Is that how he got those scratches?"

She shook her head.

"Was he using the tape for blackmail? Is that how he got to you?"

She bolted out of her seat, putting herself toe-to-toe with him. Anger glittered in her eyes. "Yes! Gloria and I found out about the videos and what he'd been up to with…with all of us." She blinked once, twice, clearly shocked she'd said so much.

"And how did Gloria feel about that?" He'd already checked out Gloria's alibi. It was airtight. She'd been at dinner and the movies with her niece. But then, he supposed, the niece could be lying. "Did she want him dead, too?'' What woman wouldn't after what Harrison had done to them?

"How do you think she felt?'' Elizabeth spat. "But we didn't kill him,'' she countered, some of the bravado going out of her. "We were victims. Don't you get it?''

That was the trouble. He did get it. It took all his willpower to restrain the impulse to take her in his arms. He urged her back down onto the chaise, then sat beside her. "Just tell me what happened, Elizabeth,'' he said gently. "That's all I want from you.''

For a long time she just sat there staring at her hands. Mac wished he knew the right words to say to somehow make her feel at ease. But no words could make any of this right.

"I'd sworn I wouldn't ever speak to him again,'' she began wearily. "He'd hurt us too much. Almost cost Gloria and me our friendship. But he kept calling. He sounded so desperate. Finally he said he would give me the tape if I'd have dinner with him one last time.'' She shrugged with the same weariness he heard in her voice. "I was desperate to get that tape. We knew he had one on each of us. Gloria found out somehow.''

Gloria seemed to know a lot of things, Mac mused. He'd read Brannigan's report on his interview with her; maybe he needed to question her himself. But Brannigan had been thorough and he'd verified all statements. Funny they hadn't found a tape of Gloria Weston. Mac wondered how she'd managed to get hers from Harrison.

"Anyway, I went to the restaurant.'' Elizabeth laughed, a dry, humorless sound. "Like a fool. Of course he didn't show up." She shook her head. "I was so angry. I wanted to tell him just what I thought."

"So you went to his place." Mac had hoped that wasn't the case, but deep down he'd suspected as much. That was what had her running scared. She'd been so close to the murder without even knowing it.

She nodded. "I had to knock several times before he answered. When he did, it was obvious he'd been in bed with someone." She pressed her fist to her mouth as the tumultuous emotions shook her again. "I didn't think. I was furious. I just pushed past him and went straight to the bedroom. The sheets were tousled. The whole room smelled of sex. I screamed at him that I couldn't believe he'd kept me waiting while he screwed someone else."

The idea that Harrison may have threatened her physically or even hurt her in some way tore at Mac's gut. Before he could ask about that, she went on.

"I demanded the tape. He wouldn't let me have it." She exhaled a ragged breath, then chewed her lower lip for a moment. "We argued and he grabbed my arm and tried to make me listen to what he had to say."

Mac tensed as fresh rage gripped him.

"I fought him." She frowned. "I think maybe I did scratch him." She splayed her hands. "I don't know. It all happened so fast." A defeated sigh hissed past her lips. "He wouldn't give me the tape, so I gave up. I warned him to stay away from me. Then I left."

His jaw aching from clenching it so tightly, he asked harshly, "But no one saw you come or go?"

He already knew the answer to that. Brannigan's men had questioned everyone in the building.

"I don't think so."

Mac scrubbed a hand over his face, the receding adrenaline leaving him weak. "Why didn't you tell me this in the beginning?"

"I was afraid you'd think I killed him."

Well, she'd been right to think that, although he'd considered her a prime suspect, anyway. "You're sure no one else was there with Harrison when you left?"

She mulled that over for a moment. "I'm pretty sure. I mean, I didn't go into the guest room or bathrooms." She closed her eyes, most likely retracing her movements in her mind. "I didn't go in the kitchen, either, but you can see beyond the island from the living room and I didn't notice anyone. But I was pretty upset."

Mac considered all she'd told him. There definitely could have been someone else there. "I'm still going to need that DNA sample from you. It's the only way I can prove you weren't in bed with him that night."

"Fine." She stiffened slightly. "Does it have to be…"

He knew what she was thinking and let her off the hook. "No. It can be as simple as a saliva swab." The pubic hair wasn't the only DNA evidence they'd eventually collected from Harrison's bed.

Her relief was almost palpable. "Okay."

"Tell me about last night."

Elizabeth had known that was coming. She'd made it through the initial part of her confession, but this part was going to be a little trickier. Her story would sound so farfetched. But what the hell. She had nothing to lose at this point and she was definitely out of options. Besides, MacBride wasn't going to give up until he had the truth. She had to respect that about him. He was trying to bring at least one murderer to justice.

"We had a kind of conference," she began.

"Who?" he interjected.

"Gloria, Annabelle and I."

"Annabelle Ford? Harrison's attorney?"

She stole a quick glance at him and almost shivered at the intensity in his eyes. And he was close. Closer than she'd realized. She resisted the urge to scoot away. Being afraid was over. She had to do this right. If anyone else died and it was in any way her fault for not telling all…

"Yes, Ned's attorney. Gloria called her when the third woman was murdered. We decided to see if we could put our heads together and figure out who was doing this."

MacBride sat perfectly still, his head inclined as he listened to her relate the details of her first meeting with Annabelle and Gloria. When she mentioned the Gentlemen's Association and the secret room, something changed in his eyes, but he masked it so quickly she wasn't sure she'd seen it.

"I guess Brian was watching me," she suggested for lack of any other explanation. "We hadn't really seen each other except at an occasional party in months. I can't imagine how else he would have known. Even Annabelle and Gloria didn't know when I planned to make the attempt at getting in."

"Did he threaten you in any way?"

Elizabeth could feel the tension vibrating in the man sitting beside her. Something she'd told him had hit a nerve. She shook her head in response to his question. "Not at first. But then he started to make me uneasy. He tried to force me to admit I'd killed Ned." She quickly gave him the condensed version of the conversation. "It was like he thought he could make me say what he wanted to hear."

Mac couldn't stop himself. He had to touch her. He placed his hand atop her clasped ones. "Listen to me, Elizabeth. I can't elaborate much on the Gentlemen's Association, but I can tell you that the people involved with that group are not to be trusted."

She looked up at him, her eyes wide with surprise behind her glasses. "So you do know about them?"

He nodded. "Did Novak say anything else about it? Something maybe you forgot to tell me?" Mac would damn well have Novak picked up this very day. His mention of the Gentleman's Association to Elizabeth was enough for probable cause.

After a moment's thought she shook her head. "No. That's all he said before I hit him."

He couldn't help the smile that broke loose at the idea of her crowning Novak. The self-serving bastard. "Okay. Shall we try and locate that secret room?"

She nodded jerkily and his protective instincts surged. Their eyes met and he knew in that instant she was without doubt completely innocent. He reached up to touch her face. He heard her breath catch, but she didn't draw away.

The ring of the cell phone shattered the moment.

It took a second ring for him to pull himself together enough to answer. "MacBride."

"Mac, it's Driver."

He stood and moved away from the temptation she represented. "What's up?" The urge to loosen his tie had him reaching for his throat. The room was suddenly too damned hot.

"That guy Novak."

"Yeah." The newest addition to Mac's I-wanna-pound-him list.

"Well, his body was found in Central Park about an hour ago."

The tangle of scenarios and possibilities fighting for attention in Mac's thoughts stopped dead. "You're sure it's him."

"Brannigan's partner ID'd him. It's him."

Mac let go a heavy breath. "I'm on my way."

"Wait," Driver said before he could hang up. "You haven't heard the most bizarre part."

Mac braced himself for cause-of-death details. He always hated that part although those were the very details that gave an investigator the most information about the killer.

"The ME called your office this morning. It seems he found a match to the DNA evidence collected from the female victims in the Princess case."

Before Driver continued Mac was certain it had to be Novak, even though he wasn't sure how the ME had run across a DNA workup on Novak unless he'd been previously entered into CODIS under an alias.

"Remember all the DNA evidence that had to be checked out from Harrison's apartment? Well, Harrison's DNA had to be cross-matched to eliminate body hair, etc."

"Get to the point, Driver." Mac was getting impatient here. He knew the drill. It had to be Novak.

"Well, the specimen in the first two victims was a match. The last two aren't completed yet, of course."

"A match to whom?" Mac snarled. Dammit, why didn't he just spit it out?

"To Harrison," Driver said. "The DNA in both cases is a perfect match to Dr. Ned Harrison."

Chapter Eleven

Elizabeth stood numbly by as MacBride spoke quietly to the caller. She was afraid to even imagine what had happened now. But it was surely bad. The tone of his voice left no doubt. Cold, flat. Whatever news he'd just received, it was not something he'd wanted to hear.

Elizabeth thought of her friend. MacBride had people watching her, but what about Gloria? She needed protection, too. She remembered what Annabelle had said that morning. Four more. Four more female patients she had reason to believe had carried on a personal relationship with Ned. Two of which were Gloria and Elizabeth. She shuddered. What if that was what the call was about? What if another victim had been found?

MacBride ended the conversation. As he closed his phone and dropped it back into his pocket, she told herself she had no choice but to trust him. The suspicions Annabelle had offered were relevant to the case. Elizabeth had come clean with him about everything else that happened last night and he'd listened. He'd covered her hand with his own, comfort-

ing her. She should tell him this part, too. She warned
that more vulnerable part of herself not to read too
much into his comforting gesture, but she just
couldn't help it. She was drawn to him, seriously
drawn to him. Somehow the attraction went beyond
the physical.

*Right, Elizabeth. You're doing it again. Falling for
the wrong guy. Who probably felt nothing for you but
sympathy.*

But he felt something. Elizabeth had noticed the
way he looked at her, had seen the hunger in his eyes.
She saw the emotion in his eyes as he turned to face
her now. There was a dread, not at seeing her, but at
telling her the news he'd just received. Why would
he care how it affected her if he didn't feel something
for her? He'd rescued her from Brian even after she'd
given the guy watching her the slip. MacBride had
likely sensed where she would go when the other man
hadn't had a clue. He was tuned in to her on a very
primal level. Or maybe he'd simply had someone
watching Ned's office. A good thing, too, whatever
the case. She felt reasonably sure that Brian would
have come after her if he hadn't seen MacBride outside with her. Brian had clearly snapped out of the
dazed state the whack on the head had sent him into
and managed to slip away unseen. Tracking her down
wouldn't have been a problem for him—except that
MacBride had been watching over her. Like a guard-
ian angel.

He moved toward her now, drawing her full attention back to the moment. Those intense blue eyes
were guarded, which made her even more nervous.
''Novak didn't mention talking to anyone else or ex-

pecting to meet with anyone else last night?'' he asked, his words measured.

A tendril of trepidation coiled inside her. They were back to Brian again. "No." Where was he going with this? "I don't know where he went afterward. He...he didn't call or anything." A burst of irritation chased away the trepidation. "I'd have had a few things to say to him if I'd heard from him." She was sick to death of being vulnerable—to MacBride or anyone else. Annabelle's theory nudged her again, shaking her newly found bravado.

"I'm not accusing you of anything, Elizabeth," Mac said more softly as he came nearer still. "But there's been another development and we need to know if Novak mentioned meeting or speaking to anyone else."

Development? A chill raced over her. He meant another murder. "Who's dead?" Her voice gave away the fear building in her. "Don't try to hide anything from me, MacBride," she added with surprising strength.

He touched her. Placed his hand on her arm, nothing complicated or serious, just a touch. But the feelings the gesture engendered were entirely serious.

"Novak is dead. His body was found in Central Park a little while ago."

Mac hadn't wanted to tell her like this, but she'd limited his options. She wanted, needed to know what was going on.

"How?" Her chin trembled ever so slightly and it was all he could do not to take her fully into his arms.

"I can't answer that for you just yet. But considering the speed with which these murders are occurring, I'd like to place you into protective custody for your own safety.''

Fear, followed quickly by uncertainty, danced across her face. "I...I can't. I have to work."

"Elizabeth, it would be best—"

"Is someone watching Gloria, too?" she demanded abruptly.

Mac's worry began to manifest itself in an annoying ache behind his eyes. "Brannigan has one of his men keeping an eye on her, if that's what you're asking."

Her eyes glittered. "I want to know if someone is watching her every minute of the day and night."

He wondered if shock was setting in. She'd gone from wanting to know how Novak was killed to whether or not Gloria Weston was being protected. The way she demanded a more precise response after he'd already given her an answer made him wonder if there was something more he should know. "Are you trying to tell me something, Elizabeth?"

A tremor went through her. "Annabelle has a theory. The murders—" she cleared her throat of the emotion thickening there "—have occurred in alphabetical order. Bumbalough, Dell, Fowler, Landon. Annabelle thinks there are approximately four others she can pinpoint as having had a sexual relationship with Ned. Gloria and I are among those four. She thinks he won't stop until...we're all dead."

Mac had already suggested to Brannigan and his newly formed task force that the killer might be working in a non-random manner. The only difference in Mac's theory was that, judging by the number of videotapes they'd found in Harrison's apartment, there were a lot more than only four more potential victims.

"All the more reason for you to go into protective custody," he suggested, keeping the numbers to himself. The alphabetical theory had been shot down to an extent, anyway, when the Landon woman was found. The killer had skipped over at least three names between Fowler and Landon—names that went with tapes they had found.

She shook her head. "I have to finish this job." She looked directly at him, the urgency in her manner relaying just how important this was. "It can't wait. Boomer will be with me."

"And who wouldn't be comforted by that?" Mac said dryly, regretting it the instant the words escaped.

"Look," Elizabeth said hotly, "I know you don't like him, but he's a good guy and I can depend on him."

Therein lay the crux of the matter, Mac realized. Elizabeth Young had been let down by too many people in her life. Her mother, her fiancé, her brother-in-law, even her father, who'd left her all alone when he died, and finally by her shrink. Trust didn't come easily to her. Being able to count on someone would mean a great deal to her. Even if it was a former scumbag like Boomer.

"You're right," he admitted to her surprise. "I want you to know that you can depend on me, as well. I'll see that someone is keeping an eye on Gloria."

Not bothering to hide her amazement, she murmured, "Thank you."

"I'm going to trust you with something, Elizabeth," Mac told her, only now making the decision to offer the information. "The Gentlemen's Association is why I'm here. These guys are nasty business. They're deep into Internet porn, mostly pretty young women like you, but some even younger. They have to be stopped. Harrison was my only bona fide connection. Novak was a close runner-up. Now they're both gone." He cranked up the intensity of his gaze, hoping to relay the utter desperation he felt. "I have to nail these guys, Elizabeth. I don't want anyone else hurt the way you were. I need evidence. Something. Anything to bring these guys down."

"The secret door," she said softly. "I know where it is."

MAC INSPECTED the loft where Elizabeth and Boomer would be working today. He'd stationed Driver in the corridor just outside the door and given him orders not to leave Elizabeth under any circumstances. Boomer, after a show of belligerence toward Mac's orders, had calmed down and told Mac in no uncertain terms that nothing would happen to Elizabeth while she was with him.

Mac didn't want to leave her. Dammit, he had a job to do, and still he didn't want to go. Apparently it had taken just that one kiss to skew his judgment completely.

As he pointed his sedan in the direction of midtown, he forced his attention back to the case. The hidden room had proved to be the break he'd been praying for. The room was completely sealed, shielded from any sort of detection, similar to the way the CIA insulated their buildings. Harrison had covered every base. The room was totally self-sufficient and separate from the rest of his office. The power feed and telephone lines were split from a neighboring system, that of a legitimate business with nine-to-five operating hours. Never in a million years would their system have been checked. No one, not even Mac, would have thought of that. The lines weren't connected to Ned Harrison in any way. Running lights and a few electronics wouldn't constitute enough of a draw to alert the other business that they were being systematically robbed.

This provided new insight into the way others in the association were probably getting away with their evil deeds without being caught.

An entire forensics team was at this very moment going over the room. The elaborate computer system would likely hold all the evidence they would need to lead them to others.

Mac should be back there himself, but first he had to see Brannigan. They needed to discuss this latest turn of events. There had to be a reasonable explanation for Harrison's DNA turning up at the crime scenes. Harrison was dead. Mac had viewed the body, read the autopsy.

A theory churned in the back of his mind, but first he wanted to hear Brannigan's take.

Since the detective was still at the crime scene, Mac parked near the entrance to the walking zoo. The body had been found next to a park bench where pigeons hung out hoping to be fed by the numerous daily visitors. Vaguely he wondered if the location was significant. Maybe someone thought Novak had talked.

Five minutes later Mac stood next to Brannigan as

the ME's office took away the body. The autopsy would be needed for confirmation, though it appeared Novak had been bludgeoned to death. The irony that Elizabeth had hit him on or near the temple wasn't lost on Mac. According to the ME, time of death was possibly within mere hours of that of Marissa Landon. Even the location wasn't that far away from the Landon apartment.

"No signs of struggle," Brannigan said, then added dryly, "other than the pulp his head was beaten into."

"You think someone just sneaked up on him out here in the dark?" Mac queried, not certain he agreed with that theory.

"His wallet is missing," Brannigan said. "But it seems a little overkill for a simple robbery."

Mac made an agreeable sound. "Whoever did this wanted to make sure he didn't survive."

"Well, that takes Novak off the suspect list." Brannigan sighed wearily. "Damn, I thought for sure he might be our man. Especially after he disappeared on us last night. It seems every time a murder has occurred, he managed to be AWOL."

"What about the DNA connection to Harrison?" Mac asked, getting to the heart of the matter. "How's forensics explaining that little quandary?"

"They're checking to see if it had been refrigerated or frozen prior to use." The older man shrugged, the movement calling attention to the poor fit of his jacket. "Maybe Harrison had been storing up for a rainy day and somebody decided to use his stash to throw us off."

Mac rubbed his chin, absently noting that he needed a shave. "We need to check into the brother," he suggested. "We know Harrison is dead, there's no question. And yes, someone could be planting the evidence. It isn't impossible, but neither is the possibility that the dead brother isn't dead. We haven't seen his body for confirmation. Who's to say the guy isn't alive and well and seeking his vengeance for his brother's death? We both believe Harrison was killed by a woman, so what if the brother believes it, as well? He can't be sure which of the former lovers is guilty, so he takes them out one at a time, knowing that eventually he'll get the right one."

"Hell, Nigel Harrison was supposed to have died four years ago," Brannigan countered. "He's buried in some shit hole down in Mexico. How the hell am I supposed to verify that he's really dead? We damn sure can't rely on any paperwork they send us. And if he's alive, where the hell has he been all this time? No one I've interviewed even knew Dr. Harrison had a brother."

"I want him exhumed," Mac said grimly, fury pumping through him. "We've got four murder victims with Harrison's DNA fingerprint swimming around inside them." The idea that Elizabeth could be next screamed at him. He clenched his jaw until he regained some semblance of self-control. When he'd investigated Harrison's background months ago, he'd learned about the brother, but that detail hadn't mattered—he was dead. But now they had reason to believe otherwise. Especially considering this latest turn of events. "The brother is an identical twin—he could have the same DNA structure. I want to know if the bastard is really dead or if he's alive and avenging his brother's death." The whole scenario was different now.

"So we're going ghost hunting now?" Brannigan mused, only half joking.

"Maybe," Mac allowed, "but we're not going to overlook that avenue just because we *think* it isn't viable. I want to *know*."

Brannigan shoved his hands into his trousers and ducked his head between his shoulders in an uncharacteristically humble manner. "Your people can get an order like that faster than I can. You know the chain of command I'm forced to work with."

Mac reached for his cell phone. "I'll take care of it." He hesitated before entering the necessary number. "If you're not keeping Gloria Weston under surveillance 24/7, I think you should. Annabelle Ford, too."

"We got someone watching the Weston woman 24/7. You think the mouthpiece needs surveillance, too?"

"She seems to know an awful lot." Mac tried to pinpoint his reservations where Annabelle Ford was concerned, but couldn't. "There's something about her that nags at me."

Brannigan scoffed. "She's a freakin' lawyer. 'Nough said."

"Push the ME for DNA analysis on Novak, too," Mac added as an afterthought. "He's about the same size as Harrison was. A little more muscular, but the height is right. He could be the brother. Who knows? With the cosmetic-surgery possibilities out there today, it could be anyone with a similar build."

Brannigan gave him a two-fingered salute and then

strode in the direction of the ME's van where Novak's body was now safely ensconced. Mac stared at his cell phone for a second and considered that it would take some powerful influence to get this exhumation under way ASAP. He had a friend or two in D.C., so he might as well start there. Why bother with the bottom when he could start at the top?

ELIZABETH PACED the room again, stopping every few minutes to peek out the window. Agent Driver was still there, watching her apartment. It was past seven and she was exhausted. She and Boomer had worked until six and had made a good deal of progress. By then she'd been so wired up thinking about all that had happened she'd just had to call it a day. Boomer had offered to come stay with her, but with Driver right outside she didn't see the point. Besides, he probably had a date. Boomer always had a date.

She'd called Gloria to make sure she was at her sister's, and she was. Elizabeth couldn't help feeling hurt all over again as Brian's words echoed through her. He had to have been lying. She refused to believe that Gloria would do that to her. Elizabeth closed her eyes and collapsed on the sofa. No matter that she'd firmly decided to put that behind her, it pushed to the forefront yet again.

Brian was dead.

No matter that he'd been a jerk who hurt her, she couldn't help feeling bad that he was dead. No one deserved to die a violent death like that. She shuddered when she considered that the last two men with whom she'd been involved had come to tragic ends. But then again, she doubted it had anything to do with her. Both had been deeply involved in very dangerous hobbies. A shiver ran through her when she thought of all she'd seen in that hidden room this morning.

Dozens of pictures of women, some far younger than she, in degrading poses. How could she not have seen how utterly sick Ned was? And if Brian were— had been, she amended with another quake of dread— involved with that kind of thing, he was pretty damned sick, too. Where was her intuition on the subject of men? It seemed she was utterly blind when it came to men. Her naiveté had gotten her into real trouble this time.

Did the members of the Gentlemen's Association see women as nothing more than pieces of meat? Or as mere playthings?

The idea that she had been a part of that, even unknowingly, made her ill. She wanted—needed—to be able to depend on Mac. She rolled her eyes. There she went, calling him Mac again. She wrung her hands and tried to reason out the issue. What if she trusted him and he let her down the way everyone else had? But she needed him. She closed her eyes and confessed that truth. She needed him. She wasn't sure she could get through this alone, and her relationship with Gloria was up in the air right now. At the same time that thought went through her mind, she told herself it was foolish. She could trust Gloria. Brian had lied. That was all.

A knock at her door startled her from the troubling thoughts. She stood, propelled as much by fear as by the instinct to answer the door. She peeked out the window. Her heart almost stopped. Driver's car was gone. Frantically she scanned the area surrounding the house. With immense relief she noted Mac's sedan in the driveway.

Letting go the breath she'd been holding, she hurried to the door. As she reached for the lock she remembered what he'd told her about that and asked, "Who is it?"

"It's me," his deep voice resonated through the wood between them.

Something warmer than relief washed over her, and she quickly unlocked and opened the door. "Nothing else has happened?" She was suddenly afraid he'd come here to tell her more bad news. She'd just spoken to Gloria...

He shook his head. "Nothing new. I just wanted you to know that I'd be out there watching tonight."

She nodded mutely. He looked exhausted. She wondered why he didn't just assign another of his men to take over.

"Call me if you need me," he said.

When he would have headed back down the stairs, she abruptly regained her voice. "Could you come in for a while?" He stopped but didn't turn. She snapped her mouth shut and called herself an idiot. What was she doing?

Slowly, as if considering the prudence of that offer, as well, he turned to face her. Those blue eyes directed that very question at her.

She attempted a nonchalant shrug but managed only a stiff jerk of one shoulder. "I just thought we could talk for a while." She folded her arms to hide the way her hands had begun to shake. "I guess I'm a little rattled." She heaved a mighty breath. "Or restless."

"Just for a little while," he relented, moving deliberately toward her. When he stood in the doorway staring down at her, he qualified, "I'll leave it up to you to let me know when it's time to go."

She nodded and stepped back so he could come inside. When she'd locked the door, she turned to find him standing in the middle of the room watching her. She summoned a smile. "Would you like coffee or tea?"

He shook his head, his gaze seeming somehow more potent and focused solely on her.

She told herself she was simply tired. It had been a long day. Hell, it had been a long week. The faces of all those women floated briefly before her eyes. The realization that Ned and Brian were dead. Murdered. And then the undeniable fact that she could be next...well, it all kind of crashed down on top of her at once and she swayed.

Mac was at her side in a flash. "You should sit down."

Elizabeth leaned heavily on him as he walked her to the sofa. Damn. What was wrong with her? Was everything just catching up to her?

"Thanks," she mumbled as he released her.

"Maybe you're the one who needs some tea," he suggested, concerned.

For just a second she basked in the warmth of his genuine concern. It felt so good to have someone worry about her. Then she shook her head and chastised herself for behaving so foolishly. "Please, just keep me company for a while."

He dropped into the ancient overstuffed chair directly across from her and appeared content to simply watch her.

She looked away, suddenly at a loss as to what they should talk about. Here she'd practically begged him to stay and now she'd apparently turned mute. Well, she might not be able to instigate a conversation, but her blood was rapidly reaching the boiling point. Her gaze flicked toward him and she reveled in simply looking. He'd shed his jacket and tie. She couldn't recall ever seeing him without his tie. A couple of buttons were loosened and she could see a tempting V of bronzed skin. A dreamy sensation tingled to life inside her. She almost laughed out loud. What was wrong with her?

Her gaze bumped his and for several beats she couldn't look away. Naked hunger flashed fleetingly in his eyes. That awareness sent need swirling through her. She wasn't the only one having trouble with the building tension. She felt a smile tickle her lips at the idea he could possibly want her. It seemed so…so unlikely, and yet she'd known from the very beginning that something sizzled between them.

With effort she directed her gaze elsewhere. To the faded rug, then the tattered fabric of the sofa.

"You checked in with your friend Gloria?" he said abruptly.

Her head came up. Was it her imagination, or was his voice strained? She blinked and searched his face for any hint of that sexual hunger she'd seen moments ago. But he'd banished it, assumed his professional demeanor.

She bobbed her head, the movement awkward. "She's fine."

He nodded once. "Good."

The seconds turned into minutes as the silence thickened around them again. What had she been thinking? She should have known this wouldn't work. She just wasn't the type to play the part of seductress and he obviously wasn't that interested or he'd make a move.

She closed her eyes in self-disgust. What was wrong with her? People were dying all around them. How could she be thinking about sex?

"Well." Mac stood. "I'll be outside if you need me."

Her eyes popped open and she scrambled to her feet. "Um...okay." She didn't want him to go. It was crazy. She'd never been good at this, always made the wrong choices. But God, how she hated being weak and uncertain, being unable to go after what she wanted. For once in her life she wanted to be the one in charge. She wanted *him*.

Mac paused at the door. "Good night."

Refusing to hesitate long enough to think, she grabbed him by his shirtfront and pulled his mouth down to hers. She closed her eyes tightly and she kissed him. For one terrifying moment all she could think was, this wouldn't work. He resisted...didn't take her in his arms...didn't kiss her back. Defeat tugged at her fledgling determination. She couldn't do this. Then the marvelous textures of his lips and mouth penetrated her senses as he surrendered to the kiss and abruptly took charge.

He devoured her with his mouth, his jaw scratchy and rough but more tantalizing than any sensation she'd ever known. His fingers plunged into her hair as he deepened the kiss. She could feel the fierce energy radiating just beneath the surface of his hot skin. Those skilled hands slid down her back and suddenly he was touching her everywhere at once, stripping off her clothes, baring her skin to his greedy mouth. His fingers set her on fire every place he touched. His tongue laved her body. She was losing control and she wanted him to lose control with her.

She tugged at the buttons of his shirt until her hands flattened fully against the muscled terrain beneath. The heat seared her palms. She moaned and somehow his mouth found hers again, his kiss insanely sexy and breath-stealingly savage. He pulled her body hard against his, kicked the door shut and carried her to the bedroom, all the while his mouth plundering hers. He tasted hot and strong, like dark, fragrant coffee, full of delicious flavor and the promise of relentless energy. She wanted him to sweep her away, to awaken every part of her body and to stimulate her long-slumbering libido. To turn her into the kind of woman who could bring a man like him to his knees.

She wanted to see his vulnerable side, to find his weakness if it took all night long. She wanted to forget everything, to make the world go away for just this one night.

Their mouths mating hungrily, possessively, they stripped off the last of the restrictive garments, touching, teasing each new expanse of skin they uncovered. He felt so incredibly hot and hard. His muscles were beautifully defined, his body perfectly proportioned. His entire anatomy was a source of perpetual amazement. She wanted to learn all of him, wanted to taste the sweet and the salty.

Broad, broad shoulders and a sculpted chest that narrowed into a lean waist and hips. Incredibly strong arms that lifted her nude body against that tempting torso and lowered her to the bed. Long, muscular legs and strong, confident hands. He came down over her and she smiled as she considered the other generous part of him. His thick sex nudged ambitiously between her thighs, and for the first time in her life she opened freely, without undue coaxing.

She wanted this. She wanted him. She stared into the fiery blaze of those dark-blue eyes and knew this was going to be special. Whatever repercussions tomorrow brought, this moment was worth it.

She gasped when his body drew away from hers, but she soon discovered that he had other plans. He trailed hot, wet kisses along her flesh until he reached his ultimate destination. With the first flick of his tongue she melted into a tangle of shivery sensations. Moan after moan drifted from her lips as he positioned her for full access and lapped hungrily at her sensitized flesh. He pushed her closer and closer to the brink until she was writhing and pleading for him to finish it. She felt ready to combust, to implode with the swelling pleasure.

She screamed his name and somehow his mouth came down on hers as he simultaneously drove into her. He thrust fully, deeply and for the first time she was utterly primed, slick and yielding. Muscles that had once resisted this very moment opened eagerly to him, welcomed the marvelous friction of his rigid male body along her skin and thrusting deep, deep inside her. He cupped her face in his hands and kissed her tenderly, his hips setting the perfect rhythm, not too fast, not too slow. The world narrowed until there was nothing but his weight, his breath, his strong hands, and the plunge and slide of his velvety smooth shaft.

The spiraling sensation started so, so far away and then suddenly she was caught up in a hurricane. She reached frantically for him, called his name as his slamming thrusts brought her closer and closer to that moment of final exultation. Something snapped inside her and a pang of longing, fierce and feminine, erupted, shattered some imaginary membrane that had held her captive for so very long, allowing the final burst of climax to rain wildly down on her, capturing her breath and sending ripple after ripple of pleasure cascading through her.

He followed her over the edge, coming with such force that her body arched like a bow, and with one completing thrust he made her forget everything but him and his touch.

Chapter Twelve

Mac lay in Elizabeth's bed as the sun rose the next morning. They'd made love over and over again during the night. She'd come alive in his arms just as he'd longed for her to do. His gut clenched when he thought about how she could tear him apart with that luscious mouth.

She lay in his arms now, sleeping peacefully, trustingly. Her glasses were on the bedside table and their clothes were spread all over the apartment. His pulse began to race as he inventoried the way her body was wrapped around his. One creamy thigh was draped across his hip. Her arms were curled around his neck. Her sweet face was nestled in the curve of his neck. And those lovely breasts were flattened against his chest. Her long hair splayed over his flesh like raw silk. There wasn't a part of him that didn't ache for her still. Even after hours of mind-blowing sex.

No coddling or coaxing had been necessary. She'd kissed him first and she hadn't slowed down until she fell asleep, exhausted and sated. She'd explored his body without hesitation. After her first climax she'd rolled him over and climbed atop to ride to completion once more. Her appetite and eagerness had matched his in every way. She'd licked and sucked and kissed him until he'd thought he would go crazy or simply die.

And she was his.

His arms tightened around her.

Whether Elizabeth Young suspected it or not, he never intended to let her go.

"What time is it?" she murmured sleepily, those tempting lips moving against his throat.

"Time for both of us to get to work." Mac knew she kept long hours just as he did. On the job early and didn't stop until it was done. That was something they had in common, loyalty and determination. He respected those traits in her. He also respected her ability to make him hard with scarcely a touch even after a night like last night.

"Hmm...I see we're *up* already," she purred.

He rolled her onto her back and smiled down at her. God, he loved how she looked first thing in the morning. All soft and pretty and relaxed. "Honey," he growled, "up will never be the problem as long as I'm within three feet of you."

They made love again and then they showered together. Mac swore as he wrapped a towel around her damp body that he would not let this moment end. He would not let her down.

And no one would ever hurt her again.

ELIZABETH COULDN'T remember ever being this happy. Not even when she thought she had the world by the tail after Brian's proposition that she come away with him. A flash of regret stung her at the memory that Brian was dead, but she forced it away. She'd cared for him, was sorry that he was dead, but never in her life had she felt the way she did at this moment about any man.

She studied Mac's profile as he parked in front of the building where Boomer was already at work. He'd insisted that he would see her to work, and Driver would take over from there for a few hours. After all, he had a case to solve. But he wasn't about to leave her vulnerable. A warm glow started deep inside her at the idea of how protective he was of her. She'd never known that feeling of security with anyone except her father.

This was good. She knew it with complete certainty.

She smiled.

This was very good.

She didn't want it to end.

Mac switched off the engine and turned to her, propping his arm on the back of the seat. "I've debated whether I should tell you this or not, but I feel like I have to."

Fear trickled into her veins. "What?" She didn't want to hear anything bad. She wanted desperately to hang on to this wondrous moment.

"The killer left behind some evidence at each scene. DNA analysis is back on the first two victims."

She nodded, not sure exactly what that meant.

"All of the victims were sexually assaulted." She shuddered visibly and he winced, clearly not happy at having to tell her this.

"Do you think it was Brian?" she asked.

Mac hesitated before answering, and in that moment her instincts warned her that it was far worse than that. "The DNA was a perfect match to Harrison's."

Shock plowed through her. For a moment she couldn't breathe. "But he's dead," was all she could say.

Mac nodded. "Yes, he is. That's confirmed." He searched her face and she knew that the pain on his was related to the anxiety he saw on hers. "Did you know he had an identical twin brother?"

That news startled her all over again. "No. I mean yes. Annabelle told us he had a brother who'd died, but she didn't mention he was a twin."

"They grew up in an orphanage. Both managed to make a better life for themselves—or, at least, it seemed so." Mac tapped the steering wheel as if contemplating how much more he should tell her. "His brother reportedly died four years ago."

Just when she'd thought nothing else could shock her. Ned had never let on about any of that. "If he's dead and Ned is…"

Mac leveled his gaze on hers. "Ned Harrison is dead," he confirmed. "Don't even go down that road. He's definitely dead. But we haven't confirmed the brother's death as of yet. We're working on it. I just wanted you to know that someone out there might be out for vengeance. If he thinks you killed his brother…"

No further explanation was necessary. "I get it." Icicles formed in her chest. "So I should be on the lookout for a carbon copy of Ned," she said sardonically. This was too much. One Ned Harrison was more than enough.

"Not necessarily," Mac countered. "He may have altered his appearance, surgically and otherwise."

Great. Just great. She released an exasperated sigh. "So basically, he could be anyone."

Mac nodded. "Basically. If he's alive."

His fingers trailed along her hairline, sending delicious shivery sensations through her as he tucked a stray tendril behind her ear. It didn't pay to braid one's hair while being kissed by a man like Collin MacBride. She probably had dozens of wisps hanging about.

"Don't take any chances, Elizabeth. Stay close to Boomer. He's safe. He was in prison when Harrison's brother supposedly died, and besides, unless the identical twin was less than identical, he's far too tall. Don't wander out of Driver's watch. I need you to be careful while I go do what I have to." He shook his head and looked away for a moment. "To be perfectly honest with you, I'm tempted to arrest you and force you to go into protective custody—"

"You promised," she interrupted. "I have to work."

He sighed. "I know. I won't break that promise." His gaze found hers once more. "But I need you to swear to me you won't take any chances. We can't be sure who we're looking for here. It could be someone from the Gentlemen's Association who had a thing for Harrison."

"I won't take any chances, I swear."

His reservations evident, Mac walked her to the door of the loft where Boomer was already hard at work. Driver took up watch right outside the door.

She was pretty sure she wouldn't soon forget his

goodbye kiss. If the desperation behind it was any indication, he was as deep in this as she was.

And she was in way too deep.

AROUND LUNCHTIME loud voices erupted in the corridor outside the loft. Boomer and Elizabeth exchanged questioning looks. But then Elizabeth recognized the voice railing at Driver.

Annabelle.

Elizabeth put her paint roller aside and rushed into the corridor to intervene. In one glance she summed up the situation. Driver was hell-bent on doing his job protecting her, and Annabelle was equally determined to see her.

"It's okay, Agent Driver," Elizabeth said quickly. "Annabelle is a friend."

Giving the resigned man a triumphant glare, Annabelle stormed past him and into the loft with Elizabeth.

"We have to talk," she whispered from the corner of her mouth. Her gaze flickered to Boomer on the other side of the loft.

"Sure." Nerves jangling, Elizabeth ushered her toward the one small area that was separated from the main part of the loft—the bathroom.

Once within the confines of the tiny room, Annabelle blurted her statement in what was probably an attempt at whispering: "Brian Novak is dead."

Elizabeth nodded solemnly. "I know."

Annabelle took her hands in hers. "I'm so sorry, Elizabeth. I just had to be sure you were all right. I know how close the two of you once were." She glanced toward the open door. "I don't want you to worry. I didn't tell them anything about the other night.''

A frown of confusion worked its way across Elizabeth's brow. "You didn't tell who?"

Annabelle rolled her gray eyes with something akin to disdain. "That brutish Detective Brannigan. He spoke to me and to Gloria. She called, extremely upset. I rushed over here immediately, since you don't have a cell phone." She cast Elizabeth an annoyed look. "You really should have one, you know."

Elizabeth nodded. "I know. But you didn't have to worry or hide anything about the other night in Ned's office."

Annabelle squeezed her hands knowingly. "Oh, but you're wrong. That ridiculous detective thinks you killed Brian. He thinks you killed Ned, too!"

A little jolt of shock rumbled through her. "What...what makes you think that?"

The older woman huffed a sound of derision. "Why, the imbecile said as much. He was rambling on about how the FBI had been watching you from the beginning and how they'd taken the case away from him." She released Elizabeth so she could throw up her hands. "He was furious with MacBride for horning in on his prime suspect."

"Me?" Elizabeth could hardly believe her ears. This didn't make sense. She and Mac had—

"Talk to Gloria," Annabelle urged. "She came away from the meeting with the same feeling. You've got to call that criminal lawyer you put on retainer before you find yourself appearing before a grand jury."

"I will." Her words were thin, since it took all the

strength Elizabeth possessed to hold back the misery mushrooming inside her. "I'll call him today."

Apparently satisfied with that assurance, Annabelle warned her again to be careful and left in the same rush with which she'd arrived. Agent Driver looked none too happy about the visit, but Elizabeth didn't care. Right now the only thing she cared about was confirming the worst.

If Mac had used her... She closed her eyes and fought back the tears. She couldn't believe that just yet. Mac had protected her. Made love to her as no one else ever had. She'd opened up to him, been the wanton woman she'd secretly longed to be with the right man. It couldn't have been a lie.

She wouldn't let it be.

Annabelle was upset. She'd probably taken it all out of context. Elizabeth knew from experience that Brannigan could be a brash SOB. On that thought, the pain subsided just a little bit.

She would not lose trust in Mac—not without solid proof, anyway.

ELIZABETH FORCED herself to work another hour. When she'd reached a good stopping point, she gave Boomer instructions for the rest of the day. Not that he really needed any. He worked well on his own and was good to take the initiative.

Now came the hard part. She exited the loft and found Driver propped on the window ledge at the end of the corridor, sipping coffee from his thermos. The window's view was only of the uncommonly wide alleyway between this old industrial building and the next, but at least it allowed sunlight into the otherwise dark corridor.

"I need to go to Gloria Weston's office."

Driver stood abruptly. "I'm not sure that's such a good idea. We'll have to check with Mac on that."

Elizabeth wasn't about to be thwarted. "You can either take me now or I'll use Boomer's van."

"Let me just give Mac a quick call." Driver flipped open his cell and punched the number. After thirty seconds or so it was obvious he wasn't going to reach Mac. "He must be on another call."

"I'd like to go now, please," she informed him, leaving no room for argument. She was going to Gloria's office one way or another. Something wasn't right. Whatever it was nagged just beneath the surface—she couldn't quite grasp it. She kept replaying the conversation she'd had with Annabelle. Something felt wrong.

Driver finally relented. "All right. I guess it won't hurt."

Half an hour later they were on the elevator headed toward the eighteenth floor and Gloria's office. Driver fit right in with all the suits and ties. Elizabeth, however, stood out like a sore thumb. Her jeans and T-shirt, both dappled with white paint, looked vastly out of place.

"You can wait here," she said to Driver when they reached Gloria's door.

"I'll need to check it out first."

Blowing out a puff of frustration, Elizabeth stood back and allowed him to knock and then enter Gloria's office.

"Miss Young would like to see you." She heard

him say. Wow, finally, she had her own secretary, as well as bodyguard. All it had taken was a few unsolved murders.

He stepped back into the corridor as Gloria peeked out from her office, her green eyes wide with surprise. "What's going on?"

Elizabeth shot Driver a look that told him to stay put and quickly followed Gloria into her office, then closed the door behind them. "You know Brian is dead."

Gloria nodded grimly. "I can't believe it. Do you know that they think he's the one who's been killing all the women?"

Elizabeth didn't remember Annabelle saying that. "They do?"

"It's hard to believe, I know. But that's the impression Detective Brannigan gave me."

"But he didn't say that," Elizabeth pressed. She had to know how this was going down.

Gloria frowned thoughtfully for a moment. "No, he didn't exactly say it. I just got those vibes from him and the slant of his questions."

"Did he say anything about me?" Elizabeth held her breath, not sure she could cope with the answer if it matched what Annabelle had said.

Gloria flipped her hands palms up in a noncommittal gesture. "He did mention you." She dropped onto the edge of her desk. "It was odd. He didn't exactly accuse you of anything, but I got the impression he somehow thought you and Brian were in on this together." She pulled a cocky face. "But I set him straight on that one. You and Brian hadn't been in on anything together in months."

Her words warmed Elizabeth. "Thanks." She moistened her lips, then gnawed on her lower one for a second. "Annabelle came by. She was extremely upset. She said that Brannigan considered me the prime suspect in Ned's, as well as Brian's murder. And that he'd gotten the impression the FBI thought so, as well. She…she…I don't know. The more I think about it, the weirder the conversation seems."

Gloria shook her head slowly. "He didn't say anything like that to me, but he did ask a lot of questions about you and Ned and you and Brian." Her frown deepened. "Now that you mention it, he did lean heavily toward that line of thinking. He kept bringing up your name each time he talked about Ned or Brian's murder."

That too-familiar chill crept into Elizabeth's bones. "But he didn't mention the FBI's thoughts on the matter?"

"No. I'm sure he didn't." Gloria shrugged. "Then again, I made it clear that you and I are friends. Maybe he held back, knowing I'd likely tell you whatever he said."

That was true. Since there was no reason for him to suspect Elizabeth and Annabelle had any sort of relationship, he would likely speak more freely around her. Anxiety coiled in her stomach. Still, she had no real proof against Mac.

"And don't sweat Annabelle. I've gotten the occasional creepy vibe from her, too." Gloria rubbed her forehead with her thumb and forefinger. "I just wish this were over."

"Me, too." Elizabeth leaned against the corner of

the desk next to her friend. Maybe that was what had been digging at her. A "creepy vibe" was a damned accurate description. But she supposed Annabelle couldn't help how she was. Still, Elizabeth had bigger problems than trying to figure out the woman. "There's something I have to ask you, Gloria."

Her friend turned to look at her, her gaze expectant. "You know you can ask me anything."

"When Brian confronted me at Ned's office, he said some hurtful things." She'd sworn she wasn't going to bring this up…but, dammit, she had to know. She was feeling so uncertain right now.

Gloria shook her head. "Well, I hate to speak ill of the dead, but there's no surprise there."

Elizabeth moistened her lips and worked up the nerve to say the rest. "He said that you recommended me to Ned after *he* told you to. That you were in on the whole thing. His using me and then Ned doing the same."

Gloria's expression had gone from calm and patient to outraged in less than three seconds. "You're kidding, right?"

Elizabeth gave her head a little shake. "I didn't believe him, but I wanted you to know—"

"What do you mean, you didn't believe him?" Gloria demanded, her tone filled with hurt. "You're asking me, so you must have believed it to some degree." She threw up her hands and pushed away from her desk. "I can't believe you would even consider his lies as having any basis whatsoever."

Driver stuck his head inside the door. "Everything all right in here?"

The two severe glowers thrown his way sent him ducking back into the corridor.

"Gloria," Elizabeth urged, "I didn't believe him. I—"

"You didn't?" Her friend was angry now. A flush had turned her pale skin a deep crimson. "Oh, really. Well, you could have fooled me. Why would you bother asking if you didn't?"

She was right. Elizabeth stared at the floor, ashamed of herself for believing Brian even for a second. "I'm sorry. I don't know—"

"I do," Gloria snapped, her arms folded over her chest in an unyielding manner. "You have that little faith in our friendship." Mouth set in a grim line, she skirted the desk and began to shuffle through the mound of papers lying there. "If you'll excuse me, I have work to do."

"Let's not leave it like this, please," Elizabeth pleaded. "I was wrong to let him get to me, but I—"

Gloria held up a hand and fixed her with a hard glare. "I can't talk about this right now, I'm too upset. Please, just go."

Knowing a brick wall when she ran into one, Elizabeth admitted defeat. She moved to the door, but hesitated before going through it. "Just remember one thing," she said softly. Gloria didn't respond. "This isn't your fault. It's mine. I'm the one with the trust issues. I jumped the gun here and I'm sorry. No matter what happens with all this insanity, you're still my best friend."

Elizabeth didn't wait for a reply; Gloria was too hurt right now. But they would work it out... somehow.

SHE SAT NUMBLY in Driver's car as he headed back toward SoHo. His cell phone rang and she jerked at the sound. Swiping the infuriating tears from her cheek, she forced a deep breath and kept her gaze straight ahead. She tried not to think, but it was impossible. The events of the past ten days were whirling in her head, crashing down on her with a sense of finality that threatened her tenuous grip on her composure. Ned's deceit. His murder. The police. The murdered women. Brian's preposterous accusations. His murder. Making love with Mac.

God, please let her be able to trust him. To count on that one thing. She couldn't live with another letdown.

"It's Mac," Driver said. "He needs to talk to you."

Her hand shaking, Elizabeth took the compact phone. "Hello." She cringed at the quaver in her voice. Strong. She had to be strong.

"Elizabeth, listen to me." The sound of his voice was reassuring. "There's been another murder. I've instructed Agent Driver to take you home and to stay with you until I can get back there."

She just listened, too stunned to reply. Some part of her brain niggled at her, reminding her that she really needed to work, but she couldn't quite grasp the initiative.

"Brannigan is sending another man over to keep watch on Gloria."

Her friend's name startled her out of her trance. "Annabelle said there's still one more before he gets to Gloria and me." God, she prayed her information was correct. What was she thinking? She was wishing the danger on someone else, someone just as innocent as they were. "Whoever she is, she'll need protecting, too."

Silence roared between them for a moment that felt like an eternity. Why didn't he say something?

"If Harrison had another female patient whose name comes alphabetically after the latest victim and before Weston, I can't find it in his files."

Fear broadsided Elizabeth.

If that was so, Gloria was next.

Chapter Thirteen

Elizabeth retraced her steps across her suddenly too-small living room. She'd never noticed before that the old wooden floor creaked in a certain spot about three feet from the rear wall. It squeaked smack-dab in the center, too. Guess she'd never really had time to pace the floor that much or to be aware it made any sounds. Or maybe she'd simply been too exhausted by the time she dragged herself home at night. Whenever her panic attacks had struck at home, she'd done her pacing outside. It worked better that way. Now that she thought about it, this apartment had really served as nothing more than the place she slept and showered. It hadn't really been a home.

Her life had been in too much of an uproar and she'd been far too busy attempting to make ends meet to worry about anything else. The worn area rug and meager furnishings had been included with the place, for which she'd been immensely thankful—she'd had nothing of her own.

Nothing but her clothes and a boxful of mementoes from the life she'd once lived in a small Maryland town. It felt like a dozen lifetimes ago now.

She hadn't even bothered calling her sister, the only family she had left, and telling her about the murders or her connection to any of it. Her only sibling had enough troubles of her own. Fortunately for the kids, Peg had straightened out her life since becoming a widow. No more drugs or drinking. She even had a job. While working at the local Wal-Mart might not have sounded like much to most, it was a huge step for Peg. Elizabeth's little sister had never been much for responsibility, and she hadn't really grown up until her third child was born.

But then, Elizabeth couldn't blame it all on her sister. With a mother who deserted them and a father who'd been too busy working to keep a roof over their heads to influence their raising to any degree, what else could one expect?

She knew she was rambling down memory lane, as fruitless as it was, to avoid facing reality.

In the past a situation this stressful would have thrown her into full-scale panic, but strangely she felt an odd sense of calm. Her concern for her friend had overridden all else. Elizabeth turned and started across the room, once more silently willing the telephone to ring. She needed to hear from Gloria. She'd called her office as soon as she arrived home, but her assistant had informed her that Gloria had gone for the day. She'd called Gloria's sister's house, and there hadn't been any answer. And her cell phone was either out of range or not activated.

Uneasiness plugged away at Elizabeth, but she stayed strong. She should have heard from Mac by now. What was going on with the latest victim? Had he gotten in touch with Brannigan about Gloria?

Elizabeth deviated from her usual route and pushed the curtain aside just far enough to see Driver's car outside. She didn't see him in the fading daylight, but she knew he was around, watching the grounds, checking the doors and windows. She'd offered him some coffee, but he'd declined, saying that his wife always made him a thermos of it each morning. Elizabeth wondered vaguely what it would be like to have that kind of relationship. Taking care of each other's needs, always knowing someone was there to depend on. She closed her eyes and thought about making love with Mac. Long nights, cradled in his arms, sated emotionally, as well as physically.

Never count your chickens before they hatch, darling, her daddy had always said. She, of all people, should know that old adage was true. She knew better than to start thinking about forever where Mac was concerned. They'd shared one night, nothing more. When this case was over, assuming she survived it, they would probably never see each other again. He could have a girlfriend...or a fiancée.

The bottom fell out of her stomach. They really hadn't talked that much. What did she actually know about him? He'd been born and raised in Washington, D.C. Had a degree from Columbia. He was thirty-five and he'd been with the FBI for ten years. She had no idea if he had any family or even what foods he liked or what his favorite color was.

The panic she'd been certain wouldn't strike suddenly did. It tightened her throat, made her skin crawl, as her heart kicked into overdrive and unneeded adrenaline shot through her veins. "Walk it off," she muttered, disgusted with her inability to control the reaction. Damn, she hated being vulnerable to her traitorous body. And just when she thought she'd get through this without a problem.

She grabbed the phone and punched in the number for Gloria's sister's house. When she got no answer she tried the cell phone again.

Still no answer.

Still no word from Mac.

She couldn't take it anymore.

She punched in another number and the answer came after the first ring. "Speak."

Despite the pressure building inside her, she almost laughed at Boomer's barked greeting. "Boomer, I need your help."

Forty-five minutes later Elizabeth climbed into Boomer's truck and shouted, "Go!"

He floored the accelerator and the vehicle shot forward like a rocket. She buckled up and collapsed against the seat. She'd made it.

She'd known that Driver would be watching her truck, so she'd waited until he was doing his perimeter search on the far side of the yard and slipped out. Boomer had waited for her three blocks away. Even now Driver was probably knocking on her door, wanting to know if she was all right. But it was too late; she and Boomer were well out of sight. Mac would be angry. He didn't want her leaving the house for any reason.

"Hurry, Boomer," she pleaded. "I'm really worried about Gloria."

Keeping an eye out for the cops, Boomer made Brooklyn in record time. Gloria's sister lived in a cop neighborhood. Half the residents were on the force, as her husband had been. When her husband had died, she'd known she had to stay. Her neighbors were like family; she couldn't possibly leave.

"Just let me make sure someone is there," Elizabeth said when Boomer parked in front of the small, neat cottage. "I'll wave for you to go on if all is well."

"I can come in with you," he offered, his face scrunched with worry. "I don't like leaving you here."

"As long as Gloria is here and safe and sound, everything'll be fine. I'll call Mac and let him know I'm here. He won't like it, but it's too late now."

Boomer nodded reluctantly. "I'll wait for your go-ahead."

"Okay." Elizabeth slung her purse on her shoulder, slid out of the truck and walked to the front stoop. She pressed the doorbell, but not sure if it worked, she followed with a couple of firm knocks. A moment later the door opened.

"Elizabeth?" Gloria frowned at her. "Are you all right?"

"Are you?" Elizabeth countered, quickly sensing the subtle differences in her friend's voice and posture. Something wasn't right.

Gloria started to say yes, but Elizabeth read the lie in her eyes a split second before she admitted defeat. "I can't do this anymore." She opened the door wider for Elizabeth to come in. "I have to tell you…"

Really worried now, Elizabeth waved at Boomer to send him on his way, then went inside the house. Gloria quickly locked the door behind her. "Where's your sister?'' Elizabeth asked. The silence in the house seemed to close in around them.

"I sent her and my niece away."

"What do you mean, you sent them away?" Fear inched its way into Elizabeth's being. Things were definitely getting stranger by the second. Maybe she should have kept Boomer around a little longer. "Where are they?"

"I can't tell you, but they're safe from that madman." Gloria moved about the room, peeping between the slats of the blinds at window after window. "It's better if you don't know. I don't want him to find them."

Elizabeth moved to stand beside her friend as she peered out the front window. "What is it you have to tell me?" she asked softly, not wanting to push, but Gloria had said she had to tell her something. Abruptly she wondered where the police officer was who was supposed to be watching Gloria. "Have the cops been by to see you?" she asked, irritation climbing into the mix of emotions.

Gloria spun toward her. "No!" she practically shouted. "I haven't seen anyone."

This was too bizarre. "Gloria, tell me what's going on."

Those wide green eyes suddenly glistened with emotion. "That bastard is after my niece. I had to save her. I don't care if he kills me."

Elizabeth had missed something here. This didn't make sense. "I don't understand."

"Ned, the son of a bitch, took advantage of my niece, too," Gloria spat.

At first Elizabeth wasn't sure what she meant, then it dawned. "Oh, my God. Not Carrie."

Gloria nodded jerkily. "I couldn't believe it." She swiped at the tears falling freely now. "I wasn't really that surprised when he used us, but she's just a kid. Barely eighteen." Gloria shook with rage, her face turning beet-red. "She kept having all those problems after her father's death. Ned was certain he could help." She clenched her jaw, a muscle jerking in her cheek. "He helped all right. Carrie didn't tell me what happened until a couple of weeks ago."

Elizabeth put her arms around her friend and hugged her stiff shoulders. "I'm so sorry. You're right, he was a son of a bitch."

Gloria went completely rigid. "That's why I killed him."

For a couple of seconds her words didn't fully penetrate the wall of disbelief that instantly formed. Then they did, and Elizabeth felt a jolt all the way to her soul.

"Gloria, you can't mean that!"

She pulled out of Elizabeth's arms and stared at her. "I did. I killed him." Her eyes were glassy now. Elizabeth felt certain she was edging into shock. "I'm glad he's dead." She turned away.

Elizabeth tried to gather her wits. What the hell did this mean? Could Gloria be serious? "Tell me what happened," she urged, moving up behind her friend, hoping to lend support with her nearness.

Gloria lifted one shoulder in a shrug. "I didn't actually mean to kill him. I went there to teach him a lesson. I screwed his damn brains out, making him vulnerable, and then I pulled out my dead brother-in-law's service revolver.'' She laughed, the sound empty, so unlike her usual tinkling laughter. ''He was scared shitless. I had him trussed up like a Christmas turkey in that chair, buck naked, and then I tortured him. Mentally mostly.''

She lapsed into silence for a time and Elizabeth struggled to be patient. Gloria was definitely close to a breakdown. Elizabeth could feel it.

''He'd taken out that dagger you'd given him. Cleaning it or admiring it, who knows? Or maybe he intended to scare you with it when you showed up.'' A laugh tore out of her again. ''Oh, yeah, I was there when you came over mad as hell that he'd stood you up. I was hiding in the master bathroom, praying you didn't find me. I couldn't hear everything you said…just parts. Then you left and I tempted him into a game he couldn't resist. He loved every minute of it as I tied him up. He even liked it when I stuffed those panties in his mouth. I brought them with me— brand new cheap ones. I knew he'd hate that they weren't silk. But then I picked up the dagger. That's when he got worried. I taunted him with it, drew blood a couple of times just to hear him whimper.'' She paused for so long Elizabeth wasn't sure she intended to continue. ''And then he laughed at me.''

Her voice had gone arctic cold.

''I didn't mean to kill him…but I was so angry,'' she said tightly. ''The next thing I knew the dagger was in his chest. I don't even remember doing it.'' She pulled in a shaky breath and exhaled loudly. ''I don't remember anything after he started laughing except the look in his eyes when the knife thrust into him. It made this…awful sound…''

Elizabeth fought back the images her friend's words elicited. "Gloria, I know this is hard, but why didn't you call the police? You could have explained everything."

She whipped around, pinning Elizabeth to the spot with a piercing glare. "And then what? Spent the rest of my life in prison? For killing a piece of scum like him?"

"Okay, okay," Elizabeth said placatingly, holding up her hands. "I understand. Hell, I would probably have done the same thing if it had been my niece."

"You would've?" Gloria's bravado wilted. "God, I can't believe I did it." She peered out the window.

It was dark enough now that, with only the dim slice of moon hanging in the sky, there wasn't much she could see. Just a streetlight struggling valiantly to send its glow across the small expanse of grass.

"It's like a bad movie playing in my head," Gloria said quietly. "I see myself doing it, but I still can't believe I did. It's like it really wasn't me, just someone using my body. I took the tapes he'd made of Carrie and me. I couldn't find yours." She looked at Elizabeth in earnest. "I swear I tried to find it, but I was so upset..."

"It's all right." Elizabeth thought about how Gloria had urged her not to tell the police anything, not to give them any extra information. She'd been trying to protect Elizabeth, as well as herself. But everything had gone wrong.

"Now he wants her dead," Gloria murmured. Her whole body seemed to quiver with a new, building emotion. "Well, I'll see him in hell first," she snarled. "Since it obviously wasn't Brian, I may not know who *he* is, but I'll be here waiting when he shows up.''

Ignoring her resistance, Elizabeth pulled her friend into an embrace once more. "And I'll be here with you. If he comes, we'll take him on together.''

Surrendering just a little, Gloria burrowed her face in Elizabeth's shoulder. "We have to!" she cried. "If we don't he'll kill us all.''

"No way," Elizabeth argued, "because we'll be right here waiting for him. He has no way of knowing we're on to him now. We know what he wants next.''

Gloria drew back. "I'm sorry I let the police suspect you. I should have come forward. I should have at least told you." She blinked back a new surge of liquid emotion.

"It's okay." Elizabeth hugged her tightly. "It'll be over soon.''

And it would be. Elizabeth could almost feel him coming. Things had been building toward this moment ever since Ned's death. The momentum had been unstoppable. She closed her eyes and prayed that God would keep an eye on them. And that somehow Mac would find her, would swoop in and save the day.

Her courage shored up at the mere thought of him, Elizabeth drew back and looked at her friend. She brushed away the tears glittering on her cheeks. "I think I'm going to stack the deck to our advantage.''

Gloria frowned wearily. "What do you mean?''

"I'm going to call us a hero.''

MAC WAS ON THE PHONE with forensics, pushing for a speedy analysis on the latest victim. He had a few last-minute details to handle and then he was going to Elizabeth. He didn't want her in anyone else's care tonight.

Of course her safety was of primary importance, but a major part of him wanted a repeat of last night. He wanted to make love to her over and over…tonight.

If he could just get these damned people to commit to a time.

The intercom buzzed, sending a fresh bolt of pain through his aching head. He could sure use a neck rub about now.

"Agent MacBride, there's a call from Mexico for you on line four. And that other call is still holding on three. When I asked her if she wanted to continue holding, she said it was extremely important that she speak to you."

She? "Who is she?" The receptionist hadn't said a damned thing till now about the caller being a woman. His first thought was Elizabeth. But Driver would have called if Elizabeth had needed anything.

"She wouldn't give her name."

Uneasiness sliding into his gut, he barked a thanks and stabbed the blinking button that represented line three. He could call forensics back later. "MacBride." Nothing. It was dead. The caller had hung up.

Mac swore and poked the final flashing light. He'd been anticipating this call all afternoon. He couldn't risk missing it. He just needed one damned clue as to the identical twin's whereabouts. Just one. If the guy actually was dead, Mac needed to know it.

"MacBride."

"We've got your body, MacBride," said the man who worked in Mexico as a liaison between the FBI and the CIA, "but I think you're going to be a little startled."

Why the hell not? Mac mused. Everything else about this case had been screwy. What was one more wacked-out item on the list?

"Nigel Harrison may very well be dead, but he isn't buried here. The corpse in the coffin at his grave site is female, and in damn good condition, too. Incredibly well preserved."

A woman. "Do you have any idea who she is and why she would have been buried in Harrison's stead?"

"Sure do. I have a nice thick file on Nigel Harrison. He was a rather naughty boy when he lived down here. When the Harrison brothers were growing up in that orphanage they called home, they became close friends with a girl there. According to one of the overseers who's still on staff there and remembers the Harrison brothers, the three were inseparable. Apparently they started planning their dastardly deeds way back then. Whenever they got caught in something underhanded, none of the three would admit who actually did the deed. Loyalty was the mainstay. The three stayed in contact when they went off to college. Nigel and the girl became lawyers, and Ned became a doctor. All three apparently rose well above their beginnings."

Mac was becoming impatient. He knew some of that already. "So you don't know where the hell Nigel Harrison is or even if he's dead."

"That's right. He supposedly died in the jungle and

his body was carried out by the cave dwellers his companion on the journey allegedly hired.''

Mac swore viciously. ''I have to find this bastard,'' he muttered. ''What you're telling me isn't giving me what I need. Why would he have faked his death?''

''I can't help you with where he's at,'' the man explained. ''But I can speculate about why he faked his death. The corpse in the coffin belongs to a murder victim. Her throat had been slashed. She might have been well preserved, but the morticians down here aren't so good at covering up the cause of death. I imagine Nigel Harrison faked his own demise to conceal his handiwork. From the looks of the wound, he all but decapitated her.''

Realization slammed Mac. ''Do you have a positive ID on the woman?'' Hell, she could be anybody, but he had a sneaking suspicion it was someone very close to the Harrison brothers.

''That I can give you, as well. Since her practice was in California and they fingerprint everyone who applies for a driver's license, her prints were on file. It's a positive ID.''

Mac wished he could reach into the phone line and give the man a shake. ''Well, do you have a name?''

''Oh, yeah. Sure. She was the girl who befriended the Harrison brothers in the orphanage. Her name was Annabelle Ford.''

''IT'S ANNABELLE,'' Elizabeth whispered as she peered through the door's peephole. ''What do you want to do?'' She punched the ''end call'' button on the cordless phone. She'd have to try Mac again in a few minutes. She couldn't keep holding on. Maybe she should have given the receptionist her name, but she'd feared it would set off some sort of alarm, since Agent Driver had no doubt already called in. She didn't want anyone but Mac to know her whereabouts. "I don't know, Gloria." Elizabeth tried to rationalize her hesitation. "I know you trust Annabelle, but there's something wrong about her. The longer I think about it, the stronger the feeling."

Gloria chewed her lip thoughtfully for a moment as a fourth knock echoed, startling them both even though they'd known it was coming. "I...I guess we should let her in. She's a lawyer—she could help. She could have news."

Elizabeth still hesitated. "How well do you really know her?"

Gloria cradled her face in her hands for a moment, then shrugged. "Not that well, but it seems like she's tried to help us."

Maybe so. Pushing aside her nagging reservations, Elizabeth opened the door. "Hurry," she urged the older woman. "Come in. We don't want anyone to see us here."

Annabelle hurried inside, the same look of desperation on her face that no doubt was on Elizabeth's.

"There's been another murder," Annabelle said quickly. "I'm really getting worried. I'm not sure the authorities are going to be able to stop this."

Elizabeth hugged herself. "I'm wondering that myself." She studied Annabelle, tried to pinpoint the rub. What was it?

Annabelle looked from one to the other, a worried expression on her face. "Are you two all right?"

Elizabeth and Gloria exchanged a hopeless look. "Well," Gloria began, "it's…"

"It's just that we're sick about this latest victim," Elizabeth said quickly. She suddenly didn't want Annabelle to know the truth. "It could be either one of us any time now. Wouldn't we be next?"

Annabelle's gaze turned wary. "Good idea to feel that way." She focused on Gloria. "But something isn't right here," she said slowly. "What's going on?"

"I killed him!" Gloria blurted, a new gush of tears punctuating the admission. "It was me. I…I…" Her words faltered, replaced by a high-pitched keening sound.

"It was an accident," Elizabeth hastened to add as she quickly enveloped her friend in her arms once more. "It's okay, Gloria. We'll tell the police everything. There were extenuating circumstances."

"You don't get it," she wailed. "I screwed up! Made a mistake! And now he's after my niece. She's the last one before the two of us."

Carrie Underwood. Elizabeth shook her head in confusion. "But why wasn't she on Ned's patient log?"

"He agreed to keep her name off the record so her psychiatric care could never come back to haunt her. She's so young. I didn't want her to start out with that hanging over her head. You know some of the big corporations and even some of the universities look for crap like that."

That was why Mac couldn't find another name.

"And now she's in danger because of me!" Gloria

trembled violently. "She may die for my stupid mistake!"

Elizabeth reached for her to comfort her, but Annabelle reached her first.

"Don't worry, Gloria, you won't have to witness anything bad happening to your niece. You can go first."

Annabelle whipped a long-bladed knife from beneath her suit jacket and held it to Gloria's throat. "I don't mind deviating from the plan."

"What're you doing?" Elizabeth shouted. The stark fear that had momentarily paralyzed her propelled her into action. "Put that knife down!" She wanted to take it away from her, but it was pressed so close to Gloria's flesh. Instantly Elizabeth remembered Mac's description of arterial spray. She shuddered, her knees almost buckling beneath her.

"Did you really think I'd let you get away with it?" Annabelle growled, her usually gravelly voice even deeper now. "I knew if I picked you off one at a time, I'd eventually get the right one. I knew the few who'd made an impact on my brother's emotions. The ones he toyed with the most...who resented him the most."

Elizabeth tried to make sense of the scene. Annabelle was threatening to kill them. Her voice had deepened considerably. She'd called Ned her brother.

Oh, God.

The twin.

"You're Nigel," she said almost to herself.

"Well, give the girl a cigar," he said facetiously, not even attempting to hide the masculinity of his voice anymore.

Elizabeth looked at his meticulous chignon and then at the perfect fit of his suit over undeniable mounds of breasts. The toned legs, free of male hair, below the hem of her skirt. She'd known something wasn't right, but this...

"Get a good look, Elizabeth. It'll be your last." He laughed cruelly. "Just so you know, the hair is all mine. It took me two years to get it this length. Of course the color is different, just like my eye color. Aren't colored contacts marvelous?" he taunted, all the while pressing the knife firmly against Gloria's throat. He inclined his head sheepishly. "But the breasts are expensive fakes. You know the kind cancer victims can get? A little surgery here and there and no one could tell we were brothers." His evil smile sickened Elizabeth. "Or that I wasn't a woman. Even you didn't know."

"Why?" Elizabeth asked.

"It was either take over Annabelle's identity or admit that I'd killed her." He lifted one shoulder in a shrug of indifference. "Stupid bitch. Annabelle should have known I wouldn't marry her. But no, she'd wanted children. She was tired of all the games we'd played together all those years, just me, her and Ned. She'd heard her biological clock ticking. Too bad for her. There was no contest as far as I was concerned regarding how to handle it. All it took was a little extra money to the mortician and one dirty cop. But then I had to kill them both. Hell, I'll bet they're still trying to figure out what happened to those two. Then again, maybe not. I did leave them in a rather compromising position. In that macho culture they're not about to own up to one of their own being homosexual. I just couldn't take the risk that one of them might grow a conscience one of these days and spill the beans. Or get greedy," he added with a sinister snarl, "and start attempting blackmail."

Annabelle…Nigel…whoever the hell he was laughed at her horrified expression. Gloria stood stock-still, frozen in fear, or perhaps defeat.

"Why did you come here?" Elizabeth asked, her voice hollow.

"Here in New York?" he demanded as if she was stupid. "Or *here?*" He looked down at Gloria briefly, then leveled that satanic gaze on Elizabeth. "Well, I came to New York to be with my brother, of course. We'd never been apart for long. And everything was perfect until you bitches had to go and ruin it! You made him what he was. All of you. And that filthy Gentlemen's Association," he accused. "I got them, too, and it was so easy."

Elizabeth knew what he meant by that. He'd set her up to lead Mac to the hidden room and, ultimately, to the Gentlemen's Association.

"So he knew," Elizabeth ventured, trying to keep him calm until she could think of some way to help Gloria. "Ned knew you'd killed the real Annabelle."

Another hateful laugh. "Of course. He was glad to be rid of her, too. We'd always liked it better when it was just the two of us. Even now, he's with me."

Elizabeth didn't want to know what he meant. Nigel was obviously insane. She had to find something else to ask, something to keep him talking. Her heart rocketed into hyper mode. "How did you get into all those women's apartments? Did you use a gun?"

He smirked. "That wasn't necessary. All I had to do was tell them Ned had mentioned them in his will and that we needed to talk. It was incredibly easy. They were all so stupid and we're so smart."

"Why...why have you been pretending to help us?"

"Partly because I needed you to help me lead the police to the association since they're the reason my brother is dead. They made him weak...made him stupid. Women like the two of you were the catalysts they used. So just for the fun of it," he confessed smugly. He waggled his brows suggestively at her. "I went in alphabetical order so I could save you for last. You were special to my brother. I owed you that much." As suddenly as this persona had appeared, it changed again. "But now the fun is over. We're through playing," he said grimly. "Time to die."

Out of options, Elizabeth lunged for him, the first bloom of blood sliding onto the shiny blade as it pierced flesh. She grabbed his arm, pulled with all her might. Gloria screamed, snapping from her paralysis and fighting to free herself.

With a lionlike roar Nigel shoved Gloria aside and grabbed for Elizabeth. She felt the pierce of the cold steel on her forearm as they struggled, but she didn't let up. She had to stop him.

Suddenly the knife was poised high above her.

She couldn't move fast enough.

She was going to die.

An explosion rent the air.

Halfway to its destination the knife suddenly dropped from Nigel's limp hand.

He slumped to the floor.

Gloria scrambled out of his way, her hands clutching at her throat where blood seeped like crimson tears between her fingers.

"I need an ambulance!"

Elizabeth swung around at the sound of his voice. It was Mac. He'd shouted the order into his cell phone.

He'd saved them. Her hero had come.

As much as she wanted to dive into his arms, Gloria needed her more. As if reading her mind, Mac dropped to the floor next to her doing what he did best: saving the day.

MAC SAT NEXT to Elizabeth in the lobby of the surgical wing of New York General when she received the good news.

"Miss Weston will fully recover," the doctor told her. "The damage was mainly superficial. She'll need some cosmetic work in the future. But otherwise she'll be fine."

"Thank you." Elizabeth blinked at the tears Mac saw shining in her eyes, but still they slipped past her lashes. When the doctor walked away, she turned to him. Her bandaged forearm and her friend's blood staining the front of her T-shirt the same way it marked his shirt served as vivid reminders of the horror they'd survived. "Thank God it's over."

He slid an arm around her and pulled her close. "Amen."

They sat in exhausted silence for a while and then she asked, "Mac, what will happen to Gloria when the grand jury convenes?"

"That fancy lawyer you put on retainer will get her off the hook with no problem."

Elizabeth looked up at him, hope glittering behind the tears. "Are you sure?"

He nodded. "Definitely. If he's only half as good as his reputation, he'll sail through this on a temporary-insanity plea. Gloria admitted to you that she doesn't even remember doing it. She was out of her mind with worry for her niece. She went over the edge."

"Annabelle—Nigel," she amended, remembering those final moments, "kept saying *we,* like Ned was still with him."

Mac made a disgusted sound. "I think he went over the edge long ago—to the point of no return."

Elizabeth shuddered, then nestled against Mac's shoulder and prayed it would be that easy for Gloria to be absolved from what Ned had pushed her to. Her friend had made it past the first hurdle—she was going to recover. Now she just had to get through this. Elizabeth would be there for her.

"What about the Gentlemen's Association?"

"They're going down. The whole task force has descended on that secret room. This group has a lot to answer for, including pushing men like Harrison, who already have a penchant for the unsavory, over the edge."

She sighed wearily. That was good news. She wanted all of them to go down for what they'd done. "What about us?" she asked without looking up. That question had haunted her all those long hours they'd waited to hear about Gloria. Worrying about her friend had kept her from focusing on the other.

But now, as relief sent the stress draining away, there it was.

Mac drew back and looked into her eyes. "I happen to know you have a problem with trust and, considering what you've been through, I can't blame you. I'd like to spend some time proving to you that you can count on me."

She smiled, her lips trembling with the effort of holding back the tears that thickened in her voice when she spoke. "I already know I can count on you, Mac."

He pulled her close once more. "Then all we have to do is get to know each other better."

She smiled. "That sounds like the right thing to do."

"Definitely," he said, those amazing lips spreading wide in a beautiful smile. "It wouldn't be proper to marry a stranger."

Her eyes widened. He couldn't mean that. "We hardly know each other," she protested though she actually had no reservations whatsoever. For the first time in her life she was completely certain about a man.

He kissed the tip of her nose. "That's why we're going to do this one step at a time. And then when we're ready, whether it's next month or next year, we'll take the plunge. Deal?"

Her smile broadened to match his. "Deal."

Like all good deals, they sealed it with a kiss. A long, passionate kiss.

"We could leave for a little while now, you know," he whispered as he nuzzled the shell of her ear.

"Hmm...I hate not to be here when Gloria wakes up." Her breath caught when his tongue slid along her throat.

"Well—" he blew on the wet path he'd made and she shivered deliciously "—we'll just have to find ourselves a handy supply closet, because this isn't going to wait."

"Are you always this impatient, Agent Mac-Bride?" she teased.

He drew back and that blue gaze collided with hers. "I almost lost you today," he murmured thickly. "Never have I wanted anything more than I wanted to do my job—until now. Whatever's happening between us, it's special. Very special. I'm not about to waste any time, and I'm damn sure not going to risk losing you now that I've found you."

His words touched her deeply. No one had ever made her feel this way. Mac was right. This was special.

His lips found hers once more, and just like before, the whole world fell away, leaving only her and the man she trusted.

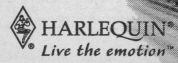

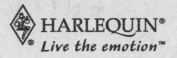 

Harlequin Books and Konica present
The Double Exposure Campaign!

Expose yourself to Intrigue. Collect original
proofs of purchase from the back pages of:

UNDER WRAPS 0-373-83595-7
GUARDED SECRETS 0-373-83593-0
WHISPERS IN THE NIGHT 0-373-83596-5
KEEPING WATCH 0-373-83594-9

and receive free Konica disposable cameras,
each valued at over $5.99 U.S.!

Just complete the order form and send it, along with your proofs of
purchase from two (2), three (3) or four (4) of the featured books above,
to: Harlequin Intrigue National Consumer Promotion, P.O. Box 9047,
Buffalo, NY 14269-9047, or P.O. Box 613, Fort Erie, Ontario L2A 5X3.

---

093 KIL DXHU

Name (PLEASE PRINT)

Address   Apt. #

City   State/Prov.   Zip/Postal Code

Please specify which themed gift package(s) you would like to receive:

❑ I am enclosing two (2) proofs of purchase for one free Konica camera
❑ I am enclosing three (3) proofs of purchase for two free Konica cameras
❑ I am enclosing four (4) proofs of purchase for three free Konica cameras

---

Have you enclosed your proofs of purchase?

Remember—the more you buy, the more you save! You must send two (2) original proofs
of purchase to receive one camera, three (3) original proofs of purchase to receive two
cameras and four (4) original proofs of purchase to receive all three cameras.

THE
DOUBLE EXPOSURE
CAMPAIGN
One Proof of Purchase
SEPTNCPPOP4

Please allow 4-6 weeks for delivery. Shipping and handling included.
Offer good only while quantities last. Offer available in Canada and
the U.S. only. Request should be received no later than **December 31,
2003.** Each proof of purchase should be cut out of the back-page ad
featuring this offer.

© 2003 Harlequin Enterprises Limited

Visit us at www.eHarlequin.com

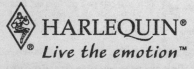

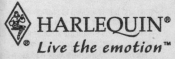